NO REGRETS

He closed the gap between them and pulled her to him. She laid her cheek against his chest. One of his hands rose to stroke her nape while the other banded around her waist, holding her closer. "Don't cry, sweetheart," he whispered against her ear. "Not one person caught up in this is worth any of your tears."

Cradling her face in his palms, he tilted her face up to him. He brushed away her tears with his thumbs. "Don't cry." Without thinking, he brought his mouth down to hers.

Immediately her arms closed around him and she kissed him back with a fierceness he had yet to see in her. It was as if she channeled all her emotions into that one kiss. He understood that, too—the need to sublimate that which you couldn't change.

Her fingers went to his shirt, pulling it from his waistband and over his head before he had the time or the will to stop her. He couldn't help the groan that rumbled up from somewhere deep as her lips touched down on the center of his chest. Damn, he wanted her, but he didn't want any replays of the previous night. He didn't want her to come to her senses sometime later and regret whatever happened between them.

He tilted her chin up to see her face. "Seems we've hit this spot in the road before."

Her eyes narrowed. "What's your point?"

"There might not be any backfires to raise an alert. No last minute saves." She looked at him more confused than before. He may as well ask her straight out. "Do you want to be with me, Dana?"

She averted her gaze to his chest, where her fingers made a lazy exploration of his bare flesh. He held his breath waiting for her answer.

When she looked at him again, it was with a sideways glance and a smile he didn't at first comprehend. "Only if you do me a favor."

"What's that?"

"Take me upstairs."

BOOK YOUR PLACE ON OUR WEBSITE AND MAKE THE READING CONNECTION!

We've created a customized website just for our very special readers, where you can get the inside scoop on everything that's going on with Zebra, Pinnacle and Kensington books.

When you come online, you'll have the exciting opportunity to:

- View covers of upcoming books
- Read sample chapters
- Learn about our future publishing schedule (listed by publication month *and author*)
- Find out when your favorite authors will be visiting a city near you
- Search for and order backlist books from our online catalog
- Check out author bios and background information
- Send e-mail to your favorite authors
- Meet the Kensington staff online
- Join us in weekly chats with authors, readers and other guests
- Get writing guidelines
- AND MUCH MORE!

**Visit our website at
http://www.kensingtonbooks.com**

Body of Truth

Deirdre Savoy

Kensington Publishing Corp.
http://www.kensingtonbooks.com

DAFINA BOOKS are published by

Kensington Publishing Corp.
850 Third Avenue
New York, NY 10022

All Kensington titles, imprints and distributed lines are available at special quantity discounts for bulk purchases for sales promotion, premiums, fund-raising, educational or institutional use.

Special book excerpts or customized printings can also be created to fit specific needs. For details, write or phone the office of the Kensington Special Sales Manager: Kensington Publishing Corp., 850 Third Avenue, New York, NY 10022. Attn: Special Sales Department. Phone: 1-800-221-2647.

Dafina Books and the Dafina logo Reg. U.S. Pat. & TM Off.

ISBN 0-7582-1228-3

First Printing: November 2005
10 9 8 7 6 5 4 3 2 1

Printed in the United States of America

For all my buddies at P.S. 178,
and to all the children I've taught,
who have enriched my life
more than they imagine.

ACKNOWLEDGMENTS

Thanks to my sister, Elyse Savoy, R.N., for letting me borrow her life. Thanks to Arthur Brown, Deputy Inspector, Ret., NYPD, for pointing me in all the right directions. Special thanks to Wally Lind and all the folks at crimescenewriter@yahoogroups.com for their excellent advice, camaraderie and willingness to share.

Prologue

Twenty-five years ago

God helps those who help themselves.

Father Malone had drummed that saying into heads so often he could hear it in his sleep. As they stood in the burning light of the growing fire, he wondered if Father regretted teaching them those words.

They looked at each other, their faces carefully blank, not knowing what to feel, what to say to one another. They had taken Father Malone's advice. They'd come here to help themselves to a share of the skim Father and his cronies were said to be taking off the top of the development fund to rebuild Vyse Avenue. But the old man claimed not to know what they were talking about, and Mouse, always Mouse, with his temper . . .

He turned back to the fire, wondering if anyone could see it—like the dancing glow of the fire—on their faces, the guilt, the onus for the tragedy they only suspected had occurred. They stood there, pin-points in a crowd, staring—equally repulsed and fascinated by the flames consuming St. Jude's.

God helps those who help themselves. But would He forgive them?

One

Nobody bothered The Nurse.

Nobody noticed as she picked her way across the street, over empty crack vials, spent condoms, used hypodermics, broken bottles and whatever other waste, sometimes human, the residents of this neighborhood in the South Bronx had strewn in her path.

Nobody bothered The Nurse, because they knew why she was here. She came to the bedridden, the chronically ill or the injured, the mothers, wives, aunts, and children of the men and women who let her pass on the street, unnoticed and unmolested.

Or, perhaps one day, she would come for them.

So her car went unvandalized, nobody rushed up to her in dark corners intent on robbery or worse. No catcalls followed her as she entered the four story walk-up on Highland Avenue, no cries of "Yo Baby, *Mira Mami*, Hey Honey," or a thousand other variations, no propositions or promises of masculine prowess. Well, not many.

But then the only time she ventured into this alien territory was after eight o'clock in the morning, when most of the real predators that ravaged the neighborhood had finally gone to bed, and before three, when they went back on the prowl.

Every day she spent in this place preceded a night when she thanked God for her own humble home in Mount Vernon, a northern suburb of New York City. And now she had something else to look forward to. In exactly one day, she would board a plane to Paradise Island to take the first real vacation she'd had in years. She owed herself that vacation for all the years she'd spent looking after her ailing mother while she was alive, and raising her younger brother after she had passed away.

She'd promised herself that after Tim graduated from high school, she'd treat herself to somewhere nice and warm and sunny, even if it were for only a few days. The trip hadn't become real to her until this past Thursday, when she'd attended St. Matthew's Commencement Ceremony to watch her brother receive his diploma. Now anticipation flooded her nervous system, as well as anxiety that something would happen to make her cancel her trip.

She walked the three flights of stairs to her client's apartment and knocked on the door. The bell had long since expired, and, like everything else that broke in this apartment building, it went unfixed.

"Who?" a masculine voice called.

She was tempted to answer "The goddamn Avon Lady." Who else would be showing up in this godforsaken neighborhood at nine o'clock on a Friday morning? She decided better of it and gave her standard answer. "Dana Molloy from At-Home Health."

A few moments later, the door was pulled open to the extent the chain allowed. Wesley Evans, her patient's grandson, appeared at the door. She gave him a quick up and down look through the thin opening. He wore a black do-rag on his head and a pair of jeans low enough on his hips to expose the waistband of a pair of red boxers. His bare chest sported the muscles earned from running the streets instead of running to the gym. He was tall, probably six-three or better. If it weren't for the sour expression, he would remind her of her own brother. Wesley sucked his teeth. "Hold on."

As he shut the door to take the chain off, she caught the flash of a dull black object in his hand. Some sort of handgun, she assumed—just the fashion accessory every young thug needed.

Dana shifted the strap of the bag that housed the heavy laptop provided by the company. On it, she would record patient information obtained from this and her other visits. The only reason she carried it was that if it were stolen and not on her person at the time, At-Home Health would deduct the cost of it from her salary. And even the junkies knew not to bother. The laptop could only be programmed to record medical information. There wasn't even a game or two on the damn thing to make it worth stealing.

When Wesley pulled the door open, an oversize football jersey had been added to his ensemble, and the gun was nowhere in sight. Rather than hold the door for her, he let it swing closed so that she had to either dash inside or let the door hit her to keep from getting closed out.

Dana settled for the latter, muttering under her breath, watching as he sauntered toward the decrepit couch at the center of the living room. He propped his feet up on the scarred and chipped coffee table. "Granny's in back."

No shit. Considering that Granny was a bed-ridden diabetic, there weren't many places Granny might be.

Dana stepped out of the way, letting the door close behind her. Despite the foolhardiness of antagonizing a teenager with a firearm, she said, "Shouldn't you be in school?"

His eyes narrowed and his mouth drew into a tight line. "I would be if that home care lady had shown up today." He implied that the other woman's absence was Dana's fault. In a way it was, because as the nurse on her grandmother's case, it was her responsibility to coordinate all services, which included making sure the home health aide arrived on time and didn't take anything.

To her knowledge, the aide assigned to Wesley's grandmother was a conscientious woman, but there were enough who weren't to give the profession a bad name. Then again, how much could you expect from people doing a demanding job that paid barely more than minimum wage? To Dana's thinking, it was a set-up that could only lead to failure.

"I'll speak to the aide about being here every day."

"Yeah, you go 'head and do dat." He turned up the sound on the large screen TV that sat against the wall next to her.

With a sigh of resignation, she headed toward the back of the apartment. The smell of fetid flesh reached Dana's nostrils before she reached the open door. Nadine Evans, though nearly seventy and morbidly obese, had once been a handsome woman. It was evident in the old woman's lined and wrinkled face and the framed photographs scattered around the cluttered room.

"Hi, Nadine," Dana said, trying to inject a note of cheer into her voice.

"Dana. Come in." Nadine waved her forward with a meaty arm. "It's so good to see you."

Like with many of Dana's homebound patients, the visit from the nurse was the only one they could count on. "How are you doing today?"

"More of the same."

Dana got the chair from the corner of the room and placed it by the foot of the bed. "I'll change your dressing first, then I'll test your blood sugar."

"However you want, honey. I'm not going anywhere."

After rolling on a pair of surgical gloves, Dana rolled back the covers to expose Nadine's right foot. Dry gangrene claimed the smallest toe. The stench of it was worse than wet garbage rotting in the can for a week during an August heat wave. The smell got in Dana's nose and stayed all day. Dana suffered through it only minutes at a time, but how did Nadine stand it hour after hour? If it were Dana, she'd tell the doctor to cut the damn thing off rather than waiting for nature to take its own course.

Then again, Dana wouldn't complicate her own medical condition by refusing to follow the diet prescribed for her by her doctor, either.

Dana gently unwrapped the toe and removed the old gauze, damp with thin, straw-colored mucous. The toe was black and crusty, resembling a Brazil nut more than a human digit. One day soon she'd probably find the toe in the bandage as well, but she was glad today was not that day.

"How's she healing?" Nadine asked.

"She isn't." Nadine chose to believe that all this fuss was about making her toe better, the same way she chose to believe that eating Ho-Hos for dinner wouldn't affect her blood sugar level. Dana rewrapped it in sterile gauze, and secured it with paper tape. "How have you been doing with your diet?"

"Real good. No sweets."

Dana cast the old woman a skeptical look. "How long ago did you last eat?"

"I had a couple of eggs around seven."

"Good." Two hours after eating was optimum time for checking blood sugar. By then whatever had been consumed had made its way into the blood stream. Dana moved the chair to the side of the bed next to Nadine. She got a lancet, a test strip and an alcohol swab from her bag. "Come on," she urged.

"I hate them little needles," Nadine protested, but she stuck out her hand.

"I don't blame you." She swabbed the pad of Nadine's thumb, pricked it with the lancet and caught the droplet of blood that appeared on the test strip. She fed it into the blood glucose monitor Nadine kept on her ancient nightstand. They would have the verdict in a moment. In the meantime, Dana asked, "How is Wesley treating you?"

"He's a good boy. In his heart he's a good boy."

Dana didn't comment. In the nine months Nadine Evans had been her patient, the old lady had filled her ears with stories of her grandson. Stories about a sweet young boy whose mother lost herself in crack and the arms of the wrong man. Nadine hadn't heard from her daughter in years, and didn't expect to. She was grateful that he remained in school and somehow managed to maintain an A average while dealing crack and without studying.

Although she knew about his activities, she was powerless to stop him. Not only did she lack the influence, but the money that bought the food and the big screen TV and the medical supplies Medicaid did not cover came from drugs. It wasn't an unusual arrangement, but it galled Dana to see a young man with such potential sucked up into what this neighborhood could do to a person, rob them of any life other than perpetuating what had gone before.

She glanced down at the monitor, then over at Nadine. Normal blood sugar level was between 70 and 120. "Two sixty-five. Tell me you didn't wash down those eggs with a glass of juice."

Nadine huffed. "Just a little."

"Even a little is too much. Come on, Nadine, you know the drill. No cake, no cookies, no pudding, no pie, no *juice.*"

"No fun."

"And losing your baby toe is a real laugh?" Annoyed, Dana threw the test strip in the trash and snapped off her gloves. Sometimes it wore on her that many of her patients refused to follow medical advice yet somehow expected to improve. Kids, she could understand, but a sixty-nine-year-old woman ought to know better. "I'll see you tomorrow," she told Nadine.

Out in the living room, she paused by the TV. Wesley sat sprawled in the same position she'd left him. "I need to talk to you about your grandmother."

Wesley stared straight ahead, his focus on the screen. "So talk."

She stepped in front of the picture. "Someone has to do a better job of monitoring your grandmother's sugar intake."

He shrugged and continued watching, as if she weren't there. "She's an old lady. She should be able to eat what she wants."

"She might live a while longer if you didn't indulge her sweet tooth."

He fastened a cold, menacing stare on her. "Why do you care so much, anyway?"

"Because it's my job," she answered, but it was

also in her nature to care, to nurture. Most of the time, she considered it a blessing, but sometimes, like now, it was a curse, since she directed her regard toward people who would not help themselves.

"One a these days I'ma get tired of you bein' all up in my face."

If she had a dollar for every time she pissed someone off by asking a question they didn't want to answer she could retire. "Being all up in people's faces" was often part of the job, especially with clients or relatives that refused to follow the plan of treatment prescribed for them.

Dana glared at him, refusing to back down. "Do what you're supposed to and you won't hear a word out of me."

Dana let herself out of the apartment and descended the stairs to the first floor. She pulled open the front door of the building. As she stepped out into the brilliant June sunlight, she noticed a tall white woman, perhaps the only true blonde for miles, getting into the passenger side of a dark sedan parked by the curb. Dressed in a white blouse, black pants and high-heeled black pumps, she had a black and white scarf tied around the strap of her shoulder bag.

Dana snorted. Probably a social worker or some other do gooder who hadn't figured out you don't wear your Bergdorf's Best in the neighborhood if you didn't plan on getting mugged. At least she was smart enough to catch a ride out of this place.

As the woman pulled the door closed, Dana caught a glimpse of the dark-haired man in a short-sleeved black shirt behind the steering wheel. Oh goodie, matching yuppies.

Dana turned in the direction of her car to see a

man in filthy, tattered clothes urinating against the side of the building.

She shook her head contemplating the dichotomy of rich and poor in the neighborhood and walked back to her car. "One more day," she told herself. "One more day."

At two thirty, Dana walked into the offices of At-Home Healthcare. Her supervisor, Joanna Haynes, also happened to be her best friend. Joanna was almost nine months pregnant with her first child by her new husband, Ray Haynes. As Dana entered her office, Joanna waddled from the file cabinet to the chair and sat down, bringing a smile to both women's faces. "It's a good thing I don't have much longer to go, or I wouldn't make it."

"Seems like you're going on leave just in time."

"I know. Speaking of which, where is everybody? I wanted to say good bye to some of the girls."

Dana shrugged. "Maybe it's been one of those rough days where no one gets out of the field before four." Dana nodded toward the bag of presents leaning against the other side of the desk, a few token gifts, given so that Joanna wouldn't get suspicious. "Who's picking you up today?" Joanna had given up driving in her seventh month, since she no longer fit behind the steering wheel.

"My brother Jonathan. I just called him. He should be here in about an hour."

"Which one is that?" Joanna had three brothers, all taciturn, somber-faced men, all cops in one form or another. The lot of them gave her the willies. Dealing with cops was like dealing with doctors: both had delusions of grandeur. Doctors thought they were GOD; cops thought they were THE LAW. Of the two she preferred doctors. Doctors didn't carry guns.

"The baby."

Dana shook her head. The way she spoke made him sound like some angelic cherub, when from what she remembered of "the baby" he was six-foot-three, rock-solid and mean. Joanna claimed his lousy disposition came from being the youngest and always having to prove himself. Dana thought he was just plain crazy. While other cops were doing their damndest to get transferred out of the Forty-Fourth precinct, he'd transferred in. If that didn't speak for a profound lack of judgment, she didn't know what did.

Joanna must have read her thoughts from her expression, because she added. "I know. He's arrogant, he's a pain in the ass, but he's my brother. I'm stuck with him."

Dana snorted. "I know what you mean. Sometimes I could gladly take a bat to Tim, but then they'd get me for child abuse."

Joanna laughed. "Some kid. He's a foot taller than you are."

"And still growing. I've got the food bills to prove it."

Joanna shifted in her seat. "Why do you want to know who's picking me up?"

Dana lifted her shoulders. "I was going to pick up something for dinner from across the street. Tim's leaving tonight to spend the week with the family of one of his friends. They're heading down to Florida and I hate cooking just for me." She gestured over her shoulder toward the door with her thumb. "Why don't you come with me? We can hang out in more comfortable surroundings until he shows up."

"Sounds like a plan. This chair and my back do not get along."

Dana helped Joanna gather her things and tape an unnecessary note on the glass outer door of the office. Dana had already told Ray about the party in the hopes he'd pass that information on to whoever came for Joanna that night.

As they crossed the street, Dana hid a smile. She only hoped the women assembled inside the Italian restaurant didn't send Joanna into premature labor when they yelled, "Surprise!" Joanna had worked for At-Home for twelve years in one capacity or another and was one of the few supervisors the nurses respected. Over thirty women had responded to the invitation saying they were coming, but the number who turned up could actually be higher.

Fiorello's had been selected as the party spot for three reasons: the food was divine, it was large enough to seat fifty diners in the front room, and its tinted glass allowed diners to look out but not passersby to look in. Dana pulled open the door to let Joanna enter ahead of her. A second later, a roar of "Surprise" hit them like a wave.

Joanna staggered back a step, but Dana pushed her forward. "Surprise," Dana echoed.

Joanna pursed her lips and sent Dana an evil glare. "I'm going to get you for this later."

Dana stuck out her tongue. "Promises, promises."

A couple of the nurses rushed forward to help Joanna into a white wicker chair at the center of the room, decorated with pink and blue ribbons. Dana took a seat at one of the tables. She'd served as chief organizer of the event, but being one of the few childless women present, she had no gruesome childbirth stories to share, no tales of late night feedings or lactation woes. She had raised her brother alone for the past six years, but it wasn't the same. So she was content to remain on the perimeter and let the moms have their day.

Joanna said her brother would come for her, but it was her husband Ray who walked in the door a half-hour later to collect her. Although Ray was tall, handsome and a doctor, the product of a privileged upbringing—every mother's wet dream for her female offspring—Dana had never liked him. Something about him seemed disingenuous, too slick, though she couldn't say what. She also did her best to disguise her dislike, as expressing it would only form a rift between her and Joanna. Joanna might be clueless, but Dana was certain Ray knew, and made her pay for it at every opportunity.

"Good evening, ladies," he said, letting the door close on its own steam behind him.

The other women greeted him warmly with jokes and laughter and demands that he make sure to take care of their friend during her maternity leave. Dana got up and busied herself getting Joanna's things together to take them out to Ray's SUV. She didn't look up until she noticed him standing in front of her.

He smiled one of his slick smiles. "Don't worry about all this. I'll get it."

She forced a smile to her lips. "It's no problem." She hefted the bag she'd packed against her hip. "I'll take this stuff out to the car. Is it open?" She didn't wait for his answer before starting toward the door. She made it outside to the Navigator parked at the curb before she felt Ray come up beside her.

He beeped the trunk open. "What did I ever do to make you hate me?"

Dana shoved her bag into the back seat a little

more forcefully than necessary. "I don't hate you."
She stepped back and glanced at Ray. The smugness
of his expression told her he didn't believe her.
"Look, Joanna had a hard time with her first husband. I hope she doesn't have to go through that
again." She turned to walk away from him.

He pulled her back with a hand on her upper
arm. "I love my wife, Dana. I'm adopting her kids.
We're about to have another one together. What
more do you want from me?"

She bit her lip, contemplating him, their situation.
She didn't doubt the sincerity in his softly spoken
words. But she wondered why he cared enough to try
to change her mind about him. And what could she
answer him? What did she want from him? She
shrugged. "I don't know."

"Then cut me some slack, huh, Dana?"

She sighed. Refusing would serve no purpose
except to be contentious. "I think I can manage
that. As long as you make sure Joanna doesn't go into
labor while I'm gone. I want to be here when the
baby's born."

"I'll see what I can do."

Finally, Dana let go a hint of a smile. They went
back inside to finish packing up the truck.

Later that night, after Tim had gone, Dana sat
alone in the white rocker she kept on her enclosed
front porch and sipped from a glass of Chablis. She
liked nights like these: quiet, sultry, when the wind
that rattled her screens brought the scents of summer
to her nose and stirred tendrils of her hair. Nights
like these she felt a world away from the area in

which she worked. She felt at peace with her life and what little she'd been able to accomplish with it.

Her father had disappeared almost the moment her mother had been diagnosed with multiple sclerosis. Her mother had held on for another ten years, becoming, in the end, almost totally dependent on her daughter. It had taken her an extra year to finish her nursing degree while working full time as a clerk in the bursar's office at Lehman College where she studied. She'd accepted the job with At-Home Health because it was the first one offered. The base pay alone afforded her the opportunity to save for a real house instead of the apartment in Co-op City where she'd lived since childhood.

What she had now belonged only to her, her and Tim. She'd managed to eke out a decent life for them. She'd survived what life had thrown at her and flourished. She was a survivor, always a survivor, never a victim. Life didn't get her down.

But tonight was different. Thoughts of Wesley Evans intruded on her solitude. Thoughts of Wesley and the obvious comparison to her own brother. Neither teenager had really known their father and both had lost their mothers at an early age. But while Tim was getting ready to start Cornell in the fall, Wesley was headed for a life of crime, jail or worse. A scant ten miles separated their homes but their lives were worlds apart.

She thought of the Robert Frost poem. "Two roads diverged in a yellow wood." She was grateful she could offer Timothy the right one.

"I won't be seeing you next week," Dana told Nadine Evans the following morning.

Nadine pouted. "Why not?"

"I'll be taking a much needed vacation. I'm leaving after my shift tonight." God willing, anyway. Her bags were in the trunk of the car, which hopefully hadn't been vandalized. Tonight she planned to eat freshly caught fish instead of frozen fish sticks. And have a piña colada. She had to have at least one piña colada before she went to bed that night.

Nadine's frown deepened. "I hope they don't keep sending that girl that comes on weekends. I think she steals from me."

Dana paused in her task of repacking her supplies into her bag. Anything worth stealing that had ever been in this apartment had either been pawned or left to rot away its value. Nadine was trying to guilt her for leaving her in someone else's care, but Nadine wasn't a heavy enough hitter in that department to faze Dana.

Dana zipped her bag closed. "I'll see you when I get back."

"If I'm still here."

Dana sighed. So maybe Nadine wasn't so bad at this after all. Dana patted her meaty shoulder. "You'll be fine. And behave yourself while I'm gone. You know I'll hear all about what you've been doing with yourself when I get back."

Nadine rolled her eyes. "I'll try."

Dana left the bedroom and walked out to the living room where the home health attendant was watching BET on the tube. Dana said nothing, but let herself out of the apartment. As she walked down the stairs to the first floor she saw a man standing outside the building, leaning against one of the faux pillars that decorated the building. Or rather, she saw a man-child, Wesley Evans, who had obviously skipped school again.

Wesley's head swiveled around as she opened the door. He frowned, probably figuring she'd give him more of her usual harangue. Not this time. She figured if she got on his case when he didn't do right by his grandmother she ought to be equally appreciative when he did.

He shifted, standing a bit straighter. "How's my granny?"

"Better. You must have gotten her to cut back on the juice."

He shrugged. "I heard what you said. I'm not stupid."

"I never said I thought you were stupid. I know how hard it is to get someone to stick to a diet they don't want to follow." Especially when you were the child and the grown-up ought to know better. "Thank you."

He shrugged again, shoving his hands in his front pockets, and she suspected her simple words of praise embarrassed him. Dana shook her head. She knew plenty of kids like him, all hard edges on the outside, needy and scared on the inside—scared most of all of showing they needed anything. Again, she wondered how differently he might have turned out if life had dealt him a better hand of cards or he better understood how to play the ones he had.

Sighing, Dana focused on his face, but he'd already turned away to watch the street where a black Oldsmobile with tinted windows rolled down the block. DMX blasted from the souped up automobile, drawing the attention of early morning passersby. The car moved with such deliberateness as to suggest its occupants were looking for a non-existent parking space . . . or cruising for trouble.

Dana stepped farther out of the building to stand beside Wesley. The young man seemed not to notice her, his attention taken up by the trajectory of the car. "You could do something else."

Only after the car turned right onto Sheridan Avenue did he look at her. His expression was distracted. "What?"

"You're graduating from high school. You could get a decent job. Maybe something civil service. Get your grandmother out of here. Go to college at night." It was how Dana had survived after her mother passed.

His face contorted in a mask of anger. "What do you know about it, lady? You ain't never been poor. You ain't never had nothing. You ain't never had it that all that stood between you and the street was you. So don't talk to me about getting no job. I put food on the table, so you got no right to judge me."

She didn't try to argue with him. He saw her now, not as she had been, barely older than he, charged with the care of her younger brother and no clear idea how to manage. He only saw the woman, who today could pay to live in a nice house and afford most of what her heart desired. Given that, she understood his outrage, especially considering the tiny bit of vulnerability he'd just shown her. He'd want to back her off, but she didn't back down. "You could start your own business. Don't tell me living in this place eats up all of the money you've made. Sell T-shirts. Anything where you don't have to watch the block to make sure someone isn't gunning for you."

Wesley leaned down so that his face was almost in hers. "Yeah, well if they come for me, I'ma stand up like a man, not go running like some punk. Anybody wants me, I'm right here."

He spoke in a quiet voice, his words made more chilling by his tone. One thing Dana had never felt was that her life was so hopeless that dying was as viable an option as living. "Who will take care of your grandmother then?"

He straightened away from her, but she could tell she'd gotten to him just a little. "That was low, lady. That was—" His words were cut off by the squeal of tires coming from a car rounding the corner. Wesley's head snapped up and his body stiffened. "Get inside."

Alarm prickled at her nerve endings as she watched the same car head down the street, much faster this time. No one needed to tell her that the car's driver and occupants were up to no good. She fumbled to get the door open, and doing so, she turned to pull him inside with her. She didn't want to find out if he'd do what he said he would. "Come on, Wesley," she pleaded, grabbing at his arm.

"Get inside." He shoved at her, a backhanded swat that caught her in the solar plexus, winding her. She gasped for air, watching the car speed closer to them. As if in slow motion, the rear driver's side window rolled down and the barrel of a gun appeared in the window.

For a split second, she contemplated the unreality of her situation, the beauty of the cloudless day marred by the ugliness of the black gun pointed at her and the murderous intentions of the man who held it. She inhaled and air whooshed back into her lungs. She lunged forward, grabbing hold of Wesley's arm. "Come on," she shouted. Yanking as hard as she could, she drew him toward her.

But she froze as a bullet whizzed past her ear to shatter the glass door behind her. And then her shoulder was on fire. The force of her own momen-

tum threw her backward, through the front door. She
landed on her back, still clutching Wesley's arm in
a death grip. He bounced down of top of her, pushing her backward along the floor, his weight as dead
as his eyes staring back at her. Her head snapped
back, making contact with broken glass and a concrete floor covered in a thin layer of vinyl tile. As
blinding pain and terrifying darkness claimed her,
Dana's last thought was that she wasn't going to be
getting on any airplane any time soon.

Two

Jonathan Stone pulled up behind one of three squad cars blocking the alley behind Mario's Pizza off Vandall Avenue. Earlier that morning, some poor bum looking for cans to redeem had been rifling through the trash when one of the trash cans produced an unexpected bounty: a woman's naked body.

Jonathan and his partner, Mari Velez, had taken the call an hour ago, while they were investigating a homicide on the other side of the Bronx, ironically across the street from the cemetery on Webster Avenue. The Bronx might not be the murder capital of the North America, but today it was holding its own.

Jonathan cut the engine and rubbed the back of his neck. It was barely ten o'clock and already the heat topped ninety degrees. For the second year in a row, New York had been treated to a frigid winter followed by an equally brutal, humid summer. Jonathan took one last gulp of air-conditioned air and cut the engine.

"Here we go again," Mari said, nodding toward the crowd assembled at the scene—a smattering of uniforms keeping the curious at bay; a couple of detectives he recognized from his time at the 44 talking with the uniform sarge, a few crime-scene techs combing the back of the alleyway. The same old, same old. Mari got out of the car, humming the tune to Mr. Rogers' Neighborhood.

Jonathan retrieved his jacket from the back seat and followed her. He'd inherited Mari when she'd come to the station two years ago. None of the other guys had wanted to partner with her, first because she was a woman, second because she didn't take any shit from them and third because she didn't put out.

After that they'd dismissed her as the most in-comprehensible and most hated woman of all: a dyke. Jonathan didn't know if that was true or not and didn't care. Mari was a good cop. She did her job and didn't complain about having to do it. That's all he needed to know about her. One of these days, if he ever wanted to really piss her off, he'd ask her.

He pinned his badge to his jacket lapel as he ducked under the police tape cordoning off the alley and crossed to where the two detectives he knew from the 44 stood. He'd never bothered to an-alyze the peculiar cop practice of nicknaming every-one, but he admitted he wasn't immune either. This pair he'd dubbed Mutt and Jeff, as the younger lanky one resembled a taller, fairer, more obnoxious Jeff Goldblum, and the older one, a Yaphet Kotto look-alike sans the cheesy Afro wig, sported a pot belly Buddha would have admired.

"What have you got?" He directed his question at Mutt, a.k.a. Ken Patterson, who, along with the bigger gut, possessed the greater brain power.

Patterson adjusted his belt over his ample waist. "Some old rummy finds the body of a white female stuffed in a trash can back in the alley. He pulls off the lid and there she is. Nearly scared the guy to death."

"Where is he?"

"Back of one of the squads." He nodded toward the building. "We're still waiting on the owner to show up. Lives in Larchmont and doesn't usually come in for another hour."

As they talked they walked the short distance toward where the body lay uncovered on the concrete. Mari had already squatted alongside the body, next to Bill Horgan, one of the guys out of the coroner's office.

If the girl in the can had ever been a pretty woman there was no evidence of it now. Three quarters of her face had been smashed in, leaving only her chin and a portion of her right cheek untouched. A row of purplish bruises ringed her neck, as well as several deep scratches, probably wounds she'd inflicted herself trying to fend off her attacker. Whoever she was, she probably hadn't been in that can for long, as the stench usually associated with decaying bodies in hot enclosed spaces was thankfully absent.

Whoever had left the secret surprise had probably hoped it would find its way to the dump before anyone discovered its contents. But garbage pick-up in this neighborhood was less of a scheduled affair than a game of what if. Or maybe he hadn't cared. Whoever had left her had robbed her of whatever dignity or identity she possessed by dumping her here like so much trash in an alley.

That fact galled him, as whoever she had been, she'd been someone's daughter or sister or mother. Whatever else she might have been in life, he understood his obligation to her in death. He owed her that, even if no one else did.

He pulled the Polaroid from his pocket, opened it and snapped a picture of the corpse. He lowered the camera and picked off the picture. There would be plenty of official photographs to sift through later, but the pictures he took now were just for him. His own reminder, his own incentive.

"What's your guess?" Jeff nodded toward the body. "A working girl?"

Jonathan's gaze slid to the man. His eyes were over-bright, his movements jerky. Either he was on something or he was an adult victim of hyperactivity disorder.

Jonathan shrugged. The fact that she'd been found nude might hint at a sexual motive for the crime, but Jonathan doubted it. That had nothing to do with the scene before him, but his own cop's intuition that he'd learned to rely on. Right now, that intuition told him this wouldn't be some simple open and shut case. Maybe it was just the way his luck was going right then.

Mari looked up. "She's no pro. Not on the street anyway."

"You can tell that just by looking?" Jeff scoffed. "You turn psychic and nobody told us?"

Mari speared him with one of her dark-eyed looks. "Aside from what this creep did to her, there isn't a mark on her, no tracks. How many hookers do you know with a dye job that probably cost more than you make in a week?"

Jeff laughed as if the answer didn't matter much. "Speaking of which," he nodded to a spot lower on her body. "I guess more than her hairdresser knows for sure now."

Jonathan shot the other man a look that made him take a step backward.

"Let's see if the owner's shown up yet," Patterson said, and the two of them walked off down the alley.

He caught Mari giving him a patient look. "Ease up, Stone. That's probably the closest that jerk's gotten to a naked woman in ten years."

Jonathan snorted. All the more reason not to put up with an idiot who'd use a corpse to make a lame joke. Jonathan focused on Horgan, a short stocky man with a stock of gray hair reminiscent of Spencer Tracy. "What have you got?"

"White female, or possibly Hispanic, thirty to forty years old. Signs of strangulation here." He gestured along the breadth of her throat with his index finger. "Someone gave her face a good going over, but as to which killed her, the bludgeoning or the asphyxiation, your guess is as good as mine."

"Was she raped?"

Morgan shook his head. "I don't think so. There's no sign of penetration, no evidence of fluids. I don't think I'd find any, anyway. Someone cleaned this girl up before dumping her here, clipped her fingernails. Whoever did this knew how to cover his tracks."

Jonathan frowned, which meant her killer could be someone in law enforcement, a medical practitioner or any of the millions of CSI devotees. Great to narrow down the field a little.

"Time of death?"

"Hard to say. Roasting in that can probably threw off the body temp. Rigor has set in, and judging from the posterior lividity, she lay on her back for a few hours before finding her way here. I'd say no more than twenty-four hours, but that's the best I can say now."

He nodded. "Thanks." Though he didn't really know much more than he'd started with, except that whoever killed this woman had gone to a great deal of trouble to conceal both her identity and his.

Jonathan looked up at the building across the street, which provided a perfect view into the alley. Maybe someone had seen something, and more importantly, might be willing to tell what they saw. In this neighborhood, the most likely response to police inquiries was a not-so-polite litany of what cops could do with themselves and how often.

Ironically, residents of this neighborhood, when asked what the police can do for the community, cite increased police protection as the most pressing issue. Good thing nobody ever said life had to make sense.

Jonathan sighed. Time to get down to the real work: getting a canvass started, rounding up witnesses. By the time this was over, he'd probably know this woman in the alley better than her own mother did.

He folded the camera and slid it into his pocket. "Let's go."

Coming back to consciousness, Dana opened her eyes slowly. Her head ached and her shoulder throbbed. Groggily, she took in her surroundings: a dingy white room, clunky, industrial furniture, and above, the tracks for a privacy curtain. Images of the shooting flooded her consciousness—the car, the gun pointed at her, firing, Wesley's cold, dead eyes. She closed her eyes and inhaled. *Please, God, don't let me be in Washington Hospital.*

"Welcome back to the land of the living."

Dana turned her head to the right to see Joanna sitting in a high-backed chair beside her bed. Dana licked her dry lips. "Where am I?"

"Montefiore Hospital. How do you feel?"

"Grateful to be alive. What about Wesley?"

"The kid who was with you? He didn't make it."

Dana squeezed her eyes shut. She'd known. She'd known from the moment she'd seen his eyes that he was gone, but hearing it flat out brought tears to her eyes and a sweeping sense of sadness rushing through her.

"I'm sorry," Joanna said.

Dana wiped her eyes with her hand. "I know." She was sorry, too, that a young man with such potential was gone before he'd really had a chance to do anything with his life. As sure as she knew her own name, she knew she'd been getting to him. Maybe with a little more guidance . . . Her speculations didn't matter anymore. Wesley was gone and she couldn't change that either.

"There's a detective outside waiting to talk to you. Do you feel up to it?"

She nodded. If she could, she wanted to help find Wesley's killer, though she doubted she'd be much help. "Send him in."

With a little effort, Joanna rose from her seat and went to the door. Through the opening she could see a uniformed officer outside her door. He nodded as Joanna spoke to him. Dana supposed such protection wasn't out of line considering she was a material witness to a murder.

After a few moments Joanna waddled back to her. "He'll be right here. Are you sure you're up to this? Maybe I should get your doctor."

"I'm fine." Dana smiled wickedly and appealed to her friend's nurse's pride. "Do you think a doctor would know my condition better than you would?"

"Of course not. But he is a man. You know how

they tend to pay more attention to each other than they do to us." Joanna grinned. "Besides, he's single."

Dana rolled her eyes. That was Joanna, the perpetual matchmaker. "One of these days I'm going to convince you to give up on me."

"Never."

As Joanna spoke, the door pushed open and a tall, Caucasian man walked in. He wore his dark hair long and shaggy, as haphazardly arranged as his clothes, a dark brown suit with an askew tie. His gaze went immediately to Joanna. "I'd like to speak to Miss Molloy alone."

Dana's eyebrows lifted, not because of his request, but because of his wide-legged, hostile stance at the foot of her bed. THE LAW had arrived, and he wasn't taking any prisoners. Clearly, he expected a confrontation with her, though she wondered why. Maybe he was simply impatient to find out what she knew, but she doubted it.

Joanna rolled her eyes comically, breaking the tension in the room. "I'll be right outside."

After Joanna left, she focused on the man standing at the foot of her bed. "What can I do for you, um . . ."

"Detective Moretti, 16th squad. I'd like to ask you some questions about the shooting."

"Go ahead."

"How well did you know Wesley Evans?"

"Not well. I was his grandmother's nurse. I work for At-Home Healthcare."

"That's why you were at 4093 Highland Avenue this morning?"

"Yes."

"What do you recall about the shooting?"

Dana inhaled and let it out slowly. "I came out of the building after seeing Mrs. Evans. Wesley was outside. We talked for a few minutes when this black car came careening down the street. The next thing I knew they were shooting at us."

"They? How many were there?"

"At least two. One driving and the one with the gun."

"Did you get a look at either of them?"

Dana shook her head, sending pain dancing along her scalp. She shut her eyes for a moment until it passed. "No. The windows were tinted black and I was too busy staring at the gun to see anything else."

"Did you get a license plate?"

"No." As a nurse she was trained to be observant and it galled her that she couldn't remember any information that would help in finding Wesley's killer. Looking at Detective Moretti, whose posture hadn't changed since he'd staked his claim on her room, she wondered why he hadn't taken down any of her information. "Shouldn't you be writing any of this down?"

He gave her a look that said if she'd provided him with anything worthwhile he'd have done so.

She huffed out a breath, her frustration mounting. "There were other people on the street. Didn't anyone else see something?"

"I wouldn't count on getting much from witnesses."

"Why not?"

"Evans was a small time drug dealer. Not everyone is sorry to see him gone."

She supposed that included this cop who went through the motions of investigating his death, but with little enthusiasm and no conviction. "What do you plan to do next?"

"That's police business." He pulled a business card from his pocket and extended it toward her. "If you can think of anything else, you can call me at that number. Thanks for your time."

Dana took the card and surveyed it. Det. Thomas Moretti. He was halfway out the door by the time she looked up. "You might try letting those reluctant bystanders know that he tried to save me. He tried to get me to go back inside and then he tried to shield me with his own body." That's why he'd been facing her when he'd fallen. He'd turned to protect her.

"Right," Moretti said, and continued on his way to the door.

He either didn't believe her or didn't care. She doubted what she'd told him changed his estimation of Wesley or improved his interest in solving the case. He hadn't said so, but he probably believed she'd stopped to talk to Wesley in order to score some of his product for herself.

Dana closed her eyes and rubbed her forehead with her hand. If she didn't watch it she'd be in for a serious migraine, the kind that hurt so much it nauseated her.

"How'd it go?"

As if Joanna hadn't listened at the door as if E.F. Hutton had been talking. Dana dropped her hand to the bed and laughed without mirth. "God, I hate cops."

After a long, mostly unproductive day, Jonathan parked his car at the corner of 161st and Grand Concourse and cut the engine. Darkness had already fallen, but as he got out of the car, he looked up at the building that loomed in front of him. Cut out of the far corner of the building stood a new restaurant that replaced the deli that had stood there for years. A lifetime ago, that deli had been a bar frequented by cops and c.o.'s from the Bronx House of Detention down on 149th Street.

The surrounding building had been the Concourse Arms, the hotel visiting teams had stayed at while taking on the home team at nearby Yankee Stadium. Now it was a broken-down Old Folks Home. In the Bronx, when the mighty fell, they fell hard.

Walking the block and a half to his building, he appreciated the cool breeze that wafted to him from the East River. Nights like these, he'd sit out on his fire escape cum terrace, nursing a beer and listening to the sounds of the neighborhood. Or on a game night, like tonight, he'd bring out his portable TV and when the cheering started he'd turn on the set in time to catch the instant replay.

He knew his family and most of the cops he worked with thought he was crazy for living in the neighborhood. Hell, half the building thought he was nuts. Even on a cop's salary he could afford to live somewhere where the morning wake-up call wasn't a siren from a squad car chasing down some low-life in the street. If he had a wife or kids to worry about, he wouldn't consider it, but for himself alone, it did just fine.

If he was lucky, April might have called, signaling she'd gotten over being angry with him. April wasn't very demanding of his time, but he'd stood her up on her birthday to run down a lead on the case he'd been working on. Not even a low maintenance woman like April would tolerate that without complaint. Maybe he should call her and try to apologize again.

As soon as that thought entered his mind he knew he wouldn't do it. For as accommodating as April was, he knew she was better off without him. His job as a homicide detective working out of the 48 provided all the complications he needed in his life; he'd never allowed any woman to be more than a distraction. He didn't intend to change now.

He stripped out of his clothes and showered off the grime of his day. Dressed in jeans and a T-shirt, he padded barefoot to the kitchen at the front of his apartment. The refrigerator yielded nothing more appetizing than some three-day-old chicken and a couple of beers. He'd have to settle for that as he wasn't in the mood to cook, nor did any of the places that delivered offer any fare worth the price of indigestion later.

He ate the chicken in the kitchen but took the beer out onto the fire escape outside his living room window. The night was warm, sultry in a way you only found in New York. The breeze off the river, heavy with humidity, brought the scent of other dinners cooking on other people's stoves. Somewhere in the distance, a siren wailed, but closer to home, Usher's voice blared "Yeah," accompanied by the laughter and shouted conversation of teenagers.

Once upon a time, this had been a quiet, middle-class neighborhood, populated by some of the city's largest ethnic groups: Jews, Poles, Irish and Italians. In the 1970s, a combination of white flight and financial incentives to move to the kinder, gentler North East Bronx decimated the population of the neighborhood. Unlike Harlem that had burned, paving the way for today's renewal and gentrification, the South Bronx had been abandoned to the new ethnic groups that moved in: Puerto Ricans, Haitians, Jamaicans and other groups struggling to eke out a decent living amid crime infested streets.

Every now and then, some politician would make noises about taking back the South Bronx, the Grand Concourse in particular. The only strides he'd seen in this regard were the opening of the Concourse Plaza shopping mall over a decade ago. At least the locals now had a few decent stores in which to shop.

He took a long pull on his beer before retrieving the photograph he'd tucked in his back pocket. He scanned the image of the woman's battered face. "Who are you, sweetheart?" he whispered. As of yet, fingerprints hadn't come back yet, the bum in the alleyway couldn't tell them anything and so far the neighborhood canvass had yielded the usual chorus of "I didn't see nothing." The coroner's office wouldn't be getting to the body until some time tomorrow. He'd have to wait until then to discover if the corpse held any secrets to her identity or her attacker's. Meanwhile, they'd faxed the information they had to missing persons. Maybe they'd come up with something, but he doubted it. The only distinguishing sign on her body was a small birthmark on her left shoulder. Not much to go on considering her facial features were unrecognizable.

Jonathan rubbed his temples with his thumb and middle finger. Investigating the first case they'd caught that morning hadn't proved fruitful either. Two men had gotten into a knife fight over a woman. The loser had expired on the spot. The winner, one Freddie Jackson, had been wounded, too, with a strike to the belly. But he hadn't turned up at any of the local hospitals seeking treatment, returned to any of his usual haunts. No one had heard from him, not even his mother. Jonathan suspected the only way they'd find this man was when his body, wherever he'd holed himself up, started to stink.

So, for today he was batting 0 for 2. From the sudden racket issuing from the Stadium, someone was doing better than him. He could find out who if he got the TV, but lacked the will to bother. The cell phone clipped to his waistband rumbled. He unclipped it and looked at the display. Mari's number, plus he'd missed another call.

"What's up?"

"I tried calling you before. Where were you?"

"In the shower, probably." He heard the excitement in her voice and the chastisement for keeping her waiting in her words. "What did you hear?"

"Well, to quote Samuel L. Jackson, hold on to your butt. The Jane Doe in the alley was none other than Amanda Pierce."

If Mari expected him to know who that was she was going to be disappointed. "Who?"

"Amanda Pierce, celebrity biographer, Amanda Pierce. Years back she did a book on Sinatra that made Kitty Kelly's book look like a love letter. You watch, Stone. This is going to be big."

Just what he was afraid of. How'd you find out?"

"Missing persons got back to me. The housekeeper at her East Side town house reported her missing. Yesterday was payday and Pierce didn't show up to hand out the check. The housekeeper waited twenty-four hours then called the local precinct."

"Any relatives?"

"Only a brother, some sort of movie type. He's flying in from the Coast tomorrow morning."

So what was a woman like Amanda Pierce doing in the South Bronx? Maybe she hadn't been. Maybe she'd been dumped far from the scene of the crime to confuse the investigation even more. "Any clue so far what she was doing so far from home?"

"That's the question of the hour, *amigo.* I guess we start on that tomorrow."

Jonathan clicked off the phone and sat back against

the iron railing, remembering his earlier feeling of unease about this case. So far his suspicion that this investigation wouldn't be an easy one had proved true. What remained to be seen was how gruesome this thing could get. The victim's celebrity changed things.

The press would dog him, wanting to know who'd slain one of their own. They'd be working under a public microscope—never a fun prospect. For all he knew, Manhattan would want the case if it could be proved that she was killed on their soil. He'd gladly give it up, except there was something about that battered, broken body that called to him, that whispered she wouldn't rest until he'd found out who'd killed her.

Until then, neither would he.

He sat in his study, a half-full tumbler of scotch at his elbow, looking at a picture of them from years ago. Leather jackets and wild hair and restless spirits. They'd had nothing then, no one. They'd run the streets as only those who have nobody waiting at home to question their activities could. They'd gotten into their share of trouble, but never paid the consequences until the night Father died. They'd gotten away with his murder, but they'd lost the only person who'd ever given a damn about them. He took a quick swig from the glass trying to counteract the taste of bile in his throat, with no success.

That night, the night the church went up in flames, they made a pact. They would stick together. They'd watch each other's backs. They would never tell anyone. But they'd do their damnedest to get out of that neighborhood, to make something of themselves like Father wanted.

They'd succeeded beyond what they could have conceived of at the time. Father would have been proud, if he'd lived to see them now. That's what counted most to him. He, they, had risen above what meager prospects the neighborhood had offered. They had made it.

Damn Mouse! For twenty-five years they'd kept their pact and their silence—and for the most part, their distance, as well. But thanks to Mouse, they were in it all over again. Mouse had come to him begging his understanding and his help. He hadn't meant to kill the nosy bitch, but she wouldn't leave it alone. He'd seen his carefully built life ruined because of her and panicked.

That was the trouble with lies and secrets: No matter how carefully you kept them, they sought the light, they sought discovery. He'd lived the last twenty-five years waiting, knowing time would eventually reveal what they'd done. But why now, when he'd finally allowed himself to breathe, to hope, to want, did his world threaten to dissolve around him?

More than discovery, he feared what else Mouse would do to keep the secret besides what he'd done already. But this time there would be no pact, no promises. They weren't children anymore; they were grown men. He couldn't be a party to it anymore. He put the picture back in his wallet, hiding it behind another. This time, if there was hell to pay, he'd pay it and let the chips fall where they may.

Three

If not Jonathan's least favorite place, the m.e.'s office on Crosby Avenue had to run a close second. Not that the sight of blood or gore fazed him. He'd been a cop long enough to have gotten over any innate squeamishness he might have possessed. But folks who made a career out of poking around in dead people's insides had to be one step up from crazy.

Jonathan parked in the small lot at the back of the building and got out of the car. Heat rushed up at him from the pavement. This day threatened to be as much of a scorcher as the day before. Mari came up beside him as he retrieved his jacket from the back seat and put it on.

"Ready to meet the relative?"

Jonathan snorted. Seymour Banks, Amanda Pierce's only living relative, had been met at LaGuardia airport by a black-and-white unit, supposedly as a courtesy to the bereaved. In truth, Jonathan wanted to get a bead on the man when he viewed his sister's body. Distance preventing him from seeing first-hand Banks's reaction to the news Pierce had been killed, as he would have liked. Without intending to, people

gave away a lot about themselves by the way they reacted to the news, sometimes their own culpability.

According to the detective that had spoken to the
brother, Banks had responded with neither surprise
nor much emotion. There could be any number of
explanations for that. After Jonathan had spoken to
Mari last night, he'd spent a few hours researching
Amanda Pierce on the Internet. No one but her
publisher seemed to have a kind word for the woman.

Reviews attacked her literary prowess. The subjects
of her tell-all books threatened lawsuits, though as far
as he could determine none had actually gone to trial.
The general public seemed to hate her most of all. The
"Let's Start by Killing Amanda Pierce" message board,
which appeared to be frequented mostly by fans of the
celebrities she'd skewered, featured innovative ways to
put Pierce out of everyone else's misery.

The uni pulled into the parking lot and took the
spot beside them. The officer on the passenger's
side got out and opened the back door. Banks
stepped out. A man of medium height, with a slender build and lanky brown hair, he wore a pair of gray
slacks and a summer weight sweater that appeared
casual but had probably cost as much as Jonathan
made in a week. According to an article Jonathan had
read, Banks made seven million dollars last year
playing a number of bad guys in a variety of movies.
If that were true, he might be more well off than his
sister had been.

Banks looked around with an expression of disdain
before his gaze settled on him. "Detective Stone?"
Banks checked his watch. "Is this going to take long?"

Beside him, he felt Mari bristle. To her, family
was family, which meant you showed a little respect.

Jonathan stepped forward and extended his hand

toward the man. "Mr. Banks, my condolences on your loss."

Banks ignored his hand. "Can we get this over with?"

Jonathan brought his hand to his side. "In a moment. We have a few questions for you first." Although he could just as well ask his questions inside the air-conditioned building, Jonathan decided to use the man's discomfort to his advantage. "When is the last time you saw your sister?"

Banks shrugged. "A couple of years ago, I guess. We ran into each other at some function. I haven't seen her since then."

"You and your sister weren't close?"

Banks shook his head. "Amanda and I decided a long time ago that she'd stick to her coast and I'd stick to mine. When she was alive, our mother had expressed the hope that one day we would learn to get along. For that reason alone we used to call each other twice a year, Christmas and Thanksgiving, and speak for approximately five minutes. Aside from that, we don't have much to do with one another. Amanda was a pain in the ass, but I didn't kill her, if that's what you're implying."

He hadn't implied anything, and he found the man's defensiveness telling. "These are standard questions, Mr. Banks. We ask them of everyone."

"Look, I've been in enough cop dramas to know how this goes. The first people you people suspect are spouses and relatives."

"But that's not true in this case?"

"Detective, my sister made her living pissing people off. Does it surprise you that one of them finally had enough?"

No, it wouldn't surprise him if that were the case, but he wasn't willing to concede that it was—yet.

Time might prove him right or wrong, but he wasn't willing to close off any avenues just yet. "Do you have any reason to suspect anyone in particular?"

"I wouldn't know. Last I heard she'd set her sights on Will Hudson. The one who turned up in that hotel room with two underage girls last year. That's what I heard, but you'd have to ask her assistant what she was working on. His name is Eric Bender."

Jonathan took down the man's name and contact information on his pad then returned it to his breast pocket. "Thank you."

Banks issued an impatient sigh. "Can we go in now? Or was there another standard question you wanted to ask me?"

Inwardly Jonathan shook his head, but didn't comment. He referred to Pierce's corpse as *the* body, not Amanda's or even my sister's body. He gestured for Banks to precede him toward the building.

Jonathan felt Mari come up beside him. "It's a wonder Pierce didn't off him."

Although he doubted Banks had heard her, he whispered, "Behave."

"Maybe."

Once inside, Jonathan led the way to the small room set up for family identification of the deceased. The viewer stood on one side of a large window with the body on the other side. Once the blinds were opened, the viewer could make the identification.

"Mr. Banks, how much have you been told about the way your sister died?"

"She was strangled and left in some alley."

"Someone also beat her pretty badly. You may not recognize her."

For the first time, Banks's face registered something other than impatience. "Let me see her."

Jonathan pressed the wall intercom button. "We're ready." An instant later the blinds slid open. Amanda Pierce was laid out on a stainless steel table looking much the same as she had in the alley: her body intact but her face broken. He reacted with the same visceral revulsion to violence he always did. Some cops worked at losing that, but the day Jonathan lost it he'd turn in his shield.

But it was Banks's reaction that concerned Jonathan now. The other man's eyes widened and he gasped, "Good God." He lowered his head and shut his eyes. He gulped in air in a way Jonathan had seen many times before. He had the look of a man fighting nausea. Though the man was an actor by profession, Jonathan doubted the man's response was a manufactured one.

After a moment, Banks said, "Wh-who could do that?"

"Is that your sister, Mr. Banks?"

"I don't know. It could be. She wore her hair like that."

"Did your sister have a birthmark on her left shoulder?"

He nodded. "A half moon. It's her, isn't it?"

"I believe so."

Banks nodded. "I need to make some calls, funeral arrangements. When will her body be released?"

"I'll have to get back to you. Where will you be staying?"

"I made reservations at the Pierre."

"I'll contact you there. We're going to need to get into your sister's apartment."

Banks shrugged. "I've never been there." He gave

them an address on Central Park West. "Please keep me informed on your progress."

Jonathan pulled one of his cards from his pocket. "If you can think of anything else that might be helpful, please call." He nodded to the uniforms that had followed them in. "The officers will take you to your hotel."

Banks looked at the card then stuck it in his pocket. "Thank you."

As the three others walked off, Mari turned to him. "Just when I had the guy pegged as a complete asshole."

Jonathan snorted. "Sorry he disappointed you."

"You don't like him for this, do you?"

"Not particularly. I've got the LAPD checking out his whereabouts for the last two days."

"Even if he was there, that doesn't mean he couldn't have paid someone to take her out."

"True, but so far, where's the motive? The guy doesn't appear to be hurting financially and from what he said, they were content to ignore each other." Which didn't mean he wouldn't check out every word Banks had said, he just didn't think he'd find anything going in that direction.

"That's what he said . . ."

"True." Yeah, and if Banks had lied to them he wouldn't be the first or last person to do so. "Why do you like him so much?"

"I don't, actually. It would be nice and neat, though. Brother and sister don't get along. One whacks the other. End of story. Let the press feed on that."

Instead of on them. Once the press had a name to go with the body found in back of Mario's, the fun would really begin.

Bill Horgan appeared at the window, beckoning them inside.

Stepping through the door to the right of the window, Mari said, "What brings you in on a Sunday?"

"Word came down from on high to put a rush on this, so I got called in."

That news didn't entirely surprise Jonathan. "By who?"

"Don't know. I am but a cog in the great machine." He reached for a clipboard on the counter beside him. "Let's get the preliminaries out of the way. The rape kit was negative for fluids, fibers or hairs. My guess is Ms. Pierce hadn't seen any action in a long time. The tox screen came back, too. It's negative for any of the kinds of those fun drugs we look for."

Horgan flipped over a page in her chart. "Her last meal—eggs, toast and Canadian bacon—was still fairly intact. I'd put her death between six and ten o'clock Friday morning."

Jonathan recorded the pertinent details in his notebook. "Anything else?"

"Here's where it gets interesting," Horgan continued. "Remember, I told you I thought the body had been washed before being dumped in the alley? I confirmed it. I thought from the smell it was probably rubbing alcohol and it was. But, here's the interesting part."

Horgan produced a tiny glassine envelope with a miniscule scrap of something dark in one corner. "Your killer wasn't as thorough as he thought. This scrap of fabric was imbedded in her skin, here." He pointed to an area on his own neck. "Some sort of silk material, maybe from a blouse or a scarf. I'm sending it over to your lab boys to check it out."

Horgan put down his clipboard and ran his hand through his hair, making it stand on end. "One last thing. The job on her face happened post mortem."

Which fed into Jonathan's theory that she'd been beaten for the sole purpose of hiding her identity. "Any guess on the weapon?"

Horgan shrugged. "Something round and heavy. Maybe a paperweight."

After writing down the additional information, Jonathan closed his notebook. "If you think of anything else."

Horgan winked. "I know where to reach you."

Once outside in the oppressive heat, Jonathan loosened his tie and opened his collar before they reached the car. As Mari got in, he heard her snicker.

He laid his jacket on the back seat before sliding in behind the wheel. "What's so funny?"

"You are, my friend. You and your brethren." She tugged on his tie. "How can you stand to wear those things?"

He slid a sideways glance at her as he started the car. He recognized her comment for what it was—an attempt to distance herself from the brutality they'd just seen with the aid of a little humor. He didn't mind playing along. "If men are ridiculous for wearing ties, what does that make women for wearing panty hose?"

"Yeah, well women don't like pantyhose. Besides, it's not like we wear this big sign on our chests that points to our gonads. It's like, 'There's my penis. Right there. Look at it, look at it.' It's disgusting."

Smiling, Jonathan pulled out of the space and into traffic. "Then how do you explain the push-up bra?"

"Okay, you've got me there. I guess neither sex corners the market on unbridled vanity." She sighed. "I suppose I ought to call the LT. He asked me to let him know when Pierce's identity was confirmed."

In the periphery of his vision, Jonathan watched her pull out her cell phone. Lieutenant John Shea was one of those political beings that made their way up the ranks not through intelligence or hard work but through cronyism and a certain brand of craftiness better suited to lesser animals. He was a master of serving his own ends rather than protecting his men or serving the public, and Jonathan wondered about his involvement in this case. Obviously, it concerned him enough to have Mari call him on a Sunday morning to report their progress. Jonathan hoped that keeping on top of what was likely to be a sensational case was his only motive.

They'd already decided on their course of action for the day by the time they'd met Banks. First, they'd see if Pierce's brother could identify her. If not, they were back to square one and they'd start back on it on Monday. If he could, they'd head to her apartment. Since she obviously hadn't been murdered in the alley, she had to have been killed somewhere. Her apartment was as good a bet as anywhere else.

Mari closed the phone and looked at him. "Shea's going to release Pierce's name to the press. And get this, he already heard from Banks. Banks is offering a fifty thousand dollar reward for any information leading to an arrest in his sister's death."

Jonathan gritted his teeth. Adding that kind of money to the mix would bring out another brand of crazy. Every greedy son of a bitch would be calling in looking for a pay day. "It took him all of fifteen minutes to come up with that?"

"Maybe he wants to appear the devoted brother while the world is looking."

Jonathan shrugged, not really interested in anyone's motivations but his own. He pressed a little harder on the gas pedal. "Maybe we ought to get there before the press does."

Amanda Pierce lived in a luxury apartment building on the corner of West 87th and Central Park West. The doorman, dressed in navy blue livery, greeted them at the front desk with all the disdain of an English butler trying to shoo the riff raff away from his master's door. "May I help you?"

Jonathan flashed his badge. "Who do we speak to about getting into Amanda Pierce's apartment?"

The doorman's glare shifted from him to Mari and back again. His chest puffed up, like a bird's, announcing his importance. "That would be me, but I'm under strict orders not to let anyone up without her approval. Besides Ms. Pierce isn't here."

"I'm aware of that. Are you aware of the penalty for hindering a police investigation?"

The man visibly deflated. "All right, then." He pulled a voluminous set of keys from his pocket. "When Ms. Pierce finds out about this, it's on your head."

"Not a problem," he said.

The doorman led them through the expansive marble-tiled lobby to the service elevator. When the car arrived, the doorman stationed himself at the front, leaving Mari and Jonathan to move around him to stand in back. Of all the childish nonsense. Since Jonathan needed the information the man could provide, he squeezed in behind Mari without comment. "When is the last time you saw Ms. Pierce?"

"Friday morning," the doorman answered still staring straight ahead. "I hailed a taxi for her. I don't know where she was going."

"You didn't happen to notice the medallion number of the cab?"

"I am not in the habit of monitoring taxi drivers."

The elevator stopped on the twelfth floor. The doorman got out and headed toward a door almost directly across from the elevator. There were only two other doors to choose from. In a building this size, the apartments must be tremendous.

As the doorman worked on the locks, Jonathan asked. "How long did Ms. Pierce live here?"

"At least six years. She was already a tenant when I arrived."

"Did Ms. Pierce have many visitors?"

"Not many, no. Her agent came by from time to time."

"What about her brother?" Mari put that in, Jonathan figured, in an attempt to stir the pot.

"I wasn't aware Ms. Pierce had a brother."

At least that part of Banks's story checked out. Her doorman would have known if he'd visited frequently.

The door finally slid open. Jonathan gestured for the man to wait outside.

"What is this about, anyway?" the doorman asked. "Has something happened to Ms. Pierce?"

It took him long enough to get to that. Jonathan stepped into the apartment after Mari. "She was found dead yesterday morning. If we need anything else, we'll find you." Jonathan shut the door in the man's face.

"*Dios*, would you look at this place," Mari said, drawing his attention. "No wonder the admiral didn't want us in here."

Jonathan snorted at Mari's appellation for the doorman, but her assessment of the house was dead on. He let out a low whistle as he drank in the apartment's décor: white marble floors, high, arched ceilings, a foyer he could fit almost his entire apartment into. Heavy sunlight streaming in from nearly floor to ceiling windows provided all the illumination needed. Delicate wood furniture bespoke the wealth of its owner, and everything was spotless.

He supposed that's what lent the apartment a non-lived-in feel, as if everything here were being exhibited in a museum. Most people didn't live like this. If you showed up at their house unexpectedly there might be a couple of dishes in the sink, a dust bunny or two hiding under the bed. Then again, Pierce's housekeeper had been here on Friday. If Pierce hadn't returned home that day, she'd have had no opportunity to mess things up.

Searching the apartment took a little over an hour. There were six messages on her answering machine: two were from telemarketers, one was from her editor informing her that she loved the latest manuscript that had been sent in. The remainder were from her agent. In forty-eight hours she hadn't received one personal phone call.

At the far end of the house was the room she obviously used as a home office, complete with laptop, printer, fax and copying machine. He found her address book there, but no day planner, no calendar that might have told him where she was headed that day.

Her file cabinet contained little save contracts she'd signed, press clippings, fan mail and financial records. Very little to indicate what she'd been working on. Nonetheless, they would need to take all of this back to the house to sift through it, contact the people she knew, figure out which person hated her enough to kill her. But judging by the virulence of some of her mail, the vitriol of the press against her and her brother's lack of devotion, it might be easier to find someone who wanted her alive.

Four

Restless, unused to being in the position of having someone else care for her and out of sorts at being stuck in a hospital bed, Dana flicked around the meager television offerings using the remote. Absolutely nothing interested her, but eager for some kind of sound in the room, she settled on the news. A male/female pair of anchors smiled for the camera while relaying yet another grisly story of murder and mayhem on the city's streets.

Dana sighed. What was it in the recent evolution of the human psyche that required that even the worst news be sugarcoated with a wink and a grin? Annoyed, but more at her own situation than anything on the screen, Dana tossed the remote onto the bed beside her.

She couldn't even use her proper hand. Her right arm and shoulder were encased in a sling fastened close to her body. The bullet had gone through her shoulder without hitting any vital muscle or bone. She'd been lucky, damn lucky. Tim could be picking out a casket for her at the moment. If it weren't for Wesley trying to get her out of the way, the odds on that would have been even higher. She found that thought ironic, considering that his presence had put her in danger in the first place.

A knock at her door pulled her from her thoughts. Father Michael Coyne poked his head in the room. "Anybody home?"

Dana reacted with a mixture of pleasure and surprise. Not only did she credit Father Mike with helping her push, pull, drag and cajole Tim into not only finishing high school, but excelling, but Father Michael Coyne was also one fine specimen of a human being. Like three-quarters of the schoolgirls at St. Matthew's and most of their mothers, Dana had to admit to having a slight crush on the man. Since neither crossing the color line nor seducing a man of the cloth were in her immediate plans, all she did was look. But how had he known she'd been there to begin with?

Dana formed her lips into a welcoming smile. "Come in, Father," she said. "Don't take this the wrong way, but how did you know where to find me?"

Father Mike strode into the room. Dressed in neither the gym clothes he usually wore nor the priest's frock he eschewed, he had on a pair of khaki pants and a polo shirt. "Mrs. Ryan, Stevie's mother, is an emergency room nurse. She saw you come in and called me."

Dana nodded. She'd known that she and the boy's mother shared the same profession but not where the other woman worked. "She didn't have to call you."

He pulled the one chair in the room, a green pleather number, over to her bedside and sat. "Yes, she did. We're a family at St. Matt's. We take care of our own."

Dana offered him a wan smile. She'd heard that

sentiment from the first time she'd walked through the school's doors. The idea of being part of a family community had been what drew her to the school, not the fact that its academic program ranked as one of the top in the archdiocese. Neither she nor Tim had any family; they only had each other. She liked the idea of people watching out for her brother when she could not.

In the four years Tim attended the school, she'd donated blood for blood drives, baked cakes for bake sales, offered up prayers for the needy and those in dire straits. But never before had she been in the position to need their largesse or their concern. She wasn't sure how she felt about receiving it now.

Father Mike sat back in his chair. "How are you feeling?"

She lifted her good shoulder in a shrug. "Just a little worse for wear."

"But the young man with you wasn't as fortunate."

"No." Grief welled in her, clogging her throat and bringing the sting of tears to her eyes. "He died right there."

"I'm sorry, Dana."

She inhaled, and let her breath out slowly, fighting the urge to let her tears spill. "Don't get me wrong, Father. He was no angel. He dealt drugs and probably stepped on the wrong person's toes. I don't know. It just seems like such a waste to me. He was only seventeen. He could have been anything."

Father Mike offered her a sympathetic look. "Sometimes the hardest thing to give up on is hope."

Nodding, she looked away. Despite his hostile attitude and fatalistic view of his own life, she really had felt Wesley could have turned his life around. Hope. The fact that she felt the emotion didn't surprise her, but the depth of her emotions and the breadth of her grief and disappointment at the loss of the young man did. Maybe she wasn't as much of a cynic as she thought.

She started to turn back to Father Mike, but something on the television screen caught her eye, the image of a blond woman in the upper right hand corner of the screen. Dana recognized the woman as the one she'd seen in Nadine Evans's building a couple of days ago and automatically turned up the sound.

". . . body was found behind a popular South Bronx eatery," the newscaster intoned. He gave several other details of the case before concluding, "Police are investigating both the cause of Ms. Pierce's death and how she ended up in the South Bronx neighborhood where she was discovered. Anyone with any information should contact the Bronx Homicide Division. A special hotline has been set up at 1-800-877-9241."

Though the newscaster quickly switched to another story, Amanda Pierce's image stayed with Dana. "Oh, my God, Father. I saw that woman."

Father Mike sat forward. "When?"

"Friday morning. She was coming out of Wesley Evan's apartment building. Less than a mile from where she ended up."

"Are you sure she's the woman you saw?"

"Not absolutely. My head is still a little fuzzy from the concussion, but I'd swear it was her. I wondered at the time what a woman dressed as she was could be doing in that part of town. I thought at the time that she was smart to catch a ride out of the neighborhood. In retrospect it might have been her last."

"Did you get a look at who picked her up?"

"Not really. A dark-haired man. Or at least that was my impression. For all I know, it could have been a woman. I guess that's not particularly helpful."

Father Mike shrugged. "Maybe not. What are you going to do?"

Dana sighed. "Call the hotline number, I guess." And hope she could make an anonymous report. While she felt obligated to tell what she saw, the prospect of getting involved in another police investigation in two days, when she'd done nothing to involve herself in either of them, didn't please her.

Perhaps sensing her displeasure, Father Mike said, "You can always take comfort in knowing you did the right thing."

Yeah. Her and Mother Teresa. She hadn't bothered to have a phone hooked up in the room. "Hand me my phone, Father, before I change my mind. It's in my purse in the top dresser drawer."

Chuckling, Father Mike did as she asked. Between the two of them, they remembered the number to dial. After making her waste her minutes on hold, an operator came on and took down her information with the promise of getting it to the detective in charge.

Dana leaned back against her pillows, hoping that her involvement in the matter was over. If she had seen Amanda Pierce, surely someone else had seen her as well. Besides, she'd given them the precise address she'd visited and a description of the car she'd gotten into, though she hadn't been able to provide a license plate number. Surely that was enough to go on without involving her any further. Well, she could hope anyway.

Father Mike checked his watch. "I've got to be going. The other thing I wanted to ask you is if you need any help with Tim? I'm sure one of the other mothers wouldn't mind having him over for a couple of days while you recover."

Again she felt a tinge of . . . she didn't know what to call it. Guilt, probably, over making anyone worry about her, and discomfort at being in a position of need, even if it were only perceived need.

"I've got it covered, Father. You couldn't know this, but I'm supposed to be lying on a beach on Paradise Island right now, not stuck in a hospital bed. I'd already made arrangements for Tim to stay with another family. He's with them now. Besides, they're supposed to be letting me out of here today, if the doctor would ever show up to check me out."

Father Mike pushed back his chair and stood. "I'll let you get your rest until then. If you need a ride home, I can get someone—"

Dana held up her good hand to forestall him. "I've got that covered, too. My friend Joanna and her husband are on call."

He took her hand and offered her a benevolent smile. "All right. You let me know if there is anything I *can* do for you."

Great. Now she'd offended him. The problem with the do-gooders of the world was that they resented the hell out of not being given anything good to do. "Actually, there is something you can do for me. My patient, Nadine Evans, she's bedridden. I don't know if she has the wherewithal to make the arrangements or if she has any money to bury her grandson."

Dana had called Nadine earlier, only to have the woman slam the phone down in her ear. Dana didn't know what that was about. Maybe Nadine was too overcome with grief to talk, or maybe she resented her for surviving when Wesley didn't, but Dana couldn't leave it like that. Hopefully, Father Mike would be able to succeed where she failed. Nadine wasn't Catholic, but she was religious enough not to be rude to any man of the cloth.

After taking down Nadine's address and phone number, Father Mike left, leaving her alone. Now if only the damn doctor would show up, she could get out of here and figure out what to do with herself the next few days. She had another week before she had to go back to work, not that she was in any shape to lug that computer from place to place. About the only thing she was good for was catching up on all the books she wanted to get to while on her vacation. But then she'd been planning to read them with the sun on her face and a tropical breeze blowing through her hair.

Damn. That's another bonus she hadn't thought of. She'd just lost the money she'd laid out for her trip. Her life just got better and better.

When Jonathan walked into the squad room on Monday morning, Mari was already waiting for him. She nodded toward the lieutenant's office. Shea was on the phone, and from what Jonathan could tell the conversation was one-sided with Shea doing all the listening. "He wants to see us as soon as he gets off the phone."

Jonathan gritted his teeth. Most of the time Shea could not care less what you did or how you did it as long as it was accomplished with enough speed to make him look good. If he wanted to speak to them now, it wasn't to wish them a Merry Christmas.

As soon as Shea hung up he motioned them to join him. Once they'd entered his office before closing the door he gestured that they sit. Jonathan ignored the two visitors' chairs, as did Mari. If they were going to be dressed down both of them preferred to take it standing up.

"I don't need to tell you the flack I'm getting already on this Pierce thing. Turns out the police commissioner's new wife and Pierce went to Wellesley together. She's on his back about a speedy resolution to the case, and now he's on mine."

Jonathan slid a glance at Mari, gauging if she caught his implication. Never being one not to share the grief, he was passing it on to them.

Shea shifted in his seat. "Where are we on this thing?"

Jonathan glanced down at Shea's desk where his initial report sat. He wouldn't need to ask questions if he had bothered to read them. But why do things the easy way? "Apparently, Amanda Pierce caught a taxi from her apartment on Friday morning and that's the last anyone saw of her until she was discovered Saturday morning."

He filled Shea in on their meeting with Banks and what they found in her apartment. He'd spent the previous night going through some of her paper records while Mari had gone through her computer. Most of the files were password protected, so the laptop was with the techs now, hoping they could crack the code. But nothing they had found so far suggested what she was working on or where she had gone.

He finished with, "We've got the housekeeper coming in this morning. We'll put in a call to Pierce's agent and her editor and see what turns up."

Shea huffed. "There will be a small press conference this afternoon at three at One Police Plaza. I'll expect you both there."

Jonathan gritted his teeth. Any excuse for Shea to press his mug in front of the cameras. Everyone knew Shea had ambitions beyond the office he now occupied. Jonathan and Mari would be superfluous.

Shea adjusted his jacket and hunched over his desk in a way that suggested they'd been dismissed. Jonathan opened the door and followed Mari into the squad room.

"Well, that was fun," Mari said as they walked back to their desks. "Think I need to get my hair done?"

Jonathan shot her a droll look. "What time is that housekeeper coming in?"

"A half hour."

Rosa Nuñez showed up ten minutes early. A slender, petite woman in her mid-forties, she presented the picture of propriety. She wore a pale peach dress that fell below her knee, black low-heeled pumps and a silk scarf around her neck. Her dark brown hair was pinned into an old-fashioned bun at her nape.

After introducing themselves, they showed her to the coffee room, a small office converted to a pseudo-kitchenette, its only real amenities being a small sink in the corner, a refrigerator, and an ancient microwave oven. A rectangular table and four chairs took up most of the room.

He motioned to Mrs. Nuñez to sit in one of the chairs while Mari sat across the table from her. He hung back, leaning his shoulder against the refrigerator. He and Mari had worked together long enough that they knew each other's strengths and weaknesses, knew who worked better with what sort of people. Mari had an affinity to women, particularly older women. She was their daughter, their friend, their confidant.

There was something in most people, guilt probably, that made them want to confess their sins. All they needed was a sympathetic ear and the absence of an attorney telling them it was in their best interest to shut up.

Put Mari in a room with a woman and she'd know everything from her shoe size to her kindergarten teacher's name before she came out.

Mari folded her hands on the table. "Thank you for coming in, Ms. Nuñez."

"Please, call me Rosa." Her gaze darted from Mari to him and back. "Are you the detectives working on Miss Amanda's case?"

"Yes. We'd like to ask you a few questions about your employer, Ms. Pierce. How long did you work for her?"

"About six years. Ever since she moved into the new apartment. I used to live there, too, until last year. I got married again and, well, I had to move out."

"How was she to work for? Was she friendly or more distant? Was she easy going?"

"Oh, no. She is very strict," Rosa said with a note of pride in her voice. "Miss Amanda wants everything just so. Everything spotless. She made me vacuum that whole place every day."

"On Friday when she went out, did she tell you where she was going?"

"No. Miss Amanda never told me anything like that. She was very private with me. She seemed excited, though, like she got sometimes when . . ."

Rosa's words trailed off, and Jonathan could imagine the rest. . . . When she discovered some particularly dirty bit of information on someone else.

"Do you know if Ms. Pierce was seeing anyone? Did she have a boyfriend?"

Rosa shook her head. "There used to be this one, but not for a long time. Maybe two year. The only one

I see sometimes is the agent. I make rice and beans for him."

"As far as you know, was there anyone bothering Ms. Pierce, threatening her?"

"Only the usual crazy people. People who don't like what she wrote. I would see her mail at home sometimes."

"What time were you expecting her back on Friday?"

"About six the latest. That's when I usually go on Friday. She pay me and then I leave."

"Has she ever been late before?"

"Not if she didn't call. That's why I worry. I wait a while, then I call my husband. He says you have to wait to report someone missing, so I waited." Rosa's eyes misted over. "Who could have done this to Miss Amanda? She's a hard lady to work for and I know some people don't like what she writes in her books." Rosa shook her head.

Since neither he nor Mari had an answer for that, neither of them commented on it. Jonathan straightened and took a step forward. "Thank you for coming in, Ms. Nuñez. If we need to speak to you again, can we reach you at the same number?"

Rising to her feet, she nodded. "I hope you find who did this."

"I promise you, we will."

Rosa nodded again and allowed Mari to escort her from the room. When they were gone, Jonathan poured himself a cup of coffee. How palatable it would be depended on who'd brewed it, which was anybody's guess. A couple of the guys could make a decent pot, but Mari brewed it like it was Spanish coffee, dark, strong and intended to be sweetened with milk. He added his usual splash of cream and sipped. He grimaced as it went down. Mud.

Mari reappeared in the doorway. "Let me ask you this. When did maids start carrying Coach handbags and wearing Roché scarves? Looks like I picked the wrong line of work—again."

Jonathan shrugged. He'd heard of the handbag company, but women's clothing, the type expected to be seen in public, was out of his field of expertise. "Expensive?" he asked.

"Exclusive." Mari came up beside him and poured herself a cup of coffee. "Each one signed by the creator himself, supposedly. Roche makes them out of his own special blend of raw and processed silk. Try six hundred dollars a pop—and that's the bottom of the line."

"So you think the very proper Ms. Nuñez has been helping herself to her boss' finery?"

Mari shrugged. "Maybe Pierce gave them to her. Passing your castoffs to the help is as American as cheating on your taxes." As she spoke she walked toward the table and sat in the chair Rosa Nuñez had occupied. She sipped from her cup. "Hey, not bad."

Jonathan said nothing to that. They had bigger things to worry about than the gastronomical merits of stationhouse coffee. "So, other than the fact that Rosa Nuñez might have been ripping off her employer, we don't find out anything new."

"Did you really expect to?"

"No." But learning something, anything, couldn't have hurt, considering Shea wanted it done yesterday. Mentally, he went over the leads they intended to follow that day: interviews with Pierce's agent, her editor, her assistant, not to mention sifting through some more of her files, getting a look at her computer

if the techs were done with it and requisitioning the
LUDs for her home and cell phones. Light stuff.

"There you are."

Jonathan focused on the uniformed officer standing in the doorway. He held a single sheet of paper
Jonathan recognized as the one they used to take
down information on the hotlines. "Have you got
something?"

"I'm downstairs working the tip line. Mostly
Amanda sightings. I saw Amanda on the corner of
this and that. Amanda and Elvis were at Yankee Stadium. Whatever. The lieu said to give the unlikelies
to Russell and Martinez to run down."

The story had been released to the papers saying
that Pierce had been found behind the pizza parlor,
but not that she had been discovered in a trash can
or that she'd been nude. The report said that she'd
been strangled, but nothing about the beating. Only
the person who'd done that to her would know those
details. It was another way of sorting out the real
thing from those who just wanted to be noticed.

The officer stepped forward, extending the paper
toward him. But rather than step away, the man
leaned in, looking at the paper. "This one came in last
night. Didn't know if you'd seen it. A woman claims
she saw Pierce coming out of a building on Highland
Avenue. 4000 block. Surprise of surprises, she didn't
give her name." As he spoke, he tapped the box in
which each bit of information was taken down.

Jonathan shifted the paper out of the other man's
reach. "Thanks. We hadn't seen it."

As the guy moved off, Jonathan cast a glance at Mari,
certain the other officer's snub hadn't been uninten-
tional.

She shot him a look, which showed her disgust with

her fellow officers. "Please let me know when I really do turn into a piece of furniture around here. I'm sure I'll want to have myself reupholstered." She slogged down the remains in her cup. "Looks like they got a number on the call." She turned the sheet to show the series of digits scrawled at the top of the page. "Somewhere in Westchester."

Calls to the tipline were supposed to be anonymous unless the caller wanted it that way. But the caller ID must have picked it up and someone had written it down. "Let's give her a call."

They went back to their desks for Mari to make the call. She hung up almost immediately. "The voicemail came on, which unfortunately gave no clue as to who I was calling."

"Great." Considering they weren't supposed to have the number there was no point in leaving a message advertising they had it.

"What now, Kemosabe? This is your rodeo."

Jonathan stood and put on his jacket. "Let's head over to Highland Avenue." If the caller could be believed, Pierce had to be visiting someone in that building, someone who might know what Pierce had been working on or who she'd left with. Knocking on a few doors definitely beat out heading down to the city, fighting midday traffic to speak to her agent and editor. Considering that they were scheduled to end up down there later for the commissioner's press conference, they might as well start in the Bronx and work their way down. Mari sighed. "I was afraid you were going to say that."

Jonathan chuckled. While they were out, he'd have someone run down a number for their mystery caller, just in case they needed to speak to her after all.

Five

The building at 4093 Highland Avenue was, like most other buildings in the neighborhood, a pre-war elevator building in serious need of repair. Despite the deadbolt, the front door opened without the need of a key. With the aid of four officers from the 44th, Jonathan and Mari intended to knock on each door and ask the resident if they'd seen Amanda Pierce that day.

Truthfully, he didn't hold out much hope of anyone volunteering any information. Not only would they run up against the usual brick wall, but whoever Pierce saw that day might be caught up in whatever it was that made someone want to kill her. Unless they'd been living under a rock and missed the news coverage, any person seeking the police's protection would have come forward already. To Jonathan's mind that meant that whoever Pierce had seen wanted to stay hidden.

Then again, their mystery caller could have gotten the address wrong or had made up the story seeking a few minutes' attention. There was only one way to find out.

Each pair took two floors, he and Mari claiming the bottom two. It was his turn to do the talking, Mari's to take down any pertinent information. The first two doors they knocked on yielded no response. That was the trouble with a daytime canvass—half the people weren't home. He slipped a card under each door asking the occupant to call the precinct and moved on.

He knocked on the next door. "Police Department."

When the door opened, Jonathan had to shift his focus downward. An old man in a wheelchair stared back at him, a belligerent expression hardening his features. "What y'all want?"

Jonathan held up the picture of Pierce that the department was using for identification. "Have you seen this woman in this building?"

The old man took the picture in his weathered, nut-brown hands and studied it. "That's the woman that's been on the TV." He looked up at Jonathan. "What about her?"

"We have reports of her being in this building on Friday morning. Did you see her?"

The old man's expression soured. "Now, what would a gal like that be doing up here?" He handed back the picture. "Look, my program is on." The man wheeled himself back and shut the door.

That first interview set the tone for all the others. No one claimed to have seen Amanda Pierce and no one was pleased to have their morning interrupted by the police.

"Well, that was productive," Mari said as they stepped out of the building into the oppressive midday sun.

The other four officers had already left, grumbling

about wasting their time. Jonathan couldn't blame them, since he felt the same way, like he was chasing his own tail. Hopefully their trip down to the city wouldn't be equally unrewarding.

Pierce's editor had already gone to lunch when they called, but her agent, James Burke, welcomed them into his office in lower Manhattan.

Once they were all seated in his office, he said, "This is such a shame about Amanda. I was away for the weekend and just heard about her death this morning. I'll do whatever I can to help."

"How long have you known Ms. Pierce?"

"Oh, a good fifteen years, I think. We met back when she was working for the *Times*. Amanda started out as a quote unquote serious journalist, but every editor she had complained she couldn't stick to a hard news format if her life depended on it. She wrote every story as if it were a feature for the New Yorker. I suggested she work on a book, a format where her talent for embellishment would be an asset."

Burke shifted in his chair. "Her first book was about Eleanor Roosevelt, not a celebrity at all. She kind of fell into that and it was a lucky thing she did."

"What is she working on now?"

"Honestly, I don't know. She'd finished her latest contract with Pulliam Press and wanted some time off. I couldn't blame her. She'd been turning in a book every twelve to thirteen months for the past few years. Most writers doing the same kind of work take maybe two or three times as long."

Burke leaned back in his chair. "I thought maybe she might have been working on a novel she didn't want anyone to know about yet, but that's just speculation. Her assistant might know."

He very well might, but to date they hadn't been

able to track the man down. "You knew her socially as well as being her agent?"

He nodded. "We were friends. We were each other's pity date in case we had no one else to attend functions with. She knew I had a penchant for Spanish food, so every now and then her cook would whip up something for me." He glanced at Mari. "You must know what I mean."

"I'm an American girl," Mari said, sounding like Rita Moreno in *West Side Story*. "I don't eat."

Burke chuckled. "Is there anything else I can tell you?"

"It's my understanding not everyone was happy with either Ms. Pierce's subjects or what she had to say about them."

"That's putting it mildly. These days our celebrities are our gods. As much as people love to hear gossip, they hate to examine anyone's character. In her writing Amanda said these people you admire are nothing but big spoiled overpaid babies that have no self-control. And you know what? She thrived on it. The more people hated her, the more books she sold, and the more money she made. She used to joke that she'd go for the title of most reviled woman in America if she thought she could wrestle the honor from Roseanne Barr. This was a few years back, of course."

"Was there anyone in particular who might have threatened her?"

Burke snapped his fingers. "You know every now and again, she'd send me a particularly vicious letter, you know, just to show how far some people would go to express their displeasure. We used to joke about them, but honestly, I think some of them scared her." Burke opened the bottom drawer to his desk. "I think I have it here."

After a moment, Burke pulled out a black file folder and extended it toward him. "If there's a loony responsible for her death, you'll probably find him in there—or at least his e-mail address."

Jonathan stood and took the folder. He'd gotten whatever information he could from this man. "Thanks for your time."

Burke rose, as did Mari. "If you need anything else."

He nodded, understanding Burke's implication. Once he and Mari were on the elevator on the way down to the first floor, she said, "Don't tell me we might have an actual lead in this freaking case."

"Who knows?" Jonathan opened the folder. The letter on top started with, DEAR BITCH, YOU DESERVE TO DIE, in boldface red caps. He closed the folder and checked his watch. They had more than enough time to make it down to One Police Plaza for the press conference.

"You know Shea expects us to have worked a miracle by now to make him look good with the big boss."

"I know." But covering Shea's ass was the last thing on Jonathan's mind. "He'll have to settle for what we've got."

Seized by the same restlessness that had claimed her in the hospital, Dana prowled around her home, searching for something to occupy her. She'd never been much of a TV watcher and her mind wandered every time she tried to pick up a book. She'd cleaned her apartment thoroughly the week before, knowing she'd be away. Even if she'd found some household chore to do she'd have to let it slide since she was in no shape for cleaning.

She paused at her brother's room. Maybe she was just out of sorts at being alone, lacking anyone else to worry about. She'd called Tim to let him know what happened, that she was all right, in case some news story hit the tube. He'd offered to come back home, but she saw no reason to cut short his vacation simply because her own had been sidelined.

If loneliness was her only problem she'd better get used to it. Tim would be leaving for Cornell by the end of the summer. He would be home for summers and holidays, or maybe she would visit him, but the day-to-day interaction she had known was over.

She should be happy. It seemed as if she had been waiting for this day her whole life—time to breathe, to be, without first considering the needs of someone else. Not that she begrudged either Tim's or her mother's demands on her, but she couldn't remember a time when she didn't consider her own needs last. Now it was Dana time, time for her life to really begin, and in an odd way she wasn't ready for it. Aside from her one ruined vacation, she'd never had much time to contemplate what she wanted.

The phone rang for maybe the fifth time that day, but she made no move to answer it. She'd let the machine pick it up, considering it was probably Joanna calling again to check up on her. When Joanna and Ray dropped her off yesterday, it had taken a great deal of convincing to get Joanna to return home. It was enough that they'd not only given her a ride but bought her enough food to sustain her a few days since due to her planned vacation there was nothing in the house.

Dana sighed. Maybe she should take a page from her friend's book and find some decent man, have some kids and figure out how to be happy, not just survive. Perhaps she could find some man who wasn't looking for a second mama, who could stand on his own feet and pull his own weight. Her days of catering to anyone were over.

From her bedroom she heard the sound of Joanna's voice, pleading but not as urgent as if she'd gone into labor. Since she didn't feel like talking to anyone, Joanna included, she didn't pick up.

Her stomach growled, reminding her she still had to do such mundane things as feed herself. She checked her watch. It was almost six o'clock. Ray and Joanna had bought her some frozen dinners that she could heat up in the microwave. She settled on the lasagna, nuked it for the required seven minutes, and brought her meal and a bottle of beer into the living room.

Settling in the corner of the sofa, she flicked on the TV and flipped around until she got the news. There was not one mention of the shooting on Highland Avenue that took Wesley's life and maimed her, but several minutes were devoted to Amanda Pierce's murder, even some footage from a press conference held by the police commissioner with a line of grim-faced men and women standing behind him who Dana figured must be connected to the case.

For the life of her, Dana couldn't figure out why this one woman's death should garner so much attention. For the most part, she'd profiled celebrities, though she probably had some muscle with the local politicians, as well. As the reports told it, she used her fame to fundraise for the Democratic Party. Still, all the hoopla seemed like overkill.

Or maybe it was the classic case of white chick ventures into the 'hood and gets killed or raped or breaks a fingernail and then the world rallies around to make sure the guilty are punished.

The commissioner shifted, revealing one of the men behind him: Jonathan Stone, the "baby" of Joanna's family. Joanna had told her he was working homicide now. The last time she'd seen him in the flesh had been a year ago at the family's Fourth of July barbecue in Joanna's back yard. As usual, he'd stood off to the side, distant and silent.

For a moment, she could have sworn she'd caught him staring at her. Unlike most men in that situation he'd kept on staring. She'd stared right back at him as a sort of challenge—until Joanna's youngest had come up to him, startling him. He'd obviously been lost in thought, not paying any attention to her at all.

That was fine, since she wouldn't have welcomed his attention in the first place. Her ideal man didn't suffer from a death wish and was slightly more communicative than the average brick wall.

The doorbell rang, pulling her from her musings. She only hoped it wasn't Joanna, who, fed up with talking to a machine, had decided to check out her welfare in person.

She crossed the living room and walked the short distance down the hallway. She walked to the door but didn't bother looking through the peephole. It had long since clouded over and she'd been loath to pay for a new one since she didn't get many visitors to begin with. "Who is it?" she asked.

"It's Jonathan Stone."

A mixture of surprise and alarm ran through her on hearing his voice. She pulled open the door, regretting her decision not to answer any of her friend's calls. "Is Joanna all right?"

He looked surprised at her question, the most

emotion she'd ever seen on his face. "As far as I know, she's fine."

Now it was her turn to be puzzled. "Then why are you here?"

"I'd like to speak with you about what you saw Friday morning in connection with the Amanda Pierce case."

Her eyes narrowed as she considered him. "I thought those calls were confidential."

"May I come in?"

Annoyed that her confidence had been broken and the fact he neither confirmed nor denied that it shouldn't have been, she said, "Are you sure you don't want to rifle through my trash cans first? Or maybe you prefer some other way of invading my privacy."

"It's not like that, Dana."

That was exactly what she hated about cops—they thought their ends justified any means. She didn't know how the police had figured out she had called in, and it didn't really matter. It would never occur to them to leave someone alone if they thought it would help their case.

She huffed out a breath. He was here already and he was her best friend's brother. She might as well answer his questions and be done with it. It could be worse. She could have Moretti questioning her, but this time she'd bet the case would get more than a cursory investigation.

"Come on in," she said, "but I doubt I can tell you anything more than what I told them over the phone." She turned and headed toward the living room, trusting him to close the door behind him. She took a seat at the edge of the sofa facing the door to the room. She gestured for him to take the love seat on the opposite wall, but he remained standing, looking around.

"Nice place."

Yes, she agreed with him silently, but it hadn't always been a nice place. She'd bought it as a fixer-upper since she couldn't afford many places that didn't require fixing. In the last three years, she'd retiled the downstairs bathroom and completely gutted the upstairs one. She'd retiled the kitchen floor and enclosed the back porch. This room had been the worst, requiring new hardwood floors, new dry-wall and a new ceiling. She'd painted the room a soft apricot to match her caramel-colored leather furniture. The room now exuded a warm, homey feeling that she enjoyed.

But she doubted Jonathan Stone really cared one way or another about her décor. She recognized his words as his opening gambit, the infamous lead-in question or comment designed to relax the interviewee and she didn't appreciate it.

"Don't handle me, Jonathan. Ask what you want to ask."

"All right." He unbuttoned his suit jacket and sat across from her. "How sure are you that it was Amanda Pierce you saw coming out of the building on Highland Avenue?"

"About ninety-nine percent. But I didn't see her coming out of the building. She was already outside when I got out."

"You never saw her inside the building?"

"No. I told that to the officer I spoke to." Since he didn't seem pleased with that answer, she asked, "Why?"

"What was she wearing?"

Just like a cop to ignore your questions and stick

to his own agenda. She relayed everything she remembered from the pumps on the woman's feet to the scarf tied on her handbag.

He wrote on his pad as she spoke. After a moment he looked up. "What kind of scarf?"

Dana shrugged. "I don't know. It had a pattern of piano keys on it."

"You say she got into a car with a man. Did you get a look at him?"

"To be honest, I'm not sure it was a man. It could have been a beefy woman. I only saw an arm, but my impression was that it belonged to a man."

"What kind of car?"

"Big, black. Beyond that I don't know. If it had the model on the back, I didn't notice."

"Did you get a look at the license plate?"

"I'm sure I did." Since she'd found out about Pierce's murder she'd tried to recall whatever numbers or letters might have been on it and had come up blank. "I didn't know there was going to be a quiz later."

"Is there anything else you can remember that might be helpful?"

She scanned her memory, wishing she could tell him. "There was an old homeless man urinating on the building. He was outside when I got there, too." Knowing he'd ask for it, she gave a description of him, adding that she'd never seen him in the neighborhood before.

He closed his notebook and slipped it into his breast pocket. "Thank you." He nodded toward her with his chin. "What happened to your arm?"

For a moment, she wondered if this was another police interrogation tactic or he truly wanted to know. "It's my shoulder, actually. I got shot in a drive-by yesterday morning."

"Who's working the case?"

"Detective Moretti out of the 44th precinct. Do you know him?"

He nodded rather than spoke. "How did he treat you?"

"Like I was the one who shot somebody." It occurred to her that Joanna had been there at the time, outside the room. Not only had Dana told Joanna how the interview had gone, she'd probably listened to the whole exchange herself. She couldn't imagine that Joanna hadn't gone straight to Jonathan to complain, knowing that he'd worked in the 44 and probably knew Moretti. "I'm sure Joanna told you all this already."

"I like to check things out for myself."

"You don't trust your own sister?"

"Joanna's been more stressed than usual lately."

Dana snorted. "You mean hormonal."

For the first time, a hint of a smile tilted his lips. "You said it, I didn't."

For the first time, she really looked at him. He was a handsome man in a rugged sort of way, his face a study of hard lines and stark planes. She'd always acknowledged that, the same way she knew the suit he wore camouflaged the kind of muscular body most women lost their heads over. Too bad crazy didn't cancel out sexy as hell.

But today he looked tired, not fatigued but strained. She could imagine the pressure on him to find Amanda Pierce's killer. The fact that he resorted to seeking her out told her that he hadn't much to go on.

"Does this mean you're going to, what is it you people say? Reach out to him?"

"If you want me to."

She nodded, unable to bring herself to actually ask

any cop for help. "The young man who was killed was one of my patients' grandson. I'd like to know who did this to him."

Jonathan stood. "I'd better be going." He pulled a card from his pocket and extended it to her. "If you think of anything else, please call me."

She rose to her feet and took the card. She scanned it briefly, noting it had numbers for both the precinct and his cell phone, then stuck it in the back pocket of her jeans.

She showed him to the front door and let him out. He walked to a black car parked across the street, got in and pulled away from the curb.

Dana shut the door and leaned her back against it. If nothing else, Jonathan's visit had killed another hour in her day. She still had nothing to do and more than enough time to do it in. She only knew she was ready to give up on the pity party for one she'd indulged in that day. She was whole, save for a bullet wound that had mostly healed already. She was safe, she was healthy, Tim was all right. Two people had lost their lives in two days. What the hell did she have to complain about?

The stairs leading to her bedroom were in front of her. She ascended them and went to her bedroom. She played back her tape of messages, all of which were from Joanna. Picking up the phone, she dialed her friend's number.

For the second time in three days, Jonathan found himself sitting out on his fire escape, but tonight he had a purpose.

Snowball, an all white Persian cat who sometimes joined him, sidled up to him looking for food. He'd brought two sandwiches out with him tonight. He took the ham from one of them and gave it to the cat. He didn't mind Snowball's company, but it was the other stray he was hoping to see tonight.

He'd already heard about the shooting on Highland Avenue, even before Joanna had a chance to call him to complain about Moretti. He'd known that a civilian had been wounded in the process, but not that it was Dana. Hearing that Moretti had been assigned to the case signaled its lack of priority in the scheme of things, since Moretti had earned himself the nickname Lessetti by expending only enough effort on a case to keep his shield.

When Joanna first called he'd been hesitant to do anything about it. First, he resisted the idea of looking over another cop's shoulder. Cops had enough folks scrutinizing what they did, how they did it and how quickly it was accomplished. Plus, he knew how Moretti would take it—not as one cop reaching out to another but as an attempt to make trouble for him, which it wasn't.

Seeing Dana had changed his mind. He appreciated her no-nonsense attitude and her candor. Most of all, he admired her desire to find the killer, not for her own peace of mind but on behalf of a young man she barely knew.

He heard the creaking of the fire escape above him and knew his vigil hadn't been for nothing. Fourteen-year-old Tyree Owens descended from two floors above and sat on the stairs facing him. "Hey, Jon."

"Hey, T. What's up?" As usual, Jonathan was careful to play it casual around the kid. Tyree spent most nights making himself scarce while his mother brought home men who paid her for her favors. He spent most nights alone in his room or out running the streets. Tyree only sat out with him when he wanted something. But Jonathan knew he couldn't push him, or the kid would bolt. He'd say what he had to when he wanted to.

"You eating that sandwich?"

"Nah, man. You can have it."

He passed the plate to Tyree. Like the cat, the kid gulped down his meal as if he thought someone might take it from him. When he was finished he wiped his sleeve across his mouth. "Thanks, man."

"How's your moms?" Jonathan asked, a question he always asked to which the boy usually answered, "She's all right." Tyree would have to be a fool not to know how his mother earned a dollar, but he never said anything bad about her.

Tonight the question was met by silence. Tyree looked heavenward, breathing heavily. The kid was a moment from crying, which surprised him. "What happened?"

"Her boyfriend beat her up. She's in the hospital."

Her boyfriend being the latest trick she'd brought home, he assumed. He wondered how much of this beating Tyree had seen. "Were you home?"

"Nah." He hung his head. "I found her when I got home from school."

Then Jonathan understood. Tyree felt guilty for not being around to protect his mother. It was on the tip of his tongue to remind Tyree that life wasn't supposed to work that way. His mother was supposed to look out for him. Jonathan supposed she did in her own way. One of the neighbors had called Social Services on her, but when they came the apartment was neat and there was food in the place. She didn't have a man with her at the time. So that was that.

Tyree wiped his eyes. "You came out here looking for me tonight."

He wondered how the kid had picked up on that. Maybe cops and shrinks weren't the only ones who made a habit of studying people. "Yeah, I wanted to ask you something."

"Well, go ahead, man. I'm here."

For a moment he debated the wisdom of bringing Tyree into this, especially in his present mood. But all he wanted was information the boy already had, so what was the harm? "You know a kid named Wesley Evans, who lives on Highland?"

"I heard of him. He go to the same school I do. They call him Double U. That dude got smoked the other day right in front of his building. Pow. I hear they got some lady, too. The nurse."

"Any word on who did it?"

Tyree shrugged. "Man, I don't know. Probably he stiffed somebody he shouldn't have, or over some shorty. You want me to find out?"

"Nah. Let it slide." He'd only wanted to know what was common knowledge about Wesley's death, not deputize a teenager.

"All right. This heat is killer." Tyree stood, gesturing toward his apartment above. "I'm gonna go and lay up under the fan."

"How long until your mother gets out of the hospital?"

"At least a couple of days."

Jonathan didn't doubt that the boy could take care of himself, but he didn't feel right about allowing a teenager to fend for himself for that length of time. If the kid had anyone else to stay with, he'd have been there already. "If you want, you can camp out on my sofa until she gets back."

Tyree waved his hands. "Nah, I'll be all right."

He should have known better. Any adult approaching a kid with a place to stay most likely had some fun and games planned that had nothing to do with Nintendo.

"You have any money?"

Tyree's expression hardened. His eyes reflected both anger and disappointment. At that moment, the boy probably saw him as nothing more than another man looking to take advantage of him or his mother. Besides, he knew Tyree liked the illusion that they were just two buds hanging out on the fire escape shooting the breeze, which was why Jonathan had always been careful not to push him. In two minutes he'd ruined all the headway he'd made.

He opened his mouth to try to smooth things over, but before he got a word out, Tyree said. "I don't need nothing from you, man." He turned and raced up the fire escape steps. A few seconds later, Jonathan heard the sound of Tyree shutting the window behind him.

Damn. He'd screwed up big time. He hoped that when Tyree cooled down, he'd be back, but he wasn't counting on it. Sometimes one shot was all you got with these kids.

Jonathan gathered up his belongings and went inside. For some reason unfathomable to himself he picked up the phone and dialed April's number.

Six

It didn't take any advanced police work to find the author of Amanda Pierce's mash notes. Barry Sheffield had filled out every section of his AOL profile, including his age—62—his former occupation, school custodian, and the fact that he lived in Hoboken, New Jersey. A quick trip to the phone book produced his street address and current phone number.

Once upon a time, Hoboken had been a solidly working class New Jersey town where every bar and restaurant hung the obligatory portrait of Frank Sinatra, local boy who made good. In the '80s, when the average yuppie started not being able to afford their Manhattan apartments, towns across the river, like Hoboken and Jersey City, suddenly found themselves in need of gentrification. New bistros and markets catering to the go-go crowd sprang up replacing older establishments.

The landscape of the town changed again after 9/11. Many of the businesses displaced by the loss of the towers set up shop here, giving workers a bird's eye view of lower Manhattan and the site that could have cost them their lives.

During the drive through the midtown tunnel that connected New York and New Jersey, Mari said, "How much do you want to bet Pierce got on this guy's hit list because she was less than kind to Francis Albert?"

Jonathan shrugged. None of the e-mail Sheffield sent to Pierce mentioned any reason more specific for his vitriol, only generalized threats and complaints about her work and none of them dated back to the time the Sinatra book had been written. Even so, he agreed with Mari. "That's probably what started him off." But not what set him off. If Sheffield had done this, something pushed him from simply writing letters to committing murder. Pierce's last book had come out six months ago—a stinging portrait of some actress he didn't know except from the dust jacket. If that's what sent him over the edge, why'd he wait so long to seek retribution?

Feeling Mari's assessing gaze on him, he glanced at her. "What?"

After a moment, she said, "So, Stonewall, what's up?"

He slid another glance at her. She rarely referred to him by that nickname, the one other cops had given him but very few ever called him to his face. She only used it when she thought he was stepping on her toes or keeping something from her, neither of which happened very often. She lifted her eyebrows and stared back at him in challenge, leaving him to wonder which of the two offenses she believed him to be guilty of.

"Why do you ask?"

"I'd think you might be a little jazzed seeing this guy. You know, man threatens woman. Woman ends up dead. Man makes full confession. Film at eleven. That's what we do this for, isn't it?"

True, and finding out who killed Pierce sooner than later would make both their lives easier. When Shea heard about Sheffield's existence he was ready to announce to the police commissioner and the media that they had a suspect in the case, when all they really had was a guy who liked to write letters.

He didn't think Mari was any more certain than he was that Sheffield was the guy. From what they knew about whoever murdered Amanda Pierce, he fit what law enforcement called an organized killer. Both the crime scene and the body were clean, save for the miniscule piece of fabric embedded in her skin. The killer had obviously moved the body from wherever the murder had occurred. Such a killer was usually highly intelligent, socially and sexually competent— one of the last people you'd suspect had violence on their minds.

Sheffield's letters, aside from their colorful salutations, showed a greater facility with language than his job would require, suggesting an underemployed innate intelligence. To some degree, whoever killed Pierce must have planned it since they made arrangements to pick her up—unless her killer and the person offering her a ride were not the same person.

The rest of it they would have to see, especially since one thing about the crime didn't fit the profile. Strangulation often suggested a crime of passion or at least some sort of sexual overtone. As far as the Medical Examiner could tell, Pierce hadn't been raped or sexualized in any way. Not only that, if, as he suspected after speaking with Dana Molloy, the killer had strangled her with her own scarf, that

suggested an impulsivity not consistent with an organized killer. Most of these bastards planned ahead.

In either event, they'd found yet another Roché
scarf in Pierce's apartment and given it to the lab to
compare fibers. Only time would tell about that, too.

But he also knew that Mari was referring not to his
enthusiasm, but his focus. Truthfully, he'd zoned out
during the ride, his mind not on the case but instead
replaying his conversation with April last night, trying
to figure out what about it bothered him so much.

April had answered the phone and said a sleepy,
"Hello."

Since he hadn't thought up anything more clever
to say, he just said, "It's me."

"Jon?"

The incredulousness in her voice prompted him.
"I know I haven't called in a while."

"Why did you call now?"

"I wanted to see you."

"Tonight?"

He hadn't thought that far ahead, but, yes, he
did want to see her tonight for reasons that had
nothing to do with sex. With his case going nowhere
and after his misstep with Tyree, he needed . . .
something. He resisted putting a name to it, fearing
what he'd come up with. But his coming over this late
or later had never been an issue before, especially
since April refused to set foot in the South Bronx. "Is
that so unreasonable?"

He heard her long-suffering sigh. "I know you're
married to your job, Jon. I get that. But I told you
from the beginning that I wasn't going to sit around
waiting for you to get horny or lonely or however it
is you get before you start thinking about me."

In other words, she'd done a better job of understanding him than he'd done of her. And the weariness in her voice told him she was tired of making the effort. "That's it, then?"

"Look, Jon, I'm in bed right now and I'm not alone. You figure it out."

She'd hung up and he'd cursed himself a couple of dozen ways for being a fool. He'd deserved every thing she'd said and probably a few things she hadn't. She'd been good to him and he hadn't returned the favor. Now, he wished he felt something more than a vague disappointment, but any stronger emotion eluded him.

As they emerged on the New Jersey side of the tunnel, he pushed thoughts of April from his mind. He had more important concerns than his love life, chief among them watching the road. Hoboken's one square mile boasted a number of stoplights, but no stop signs. Drivers sped through intersections as if getting there first was some sort of prize.

Beside him, Mari crooned, "My kind of town, Hoboken is," parodying one of Sinatra's songs.

The woman would never make it as a singer, but at least she didn't seem to be upset with him anymore.

Sheffield was bent over a patch of flowers when they pulled up in front of his house. As they approached, he turned to squint at them over the rims of his glasses.

"Barry Sheffield?" Jonathan asked.

Sheffield rose to his feet. Six feet tall and almost bald except for a rim of salt-and-pepper hair that ran between his ears, Sheffield wore a short-sleeved plaid shirt that stretched over a broad chest and strained even further over a protruding belly, but his arms were still muscular from a lifetime of physical labor. It was only nine o'clock in the morning, but perspiration stains darkened the fabric beneath his armpits and at the center of his chest.

Sheffield gave each of them a once over, then wiped his arm across his damp forehead. "I figured you people would show up sooner or later."

"Why is that, Mr. Sheffield?"

He cast them a look as if they had the intelligence of newborn ants. "Because of the letters I wrote her."

He cast a look at Mari. At least they were all on the same page. "Is there somewhere that we can talk?"

With a flick of his arm, Sheffield gestured toward the house. "We can go inside if you want, but don't expect no air conditioning." He led the way up the white stone path.

Inside the house looked like something out of an old-time Sears Roebuck catalog—old home furniture and lots of it—and all of it neat as a pin.

Sheffield settled on the sofa. Jonathan sat in the wing chair facing him, while Mari prowled around, looking at the furnishings. A photograph of Old Blue Eyes in his heyday hung on the wall above Sheffield's head. It was the only picture in the room.

"Why did you write those letters, Mr. Sheffield?"

"Why shouldn't I have written them? She was a vulture that one, but she didn't even wait until the bones were clean to pick them. She got rich, made herself famous, trashing the lives of people she didn't deserve to be on the same planet with."

Jonathan nodded toward the portrait. "Like Sinatra."

Sheffield's fair complexion became mottled with red around his eyes and throat. "Damn right. The man was a musical genius, a philanthropist. He was a good man who didn't deserve what she or that other one did to him. He was practically on his death bed when she wrote that." Sheffield's voice rose in volume and pitch. He brought his fist down on the arm of the sofa. "Who did she ever help but herself? What did she ever do but try to ruin other people's lives?"

"So someone needed to end hers?"

Sheffield lowered his gaze, and the emotion seemed to drain out of him, as well as the color. "Someone, yes, but not me."

"Where were you last Friday morning?"

"Where I always am. My wife, she's at her sister's now, she gets dialysis three times a week. You can check with the hospital."

"We will." Jonathan took down information on where he could reach Sheffield's wife and her doctor. It didn't take them long to reach either of them and confirm Sheffield's story. Both he and his wife were at the hospital from six o'clock that morning.

As they walked to the car in the hospital parking lot, Mari said, "You know what gets to me. That poor bastard probably feels guilty for not killing her."

Jonathan had sensed it, too—Sheffield's rage, not completely directed at Amanda Pierce but also at himself for his own impotence to do what he felt needed to be done.

He'd leave it to the shrinks to analyze the Sheffields of the world. All he knew was that the man's innocence closed off one more area of investigation. Once again, they were back to square one.

"Frankly, Father, I'm going a little stir crazy."

Father Mike, still dressed in shorts and a T-shirt from his morning run, chuckled. He'd claimed to have stopped by simply because he'd passed her house on his run, but she didn't believe him. He was checking up on her. As much as she hated it, she made the decision to let all those busy bees in her life have their way, since none of them seemed capable of taking no for an answer. Joanna was due to visit in another half hour. If she could withstand Joanna's mothering she could survive anything.

Father Mike had shown up fifteen minutes ago, and after commenting on the continuing heat of the weather, he'd asked her how she was coping. The comment on going nuts had been her answer.

"Don't they say doctors and nurses make the worst patients?"

"That's because we know all the things than can possibly go wrong once you put that hospital gown on. Sometimes the injury or ailment that caused you to seek treatment is the least of your worries."

He regarded her for a long moment in a way that left her clueless as to what he was thinking. "You've seen a lot, haven't you," he said finally.

Yes, she'd seen her share of misery. If she wanted to shock him, she could share some of it with him. But she didn't. Instead she offered him a rueful smile. "I suppose you have too, Father."

He offered back the same rueful smile, then shook his head. "Actually, I did have a purpose in stopping by. I spoke to Ms. Evans as you asked me to."

"How is she?"

"As well as can be expected under the circumstances, I guess. She asked me to apologize to you for hanging up on you the way she did. She thought you'd be angry with her considering that you were almost killed because of her grandson."

Dana shook her head. It had never occurred to her

to blame Nadine for what happened. "She should know me better than that."

Father Mike shrugged, a gesture of helplessness to explain the workings of another's mind. "I helped her make the arrangements for the burial tomorrow morning. We can go together if you like."

Considering that she was in no shape to drive an automobile, that sounded fine. "Thank you, Father."

He stood. "I'll come by at seven-thirty to pick you up."

She walked him to the door. "Thanks again."

He winked at her. "That's what I'm here for." He jogged down the stairs and headed south toward the school.

The sound of a car door slamming alerted her to the blue and yellow taxi parked across the street. Joanna was making her way from it toward the house, but her gaze was focused in the direction Father Mike had taken.

The minute Joanna hit the bottom step, she asked, "And who was that I just saw leaving and awfully early in the morning, at that?"

Dana almost laughed. She should have known what Joanna would read into the situation finding any man leaving her house, much less one who looked like Father Mike. "It's not like that, Joanna."

"Well, why not? You aren't getting any younger, you know." Joanna passed her on the way toward the back of the house.

Dana shut the door behind her. No kidding. Who was? "There's always the racial divide," Dana said, more to goad Joanna than anything else.

Joanna stopped and turned to face her. "Is this the twenty-first century or the Stone Age? You'd really let that stop you?"

"No, but the fact that he's a priest would."

Joanna sucked her teeth in disgust. "Why didn't you say that in the first place?" She continued on to the kitchen at the left. She lowered herself into one of the chairs at the kitchen table. "Damn. It's bad enough that half the decent looking fellas are either gay, on something, or in jail. Couldn't God just take the ugly ones?"

Dana laughed. "Sorry, but it doesn't work that way. Those who are called must answer."

"Listen to you, Ms. Agnostic. I thought you didn't believe in any of that stuff."

"I don't, but sending Tim to Catholic school for four years I had to pick up something."

"Yeah, too bad it couldn't have been him."

Slumping into the chair beside Joanna, Dana made a disgusted sound in her throat.

"Don't give me that. You know I worry about you. You act like you don't need a man, like you don't need anybody. But, girl, you're just as human as the rest of us. We all need. Tell me, how long has it been since you let any man get even a little bit under your skin?"

Unbidden, her mind traveled back to the day before, when *he'd* been here. There had been a moment there when she'd looked at him, seen the weariness in his face and wished she could smooth it away. It must be that nurse thing in her, some defect of her genetic make-up that . . .

"Well?" Joanna prompted.

"Too long." Especially if the first man who came to her mind was Jonathan Stone.

Hanratty's on East 163rd had taken over where the spot on 161st had left off as a cop bar and hangout.

When Jonathan had worked in the 44, Moretti had been a regular at the bar almost every night of the week. Tonight was no exception.

Hanratty's didn't look much different than any other Irish bar in the city: lots of wood, lots of smoke, lots of guys losing the day's frustrations in a bottle of their favorite booze. Jonathan spotted Moretti at the bar the moment he walked in the door. But there were also plenty of cops he knew from his days working among them. There were hands to shake, jokes to be made at his expense, new faces to be introduced to. All the while, Jonathan could feel Moretti's gaze on him as he made his way to the bar.

Finally someone got to the question they'd all been wondering. "Hey Stone, to what do we owe the honor?"

"Yeah, what brings you here, Stone?" Moretti smiled back, but the belligerence in his gaze belied any friendliness in his tone.

Jonathan took a step toward him. "You got a minute for me?"

"As long as you're buying."

Moretti turned back to his drink. He lifted his empty glass and said to the bartender. "I'll have another one of these." He turned to Jonathan as he slid onto the stool beside him. "Now what does a big-time homicide detective want with little old me?"

Jonathan ordered a beer from the waiting bartender before answering. "I hear you caught the Wesley Evans case, the shooting on Highland Avenue."

"Yeah. What about it?"

"How's it going?"

Moretti downed a gulp from his glass. "It's going. Don't you have enough to do with your celebrity cases without worrying about mine?"

"Dana Molloy, the woman who was shot with Evans, is a friend of mine."

That perked Moretti up. He tilted his head to one side, his eyes narrowing. "You want to ride my ass 'cause your squeeze almost got popped. Maybe you should tell her to meet her connection inside next time."

Jonathan ignored Moretti's comment because to acknowledge it would mean putting his fist in the other man's face. "Actually, I was hoping for a little professional courtesy, but that would require you to be both professional and courteous."

"Fuck you, Stone. I don't owe you a damn thing."

No, Moretti didn't owe him anything, especially not the hostility that radiated from the man. Jonathan tried to think of anything he'd done to Moretti to warrant his level of anger and came up with nothing. Then again, Moretti resented anyone smarter, more capable or harder working than he was, as if the other person had stolen those qualities from him in order to possess them.

Whatever the case, Jonathan knew he wasn't going to get anything from this man tonight, probably not ever. "How about you just do your damn job, then." He left his untouched beer and enough money to pay for both their drinks on the bar and headed for the door.

Out on the street he heard a familiar voice calling his name. He turned to find one of the older guys jogging up behind him. The guy, an instructor at the police academy, had earned the name T.J. after T.J. Hooker, a TV cop with the same profession. Jonathan couldn't recall what the man's real name was, if he ever knew it. The two of them had never been friends, so the fact that T.J. had followed him outside surprised him. "What's up?"

"Hey, man, what you want with Moretti?"

"A witness in one of his cases is a friend of mine. Why?"

"That kid who got shot?"

Jonathan nodded.

"Wonder why he's working that case alone? No one else will touch him. IAB's on his back big time."

"What for?"

"Shaking down dealers, taking payoffs. Anything that you can get into that's dirty, he's there."

Jonathan exhaled heavily. That didn't bode well for Dana's case or for Dana herself. A dirty cop on the way down might try to pin his misdeeds on the handiest person, to take anyone down with him that he could.

Moretti had already hinted he believed Dana had been with Wesley for reasons having nothing to do with his grandmother. Moretti could try to make that accusation against her just to spite him. Moretti wouldn't even have to bring such a charge to his superiors. A news tip from an anonymous police source to the newspaper of his choice would suit Moretti's purposes just fine.

A nurse purchasing drugs from one of her clients would make an interesting story. No charges would ever be brought, but in the meantime she might lose her job and her reputation could be ruined.

T.J. chucked him on the shoulder. "You look out for yourself."

"I will," Jonathan said, but it wasn't himself he was worried about.

Seven

Nobody came. Nadine Evans sat in the wheelchair provided for her at her grandson's gravesite, surrounded by a small group of people, none of whom she knew. The man from the cemetery told her that they were folks who liked to show up at funerals, they didn't care whose.

Her heart heavy and cold in her chest like a stone, she wrung her hands in a futile gesture. For five years, she had scrimped and pinched pennies to buy this site for herself, not an underground plot but a space in an aboveground mausoleum in Woodlawn Cemetery.

Some of the most famous people in the world were buried here. She didn't really know who and didn't really care. But she liked the idea of spending eternity next to senators and musicians, authors and composers. She never did have nothing in life. The least God could provide for her was a decent resting place.

But now that spot was going for her grandson Wesley, the sweet baby the Lord and her wayward daughter had left for her to raise. Only a fool would think she'd been able to do right by that boy. Verna had come home, supposedly for an overdue visit, bringing her seven-year-old son with her. Until then, Nadine hadn't known she had a grandchild, much less this tall, skinny stick of a boy with dark, knowing eyes.

Verna left two days later, in the dead of night and alone. When Nadine awoke the next morning to find her daughter gone, she agonized about what to say to the boy. But he already knew. It hadn't been the first time his mama had left him somewhere and cut out. "I don't think she's coming back this time," he'd told her as matter of fact as if he told her it was supposed to rain. Then he sat down and ate the bowl of corn flakes she'd set out for him.

She'd wanted so much for that boy, but what could she do for him? She was poor, alone, sick with the sugar and old age, sick from life. Knowing how his mother had done him, she never could bring herself to discipline the boy much or show him the back of her hand when he needed it. And the older and sicker she got, the more she relied on him. He was her little man who took care of everything. She never could abide his selling that junk on the streets, but what could she do about it? He'd told her, "I don't sell to no kids, Granny. If grown folks want to give me their cash, I'm happy to take it."

"Messing with those people will get you killed," she'd warned. It gave her no comfort to know she'd been right. She'd found no solace anywhere. Those old heifers in her building, even those that came to her supposedly expressing their condolences, couldn't wait to inform her that Wesley had gotten no better than he deserved. It had been on her mind to ask them who the hell did they think kept him in business except their sons and daughters and probably their old men besides, but she'd held her tongue. Let them go on deluding themselves there wouldn't be someone else out there tomorrow who wouldn't have any compunctions about selling their babies anything they wanted.

So she had taken the money they pushed into her hand as they hustled out her door, congratulating themselves on their beneficence to someone who deserved nothing. She'd mumbled her thanks through a throat clogged with emotion. Where had all these people been when their money could have done some good?

She hadn't voiced that sentiment, or any other that might make her appear ungrateful. She didn't mind taking these peoples' money whatever the circumstance. For another, she still had to pay for the casket, the flowers, the fee for a minister. She'd wanted the pastor from the church she'd attended, before her illness had robbed her of the chance to go, but he'd claimed to be busy. Instead, some stranger with hound dog jowls and a sour expression would say the last words anyone would speak for her grandson.

She gazed at the man now as he approached. "We'll start in a minute, Sister Evans."

She wondered what the man was waiting for, considering only her and a handful of strangers awaited whatever he had to say. Hearing a car door close behind her, she glanced over her shoulder. That cop Moretti or whatever his name was, had just gotten out of a black sedan. He sauntered toward her with the sort of swagger she expected from the man.

Though she hadn't expected any better, it galled her that the lone detective the police had sent to investigate her grandson's murder couldn't give a damn who'd shot Wesley or why. The whole city seemed to care about some blond bitch who probably stuck her lily white nose where it didn't belong, but not one soul shared in her grief or her desire to see Wesley's killer brought to justice.

So, what was he doing here? Considering his disinterest in the case and disdainful expression on his face, it certainly couldn't be to pay his respects. In fact, he didn't approach her at all. He took up a spot to her left and behind her, apart from the small group. The man was up to something, but what?

Before she had long to wonder about it, the minister took up a spot behind the bower and folded his hands in prayer.

"Brothers and sisters," he began, as if speaking to a multitude instead of a handful of people. "We have come together today to mourn the passing of another young brother cut down before he had a chance to . . ."

Nadine shut her eyes and let the Reverend's melodious voice wash over her like a river. The words didn't matter, only their cadence and the rhythmic punctuation of amens and sounds of approval from those assembled.

As the Reverend's sermon ended, Nadine opened her eyes. She hadn't felt the dampness on her cheeks until the man next to her, the man from the cemetery, offered her a handkerchief. She blotted the dampness from her cheeks and tried to sit straighter in the unfamiliar chair. The short service was over, and the few people assembled started to leave.

"Nadine."

The sound of Dana's voice brought her back into herself. Nadine blinked and focused on the girl's face. She hadn't noticed Dana's arrival, but knowing Dana the little bit she did, she should have known she'd hang back rather than push herself to the forefront.

She had to take back that earlier thought about no one but her caring about Wesley. She knew Dana had tried to talk some sense into the boy and had no better luck than she did. Nadine might be old and bedridden, but she heard just fine. Dana had sent her that handsome priest to help her. He'd been a godsend, relieving her of the burden of seeing to Wesley's arrangements herself.

The pair of them walked toward her now. "Hello, Nadine," Dana said when they reached her. "How are you holding up?"

"Jus' fine. Though there is a hole in my heart today."

Seeing the look that came over Dana's face—not quite disapproval, but close—Nadine supposed she'd laid the drama on too thick. It wasn't a lie. Her heart lay in her chest like a dead thing knowing her boy was gone. But Dana didn't hold with no theatrics. Many a time Nadine had tried to win her sympathy the way it worked with other nurses, play their heartstrings, but Dana wouldn't have that. Sometimes she felt sorry for that brother of hers, as tough love seemed the only type Dana knew how to give.

"Mrs. Evans," Father Mike said, drawing her attention. He pressed an envelope into her hands. "The parish of St. Matthew's extends its condolences, and so do I."

She looked at the envelope. In the corner was the school logo, a candle flame with the school motto written beneath it. A blank address label was pasted to the center, but even her old eyes could make out the single word underneath it: "Dana."

Nadine's eyes flew to hers, but read no emotion

there. Obviously whatever money was enclosed in this envelope had been intended for her, but she didn't take it.

"Do you need anything? A ride?"

Nadine shook her head. "The people here will see me home."

"Take care of yourself, Nadine. I'll see you when I get back to work."

Nadine nodded. She watched the pair until they got into a dark blue sedan and drove away.

In the next moment, Nadine decided she really hated Detective Moretti. He sidled up to her and nodded in the direction Dana had driven off. Without preamble he said, "I'd like to ask you a few questions about that woman who was just here, Dana Molloy."

"What about her," Nadine answered, determined not to tell the man one damn thing.

Seated in the car as Father Mike drove toward Westchester, Dana stared out the window trying to quiet her thoughts. Wesley's funeral had affected her profoundly, and she wasn't sure why. To top it off, she couldn't put a name to the emotion that churned her stomach and put her nerves on end.

In the periphery of her vision she noticed Father Mike sneaking another glance at her. He might be curious about her silence, but she doubted that was the reason for his attention. She sighed. "If you have something to say, Father, why don't you say it?"

"It's a question, really. Why wouldn't you take the money? It's not because you're not Catholic is it?"

He'd been surprised this morning when he tried to press the envelope in her hands and she refused to accept it. He hadn't questioned her about it, and she'd figured that was the end of it. She should have known better than that. Priests made their stock in trade out of confessions.

"I didn't take it because, to me, it's blood money. Someone died for that money. I don't want any part of it."

"That money was collected on your behalf," Father Mike said in a patient voice. "You were injured. You missed work."

"I was on vacation. I've got plenty of time accumulated if I need to take it. I don't need money."

Father Mike slid her a droll look. "Don't tell me that anyone with a child about to start college doesn't need money."

She groaned. He had her there. "Okay, so the money could have come in handy. I'm sure Nadine needs it more than I do."

He said nothing for a while, leaving her to hope that was the end of the discussion. They were nearing the point on the Major Deegan where they would veer off onto the Cross County Parkway. They would reach her house in fifteen minutes if the traffic didn't snag.

"Then why are you so angry?"

Anger. She hadn't considered that possibility when she was trying to decipher her feelings. She supposed that fit, though she couldn't say what about the day had inspired it. She rarely allowed herself the luxury of that emotion. Annoyance, yes, irritation, maybe, but never the full breadth of the deeper emotion. There was a well of anger in her, deep and murky, and she didn't care to analyze who it was directed at. Letting even a little of it out was like uncorking a dam that she feared she could not recap.

She inhaled, fighting to regroup, to quell the emotions churning inside her. "She wanted me to feel sorry for her. Nadine actually wanted me to feel sorry for Wesley dying the way he did. And I do. I really do, but she didn't have to be in the position she was in. Her own self-indulgence led her to a point where she couldn't take care of him properly.

"And don't believe I hold Wesley blameless in this. He was seventeen. He made his own choice. There were hundreds of other ways he could have helped support his grandmother, if that's what he wanted to do. But there's this mentality, like 'I can't demean myself by getting an honest job in McDonalds, but I can knock your mama over the head and steal her few pennies or I can sell your child crack.' That's the way to earn your props."

"And that's the way of the world, Dana. Some people will always seek the easy way out. You know that."

She did and she hated it. "You know, Father, you hear so much about the tyranny of the strong. The strong preying on the weak. What about the tyranny of the weak, Father? That's much worse. What about those people who can but will not rise up to help themselves? I see it all the time, Father. Clients who absolutely refuse to do what they need for their own well-being. And what kind of louse must you be to refuse them?"

A voice droned in her head, but it didn't belong to Nadine or any of her other clients. It belonged to her mother. "Dana, I can't do it . . . Dana, I need you to help me . . . Dana . . . Dana . . . Dana . . ." Her mother had called on her so often the sound of her own name had sickened her. Long before her mother had been debilitated enough to require constant care she'd relied on Dana for everything. Dana had never begrudged her mother her illness; she couldn't help that. But she did begrudge her mother's helplessness, her refusal to do as much as she could for herself.

Thank God, she'd been able to spare Tim from bearing the brunt of their mother's demands. On top of that, she'd raised him to be self-sufficient. When he went off to college, he wouldn't have to wait on anyone to feed him or pick up after him. He'd be able to survive without having to depend on anyone else, though with his looks and easy-going temperament, he'd probably have some girl doing his laundry within a week.

That thought brightened her a little, enough to drag her outside herself. "I'm sorry, Father. I didn't mean to unload on you."

He offered her a kindly smile. "I keep telling you that's what I'm here for. Feeling better?"

She nodded. "Maybe I'm just a little burned out. Maybe I just really, really needed that vacation."

"Maybe you just needed someone to talk to."

Maybe, but she wasn't sure she was ready to admit that yet. Joanna had accused her of acting like she didn't need anybody, and Dana couldn't deny it. She didn't want to need anybody, not to the point where she became one of those women like Nadine and her mother, simultaneously victim and predator. She knew that was one of the things she needed to work on in herself, but hadn't gotten very far with it. But she had to acknowledge that she did feel better having spoken aloud the feelings she'd bottled up inside for so long. "Thanks for listening, Father."

"Anytime. But you have to promise to do something for me."

"What's that?"

"Stop calling me 'Father.' The way you say it makes me sound as if I've been dead long enough to be canonized."

For the first time that day, she laughed. "What should I call you then?"

"Just Mike will do."

"Okay, Just Mike," she said and heard him chuckle. She settled back against her seat, looking out her window at the passing scenery while she contemplated her growing friendship with a priest.

On the ride back to the city, Jonathan got a call from Ferguson in the tech department letting him know they'd broken the password on Amanda Pierce's computer. He damn sure hoped there was something pertinent on it or on the numerous CDs they'd culled from her apartment, as their one good lead had bitten the dust that morning.

Ferguson, the chief tech, was waiting for them when he and Mari arrived. The other techs called him Porcupine because he had a habit of running his hand through his short black hair in a way that made it stand on end. He motioned for them to take seats next to his work station.

"What have you got?" Jonathan asked.

"I got plenty, but you'll have to figure out what it all means."

"That's why they pay us the big salaries," Mari said.

"Yeah, right." Ferguson pressed a few keys on the computer. One thing I'll say for this lady, she has a devious mind. Wanna know what her password was?"

If Jonathan had bothered to give an answer, it would have been, 'Not particularly.' But Ferguson seemed intent on dazzling them with his brilliance,

Deirdre Savoy

or maybe it was only Mari he wanted to impress, as his gaze rested solely on her.

"Sure."

"Archipelago. A body of land surrounded by water on three sides. You know, the Bronx is the only borough that isn't an island. It's an archipelago."

Jonathan slid a glance at Mari, who looked back with a blank stare. For want of anything better, Jonathan said, "Okay."

"Well," Ferguson ran his hand through his hair. "Since you wanted to know what she'd been working on, I focused on the last files she started. Most of it is on one CD, a lot of information about someone named Brendan Malone, a priest who died in nineteen eighty something."

Jonathan remembered seeing something about the man in the files they'd taken from Pierce's office. But those clippings had already yellowed with age, leading him to believe that they bore no relation to her current work.

"Malone had presided over a small church in the 140s," Ferguson continued. "St. Jude's."

Jonathan touched the medal that rested against his collarbone. His sister had given it to him the day he graduated from the academy. St. Jude—the patron saint of cops and lost causes, which were often one and the same thing.

"What did Pierce want with him? Another priest pedophile?"

"Yeah, that was my first thought," Ferguson said. "But if that was her angle I don't see any evidence of it. Mostly it seems to have something to do with some housing development. That's the weird part. He seemed to have some sort of financial involvement. Aren't priests supposed to take a vow of poverty?"

"Them and every other working stiff in the city," Mari shot back.

"Well, that's as far as I got." He reached under his console. "I took the liberty of printing out most of this stuff for you. I know how much you detectives like paper."

Mari took the folder from him. "Gee, thanks, Fergie."

"Anytime."

"Cultivating a fan club?" Jonathan teased as they walked away.

"What else have I got to do with myself?" They stopped at the elevators. Mari pulled open the file. A copy of the CD lay on top of the sheaf of papers. "Here's what I don't get. Pierce is used to going after the Sinatras of the world, cultural icons. What was she doing slumming with the boys from the barrio, pedophile or no?"

"I guess that's what we're about to find out." The cell phone clipped to his belt rumbled. Jonathan checked the readout, not entirely surprised to see his brother Adam's number. He accepted the call and brought the phone to his ear. "What's up?"

"Zack just called me. Ray took Joanna to the hospital. She's in labor."

Uneasiness settled in Jonathan's belly. Joanna wasn't due for three weeks. He wondered how this turn of events boded for his sister. "How's she doing?" he asked, but Adam had already hung up.

Damn. That was his brother. Why bother to have an actual conversation when a few grunted words would do? But whatever was going on with Joanna must be serious for Adam to bother to call. Ten minutes later, he was in his car headed for St. Lawrence Hospital in Westchester.

Eight

"Come on, Joanna, breathe with me," Ray urged his wife.

"I don't want to do any goddamn Lamaze. I want the baby to come."

Dana stood on the opposite side of Joanna's hospital bed, watching the exchange between the couple. She'd been at their house when Joanna had gone into labor and had come with her and Ray to the hospital.

"I know, baby, I know."

Dana suspected he also knew what Joanna was too preoccupied with the birth to notice. A moment ago, a new team of hospital personnel had entered the room, including an anesthesiologist and a surgical nurse. They intended to take the baby.

Joanna's doctor, a tall woman with a horse's long face and a mane of long dark hair re-entered the room. Dana moved out of the way so that the woman could come to stand by Joanna's bedside.

"Joanna," she said in a kind voice. "The baby's in trouble. We need to do a C-section."

Joanna nodded gravely. "All right."

The doctor patted her hand. "Don't you worry. Everything will go just fine."

The doctor moved off and Dana went back to her spot. She knew the first step would be to give Joanna the epidural she'd refused earlier. The doctor would need quiet and solitude for that. "I'll go see if Adam has gotten here yet," Dana volunteered. When Joanna went into labor, they'd dropped the boys at Adam's house. Adam said he'd follow them to the hospital as soon as his wife, Barbara, showed up to spell him.

Joanna nodded. "But you're coming back, right?"

Dana offered her friend her most solicitous smile. "You don't think I'd miss my godchild being born, do you?"

She winked at Joanna, then left.

She found both of Joanna's older brothers waiting in the small area outside the room. Zack was sitting in one of the chairs, his arms folded, his legs stretched out and crossed at the ankles, his eyes closed, looking on the verge of sleep if he hadn't succumbed already. Adam paced with his hands fisted, a grim expression on his face.

Those were Joanna's brother's: as different as night and day, from A to Z, as far apart as their initials suggested. As she walked toward them, she wondered where Jonathan fit into that equation, how he dealt with having these two men for brothers. He struck her as being as intense as Adam, but definitely his own man, not a replica of either of his brothers.

"How is she?"

That came from Zack, the supposedly laid-back one. "She's fine, but the baby's not coming. They did an enzyme test to assess the amount of oxygen the baby is getting and it looks like the baby's in distress. They're going to perform a C-section."

Both men nodded. Adam sighed. "I called Jonathan a few moments ago. I figured all those grim-faced doctors heading into Joanna's room couldn't be a good thing. He should be here soon."

Dana nodded, not knowing what to say to that bit of news. "I'd better get back before Joanna misses me."

Since neither man objected, she pivoted and went back to Joanna. The doctors had just begun to prep her for surgery when she got back. She silently slipped back to the same spot she'd occupied before, at the head of the bed. Joanna had asked her to come back, but she didn't really need her. Joanna's attention was totally taken up by her husband, who held her hand and whispered words of comfort and encouragement.

She had to admit Ray surprised her. His devotion to Joanna throughout the birth had been remarkable. Or maybe he was just such a drastic improvement from Joanna's first husband, who'd been out drinking when their first child was born and with another woman for their second.

That infidelity, which the bastard hadn't bothered to try to cover up, had been the death knell for the marriage. Joanna had ended up with a toddler and a new baby to raise alone. To this day, he hadn't paid one dime in child support, not that he'd ever been a big fan of holding down a job. He lived off women, not the other way around.

In between him and Ray, there had been a string of other men, none of them worth a good damn among them. Joanna was smart enough to not have brought any of them around her children, but Dana had met a few of them and disliked them all. Joanna seemed to be on a self-destruct mission that Dana had been powerless to help her friend through, except as being a shoulder to cry on when yet another son-of-a-bitch showed his true colors.

Dana knew that's why she'd been so hard on Ray right from the beginning. She'd been waiting for the proverbial other shoe to drop, waiting for Joanna to call her to say Ray was married, or cheating on her, or he drank too much or hit her. Whatever it might be this time that would end the relationship and send Joanna into another depression.

But that call had never come. So far, Ray had done everything right. He treated Joanna like a queen, he was good to her children, he came home at night. Considering his present devotion to his wife, maybe it was time she cut him the slack he asked for.

The sound of the doctor's voice snapped Dana out of her musings. "It's a girl, Joanna. A girl."

Dana beamed at her friend as the numerous staff members in the room gave up a cheer. After having two boys, she knew this was what Joanna had hoped for.

After a few moments, the pediatrician handed Joanna the baby wrapped in a pink, white and blue blanket with a pink stocking cap on her tiny head. Dana touched her fingers to the tiny cap. "She's beautiful, Joanna."

Teary-eyed, Joanna beamed back. "Isn't she?" The baby smacked her lips while rooting around for something to suck on. "And hungry." With Ray's help, Joanna adjusted her gown to offer the baby her breast. The baby latched on and began to feed.

"Ouch. This is the worst part," Joanna said as if she were imparting news. "The first few days are murder."

"That's what I hear."

"You could do more than hear about it if you'd . . . *ouch.* That's human flesh you're munching on, baby."

Dana offered up silent thanks to the baby for distracting her mother from her intended topic of conversation. She intended to distract her further. "What are you going to name her?"

Joanna glanced at her husband, then back again. "We've been having the great debate over that. If it was a girl, he wanted to name her after his mother, Sarah. I wanted to name her after mine, Elizabeth. Right now, Sarah Elizabeth sounds fine to me. What do you think, Ray?"

For a moment, husband and wife exchanged a look. "Whatever you want, baby. You're the one who did all the work."

Joanna laughed. "And don't you forget that, either, bub."

Within a few minutes, the room had cleared and an orderly came to transport Joanna and the baby to their room. Dana stayed behind on the pretext of checking to make sure they hadn't left anything behind. Truthfully, she wanted to give mom and dad and baby a moment to bond without outside interference. And even more than that, she wanted to settle her own emotions.

She was relieved that the baby was all right, happy for her friend, yet some other emotion shimmered on the surface of her consciousness like sunlight on water. A peculiar form of melancholia the cause of which she couldn't identify.

For some reason she was drawn to the window and its vantage point of nothing except the side of another building. She wasn't really looking, anyway. Her mind was busy analyzing the alien emotion and surprisingly, she settled on envy.

In some ways, Joanna was right. Her biological clock was sounding an alarm, not the one that demanded children but one that announced a far more earthy need. She wasn't ashamed to admit she missed sex. She missed being held and the pretense of intimacy. It had been way too long, long enough to make a less circumspect woman do something reckless.

But, never one not to learn from others' mistakes, she'd witnessed Joanna's mistakes, the missteps of her other friends, the defection of her own father and opted out of ever trying to find someone for herself. There had been men in her life, but none who hadn't known they were only temporary and that she called the shots.

She'd always told herself she had a brother to raise and not much time for any one or any thing that would demand much of her time or attention. But that was an excuse, not a reason.

She still couldn't bring herself to believe in that "happily ever after" that poets wrote songs about, but she hoped she could find someone who would fit for right now, someone who she could let in just a little bit. Someone who she could let go when things soured without too much emotional upheaval.

Maybe all she really lacked was the opportunity to get herself in trouble. She considered the way Jonathan Stone's image had popped into her mind the other day when Joanna was haranguing her about the lack of a man in her life. Aside from a devil-may-care priest and her clients—most of whom were either too old or debilitated to be of any use—what men did she meet? No wonder he was the first man she thought of. But not him. She needed neither his intensity nor his aloofness and self-possession. She realized, with a sense of irony, she still wanted a man she could control. Now what did that say about her?

She honestly didn't know, but she'd dallied long enough. Joanna would be waiting for her.

After a brief stop at the nurse's station to find which room his sister had been taken to, Jonathan found the appropriate door and pushed it open. They were all there, the doting parents, his two brothers, Dana, and as yet none of them noticed him.

What he noticed most was the way Zack's arm rested on Dana's shoulders as the two of them stood by the bed. Seeing them together, something shot through him—not anger, or even jealousy, but possessiveness, which didn't make any sense to him. Dana wasn't his and he had no intention of making any sort of play for her either. From what he knew of her, she was hard as nails on the outside and even tougher underneath. To his mind, a little softness in a woman both inside and out was a good thing. Dana didn't seem to have any.

Maybe it was seeing Zack's arm in particular that caused this reaction in him. Zack's cavalier attitude toward the opposite sex was likely to leave a woman like Dana hurt after an involvement with him. If Zack's short-lived marriage had proved anything, it was that the man was incapable of treating a woman right, not even one he claimed to love.

Jonathan stepped further into the room. "Hey," he said, drawing the attention of everyone in the room, but his eyes were fixed on Dana. When she turned toward him, he noticed her arms were folded, a defensive posture that suggested the familiarity between her and Zack had been Zack's idea. He also noticed that while the others advanced to greet him, she was the only one who turned away.

After enduring congratulatory embraces from Ray and Zack and Adam's usual sedate handshake, he went to his sister. Bending to kiss her cheek, he said, "Congratulations, Sis."

"Thanks. Wash your hands and I might consider letting you hold your new niece."

He did as she asked, using the small lavatory in the corner of the room. When he got back, he realized Dana was no longer standing, but sitting in one of the chairs on the opposite side of the bed. It flashed in his mind to wonder if she'd moved to get farther away from him.

He'd left his jacket and tie in the car and rolled up his sleeves while he was in the bathroom. He took the sleeping baby from his sister and cradled her in the crook of his arm. He'd forgotten how tiny newborns were, how delicate. The last baby he'd held had been Joanna's youngest boy. "She's beautiful, Joanna."

"That seems to be the consensus," Joanna teased.

He looked at his sister, really looked at her this time. She looked dead tired, but happy. "What did you name her?"

"Sarah Elizabeth. I think it's fitting."

He nodded. He knew she referred to honoring their mother by naming the baby after her, but she forgot that, as the youngest, he carried the fewest memories of her. "Where are the boys?"

"At my place," Adam said. "And come to think of it, I'd better be going. Barbara is going to kill me if I leave her with four rowdy kids much longer."

"I'll walk out with you."

Zack made no excuses for his desire to leave, but Jonathan would bet it had to do with some woman.

After the two men left, Jonathan handed the baby back to his sister. "I'd better be going, too."

"You just got here," Joanna protested.

He chucked her under the chin. "And you and your hubby look like you're both ready to fall out."

Joanna smiled at him sleepily. "I can't argue with you there." She adjusted the baby in her arms. "Do me a favor and see Dana home."

"I can see myself home," Dana protested. "I live five minutes from here."

"By car, and yours is waiting for you at home."

Dana sighed. For the first time that evening she looked at him. "If you wouldn't mind, I'd appreciate a ride home."

"My pleasure."

Slowly, she rose from her seat as if she were reluctant to get up. Maybe she was stalling in order to think of some way of getting out of going with him. She'd never seemed particularly fond of him. In fact, the last time he'd seen her she'd been more than a little hostile. He could understand that, considering he'd breached her confidence in order to find her.

He didn't understand her hesitancy now. If not for him she'd either have to walk or wait downstairs for a non-existent taxi. But he did know it challenged him to find out why she'd rather be inconvenienced than to go with him.

After they said their goodbyes and promised to come back the next day, they took the elevator down to the ground floor in silence.

When they got outside, heat rushed up at them, even though the sun had gone down hours ago. By the time they walked the short distance to the car and got in, his brow was perspired and his collar chafed, but she looked none the worse for it. He started the engine and turned on the air conditioner. "How do I get to your place from here?"

She gave him concise instructions, which amounted to a few turns at various intersections. Before the air conditioning had a chance to kick in he pulled up in front of her house and cut the engine.

Her hand was already on the door latch. "Thanks for the lift." She pushed open the car door. "Good night."

She got out and he did, too.

As she rounded the car, she asked, "Where are you going?"

"It's late. I hope you don't mind if I see you to your door." He'd said that with more sarcasm than chivalry, so he wasn't surprised that she huffed and pivoted away from him.

She crossed the front porch, got the front door open, flicked on the hallway light and turned to face him. "Now I'm at my door. Or do you want to check the place for sneak thieves and mad rapists?"

He picked up on the hint of humor in her voice. "Does that mean you're inviting me in?"

"It's late, Jonathan, and I'm tired. I'm—"

He forestalled her with a silencing finger against her lips. Obviously, she'd taken him seriously, but he didn't need to hear her litany of reasons why he should go home. "Just answer one question for me and I'll go."

She stepped back from him, crossing her arms over her chest while eyeing him warily. "What's that?"

"What exactly do you have against me?"

"What do you mean?"

"Aside from the fact that we can't seem to hold a civil conversation. Every time I get near you, you back away."

"I don't like cops."

He snorted. If that were true she'd sure picked the wrong family to befriend. Not only that, he didn't entirely believe her. Working where she did, she certainly had enough opportunity to witness police misconduct if there were any to see. She probably heard enough complaints from her clients. But she didn't back away when Zack's arm had been around her, even if she hadn't encouraged his touch.

Still her statement intrigued him enough for him to question her about it. "Why not?"

"You have folks like Moretti running around and you have to ask me that?"

He couldn't argue with her there. In fact, she reminded him that he had information for her that he had yet to impart. "Listen, Dana. I spoke to Moretti last night. I don't know how much good I did any of us."

She glanced up at him. "What do you mean?"

"For one thing, the man seems to hold some sort of grudge against me, for what I haven't the faintest clue. For another, he may be under internal investigation."

"Why are you telling me this?"

"Because it makes him dangerous." He doubted his warning was necessary, but he added. "Watch your step around him."

"Believe me, I will. I have. He was at Wesley's funeral this morning."

"Probably looking for suspects among the mourners," he said, but considering the insinuations he'd made the night before, the only mourner he'd been interested in was Dana. "Call me if he gives you any trouble."

She nodded, but he didn't believe she would. She

probably made the gesture only to mollify him and would try to handle Moretti on her own.

He tilted her chin up to see her face. "Will you call me? I want to hear you say it."

"Yes, I will call you. Okay?"

There was no belligerence in her voice, only the same weariness reflected in her eyes. He rubbed his thumb across her cheek. "Get some rest. You look almost as beat as Joanna."

He paused, having nothing left to say and not quite wanting to leave her. For one thing, for the first time he'd gotten near her and she hadn't pulled away. For another, there was the expectant way she looked at him when their eyes met. He didn't know what she wanted from him, but he knew what he wanted. His mouth lowered to hers, slowly, giving her enough time to move away or slap his face or whatever she might have done other than stand there and wait for him to kiss her.

Not everything about Dana Molloy was tough as nails. Her lips were soft, moist, pliant beneath his, sweeter than he'd expected. That sweetness drew him in, prolonging what he'd thought would be a brief meeting of his lips and hers. His tongue slipped inside her mouth to find hers. Their meeting was languid, unhurried, and heady as all get out.

When he finally pulled away, he scanned her face, pleased by the bemused expression he found there. At least he wasn't the only one rocked by that incredible kiss. He ran his thumb along her moist lower lip. "Take care of yourself, Dana," he whispered, then turned to walk back to his car.

Nine

Jonathan woke at his usual time the next morning despite a lack of sleep. He'd spent half the night baking in the night heat out on his fire escape, hoping that Tyree had cooled down enough to join him. That hadn't happened, and he had to admit, much of the time his mind hadn't been on what the teenager was or wasn't doing.

His thoughts kept drifting back to Dana. It hadn't been very bright of him to put his hands on a woman he'd reminded himself only minutes before that he had no intention of pursuing. He still didn't, but now he was free to torture himself at his leisure with the sweetness of her kiss. At the time, he'd had half a mind to push her a little further to see what other surprises she might spring on him. His only comfort was knowing he'd left before it had occurred to her to throw him out.

When he walked into the squad room, Mari was already at her desk. "Look what the cat dragged in. Thanks for calling me and letting me know what happened."

He shot her a quelling look, which by now she was

used to ignoring. He took his jacket off, slung it over the back of his chair and sat. "She had a girl, Sarah Elizabeth. Everybody's fine."

"See, now that wasn't so hard."

He shot her another look, then glanced at the stack of papers littering her desk. "Looks like you've been busy."

"Interesting reading. It turns out Pierce's Father Malone didn't start life as a choirboy. He did time for B&E and burglary before some jailhouse Jehovah got ahold of him and turned him around. Later, when he became head of St. Jude's he was one of the players in building some apartment complex near Third. Trinity Houses. You can see it off the Bruckner Expressway."

He thought he knew the development she meant. "So what's the problem?" He rifled through the messages left on his desk, finding nothing of interest. "The guy hasn't been dead long enough to be canonized."

"Two things. It's speculated that the Father didn't quite leave his old ways behind. Some of his partners in the deal were his old running buddies who'd taken their scams to a higher level. Supposedly some of the funds for the project were never accounted for."

"How is that different from half the buildings that go up in the city?" You couldn't exactly give mob payoffs a line on a spreadsheet.

She shrugged. "Then there's how he died. The church burned to the ground with him in it. Mind you, this is in the days before mandatory smoke detectors and sprinkler systems, so that by itself isn't so strange. But the fire investigator could never discover the cause of the blaze, except to note the way the fire burned it must have started in the priest's office."

"Don't priests burn candles?"

"Who knows what most priests do, but they found a candle holder on the desk and wax residue by the window. If it was a candle, that was probably what started the fire. Malone's body was found prone in the middle of the room."

"Maybe he was trying to get out."

"Not if he was facing the desk."

Jonathan supposed not. "Is that it?"

"The Medical Examiner found a contusion at the back of Malone's head, but not much was made of it, considering the building practically fell down on top of him."

"They left it at that?"

Mari leaned back in her chair. "There's also speculation that powerful friends of Malone's squashed a full investigation fearing the fire had been set to cover up Malone's murder. They would rather not have known than discover one of Bronx's most beloved priests had been killed by his cronies for lining his pockets with more than his share of the skim."

"Is there any proof that anyone actually skimmed anything?" No skim, no motive for anyone to have murdered him, at least not over that.

"None that's here. It's all speculation upon speculation generated by the press. There's no proof of anything except that the building went up."

"Wonderful." He took the folder she handed to him. Knowing Mari, she'd laid out all the pertinent information in some reasonable format. As he looked through it, two thoughts bothered him, one of which Mari had already voiced: Why would Amanda Pierce care about the doings of a small-time priest and why now? The building had opened in September of 1980; the church had burned down several months after that. The only rationale he could see was that the twenty-fifth year anniversary of both events was almost here.

He pushed the file away and squeezed his temples between his thumb and middle finger. Even if there was some significance to the anniversary, there was nothing here to suggest a motive for Amanda Pierce's murder—unless of course there was something to all that past speculation and someone didn't want her to dredge it all up again. If one of Malone's gangster buddies had wanted her dead, he doubted he would have had her strangled in the first place, not to mention leaving her body nude and freshly bathed in a garbage can uptown. A couple of shots in the back of the head with a clean .22 in her own bed was more their style. Less work, no mess, and dead was dead, no matter how it was accomplished.

Shea chose that moment to come stand by his desk. "Your friend Freddie Jackson just turned up. Some neighbor saw him entering his mother's house and phoned it in." He tossed a slip of paper bearing an address onto Jonathan's desk. "Maybe you want to go pick him up."

As Shea walked away, Jonathan turned to Mari. "Want to go watch the show?"

Mari was already on her feet. "Anything beats sitting here shuffling papers."

Yeah, and having an actual break on something couldn't hurt, either.

Dana woke late and stretched languidly, for the first time in a long time not caring what time she arose. Her dreams had thankfully been free of any stark images of that morning on Highland Avenue. She hadn't told anyone, but those first two nights after the shooting, she'd dreamed of falling, endlessly falling, only to reach bottom and have two disembodied dead eyes staring down at her.

Last night was different, thank God. Maybe her psyche had simply cleansed itself of those terrifying moments through her dreams. She didn't know, but if the nightmares were over, she was grateful.

She rose, showered, and dressed in a pair of low-riding jeans and a T-shirt that exposed her navel. Against her doctor's orders, she'd taken off the sling yesterday and considered herself done with it. Her shoulder was almost healed. She could withstand whatever few twinges activity sparked in that area.

She made herself a light breakfast of toast and coffee, settled on the sofa with her feet tucked under her and turned on the TV. Channel 12, the Bronx cable news station, came to life. After a brief report on the traffic, the news anchor introduced the next story, new speculation into the Amanda Pierce case. Supposedly some crazed fan might have gotten to her. The report didn't speculate as to the identity of said crazed fan, but segued instead into a story about other celebrities who were either harmed or stalked by the public.

Dana clicked off the set. A maniac fan. That made as much sense to her as any other explanation for Amanda Pierce's fate being tossed around. At least it wasn't the proverbial tall, short, young, old, fat, skinny black man blamed for so many crimes until the real culprit, usually white, was uncovered.

She was just about to carry her dishes to the sink when her doorbell rang. Three men stood on her doorstep, all of them dressed in dark suits with white shirts and striped ties. The one in the center carried a Bible. He looked vaguely familiar, as if she'd seen him in the neighborhood, but she couldn't place him. To her mind, it was a bit early for religious proselytizing, but there was no accounting for other people's schedules.

She was tempted to leave them there on her porch, but then she'd have no assurance that they went away. She pulled open the door. "What can I do for you today, gentlemen?"

"Good morning, Sister Molloy. I am the Reverend Robert Jones and these men are my associates. May we have a word with you about Sister Evans?"

"Nadine?" She hoped these men hadn't come to tell her that something had happened to Nadine. If so, she wouldn't mind having a seat for that.

She stepped aside to allow them to enter. "Please come in." Once all of them were inside, she shut the door and led them toward her living room.

Only the Reverend deigned to sit, and at that he perched himself on one corner of her sofa. The other two men stood at his side. Dana sat on the loveseat opposite them. "What do you want to tell me?"

"I received a call yesterday from Sister Evans, right after her grandson's funeral. Honestly, I wish she'd called me earlier about her plight."

"Exactly which plight is that?"

"The inattention that's been shown by the police department in bringing Wesley's murderers to justice."

Oh, that plight. She couldn't imagine what these three men hoped to do in getting Moretti and the NYPD to move its feet, but more power to them. "What has this got to do with me?"

"You see, Sister Molloy, we want to seek justice for the boy. Every cause needs a symbol. Sister Evans is too infirm to be of much help in that way. You were wounded by the same men who killed her grandson."

In other words, they wanted to parade her around as some martyr to justice. She scrutinized the Reverend's face, finally recognizing him. Reverend Bobby Jones, who billed himself as the Al Sharpton of the Bronx, the defender of the weak and downtrodden.

No matter what anyone else wanted to say about Sharpton, particularly the mainstream media, Dana had always thought that he at least believed in the causes he espoused and tried to do his best for the people he defended.

From what she knew of this man seated before her, he was just a wannabe. All he cared about was to grab as much money and publicity as he could. She had no intention of becoming just another vehicle for him to do that.

"I doubt I'd make much of a symbol for you, Reverend."

"Think of it, Sister. You're a good woman. A public servant. A caregiver. How many times have you paid for food or supplies for your patients out of your own pocket?

Too numerous to count, but she doubted he'd been speaking to enough of her clients to really know. She'd done those things for Nadine and he'd extrapolated what he wanted from that information. Regardless of what she'd done, she had no desire to be part of his public pity party. "I'm not interested in becoming a public spectacle for you or anyone."

"You weren't so concerned about making a spectacle of yourself last night."

One of the Reverend's henchmen handed him a manila envelope, which he extended toward her.

Once she'd taken it from him he sat back with a smug expression on his face.

Dana reached inside the envelope to pull out a fuzzy black-and-white photograph. If she hadn't been there, she wouldn't have recognized herself or Jonathan as the man and woman kissing in the picture.

She'd known at the time that it was a mistake to let him touch her, though her reasons had nothing to do with any Peeping Tom photographers. The only reason she had was that she'd fully expected to be able to put any attraction to him out of her mind. She'd expected kissing him to be like locking lips with a brick wall. She'd expected him to be as hard and unyielding in that arena as he appeared to be in every other. Never would she have anticipated the gentleness of that one slow, stimulating kiss. To be honest, she'd never expected him to touch her at all.

To the Reverend, she said, "You were spying on me?"

"Not spying, Sister. Watching out. Our man just happened to have a camera. He has been sanctioned for the lapse."

Yeah, but that didn't mean the Dear Reverend wouldn't try to use the by-product of his misdeed. She tossed the photograph and envelope onto her coffee table. "I don't know what this is supposed to prove other than either your photographer needs a better lens or I need a bottle of Windex."

"Think of what the media might make of the chief investigator in one homicide being involved with a witness in another."

For one thing, in this day and age no one would care. That is if anyone besides her could actually tell who was in the picture. As sure as she sat there she knew the Reverend figured her for some half-brained female who would protect her man at any cost to herself. But he'd forgotten the chief rule of black-mail: Make sure the threat is something your victim actually fears.

Dana shrugged. "Go ahead and print it, if you can find someone to do that for you. Make sure to send me a tear sheet for my scrapbook, while you're at it. But don't ever presume to come into my home again and make threats to me, no matter how idle they may be." She stood. "Now it's time you, Louie and Dewey left."

Jones rose to his feet. "Sister Molloy, I was raised in that neighborhood. My church is there. Don't you think the people of this community need a voice, someone to stand up for them?"

"Actually, I do. But I would hope that person's first mandate would be their best interests at heart, not how best to line his pockets or get his face on TV."

The Reverend said nothing to that. He and his men filed out of her house and went to a black car parked across the street. As they drove off, she wondered if Reverend Jones was through with her and decided she didn't care.

Freddie Jackson's mother Edwina Payne lived on a little stretch of houses recently built off the New England Thruway. Like many spots in the Bronx, any postage stamp-sized lot had a new house going up on it, or one recently built and occupied. The preference seemed to be for three-family numbers, with each family claiming one floor of the building. Jackson's mother's place was no different. She had a ground floor one bedroom that offered the intriguing view of two-way traffic passing on the highway.

The neighborhood had once been a hooker stroll,

drawing customers who made a pit stop off the highway before construction began. The hookers weren't giving it up that easily. Three scantily dressed ladies disappeared into the bushes as they rolled up behind one of the squad cars in front of the house.

"Isn't it a bit early for working girls?" Mari said as they got out of the car.

"Maybe they're over achievers." By eyewitness accounts and by the blood trail leaving the scene, Jackson had been hurt. How badly or where he'd holed himself up for the past two days was anybody's guess. But by now, he must know he was wanted for murder. In all likelihood, he wouldn't come along easily, but it was the uniformed cops' show. They were along for the ride.

Unlike the TV universe, real-life detectives didn't go breaking down doors or lead S.W.A.T. teams into dangerous situations or other similar nonsense. Nor did crime labs instantly come up with results to complicated tests that took days or weeks instead of minutes to process. No wonder the public often accused the police of dragging their feet. Real cops didn't have the Law and Order guys writing the scripts.

For all the effort it ended up taking, he and Mari may as well have stayed in the house. Mrs. Payne opened the door willingly. It turned out she, not a neighbor, had called in. Her son had shown up on her doorstep feverish from his infected knife wound and passed out.

Jackson was taken to the hospital under police guard while they questioned Mrs. Payne. She had nothing of interest to report except that she wasn't letting nobody, son or not, die in her house.

He and Mari got in the car and followed the ambu-

lance. For the moment, at least, Amanda Pierce would
have to wait.

They called him "Old Specs" because from the
street all you could see of him was the top of his bald
head and the thick rims of his glasses as he peered
out at Highland Avenue through a gap in his blinds.
Dana stood outside his building—the building where
Nadine Evans lived, the building in which she'd
been shot—questioning the wisdom of what she was
doing.

After the Reverend and his minions left that morning, it had occurred to her that since no one seemed
to care what happened to Wesley except a man who
wanted to advance his own agenda, maybe she should
do a little investigating of her own. Nothing major,
like hunting down the drug dealers that killed him,
but somebody had to have seen something that
could help track down the killers.

But nothing went unnoticed in this neighborhood,
no matter what the police thought. And those who
wouldn't dream of going to the police had no com-
punction about reporting to others who might not
have her best interests at heart. She had to work in this
neighborhood. What she was doing might be suicide.

But she'd paid the better part of twenty dollars for
a cab here so she might as well get what she came for
and get out of there before she drew too much attention to herself.

As she started up the steps, her breathing shallowed
and her heartbeat quickened. The back of her neck
grew cold with the sensation that someone watched
her. She glanced back over her shoulder and saw no
one but some kids playing across the street, paying

her no mind. She took another step, feeling her empty stomach come to life, burning with acid and emotion. She reached the top of the stairs and laid her fingertips to the smooth glass panel in the door. New glass to replace the pane shattered by her and Wesley and a gunman's bullets.

She inhaled, trying to quell the effects of her body's autonomic nervous system kicking in. Maybe her dreams hadn't really cleansed anything from her psyche if her fight or flight instinct got activated just by being here. She pushed through the front door and walked to the man's apartment. She knocked on the door and almost immediately it opened, revealing a dark-skinned man in a wheelchair. She'd wondered why the old man had spent so much time sitting by his window, and she supposed she had her answer.

"I know you," the man said. "You're the nurse. Shame what happened here the other day."

"That's what I wanted to talk to you about, Mr.—"

"Just call me Teddy."

"Okay, Teddy, can I come in for a minute?"

The old man wheeled his chair backward, barely enough for her to slip inside his apartment. The first thing she noticed was the smell, like old mothballs. But the place was neat and as roomy as any of the apartments in this part of the city.

He led her down the hall to the living room. He offered her a wing back chair covered with what looked like two large cream-colored doilies while he took his usual spot by the window.

She'd thought he'd peered out through the blinds, but he'd actually cut a few of the slats to afford him a view. He looked out now, tsking as he did. "Street's quiet today."

He sounded almost disappointed, as if the goings on in the street outside were staged for his amusement only.

"Were you at the window Saturday morning?" said Dana.

"Of course. I saw the whole thing. I knew them boys was cruising around for trouble."

"They drove around more than once?"

He nodded. "A few times. Like they was looking for someone or something."

"Did you recognize any of them?"

He tapped his glasses. "My eyes aren't what they should be. I couldn't make out no faces. But I did get this." He leaned forward to rifle through the papers on the wooden occasional table next to the window. "I wrote it down."

He handed her a slip of paper. A series of letters and numbers was written on it in florid handwriting. "What's this?" she said.

"The license number on the car."

She scanned the old man's face. "Why didn't you give this to the police?"

"I wasn't gonna tell them cops nothin'." A bitter, belligerent expression came over his face. "They shot my boy. Killed him in the street like a dog. Why should I help them?"

"What happened?"

"They caught him robbin' some liquor store. They told him to stop and he didn't. But they didn't have to shoot him."

Dana shook her head. She'd heard this story before: "My son, daughter, old man, next door neighbor was out committing some crime and the police shot him for no reason." She had her own beef with the cops, but only because *innocent* people often suffered the same fate as the guilty. Why didn't it occur to people that if they weren't out robbing folks or selling drugs that the police wouldn't take often justified action against them?

"I'm sorry to hear that." She was, but not for any reason he would grasp. She folded the piece of paper, slipped it into her back pocket and stood. "I'd better be going."

Disappointment darkened the old man's eyes, reminding her of Nadine's expression whenever it was time for her to leave. Like her, Teddy probably didn't have many visitors, but there was nothing Dana could do about that. She followed him to the door and left.

Out on the sidewalk she stepped to the curb to catch a livery cab to the hospital to see Joanna. It would probably cost her more than the cab down here, but it beat taking the train.

Once the maroon Lincoln pulled up and she got in and told the driver where she wanted to go, she retrieved the piece of paper from her pocket. She knew she should call Moretti and tell him what she'd found out. Maybe that would finally get his ass moving, but she doubted it. More than likely he'd accuse her of interfering in his case or worse.

She pulled out her phone and dialed the number on the card he'd given her. He wasn't in, but whoever took down her information promised to have him call her back.

She clicked off the phone feeling she'd done her good deed for the day. Now all she could do was wait.

Ten

Jonathan checked his watch for the third time in fifteen minutes. They'd been waiting an hour to speak with Jackson, but as yet he hadn't awakened. It had only taken twenty minutes to stitch up the wound in his side, but the combination of antibiotics and painkillers being fed through his veins, not to mention the infection that had knocked him out, made that impossible. Considering Jackson wasn't going anywhere any time soon, there was no point in waiting any longer.

"What's next on the agenda?" Mari asked as they headed back to the car.

He was about to say back to the paperwork when his cell phone buzzed. "Stone." Mari looked at him with interest during the brief call. When he disconnected the call, he said, "That was Horgan. He's got something for us."

Horgan was sitting at one of the counters having his lunch when they came in. "Just the people I've been waiting to see."

"What have you got for us?" Jonathan asked.

Horgan sloshed down one more gulp from his cup. "The fiber analysis came back." He sorted through a stack of file folders beside him. Horgan found the folder he wanted and handed it to him.

"What's the gist of it?" Jonathan asked.

"Fibers from the scarf in the closet match exactly the fibers from the body in quality and consistency." Horgan picked up his sandwich and took a bite from it. "Congratulations, ladies and gentlemen, you've got yourself a murder weapon."

"Strangled with her own scarf," Mari said. "There's got to be some irony there, though damned if I see it."

But it supported the theory that Pierce's murder had been a crime of opportunity rather than a planned event. She might have said something or done something to provoke her attacker. Maybe she was walking away and whoever she was with grabbed hold of the scarf and choked her. He voiced his thoughts to Mari and Horgan.

"That would be consistent with the wounds," Horgan said. He dug in another file with one hand and pulled out a picture of the lower portion of Pierce's face and her throat. "You can see the ligature marks go back and upward. Whoever killed her was a bit taller than she was." He took another bite of his sandwich. "By the way, I released the body this morning."

"Thanks," Jonathan said, as they headed out the door. So now they had an impulse killer who nonetheless took the time to clean up his mess. Jonathan felt reasonably confident that whoever had killed her had something to do with what she'd been working on last. Something she'd uncovered that someone wished to stay hidden. He wished her

damn assistant would crawl out of whatever hidey
hole he'd disappeared into to tell them what he
knew. Not even the man's mother knew where he'd
gone. With a sinking feeling, Jonathan began to
question if Bender hadn't been the one to off her in
the first place. Rosa Nuñez had said she was difficult
to work for. Maybe Bender had had enough.

Either way, Jonathan hoped the APB they'd put out
on the guy would turn up something soon.

Both Joanna and the baby were awake and alert
when Dana got to the hospital a little after one o'clock.
The room was filled with balloons and stuffed animals
sent by well-wishers. Dana sat in the chair next to
Joanna's bed. "Makes me feel like the Grinch who stole
Christmas," she said, referring to the fact she hadn't
brought anything.

"You were here for what counted," Joanna said, ad-
justing herself in bed. "How are you doing? Is there
any break in Wesley's case?"

Dana thought of the paper burning a hole in her
pocket, but didn't plan on telling her friend about
that. "I haven't heard from Moretti, but I'm sure he
has better things to do than worry about me."

Joanna sighed. "You know, it's a shame. I know you
have your cop thing, but when I was growing up
our house was like the hangout for all my dad's buddies from corrections and the force. By then, my dad
was raising us by himself and didn't stay out late, so
they came to our place. I'd sneak into a corner to
listen to them swap stories, most of them whoppers.

"I loved those guys. Good guys. I think they're the
reason my brothers were drawn to their careers. But
every now and then they'd talk about some asshole

they knew who was either racist or power hungry or whatever. It always made me sad that these men were out there doing their jobs while others did their best to make the lot of them look bad."

Dana didn't bother to argue with her friend. She supposed it was the same in every profession—the ones who screwed up always got more notice and tainted everyone else in the process. But when you carried a badge and a gun, folks expected a little more accountability.

Instead she stood. "I'm going to wash my hands. Then I want to hold my godbaby. When do you want to christen her?"

"Sometime soon. Ray's mother was very religious. According to her, you have to baptize a baby before it's a month old."

"That soon? What sins could a month-old baby have on its soul?"

"You're asking me? I don't think Ray has any idea either. It's part of his family tradition, I guess. Sometimes those are harder to break than solid concrete."

Dana supposed, having few of her own to worry about. She went to the bathroom and scrubbed her hands. When she returned, Joanna lifted the baby into her arms. The little girl looked up at her and gurgled.

"Holding a baby looks good on you, kid."

Dana eyed her friend. "Let's not go there, okay?"

Joanna grinned. "All right, all right. I'll give my song a rest. I know you and my brothers are all tired of hearing from me. It's just that for the first time in my life, I'm really happy. I want all of you guys to know what that feels like."

Dana settled into her seat again, snuggling the baby closer. She had to admit, few things rivaled holding a tiny, trusting baby in your arms. She touched her fingertip to one of the dark curls peeking out from under the baby's cap. One day, maybe, but not now. Now was her time for a little freedom, to get back some of her own, what she'd lost putting her life on hold to care for her brother. Not counting her foray into the South Bronx, so far the most reckless thing she'd done was to allow Jonathan Stone to kiss her. Maybe that was all the recklessness she needed for a while.

"What?" Joanna said.

Dana's head snapped up. She hadn't realized her thoughts had shown on her face or that Joanna had been scrutinizing her so closely. "I was just thinking that she looks like you."

"Right," Joanna said, her disbelief evident in her tone.

Dana went back to looking at the baby. She had no intention of telling Joanna about that kiss and she assumed that Jonathan had enough sense not to, either. Knowing Joanna, she'd probably start buying rice to throw at the ceremony if she knew. As far as Dana was concerned that kiss was just a temporary aberration that wouldn't be repeated. Then again, if Reverend What's-his-name had his way, they'd be on the cover of the Daily News.

"How's Tim?" Joanna asked, apparently willing to change the subject.

"He's fine. I heard from him this morning. He's loving the weather down in Orlando."

"And probably the girls, too."

"Don't remind me. I don't want to be an aunt any sooner than I have to be."

"I hear you."

Dana stayed until evening when Ray showed up. He'd brought the boys by that morning to see their mother and new baby sister then stayed with them at home until Adam's wife Barbara got back from work to come back. As she walked the few blocks back to her house, she switched on her cell phone. No call from Moretti, or anyone else for that matter. She wondered if he'd bother to call back at all.

They were on the way back to the stationhouse when Mari's cell phone rang. She answered the call, mumbled a few words into the phone, then hung up. "You'll never guess who just resurfaced."

"Lucky Lindy? Or is it Hoffa? I never did believe that Meadowlands story."

"How about one Eric Bender? Seems Mr. Bender was out of the country. Airport police picked him up an hour ago, coming back from Aruba. He claimed not to know anything about Amanda Pierce's murder."

"Where is he?"

"At the house."

"Good." Jonathan was looking forward to meeting him.

Eric Bender was a rail of a man with long, brown hair that hung over his forehead, which caused him to periodically brush it back. His skin was tanned a dark bronze, suggesting he'd spent more than a day basking in the Caribbean sun. He was nervous, alternately rocking back in his chair in a rhythmic motion or tapping his fingers on the table. He checked his watch for the third time in as many minutes. Aside from the officer sent in to watch him, he was alone.

Watching him from the other side of a two-way mirror, Jonathan didn't like the look of him. He was tall enough to have been Pierce's attacker, but he doubted the man had the strength to strangle her without being overpowered himself. Damn.

He looked at Mari standing beside him. "What do you think?"

"Little Bo Peep in there? Nah."

That was the amazing thing about people, they liked to surprise you. "See you later."

He walked past Mari to get to the entrance to the room. Since Bender was nervous enough he decided to go in alone. Mari would watch from the where she was.

He opened the door and let the officer out. "Mr. Bender, I understand you just got back into the country."

"I was on vacation. Are you the detective in charge?"

"Yes." As he took the seat across from Bender he could feel the man's eyes on him gauging whether that was a good thing or not. "They tell me you had no idea Ms. Pierce had been murdered."

"None. As I said, I was on vacation."

"They have telephones on Aruba, Mr. Bender. Not to mention faxes, the Internet and most importantly cable TV from America. Yet you heard nothing."

"Not where I was staying."

Jonathan cast him a skeptical look.

"You don't understand," Bender continued. "It was my first vacation in two years. I wanted to enjoy it, so I found some place where they didn't allow contact from the outside world. I even left my cell phone at home."

"Why did you go to so much trouble?"

"Because of her." He huffed out a breath. "The last

time I went away she made me come back. She got a new lead on someone she was investigating. She threatened to fire me, so what could I do? I need this job." He breathed in and out, calming himself. "She was so mean I didn't think anything would ever kill her."

Stifling an amused look at that comment, Jonathan asked, "Do you know what she was working on before you left, possibly something to do with a Father Malone?"

"Yeah, that was her pet project. She was crazed about it the last few months."

"Why? Was she planning a book on him?"

Bender shook his head. "No, he was her uncle, her father's brother. A while back some producer contacted her wanting to interview her for some documentary he was making. He wanted to prove Malone had been murdered."

"She was helping him out?"

"Hell no. She wanted to clear her uncle's name. If he were murdered that means he had to be up to something, right?"

"Was he?"

"Not as far as I could tell. One of his partners was a little shady, but from what I can tell everything was legit. But keep in mind; this was twenty-five years ago. Half the records don't even exist anymore. Most of the people involved are dead."

"Then why did she bother?"

"The guy who approached her isn't exactly the kind known for his scruples, if you know what I mean. She was afraid he'd fabricate whatever he didn't know to prove his own conclusion. She was hoping to come out with an article on him *before* this guy had a chance to put anything out. Kind of a preemptive strike."

"But she got sidetracked?"

"Something like that. Right before I left she begged me to stay. She'd found some old guy from the old neighborhood. I'm not really sure how. She told me I was abandoning her." He shrugged. "Maybe if I'd stayed . . ."

"Why wasn't any of this information in her office?"

"She probably had it on her, in her day planner and in a notebook she carried. She liked to carry things around with her until I transcribed her notes for her."

Since Bender hadn't been there, whatever information Pierce had was probably destroyed by the man who'd killed her. Damn.

For the time being, there wasn't much more he needed from Bender except for the name of the man doing the documentary. Bender offered him a card from his wallet with the man's name and address.

Jonathan stood. "Thank you for coming in, Mr. Bender," he said, as if it had actually been the man's idea to come in. "We'll contact you if we need anything else."

"I can go?"

Jonathan nodded. "Just stay in town."

As Bender went out Mari came in. "Very interesting. Who's the guy doing the film?" He handed the card bearing the logo for Sunrise Motion Pictures to Mari; she looked at it and shrugged. "Doesn't do anything for me."

"Me, either." But it did give them another avenue in which to look. A producer wouldn't want Pierce coming out with a piece that would negate any claims he might make with his documentary. There was no telling what people would do where money was involved. A little greed could literally be a dangerous thing.

Then there was the possibility that whoever this old guy was, he'd given her some information that had led to her getting killed.

A dull headache throbbed at his temple. He massaged it with his thumb and middle finger. He was tired of possibilities. He was ready for some certainties to start presenting themselves. It was past quitting time and they'd skipped lunch. His stomach rumbled, protesting its neglect. They'd come back to this tomorrow. He wanted the night to assimilate everything they'd gotten so far. But tomorrow they'd start at the beginning. They'd go back to St. Jude's.

As she let herself into her house, she had the feeling someone was watching her, just like this afternoon only not as sharply. She turned to see Moretti getting out of a car parked at the curb. She wondered what she'd done to merit a personal visit from the man when a phone call would have sufficed.

She opened the door and waited for him to come up the steps.

"Good evening, Detective," she said as he reached her. "Thanks for getting back to me."

His already belligerent expression turned sour. "This isn't a game, Ms. Molloy."

"I'm glad you noticed. It's life and death. It almost cost me mine."

He said nothing to that. He entered her small hallway, crowding her. She could do without being that close to him. She started toward the back of the house, leaving him to close the door or not as he saw fit.

He followed her into the kitchen. "What were you doing on Highland Avenue this morning?"

"Your job apparently. I spoke to Theodore something, an old man who watches the neighborhood. He got the license plate of the car the men were driving. She pulled the paper out of her pocket and tossed it onto her kitchen table. "Think you can manage to run that down?"

He snatched the paper from the table. "Look lady, I do my job and I don't need any neighborhood nurse messing it up. Did your boyfriend put you up to this? Another nail in my coffin?"

He took a step toward her, closing the gap between them. For a moment she feared what he would do. "Stay out of my way, or I'll charge you with obstruction of justice."

He turned and stormed down her hall, slamming the door behind him.

Dana exhaled, relieved to have him gone. He'd been trying to scare her. She knew that. He hadn't done too bad a job of it. She doubted he could make such a charge stick, but it might last long enough to land her in Riker's for the night. Jonathan had told her to watch out for him. Now she understood what he meant. Moretti had it in for both of them and she doubted he cared which one of them he got.

On his way home, Jonathan double parked by the *cuchifrito* place on River Avenue. After two days of being on his own, Tyree would probably need some food to stick to his bones. That's if he showed up tonight, but Jonathan was hopeful. He bought rice and beans, *pernil*—roast pork, platanos—fried plantains cut lengthwise and tostones—green bananas cut sideways, and a couple of bottles of beer.

After taking a shower and changing into jeans and a T-shirt, he set the food out on his coffee table and turned on his laptop. He wanted to find out what he could about Sunrise Motion Pictures before he confronted its owner.

He'd barely gotten the machine turned on when he heard a knock at his window. Tyree was on the other side. "Hey Jay, you wanna hang?" he said through the glass.

Did he want to leave his air-conditioned apartment to roast on the fire escape? There were worse ways to suffer. "Sure. You hungry?"

The boy said nothing but he noticed the way the boy's gaze fixed on the food. "I'll be right out." He closed the computer and got a tray from the kitchen and loaded the containers, some plastic utensils and napkins on it. He opened the window and passed the tray to Tyree before coming out himself. "Help yourself."

Tyree opened the container of rice and beans and forked some into his mouth. "Those Spanish mamas sure know how to burn some pots."

Jonathan agreed. The food was hot, spicy, satisfying. Mari would be proud. After a moment, he asked. "How's your mom?"

"I gotta go get her tomorrow."

He said nothing more than that, just gulped down more food. Despite the kid's hunger, he knew Tyree wouldn't have shown up unless he wanted something. If it had nothing to do with his mother, it had to be something else. He let the kid fill himself, then asked. "What have you been up to since the last time I saw you?"

"Just hanging around with some of my boys. Down by Third Avenue. I heard some interesting shit too. You know that kid you was asking me about?"

"I thought you were going to leave that alone."

"People be talking. I just listen."

Tyree darted a glance at him before going back to his food, probably trying to gauge if Jonathan believed him. He didn't. "What did you find out?"

"He was with Big Pee Wee and them. You know who I mean?"

"Yeah." The drug dealer had earned his nickname for his weight, that topped two hundred and fifty pounds and his height, which was only 5'6".

"Word is the guy wanted out so Pee Wee sent some of his boys out after him."

It wouldn't be the first time Jonathan had heard of that happening. These gangs were like families, and like any other family, once you got in, the only way to get out was to die. The sad part of it was, to Jonathan's mind, that the leadership in these gangs wasn't the kids you always saw on TV, but men in their twenties or thirties or even older preying on the young ones. For every young punk on the street there was some older man pulling the strings.

"Thanks for finding that out, but that's it. Agreed?"

Tyree shot him another rabbit glance. "Guess I can't tell you what else I saw then."

"What?"

"That lady you asked about. The nurse. I saw her today."

"Where?"

"Right in front of the building. She was staring up at it like it was going to bite her. I didn't stop or nothing cause I didn't want nobody else to notice her, but I'm sure it was her."

"What time was this?"

"About lunch. We was heading to that chicken place over there."

Late enough for the criminal element to have

roused itself for the day. The woman had to be out of her mind. What could she possibly hope to accomplish by showing up there, let alone at that time of day? He remembered her frustration at Moretti not getting anything done. He hoped she hadn't become so frustrated she decided to take matters into her own hands. If Pee Wee had been involved in Wesley's death, he wouldn't hesitate to send those same boys after her.

He checked his watch. It was late but not so late he expected her to be asleep. "I gotta go, Tyree. You can take the rest up to your place if you want."

"Thanks, man." He started to gather up the containers. "I did okay?"

The boy still wanted his approval. That was a good sign. "You did great. Now lay low for a while and take care of your mom, okay?"

The boy nodded.

Jonathan slipped through his window and closed it behind him. He grabbed his keys off the coffee table and clipped his holster to his belt as he strode to his front door. Even at this time of night, the traffic flowing north was heavy.

Once he got there, he parked in the street, blocking her garage, and went around the side of the house to the front door. From the outside he noticed a flickering light in the living room as if someone were watching TV in the dark. The glass door of the porch was ajar, as was the front door. Neither by much, but enough to concern him. He pushed open the front door. The hall was dimly lit by a bulb plugged into a baseboard power socket. "Dana?" Not even the sound of a television answered him.

Considering her adventures today, his first thought was that someone had gotten to her before he had.

He eased his gun from its holster as he checked the stairs to his right. If anyone was up there, he couldn't see them from this vantage point.

He traveled along the wall until he reached a door on the left side of the hallway. He turned the knob with his left hand. Judging by the game systems hooked up to the TV and the posters on the walls— faded ones of Shaq and Jordan, as well as newer ones of some of the younger players—he'd found her brother's room. The room was neat and the bed still made, which probably meant he hadn't returned from wherever he'd been staying.

Jonathan pulled the door closed, then continued on. The kitchen in front of him proved empty, which left only the living room, the bathroom, and the back porch on this floor. He veered right, toward the living room. That's where the only light he'd seen had come from. The room's narrow archway made it difficult to see anything except what was directly in front of him. He eased forward, down the one step that separated the kitchen from the hall.

He saw her then, sitting on the sofa, her hair tousled, her bare feet propped up on the coffee table, looking as soft and alluring as he'd ever seen her. The flickering he'd seen wasn't a television set, but several candles burning in different spots around the room.

She held a glass in her hand, which she raised to him in salute. "Are you planning on shooting me, Detective? I promise you, I'm unarmed."

Eleven

Jonathan let out his breath and put his gun away. "Why didn't you answer me?"

"I did. The acoustics in this place are terrible, or so my brother Tim keeps telling me every time he claims he can't hear me calling him." She took a sip from her glass. "What are you doing here anyway? How did you get in?"

"The front door was open."

She shrugged. "Must have been your friend Moretti's doing. He was a little upset when he left here."

"Was he? Why is that?"

"I uncovered some information that I thought he should know. The license plate number of the car the men who shot Wesley were driving. He accused me of interfering with his case—not in such nice words, of course."

At least she had enough sense to bring what she knew to someone in the police department, though he wished she'd passed the information on to him or let him be here when Moretti showed up.

"What are you doing here, Dana?"

She lifted her glass. "I'm having some wine. Would you like a glass?"

"No, thank you." He looked at the half-empty bottle that sat on her coffee table. "It seems you're doing fine for both of us."

"Oh, please. I wouldn't have expected that sort of male sanctimony from you. A guy knocking one back is just mellowing out while a woman who takes a drink is a lush. And, just so you know, it would certainly take more than a couple of glasses of Chardonnay to get me drunk."

Was there any nonsense that could come out of his mouth that she wouldn't call him on? He supposed he was out of line, but he was angry with her and needed some direction in which to focus it. "Anything else, your highness?"

She surprised him by grinning. "Sit down. It's making my neck hurt having to look up at you."

He claimed a spot opposite her and sat back. "This isn't a game, Dana. I know you know that. If you put yourself in the middle of this more than you already have, you can get hurt."

"I know. And I have no intention of going back. But this morning I was feeling so frustrated. I wanted to do something. Anything. I didn't think talking to one old man would be such a big deal."

In other words, she hadn't expected to accomplish anything, but wanted to make herself feel better by trying.

She sighed. "How did you find out about it anyway?"

"I have my sources."

"Which are probably confidential, no?"

He exhaled, his anger dissipating with the knowledge that she understood the dangers of trying to do Moretti's job for him. With that emotion gone, he didn't know what else to say to her. "Do you think this qualifies as a semi-civil conversation?"

She made an exasperated sound in her throat. "I'm sorry about that. I find it hard to be around people I can't be straightforward with."

That intrigued him. "What can't you be straightforward with me about?"

He waited as she took a sip from her glass then swirled it, her gaze fixed on its contents. "I find myself in the unfortunate position of being attracted to you."

That surprised him—not the attraction, because he felt it too, had felt it long before last night when he'd kissed her. "Is that such a bad thing?"

Her eyes widened and she gestured in a way that suggested he should already know the answer. "Is it just because I'm a cop?"

"You're my best friend's brother."

"And . . ." he prompted, waiting for her to get to some answer that made sense.

"And it's time you left. I promise not to do anything else as stupid as I did this morning. I'll stay out of it and let you boys in blue do your job."

She stood and smoothed down her jeans, drawing his attention to how snugly they fit her slender hips. He had the feeling that if he pressed her on it, she'd reveal her true feelings, but he didn't do that. He stood and let her lead him to the door.

Once they reached the tiny alcove by the door, he turned to her. "Try to see what you can do about staying out of trouble."

He was teasing her, and she responded by punching him on the arm. Then she wrapped her fingers around his biceps. "Seriously, thank you for your concern."

The hint of a smile fell away from her face and she

looked away from him. He suspected it had taken a lot for her to say that, though he didn't have a clue as to why.

Just like last night, he tilted her chin up so he could see her face. But unlike before, he couldn't think of a single thing to say. It was the mixture of emotion laid bare in her eyes that did him in, the foremost of which was longing. Or maybe that's only what he thought he saw, what he wanted to see. That's not all he wanted from her, but he would settle for her kiss if she gave it willingly.

He lowered his mouth to hers, but from the start this was no unhurried embrace. Her fingers on his arm tightened as her other hand rose to grip his back. He tasted the fruit of the wine on her tongue as it met his for a wild, erotic dance.

Her back was to the wall. With his hands at her hips, he backed her against it. One of his thighs found its way between hers as he sank against her, losing himself in the sensual haze of her kiss.

He'd pulled away from her last night, but then he'd lacked the encouragement of her hands on him. They were at the back of his shirt now, trying to free it from his waistband. He obliged her by pulling the shirt over his head and tossing it away. And then her hands were on his bare skin, wandering over his chest, exciting him.

He pulled her against him, trapping her hands between them as his mouth claimed hers for a second kiss as ravenous as the first. But it wasn't enough this time. He wanted to see her, feel her skin against his. He pushed her back against the wall and lifted her shirt from her body. His eyes drank in the sight of her. Her breasts were round, tipped with dark areolas, and more than ample for her slender figure. He covered them with his palms, using his thumbs to stroke her nipples. Her eyes drifted shut and her neck arched. A soft sound of pleasure escaped her lips.

Then a car backfired out on the street, jolting them both. She looked at him, blinking, startled. She turned away from him, her forehead resting on the wall, one arm crossed over her breasts, the other hand splayed on the wall. Her ribcage moved with the labor of her breathing. Suddenly the cadence of her breathing picked up. For a moment he feared she was crying, though she wasn't making any noise.

He stroked her back. "Are you all right?"

She flopped around to face him, both arms crossed over her breasts though she wasn't really hiding anything from him. In her eyes he saw humor, not distress. He should have known better.

She lifted one hand to brush her hair back from her face. "That backfire must have been the warning bell on my sanity." She gestured in a way that encompassed both of them. "I didn't mean for this to happen."

As if he had. How could either of them have known that their acquaintance would turn so combustible the minute they put their hands on each other.

With a sigh, he retrieved his shirt and tugged it on. Even if he stayed he couldn't offer her flowery words or protestations of emotions she knew he didn't feel. He didn't even know if such things mattered to her, but at this point they weren't in him to give. No matter what, he wished he had something to offer her, aside from a warm body in her bed.

She didn't say anything as he bent to kiss her cheek. She simply looked at him with an unreadable expression on her face. "Take care of yourself," he said before letting himself out the front door, into the dark, sultry night.

After he left, Dana drew back on her T-shirt and went back to her living room, feeling out of sorts. Once again, she'd allowed herself to get stirred up by a man she wasn't even sure she liked.

No, that wasn't true. If anything, in the last couple of days he'd set every assumption she'd had about him, from the tenderness of his touch last night, to the heat of his embrace tonight. Jonathan Stone wasn't made of stone, at least not all of him. Though she'd downplayed it, his concern for her safety touched her. If his showing up in her living room, gun drawn, proved anything, the man was willing to risk his life to protect hers. She supposed such willingness was supposed to come with the job, but she couldn't imagine Moretti laying his life on the line for his own mother.

She sat on the sofa and pulled a pillow onto her lap. Despite everything, the truth was that she wanted him. There wasn't any question about that. And he wanted her, too. Things couldn't have gotten so out of hand so quickly if that weren't true. She hadn't said anything to him when he was leaving because part of her was tempted to ask him to stay. Part of her was ready to cast all other considerations aside to be with him.

Why shouldn't she be able to see what she wanted and take it? Everyone else seemed to do whatever they wanted whenever they wanted and leave her or others like her to clean up the messes. She was tired of martyring her desires to the needs of others without ever considering her own needs. Thank God,

he'd walked away from her without making her
choose, because right now, she honestly didn't know
what that choice would have been.

Sunrise Motion Pictures' office was housed on
the fifteenth floor in a building on Houston Street.
After he left Dana's house the night before, Jonathan
had spent the next couple of hours finishing the research he'd started when Tyree showed up.

The sun in sunrise was an acronym for the last initials of its three partners, Daniel Sanders, Keith
Unger, and Stan Nichols. It was Nichols's card Bender
had given him.

Sunrise's claim to fame was institutional shorts
for trade clients, but had recently begun to branch
into longer films they hoped to sell to stations like
the History Channel and PBS.

It didn't take them long to discern which office belonged to Sunrise. A giant mock-up of General
Custer in battle gear with the words, "The Definitive
Biography on Custer" along with the channel, date
and time it would be airing emblazoned across it was
tacked on the door.

Mari eyed the mock-up with disgust. "I'll have to
make sure to miss that."

Him, too. The door opened onto a small reception
area. Behind it were a few cubicles and beyond that
a pair of offices. If there was any more to Sunrise
Motion Pictures, Jonathan couldn't tell.

The girl behind the reception desk flashed him a
smile as they approached. "Can I help you?"

He flashed her his badge. "We'd like to speak to
Stan Nichols."

She rolled her eyes. "Hold on." She picked up

the phone and punched in three numbers. "Stan, the police are here," she said as if it weren't an unheard of occurrence. She nodded rather than spoke into the phone then hung up. "He said to tell you he'll be right out."

They stepped back from the desk to wait. Mari leaned closer to him. "Seems like you're the one with an admirer today."

"Oh, am I?"

Mari looked around. "What is it about this place that gives me the creeps?"

He didn't have much chance to speculate or answer. Stan Nichols approached, a puzzled expression on his face. "What can I do for you, Detectives?"

Nichols wore jeans and a black "Custer is Coming" T-shirt stretched over his ample belly. With his head of frizzy brown hair and coke bottle glasses, he reminded Jonathan of either an aging hippie or an overgrown Jim Henson puppet. Either his expression was a good act, or the man had no idea why they were there. For now he'd reserve judgment on which.

"We're investigating the Amanda Pierce murder. Is there somewhere we can talk?"

"Sure." Nichols looked a bit more nervous now. "Let's go into my office." He led the way to the office he'd come from. "Please excuse the mess."

The office was furnished with the kind of leather and dark wood you could get out of an Ikea catalog. Every surface, and the desk in particular, was covered with papers, videotapes or electronic equipment of some kind. Even the laptop on Nichols's desk was propped up on top of a stack of papers. At least the visitors' chairs were clear.

Nichols rounded his desk and sat. He offered

them a nervous smile. "Would you believe me if I told you I know where everything is?"

"No, not, really," Mari said. "We understand you were making a film about Pierce's uncle that she wasn't too happy about."

Nichols rolled his eyes. "That's an understatement. When I approached her about being part of it, she went ballistic. Threatened to report me to the police. But there was nothing she could do about it. It's taken us a few years but we're strictly legit now."

Jonathan scanned the room. A series of framed photographs lined the wall. Most were awards or stills from what he assumed were industrial films. But a couple were obviously from adult films.

Nichols must have noticed the direction of his gaze. "I suppose I should get rid of those."

"What interested you in Father Malone in the first place?"

"You have to understand, New York history and the Bronx in particular is hot now. Ever since 9/11 people can't get enough of this stuff."

"So you figured you'd cash in on it?" Mari said.

He shrugged. "Yeah. Why not? That's what you're supposed to do—take advantage of an opportunity. A few months ago I got a call from one of the yahoos from my high school asking me if I wanted to be on the planning committee for the 25th year reunion."

There was a black coffee cup resting on another stack of papers. Nichols picked it up and drank from it. "Now you know they had to be desperate if they were calling me, but it got me started thinking about the old neighborhood. And I remembered that about a year before or a year after we graduated was when all that hoo-ha went on with Father Malone.

I remember him. He was a great guy. So I started looking into it."

"How did Ms. Pierce get into it?"

"I contacted her. I mean, Amanda Pierce in one of my films talking about her uncle. That would have been hot. I could have sold that in a minute."

"What did you do when you found out she wasn't interested?"

He lifted his hands as if in surrender. "Hey, I made an ass of myself pestering her, but I didn't kill her. I even told her I hoped to find out who murdered him. You know, hoping to pique her interest. That made her even madder. But if you think I killed her over it! Why would I do that?"

"She was planning to publish an article in the *Times* refuting whatever claims you might have made later."

Nichols seemed genuinely surprised. "I didn't know that."

"Where were you last Friday morning?"

"Last Friday? Hold on a moment." He pressed a button on the phone. "Babe, where was I last Friday morning?"

The receptionist's annoyed voice came back. "You were at the dentist's. Anything else?"

"No, Babe, thanks." Nichols turned back to him. "I forgot. Root canal."

Jonathan handed the man his notebook. "Write down the name and address."

"Sure." The man scribbled something and handed it back. "Is there anything else?"

Jonathan stood and Mari followed. "Not at the moment." They'd check out Nichols's alibi, but if the man were telling the truth, he probably wasn't in any shape to have strangled anybody.

"Oink, oink and freaking oink," Mari said when they reached the elevators. "Here's what I want to know, how did she keep from strangling him? Imagine having a former pornographer being the one to do the biography of your beloved relative."

"No, thanks." Nichols had written down the phone number as well. Jonathan dialed it on his cell phone. When a woman answered, he identified himself and asked if Nichols had come in on Friday morning.

"Yeah, he was here," the woman said in a disgusted tone. "If you really are the police, see what you can do about getting the creep to stop pinching my butt."

Laughing, Jonathan disconnected the call. "Nichols checks out. Seems he left an impression on the receptionist."

"I'm not even going to ask what that means."

"Don't."

"I hope that doesn't mean you've crossed him off your list completely. I haven't."

Neither had he. Nichols definitely struck him as the type to get one of his low-life friends to remove any obstacle in his way. When he got back to the Bronx, he'd ask the receptionist in for a chat, away from the influence of her boss. He'd bet whatever was going on in that office she knew about it.

But he didn't tell Mari that, not while she was still riled up about the man. Instead, he managed to say with a straight face, "You objected to the former porno king's choice of artwork."

She shot him a disgusted look. "I'd like to see him with a dick shoved up his—"

The ping of the coming elevator distracted Mari from finishing that sentiment.

"With that mouth, it's a good thing the next place we're going is to see a priest."

* * *

The new St. Jude's sat on the corner of Prospect and Dyre Avenues, a beacon of neither beauty nor grace. A squat building, wider than it was long, it boasted little in the way of adornment of any kind. The spiked gate surrounding the property and the bars outside the few stained glass windows showed the church had more of an eye to curbing theft than comforting souls.

"It's a shame what some of these churches have to do," Mari said as they got out of the car.

Sometimes he forgot she'd been raised Catholic and didn't mind the upbringing. They'd contacted Father Masella, the current head of the church, that morning. They were a bit early for the one o'clock meeting they'd scheduled. Hopefully, the priest would be available now.

A knock at the rectory door produced a young man that didn't look any older than eighteen. Before they had a chance to introduce themselves, he said, "Come in. Father is expecting you."

They followed the boy to an office at the corner of the building. The door was already open. The man on the other side of the desk rose as they approached. He was tall, nearly Jonathan's height, but with a doughy body that foretold a lack of any real exercise. Judging by the lack of gray in his hair and the absence of wrinkles on his face, Jonathan would put the man at ten or fifteen years his senior, though he knew the man to be in his early sixties. But his cornflower blue eyes assessed them sharply as he and Mari joined him in his office.

After the introductions were made, he gestured for them to sit in the two scarred, wooden chairs across from him. "I'm sorry we have to meet under such unfortunate circumstances. I understand you are investigating Amanda's murder. Such a shame."

The priest's use of Pierce's given name prompted the question. "You knew her, Father?"

He nodded. "I had just been assigned here a few months before the fire. I saw her here a few times. A most interesting young lady."

Jonathan hid his humor. That was probably the priest's attempt at finding something nice to say rather than saying nothing at all. "Have you seen her recently?"

"She came by about a month ago. She told me about the gentlemen who wanted to do a biography on Brendan's life. She was furious. I can't say I blame her. She asked me if I could put her in touch with any of the parishioners from that time, hoping one of them could remember something important."

"Did you?" Mari asked.

"It took some time. Most of the records from that time were destroyed in the fire. It took us two years to rebuild the church. By the time we reopened many of the families had moved on."

"Why is that, Father?"

The priest tapped his fingertips together. "In many ways, Father Malone *was* this church. You had to know him to know what I mean. He was a colorful personality. He came from the streets, not here but in Brooklyn. He understood the community. He spoke to them in their own language about the problems they faced, and the archdiocese could go hang itself if they didn't like it. The boys in particular were his pet project."

He and Mari exchanged a glance, each of them

wondering how much this man's estimation of Father Malone was colored by his devotion.

Perhaps sensing their skepticism, Masella continued. "I know the reputation the church has gotten in the past years, but it wasn't like that then. Brendan had a crew of boys, the toughest, meanest kids I'd ever seen. He kept them in school, found them scholarships to college. He'd have them cleaning up the neighborhood Saturday mornings. He taught them if they wanted anything in life they'd have to make their own opportunities."

"God helps those who help themselves?" Mari guessed.

"Exactly. Those boys would have done anything for Father Malone. The whole parish would have. You have to understand, though, that this was the early eighties. While Mayor Koch was busy putting up fake windows to fool passing tourists, Brendan did something real. He used his influence with some of his friends from the old neighborhood, some who'd done good and some not so good to build some decent housing for the people of this neighborhood.

"That project earned Brendan a lot of detractors, but not in this neighborhood. One thing those people won't tell you is that the building came in under budget and up to code. And Brendan made sure the City kept its end of the bargain in maintaining the building. That's when all the rumors about him started flying. I think the politicians were trying to discredit him in order to get him to back off."

"Getting back to Ms. Pierce, did you ever find any parishioners for her to contact?"

"Yes. Thirteen names. People who stayed with the church after Brendan was gone who were still alive.

I gave them to her two weeks ago. That's the last I heard from her."

"Do you have those names, Father?"

"Yes, of course." He searched the papers and files on his desk to pull out a single sheet of paper that he handed to Mari.

There was one question that bothered Jonathan as he'd listened to the priest. He had information pertinent to their investigation and he was obviously willing to talk. Why had he kept this to himself for so long?

"Why didn't you tell any of this to the police?"

"I did. As soon as I heard about the tragedy, I called the local precinct. The officer I spoke to told me someone would get back to me. When you called, I assumed you were those somebodies."

Jonathan gritted his teeth. Information getting lost from one house to another wasn't unheard of, but he'd like to get his hands on the knucklehead responsible this time. If this new information panned out, they could have shaved a couple of days off their investigation.

"How do you want to handle the list? Geographically or alphabetically?"

"How about after lunch?"

Mari had barely gotten the words out of her mouth when her cell phone rang. After she disconnected the call, she said, "Guess who's finally conscious?"

He knew the answer this time. Now Jonathan had a few questions for Freddie Jackson to answer.

After spending the better portion of the day with Joanna, Dana decided to walk home again. The night was cooler than it had been in a while, though heavy with humidity. The weatherman predicted a

summer storm for later that night that would break
the heat wave they were having, but so far it hadn't
arrived.

She crossed the street in the middle of the block,
after the lone car she'd seen passed by. Traffic was
surprisingly light. Probably everyone had already
hurried home anticipating the storm. Walking, she
had to pass through an industrial section of town. Actually, just one block of it, if she used an alleyway between two buildings. The alley was used for deliveries
for the adjoining businesses. It was narrow here,
barely wide enough to accommodate a car, let alone
a delivery truck. The path widened down at the end
where two delivery bays faced each other.

She didn't usually take that route, but the air
seemed to be growing heavier. What the hell? In
her present mood, if there were a mugger lying in
wait on the other end of the alley, she'd probably kick
his ass. Just to be safer, maybe, she took off down the
alley at a jog. The quicker she got through, the safer
she'd be.

But suddenly there was a car behind her, close
enough for her to feel the heat of its headlights on
her skin. Didn't the fool see her? She glanced
around, still jogging. The glare from the headlights
made it impossible to notice anything about the car,
except that it was big and dark—and had begun to
accelerate toward her.

Immediately she broke into a run, her heart pump-
ing, her legs reaching as far as they could with every
stride. She had nowhere to go except forward. Her
purse weighed on her arm. She let it drop and kept
running, sprinting toward the wider part of the alley,
hoping to find somewhere to duck to get out of the
car's way.

Finally, when the car was almost upon her, she made it, darting left to vault over the high ledge of the loading dock to relative safety. The car veered after her, careened into a huge dumpster that spewed garbage onto the front of the car as it bounced off the metal surface. The car lumbered forward, continuing toward the end of the alleyway, nearly crashing into a car passing on the street.

Breathing heavily, with the blast of the car's horn echoing in her ears, Dana started to shiver. Whoever had been driving that car had intended to kill her. There was no other explanation for it, not that she could see.

But this time, as the car hesitated under the bright light of the loading dock, she'd managed to notice the license plate number.

And she realized something else that scared her right down to her toes.

Twelve

Jonathan I need to see you.

Those words echoed in Jonathan's ears as he drove from his apartment to Dana's house. Not only hadn't he expected to hear from her after last night, she hadn't elaborated on the reason she wanted him to come over. True, he hadn't exactly pressed her for one either. The only thing he did know was that it wasn't to pick up where they'd left off last night.

He'd planned on spending the evening reinterviewing the patrons of the bar where Jackson got stabbed. He'd claimed the other man had pulled a knife on him first, supposedly because Jackson was messing around with his woman. Jackson claimed not to know the woman in question, but neither Jonathan nor Mari completely believed him. That didn't necessarily negate the man's claim of simply wanting to keep his ya-yas from getting cut off, but it made him less credible. Jonathan was hoping someone at the bar had seen something that would make the case either way.

He pulled up in front of Dana's place, luckily finding a spot right out front. Even from the street he could see her, sitting in one of her rocking chairs, her legs drawn up, her cheek resting on her knees. He walked up to the house and let himself onto the porch, dread rising in him. She had to know he was there, but she didn't acknowledge him in any way.

"Dana?"

She lifted her head and looked at him. Her hair was tumbled, not in the seductive way it had been last night. Her jeans were ripped at the knee and the blouse she wore was torn at the shoulder and dirty. Her face looked tear-stained and her eyes were rimmed in red. What on earth could have happened to actually make this woman cry?

"Thanks for coming," she said, as if he'd made her social event by showing up. "I probably shouldn't have called you like that."

Maybe not, but judging from her appearance, something serious had motivated her. "Why did you?"

"I was upset. I'm calmer now."

Maybe too calm. He got the rocker from the opposite side of the porch and pulled it perpendicular to hers. "Tell me what happened."

"I was coming home from the hospital. It was stupid. I cut through this alley because it would save time and I thought it was going to rain."

Jonathan's stomach clenched. He'd heard this story before, too many times, maybe. He didn't like how it turned out. "Go on."

"All of sudden there was this car behind me. It was speeding and there was nowhere to get out of the way. I just kept running until the alley opened up and I could get on top of this loading platform. If that hadn't been there, they would have hit me."

He could imagine how terrifying that experience

must have been for her, though his first thought
was that in this part of town, she'd gotten in the path
of some teenagers drunk on their own hormones
who thought it was a great idea to terrorize pedes-
trians with the family automobile. "Did you see who
was driving the car?"

She shook her head. "I couldn't see anything
beyond the headlights. Not until the car crashed
into this dumpster next to me."

Now that didn't sound like teenagers, unless they
really were high on something. Why risk getting
grounded by wrecking their parents' cars? "They
came after you after you tried to get out of the way?"

"They, he, whoever was trying to hit me."

"How do you know that?" It wasn't that he didn't
believe her. He wanted to be as clear as possible on
what happened.

She ignored his question. "I saw the license plate
on the car. BM2 478."

"You memorized the number?"

"It was easy. It's the same number I gave Moretti
yesterday."

Alarm whooshed up through Jonathan with the
speed of a tidal wave. The same car that carried the
men who killed Wesley had also tried to mow her
down? Or the same plates, anyway. She couldn't verify
if it was the same car. But it was really the same thing,
anyway. Whoever had possession of those plates had
succeeded in hurting her once and trying to kill her
a second time, which begged the question: Why?

The simple answer to that was that someone had
noticed her snooping in the neighborhood and decided to take her out before she discovered anything that could incriminate them. But Jonathan
didn't trust simple. Especially since that would mean

that whoever had tried to run her down had ventured out of their own comfort zone to come after her. Why not wait to see if she showed up again, or hit her when she came back to work, since whatever she knew she had had time to tell the police already?

It didn't make sense, which frustrated him. He might not trust simple, but he preferred it to the niggling suspicion that nothing, neither this case nor his own, was what it appeared to be.

But for now, his only concern was Dana. She'd remained silent after dropping that bombshell on him, her gaze fixed on him as if she waited for him to say something in particular. After a moment she looked away, and he sensed her disappointment in him. That was okay. She didn't need to hear what was rolling around in his brain.

It was in his mind to pull her onto his lap to hold her, soothe her. He'd like to tell himself that impulse stemmed from some innate drive to comfort and protect, but he knew that desire came from a deeper source, one he didn't want to examine too closely at the moment.

Instead, he grasped the arm of her chair and part of the seat and turned her around to face him. "I need you to tell Moretti what you told me. Do you feel up to that?" He knew what her answer would be before he asked the question, but once again, he admired her resiliency.

"Sure. Why not? I'll make some snacks. Don't eat the one with the arsenic in it."

He chuckled. "Maybe you want to clean up a little before he gets here." His suggestion accomplished two purposes. One, he didn't want Moretti seeing her like this—vulnerable and shaken. Two, he wanted her out of the room. Aside from Moretti, he needed to

call Mari and the Mount Vernon PD, though he suspected whoever had done this to her was long gone.

She nodded. He backed his chair up so that she
could stand. After she'd gone inside leaving the door
open, he got the number for the Mount Vernon PD
from information and told the desk sergeant what
happened in the alley and that the suspected driver
was the subject of an ongoing NYPD investigation.

He called Mari next. He had two reasons for asking
her to join them. One, he wanted her opinion of
what had happened so far and, two, in the event
Moretti pulled his usual bullshit, he wanted someone
there with at least the slightest chance of pulling him
off the man.

"Are you planning on filling your friend in?" Mari
asked.

He supposed that was her way of asking why he
really wanted her there. "Yeah." In the morning, he
intended to make sure the Evans case was transferred to him, but for now he didn't want the s.o.b.
to be able to claim he pulled a fast one.

He hung up with Mari and dialed Moretti's
number. He answered the phone, "Yeah."

"I have some information for you on the Evans case.
I'm at Dana Molloy's house. I need you to come."

"Why would I want to do that? Your girlfriend playing Nancy Drew again?"

"She was nearly run down by the same car used in
the Evans shooting."

"Holy shit. Give me a few minutes. I'll be there."

The line went dead. Moretti sounded genuinely
alarmed, which was in itself surprising. He'd expected another flip response from Moretti and didn't
know what to make of the fact that he didn't get one.

Maybe Moretti was growing a conscience, but he doubted it.

Mari arrived before Dana made it downstairs from the bathroom. She lived about ten minutes away on the Bronx/Westchester border, in a two-family house she shared with her grandmother. He did a double take when he saw her walking up the front steps. Her hair was out of its usual ponytail and down around her shoulders. Gone were the ubiquitous pantsuit and serviceable shoes, replaced by a short, sleeveless black dress and heels. Obviously she'd been out somewhere or on her way out when he called her. She didn't look too happy about not being there now.

He held the door open for her to step onto the porch. She passed him, took a couple of steps and turned to face him. "Not one word, Stone, not one word."

He couldn't tell whether that comment stemmed from his obvious shock at seeing her dressed that way or whether it bothered her for him to see her dressed like a girl instead of a cop. "You mean you didn't do all that for me?" he teased.

She shot him a droll look. "Stone, you wouldn't know what to do with me if you had me."

"Hell, I didn't even know you had legs."

She laughed. "Cute. Where's your friend?"

"I'm right here."

Both he and Mari turned at the sound of Dana's voice. She stood in the open doorway. She'd changed into another pair of jeans and an oversize football jersey. With her face clean and devoid of make-up, he could see a bruise on her right cheek starting to darken. He doubted even she knew how she'd gotten it.

For the first time since he'd known her, she looked tense, on edge. It didn't surprise him. In the last week she'd been through a lot, more than most people would have withstood easily.

He closed the gap between them. "Dana, this is my partner, Mari Velez."

For a moment, neither woman said anything, obviously sizing each other up. Dana spoke first. "Killer dress."

"Thanks. Sorry we have to meet under these circumstances."

Dana shrugged. "Why don't you guys come inside? You're letting all the air conditioning out."

She turned and headed back toward the kitchen. He gestured for Mari to precede him. Bringing up the rear, he shut the front door behind him before following.

Dana stopped at the entranceway to the kitchen. "Why don't you two sit in the living room? I'm going to make some coffee. Sorry I don't have any donuts to go with it."

Mari chuckled. "Not all of us cops are donut hounds."

"Need any help?" he asked.

She shot him a droll look. "To make coffee? Please, sit. I'll be done in a moment."

Reluctantly, he did what she asked. Although she'd seemed to regain some of her composure, she still looked shaky to him. Maybe that's why she wanted them out of the way; she still needed a few minutes to get herself together. Besides, it gave him a few minutes to talk with Mari. He followed Mari into the living room and sat in the corner of her sofa that allowed him a partial view of the kitchen.

Mari took the chair at a right angle to the couch. "So why did you really drag me out here, Stone?" Mari said in a hushed tone. "What's going on?"

He couldn't account for the annoyance he heard in her voice, but answered anyway. "Like I told you on the phone, Dana was on her way home from visiting my sister when the same car from the drive-by tried to run her over."

"I got that part, but this isn't our case."

"Not yet."

Mari sat back. "Moretti's going to love you."

"Fuck Moretti," he said, but instantly regretted it. Not only did he usually leave the vitriol to Mari, he also didn't want her to know how deeply annoyed he felt.

"I'd rather not, if you don't mind. Just tell me what this has to do with us, other than whatever it is you've got going on with the woman making us coffee."

Now he understood the reason for Mari's irritation. She thought he'd stuck his nose where it didn't belong because of his relationship with Dana and was trying to drag her in too. "This isn't anything personal."

"No?"

"I'll admit I can't stand Moretti. He's a lazy cop, and probably a dirty one, too. I'll admit, too, that I don't want him anywhere near her. But, something about all this doesn't make sense."

"What do you mean?"

In the back of his mind, he'd been looking for something to link together the two occurrences in the span of two days, even though every step he took in investigating Pierce's murder took him farther away from that location. Hearing from Tyree that the word was Wesley's dealer had taken him out, had put a minor crimp in his speculation, but hadn't ended it.

"Let's look at the timeline, first of all. Friday morning,

Amanda Pierce goes missing. Dana is the last person to see her alive. The next morning Dana is shot in a supposed drive-by shooting in front of the same building. Does that suggest something to you?"

"Other than to stay the hell away from 4093 Highland Avenue? No. Given the neighborhood, it's not unusual to have two investigations in the same building at the same time."

"Involving the same person?"

Mari lifted one shoulder in a shrug. "You've got me there. So what are you suggesting?"

"Maybe the drive-by wasn't a real drive-by in the sense that a civilian, not a player, was the target."

She tilted her head to one side, considering that. "But why would a bunch of gang bangers care who killed Amanda Pierce? I'd be surprised if any of them knew who she was. And how would they know who to go after? The only people who know she has anything to do with this are cops."

He didn't have an answer for either the first or last parts of her question. He addressed the only part he did have an answer for. "She worked in the same building every day at approximately the same time. She's a fixture in the neighborhood. She might not have gotten a good look at who was in the car, but maybe the person in the car saw her through the rear view mirror. All anyone would have to do is come back the next day and see if she showed up."

"I thought you heard that Wesley was taken out by the leader of his own crew?"

He'd told her about the information Tyree had given him. "That doesn't make it true. What's to keep the guy from claiming responsibility for the shooting rather than admitting some other crew took one of his boys out without his permission?"

Mari rolled her eyes. "That's the code of the street for you. Better to be thought of as a murderer than a punk and lose face with your peeps. So, you're thinking the men who shot Wesley aren't from Pee Wee's crew?"

He shook his head. At this point he didn't know. All the pieces didn't fit in a smooth puzzle so far, but he'd bet they would if he kept at it.

"I'm not saying anything for sure. All we know about these guys is that they were wearing colors and they had guns. Put any couple guys in a tricked out car and a couple of bandannas . . ."

He trailed off, leaving Mari time to think about what he'd said. In the meantime, his gaze wandered to the kitchen. Dana was out of his line of sight, which meant she was probably over by the sink. Although he wished he knew what she was up to, her location made it less likely she'd overheard what he and Mari said.

"Why don't you go check on her?" Mari said.

He knew their conversation wasn't over, but he was more than willing to put it on hold for now. He got up and went to the kitchen, only to find it empty. A tray stood on the counter, laden with a coffee carafe, cups, sugar bowl and milk pitcher, but no Dana. He would have noticed if she'd gone upstairs. He tried the back door. It was still locked. Where the hell was she?

Then he heard the click of a door opening. Dana emerged from a door in the wall at right angles to the refrigerator. If he hadn't seen her come out of it, he wouldn't have known another room—a bathroom— existed back there.

When she looked up and saw him, she made a

sound of surprise and her hand went to her chest. "You scared the life out of me."

Good. Then he hadn't been the only one who'd gotten a good scare. He leaned his back against the edge of the kitchen counter. "I didn't mean to frighten you."

She advanced toward him. "I didn't know you cops were so impatient about your coffee."

She tried to walk around him, but he grasped her wrist and pulled her to him. She was trembling, but he doubted the startle he'd given her was the cause of her tremors. He pulled her closer with an arm around her waist. When she exhaled he smelled the aroma of fresh mint. "What were you doing in the bathroom?"

Her hands were on his chest. She pushed against him, but not enough to suggest she wanted him to let her go. "That's a little personal don't you think?"

"Maybe. Answer me."

Her gaze slid downward, maybe to his throat. "If you must know, I was throwing up."

He'd figured as much. She'd had enough time alone to really contemplate the danger she'd been in tonight and continued to be in. He thought he'd been doing her a favor by allowing her time to sift through things by herself, but he doubted now that had been the wisest course of action.

Had she been any other woman, he would have offered her some platitudes about not worrying and everything turning out all right. He couldn't bring his mouth to whisper any of those things. Right now, he didn't know what was really going on or who he was up against. He only knew he would do everything in his power to find out who wanted to kill her and to keep her safe. That's all he could offer.

The doorbell rang. It was probably Moretti. Jonathan set her away from him. "I'll get it. Do you think you can handle the tray?"

"I'm fine, really. Or I ought to be." She smiled at him wickedly. "Nothing left to throw up."

He didn't know why he did it, but as she moved away from him, he swatted her butt. He could feel her eyes on him as he walked away to answer the door. Fine. He'd rather have her indignant or angry or pissed off at him than have her frightened or vulnerable.

When Jonathan opened the door, he found Moretti with one hand braced on the doorframe and a sneer on his face—a posture and expression designed to intimidate. Almost instantly the man straightened and the expression fell away from his face. The fool had actually expected Dana to open the door. The man didn't know him at all if he'd honestly thought Jonathan would have allowed that to happen.

At any rate, Jonathan bit back the comment on his mind that it had certainly taken Moretti long enough to get here. "Come in."

Moretti sauntered past him, his usual swagger. "Where is she?"

Obviously, enough time had passed for whatever better instinct Moretti had shown earlier to wear off. "In the living room." He shut the door and followed Moretti, almost bumping into him when the man stopped short.

Jonathan thought he knew what had halted Moretti and doubted the other man had the good sense not to comment. He wasn't disappointed.

Moretti took the one step down into the living

room. "Hey, Velez. Your girlfriend lets you out dressed like that?"

Mari's eyes narrowed as a look of disgust came over her face. "You think that up all by yourself, Moretti or did you get the Cliff Notes?"

Sensing Moretti wasn't quite finished with being humiliated, Jonathan said, "Now that the pleasantries are over, let's get down to it."

Moretti's expression soured. He strode over to the loveseat across from Dana and slumped onto its cushions. Jonathan took the only remaining seat, next to Dana. Without thinking he draped his arm on the back of the sofa behind her. Any other time it would have pleased him that she instinctively moved closer to him. But he noted Moretti's leering gaze on them, on Dana in particular. As much as he disliked Moretti, his goal was to get through the next few minutes without having to deck the man.

Moretti adjusted himself in his seat and a sneer settled on his face. "So, what's the story, Stone? I hope you got me up here for something more important than getting a look at Velez's cleavage."

In the periphery of his vision he saw Mari sit forward. Not a good sign. Jonathan was a second away from telling the son of a bitch to shut his mouth. But Moretti seemed determined to get a rise out of somebody. It would annoy him more if no one took the bait.

"As I told you on the phone, Ms. Molloy was almost hit by the same car driven in the drive-by that killed Wesley Evans."

Moretti's gaze lingered on Dana. "How do you know this?"

"I saw the license plate this time. It's the same number I gave you yesterday."

"Did you see the car?"

"Only from the back. It was black. A Town Car. It had those wheels that spin."

To Jonathan's recollection, so had the other car.

"How about the driver? Passengers?"

She shook her head. "At first the headlights were in my eyes, then the windows were tinted."

"Where did this happen?"

She gave him a precise address including cross streets. He and Mari exchanged a look while Moretti continued asking all the right questions—who knew she'd be leaving or how she planned on getting home? Was this her usual route or something different? Whatever. He knew they were both thinking the same thing. Since Moretti could obviously be a half decent cop if he wanted to be, why didn't he?

"Is there anything else you remember?"

"Only that the streets were deserted. I remember thinking everyone must have hurried home because it was supposed to rain. There was one car that passed. I didn't really pay it much attention, but come to think of it, it was big and dark, but I didn't look at the plates. This was right before I went down the alley."

Which meant the driver could have doubled back after seeing her and come after her. Which also suggested they might have either been cruising around looking for her or had been waiting at her house for her and given up only to luck out by seeing her on the street. Whichever the case, or even if it was neither, she couldn't stay here. She'd be a sitting target for anyone who wanted to hurt her.

Moretti stood. "I'm going to head over to the scene. I'll let you know if I find out anything."

Jonathan doubted he would, but decided he'd not

worry about that for the moment. He'd get her out of here for now and tackle the rest in the morning.

Surprisingly, Moretti left without any more snide comments, or at least none Jonathan heard. Mari walked him to the door and came back smiling a few moments later. He wondered what that was about, but figured he'd let that slide until morning, too.

"I'm going to head out, myself," Mari said. "Why don't you do the honors of letting me out, partner?"

He'd known his conversation with Mari wasn't over and he'd bet she had a few additional comments to make about now. He rose from the sofa and followed her to the door. Once she reached the front alcove she turned to face him.

"Getting back to what we were saying before, it looks like we've got your basic chicken-and-egg conundrum. Did she get hurt because someone wanted to whack Wesley or did Wesley get whacked because someone wanted to keep her quiet?"

"That about covers it."

"This is a fine mess we've gotten ourselves into, Ollie."

"Tell me about it."

"When he wasn't too busy staring down my dress, Moretti told me he already checked out the plate. It belongs to one Oscar Grant, a gangsta wannabe. The car was stolen from one of the meters outside the Bronx courthouse. The poor sap went in to fight getting jury duty. Not only did he not get out of it, when he got back his car was gone. This happened the afternoon Pierce disappeared."

How exactly that tidbit of information fit in with everything else didn't appear to him immediately. "Anything else?"

"You know she can't stay here, right?"

"I know." There would be a squad car outside tonight, but tomorrow was another story.

She stared at him a long moment and he wondered if she suspected how he planned to resolve that. Finally, she winked at him. "Take care of yourself, Stone. If I end up having to work with one of those other yahoos at the station I'm going to be very disappointed."

He snorted. "Does that mean I'm a yahoo, too?"

"Pretty much. But you're my kind of yahoo." He opened the door for her and she stepped over the threshold onto the porch. "Don't forget we have the funeral in the morning," she added as she walked away.

How could he forget? Pierce's brother had called just before he'd left that evening to see what progress they'd made in his sister's case and let them know about the arrangements.

It would be interesting to see the mix of people who showed up at St. Pat's the next day. But for now, Dana was his focus. When he went back he found her at the kitchen sink, standing with her back to him, her head down, her hands braced on the counter. Next to her sat the coffee tray that no one but Mari had touched. As far as he could tell, Dana hadn't touched it either, only left it on the counter. But he sensed a shift in her mood, and not for the better.

He leaned his shoulder against the archway to the kitchen. "How are you holding up?"

She sighed and her shoulders drooped. "How am I supposed to feel knowing that someone else was killed because of me?"

Although he thought he knew, he asked anyway, "What are you talking about?"

She turned around to face him, crossing her arms

and leaning her back against the sink. Her distress was laid bare in her eyes. "Don't play coy, Jonathan. You and I both know what all this really means. I wasn't hurt because someone wanted to kill Wesley. He was killed because someone was after me."

He should have known that possibility wouldn't have escaped her notice. He remembered feeling as if she were waiting for him to say something and being disappointed that he remained silent. Was that what she'd expected him to say?

He hadn't voiced his supposition, because at this point, that's all it was. Tomorrow he'd work at getting the truth. He hadn't seen any point in discussing it tonight. He hadn't wanted to upset her further, but he saw now that was probably a mistake.

"We don't know that for sure. Whoever was after Wesley might have thought you saw something that you might report to the police."

"Right, that's why they followed me up here to Mount Vernon. Sure, over on Third Avenue there are places that rival any neighborhood in the South Bronx, but not here. Around here a bunch of gang bangers in a tricked out car would have been stopped by the police before they had time to breathe."

Exactly what he'd thought of the situation. "Dana," he said, trying to forestall any more speculation down that path, but she wasn't listening to him.

"If they were so worried about what I might know, why didn't they go after Old Specs, the guy who watches everything from his window?"

"I don't know. I have no idea if they did or didn't do anything to the man."

"Believe me, if they'd really wanted me, I wouldn't have made it out of the neighborhood." Tears, unshed, glistened in her eyes. "And you want to know the worst part? I didn't see anything. I've trained myself not to notice anything. If I walk into some apartment and folks are cutting drugs on the dining room table, or some hooker is doing a guy in an alley or some cop is beating the shit out of some kid in a corner, I just walk by. I keep moving. I don't see a thing."

She gazed up at him, shaking her head. "I was so busy being sanctimonious about how Wesley nearly got me killed. It never occurred to me that it could be the other way around." She lowered her head, but not before he saw the tears spilling silently down her cheeks.

He didn't know what to say to that. Intellectually, she must know that none of this was her fault, not Amanda Pierce's death or Wesley's murder. She was beyond logic, in a place where only pain mattered and the accumulated grief, sorrow and unearned guilt could eat a person whole. He knew; he'd been there.

He closed the gap between them and pulled her to him. She laid her cheek against his chest. One of his hands rose to stroke her nape while the other banded around her waist, holding her closer. "Don't cry, sweetheart," he whispered against her ear. "Not one person caught up in this is worth any of your tears."

Cradling her face in his palms, he tilted her face up to him. He brushed away her tears with his thumbs. "Don't cry." Without thinking, he brought his mouth down to hers.

Immediately her arms closed around him and she kissed him back with a fierceness he had yet to see in her. It was as if she channeled all her emotions into that one kiss. He understood that, too—the need to sublimate that which you couldn't change.

Her fingers went to his shirt, pulling it from his

waistband and over his head before he had the time or the will to stop her. He couldn't help the groan that rumbled up from somewhere deep as her lips touched down on the center of his chest. Damn, he wanted her, but he didn't want any replays of the previous night. He didn't want her to come to her senses sometime later and regret whatever happened between them.

He tilted her chin up to see her face. "Seems we've hit this spot in the road before."

Her eyes narrowed. "What's your point?"

"There might not be any backfires to raise an alert. No last minute saves." She looked at him more confused than before. He may as well ask her straight out. "Do you want to be with me, Dana?"

She averted her gaze to his chest, where her fingers made a lazy exploration of his bare flesh. He held his breath waiting for her answer.

When she looked at him again, it was with a sideways glance and a smile he didn't at first comprehend. "Only if you do me a favor."

"What's that?"

"Take me upstairs."

Thirteen

If he'd had time to think about it, he might have questioned the change in her from the previous night. More than likely her experience tonight fueled her desire more than a little bit. But she took a step toward, slid her arms around his neck and kissed him. That killed all the rational thought he was capable of at that moment. His arms closed around her, bringing her body flush with his. Her hands, nurse's hands—strong, firm and at the same time gentle—roved over his back, making him groan into her mouth.

When he finally pulled away, it was to lift her off her feet with his arms around her hips. She shrieked and hit him on the shoulder, surprised, he guessed, by his sudden move.

"I didn't mean that literally," she said.

"You know how us dumb cops are. All we know is how to follow orders."

She hit him again as he carried her from the kitchen to the hall. "Put me down. You'll give yourself a hernia."

He did as she asked, but not until they reached the stairs where the overhang from above made it

impossible to continue. He released her slowly, letting her slide down his body, exciting them both.
She ended up standing on the step above him, her
breasts at his eye level. His hand delved under her
shirt to cradle one of her breasts in his palm. When
she pulled the shirt over her head, he took her
nipple into his mouth to flick his tongue against its
peak.

She gasped and jerked against him, her fingers
digging into the flesh at his shoulders. But both excitement and anticipation thrummed in him, making
him impatient. His fingers found the snap of her
jeans, quickly releasing it. He rasped the zipper down,
then pushed the heavy material from her hips. She
backed up a step, bracing one hand on the wall and
the other on the banister, as he freed one leg and then
the other. For a moment, all he could do was stare at
her, his eyes drinking in the sight of her.

He knelt on the step below her and pulled her to
him with his hands at her waist. His lips touched
down on her belly, just below her navel. Her stomach contracted beneath his touch and a soft sound
of pleasure escaped her lips.

With one arm around her hips to brace her, he
parted her with his fingers and brought his mouth
down on her. She jerked and her breathing hitched,
coming in short gasps and sighs.

He'd only intended to taste her, but he could feel
by the tension in her that she was closer to the edge
than he'd thought. It wouldn't take much to push her
over. He wanted to push her, to make her come for
him. He slid two fingers inside her and stroked her
while he continued to lave her with his tongue.

Her back arched and her legs trembled. "Jona . . ."
she called, the rest of his name swallowed up by the

power of her orgasm. One of her hands descended to grip his shoulder as she cried out and her body spasmed against him.

When she quieted, he stood and pulled her against him. She wrapped her arms around his neck and buried her face against his neck, breathing heavily. For the moment she was sated but the fire still burned in him. He lifted her again and carried her to her room.

In a breathy voice she said, "Now you're just showing off."

His only answer was a low, wicked laugh. He set her on the bed, but didn't follow her. The only illumination in the room was the light of the full moon sifting through the windows, but he felt her eyes on him, avid and watchful as he stood. He unclipped his holster from his belt and laid it on the nightstand, then took off the rest of his clothes.

He joined her then, kneeling between her parted thighs. He paused long enough to sheath himself, then covered her body with his own. He thrust into her, his body shivering as hers enveloped him. Her arms closed around him and her legs wrapped around his waist, drawing him deeper. He thrust into her again and again, the heat of her body acting like a fever within him. Perspiration coated his skin and his heartbeat trebled. His mouth met hers for one wild kiss and then another.

He pulled back, enough to see her face. She regarded him with dark, half-closed eyes. Her hand lifted to stroke the side of his face. "Jon," she whispered. Then her eyes squeezed shut and her legs tightened around him as her hips rocked against him.

He shut his eyes and let his own orgasm overtake him, making him tremble and pulling low, ragged groans from somewhere deep in his chest. Fearing she wouldn't be able to tolerate his weight, he rolled onto his back and pulled her on top of him. Reaching over, he pulled the sheet from the other side of the bed to cover them.

For a long time, he lay with her cradled against his chest, recovering. When his breathing was somewhat normal again, he brushed her hair from her face. "How are you feeling?"

"Pretty damn good." She lifted her head to smile down at him. "But you already knew that."

He did, but he didn't mind hearing her say so.

She drew a line down his chest with her fingertip. "Don't go turning into some cocky cop on me."

"I wouldn't dream of it, for another few minutes, at least."

She groaned at his attempt at humor and laid her forehead against his chest. His hand rose to massage her nape. "Why don't you try to get some sleep? We have to get out of here early tomorrow."

"We? Where am I going?"

She really must be out of it if the danger here hadn't occurred to her. "You can't stay here, Dana. Obviously they know where you live or close enough to it to be a threat."

"I'll buy that, but truthfully, I don't have anywhere else to go."

"I'll take you to Joanna's."

"Absolutely not. The last thing she needs is to bring her new baby home and have to worry about me. I won't put her family in danger by being there. I'll get a room at the Sheraton until you catch these idiots."

He appreciated her show of faith that he'd have things resolved before she bankrupted her pocket-book, but for more reasons than one, he couldn't do that. "You want me to leave you somewhere alone?"

"What's my alternative?"

"You could stay with me."

She leaned both of her forearms on his chest and looked down at him. "I *can* stay with you?"

"Of course." His gaze narrowed. "Why do you say it like that?"

"That *can*, does it mean you are willing to let me stay with you or is it a, 'Since you've already got those lovely handcuffs on, why don't you come on and visit us at the stationhouse?' sort of *can*?"

How the hell was he supposed to answer that? "Am I planning to drag you out of here by your hair? Not unless you force me to. We both agreed that you can't stay here. I don't see what the problem is."

"*You* wouldn't."

Then he understood. There was a certain intimacy to a woman staying in a man's home, using his things. And despite the intimacy they'd just shared, he doubted she was willing to jump into a thing with him with both feet. They still didn't know a damn thing about each other beyond the case of mutual lust they'd temporarily sated. Still, he expected her common sense to overrule her need to protect her emotions.

"I'm not trying to get over on you, Dana, if that's what you think. I have a spare bedroom with two spare beds for you to choose from."

She sighed and lowered her head. "I'm sorry. I just don't like not having any choices."

He could understand that. "Is it settled then?"

She nodded. "What about Tim? He's due back two days from now."

He'd forgotten about her brother. "I'll have someone bring him here to pick up whatever else he needs, if that's what you're worried about. Is it possible he can stay where he is?"

"Right now, he's in Florida, but I suppose he could stay with the same family he went down with. I'll have to call them in the morning."

She laid her cheek against his chest. "I think I'm going to take your advice now about getting some sleep."

"Sweet dreams, sweetheart."

"I'll settle for no one trying to shoot me, maim me or run me over."

Chuckling, he wrapped his arms more tightly around her. He should probably take his own advice and get some shuteye, but he was too wound up from both the case and the woman in his arms to sleep.

As lead investigator on the case, it was his job to sort through all the information collected to separate the wheat from the chaff, the relevant from the irrelevant, the truth from the lie. In his gut he was certain that the attempts on Dana's life, Wesley's and Amanda's murders, were all tied in together and they all had something to do with Father Brendan Malone's activities and possibly his death.

He knew that somewhere underneath all the deceptions and misdirections lay a body of truth that had yet to be uncovered. He intended to find it, not only because it was his job, but because it was the only way to keep Dana safe.

That thought surprised him—that protecting the woman in his arms was more important to him than working his case. Maybe not so much that it mattered more than how much more it mattered. When had she, when had any woman, gotten so under his skin that his first priority didn't remain the job?

She stirred and mumbled something in her sleep. He couldn't make out what she said, but her distress was apparent. "Shh," he whispered, stroking her back in a soothing manner. She quieted almost immediately, sinking against him in a way that made his body harden and his thoughts scatter.

Jonathan sighed. With him unable to sleep and her plastered against him, it was going to be a very long night.

Dana woke to the sound of thunder crashing in the distance and the slap of rain against the window. Instantly, she knew she was alone in her bed, even before she caught him standing by the window. He faced half toward her and half toward the window as if he were keeping vigil over both at the same time. His face was turned toward the window now, his hands in the pockets of his jeans. Even from there she could make out the shape of his gun tucked into his open waistband.

A flash of lightning streaked across the sky, illuminating his features. He looked pensive, melancholy, maybe. Or maybe she was projecting her own emotions onto him, as listening to the rain fall often made her sad. Either way, he seemed to have gone to a place he hadn't intended her to follow. She contemplated closing her eyes and pretending to be asleep, when he spoke.

"Did the rain wake you?"

Until then she hadn't been sure he knew she wasn't sleeping. "Yes." She sat up and realized she was under the sheet and a light blanket had been spread over that. He must have done that when he got out of bed.

She drew her knees up and rested her elbows on them. Still he hadn't looked at her and her impression of his mood remained. She searched for something innocuous to say, something harmless that might somehow also lift his spirits.

That much, at least, she figured she owed him. Never before had she relied on a man for his strength or his protection or his comfort. He'd given her all three and much more. Her body still resonated with the power of their lovemaking. The scent of it still lingered in the air.

For all that she felt gratitude, and other deeper emotions she didn't want to examine too closely at the moment. For now, she'd settle for knowing what was on his mind, or failing that, erasing it from his consciousness for a few moments.

"Do you mind if I ask you a question?"

His head turned and he fastened his gaze on her. "Of course not."

"Why on earth did you transfer into the 44th precinct?"

He offered her a self-deprecating smile. "The reason isn't all that strange." He shifted to turn his back to the window and crossed his arms. "My first assignment was in the 23rd, which is a schizophrenic detail. Half the precinct's territory is the upper west side, the other half is Spanish Harlem. As you can imagine, two very different types of clientele."

She nodded.

"The rich folks treated us like dirt because we were civil servants. The poor people treated us like dirt because we were cops. At least with the poor folks, there was some chance of building up a rapport, helping out decent people in a bad situation. Holding some dowager's poodle while she got into a cab wasn't my idea of police work. I got out of there as fast as I could."

She could imagine how demeaning such treatment would be to a man like him. "Why homicide?"

"They asked for me. Not Shea, the current commander, but the one before him. You don't say no to that."

Maybe most cops wouldn't, but she suspected he had more personal motives for agreeing to the transfer. She didn't press him, though. If he ever wanted to tell her, he would. She was satisfied with that.

For now, she was concerned with him, the man, not the cop. She scanned his face as another bolt of lightning hit. Lines of fatigue showed around his eyes. She wondered if he'd gotten any sleep at all or if he'd risen from the bed to prevent sleep from overtaking him.

She swept the covers aside. "Come back to bed, Jon," she said in a solicitous voice.

He did as she asked, pushing away from the window. He left his gun on the nightstand and his jeans on the floor. As he slid in beside her, she drew the covers over them. His arms closed around her waist, bringing her down to him. She loved feeling his hard body, all sinew and muscle next to hers, under her fingertips.

The first time they'd come together had been about heat and passion, this second time was about exploring and discovering. Their hands, their mouths, touched, sampled, tasted, as if they had all the time in the world and nothing else mattered. All the while, the rain beat a steady tattoo against the windowpanes.

When finally, as they lay side by side, he entered

her, she gasped, reveling in the feel of him inside her, filling her, only to retreat and fill her again just as slowly. She wrapped her leg around his back, pulling him in deeper, but she didn't urge him to go faster. She was enjoying the sweet torture of being almost at the brink but not toppling over.

But obviously, he grew impatient. His fingers grasped her buttocks as he thrust into her deeper and with more urgency. Her neck arched and she called his name, unable to hold back any longer. A bolt of pure pleasure sizzled through her as white hot and electric as the storm outside. An instant later, his grip on her tightened and his body spasmed against hers.

Dana buried her face against his neck as their breathing normalized and their damp bodies cooled. His hand stroked over her back in a soothing motion. It took her a few minutes to realize when it stopped and his breathing had evened out. She pulled back to look at him. Sleep softened his features and lent him the look of a little boy.

She pressed her lips to his. "Sweet dreams, Jonathan," she whispered. She laid her cheek against his chest and slept, too.

The next time Dana woke it was to the sound of the shower running in the bathroom at the corner of her room. Jonathan. Her first impulse was to go join him under the warm spray of the shower and see what developed. She quashed that idea almost immediately. Jumping into his shower uninvited would smack of an intimacy that wasn't there yet. They hadn't settled anything between them yet, including whether or not last night was a one shot deal. He'd even offered her the use of another bed while she was in his apartment, though, judging by his lovemaking last night, she'd be a fool to spend any time in any bed but his.

She sighed, sitting up and drawing her knees up. What was he doing up so early, anyway? It was still dark out and the bedside clock showed four thirty-five. He probably wanted to get to his apartment before the neighborhood started waking up. Whatever the reason, he'd probably be hungry. She knew she was. She put on her robe and headed down to the kitchen.

She'd already finished the bacon and was pouring eggs into a skillet when she heard Jonathan's footfalls on the stairs. He appeared a second later dressed in the clothes he'd worn last night. But he hadn't bothered to tuck in his shirt. That and his morning stubble lent him a rumpled look she found appealing.

He came up behind her, slid an arm around her waist and kissed her cheek. "Morning."

She chuckled. He sounded as sleepy as she felt. "I made coffee. Help yourself, if you don't mind. I'll have the rest of breakfast finished in a minute."

"Thanks." He released her and went to the counter where the coffeemaker stood.

Dana gave the eggs a last turn then flicked off the burner. "I hope you don't mind scrambled. I didn't know what kind of eggs you liked."

"Scrambled is fine. I didn't intend to wake you up this early."

She shrugged as she portioned out food onto two plates. "I'm a light sleeper. It comes with the territory." She laid both plates on the table and sat.

He sat at the appropriate place and set his coffee cup on the table. "Being a nurse?"

"Raising a kid alone. Not to mention caring for my

mother a number of years before that. She died of MS when I was seventeen."

"Is that what made you want to become a nurse?"

"I guess it was a matter of getting paid for what I already knew how to do. It's amazing how much you learn about medicine when you are someone's care giver." She forked up some eggs and brought them to her mouth.

"You raised your brother alone since then?"

"Me and the parochial school system."

"Where was your father in all this?"

"If you find out, let me know." For a long minute neither of them said anything. Dana focused on her food, contemplating how similar their lives were in this regard. Both of them had lost their parents at an early age, hers to illness and abandonment, his to a car accident and a heart attack. At least he'd had the support of his brothers and sister. She'd been alone.

"How long will it take you to get ready?"

She'd been so lost in her own thoughts his question startled her. "About ten minutes. I never unpacked my bag from this trip I was supposed to take."

"Why didn't you go?"

She formed her hand into the shape of a gun and fired off a couple of mock rounds.

He let out a heavy breath. "Then we'd better get going. I'd prefer to get to my place while it's still dark."

Dana sighed. Just what she needed. Another reminder that this wasn't about two lovers sharing a post-coital breakfast. This was about keeping her out of harm's way long enough for him to find out who wanted to harm her.

She'd eaten as much of her meal as she planned to. She stood and went to the trash to scrape her plate. "I won't be long." She retreated to her room to shower and pack what few toiletries she needed to add to her suitcase.

Once they were in his car headed south on the Major Deegan, she asked, "Where is home for you, anyway?" She knew from Joanna that he lived somewhere in the Bronx, but exactly where she had no idea.

"One sixty-second off the Concourse."

The fact that he lived within the boundaries of the precinct he'd once served didn't surprise her. "Part of your plan to serve the community?"

He lifted one shoulder in a shrug. "There's some merit to living in the community you police. You get to know the people, build a rapport in a way you don't get commuting from Westchester or Long Island. I can't tell you the number of times that I've cleared a case because someone sought me out to tell me what they saw, what they heard, who they know did what. It's a well-known cop axiom that the best cop is the one with the best snitches. But no one's going to open up to you if they don't trust you."

He stole a glance at her and grinned. "Besides, where else in the city are you going to get a spacious two bedroom apartment for under six hundred bucks?"

She couldn't argue with him there. Many of those old buildings on the Concourse featured apartments with as much square footage as her entire house. Jonathan's apartment was the same, with a large kitchen, dining room, huge sunken living room, two bedrooms and two baths.

She gave herself the two-cent tour while he changed for work. It was a typical man's apartment complete with black leather sofa and manly-man big screen TV. But he had actual books on his bookshelf, mostly crime and horror fiction, and the artwork on his walls was a cut above what you could expect from most men. And the place was actually clean without him having time to neaten up before she arrived.

After peering in the second bedroom she understood why he'd put two beds in there instead of one. She recognized some of the toys in the room as belonging to Joanna's two boys. He must have decorated with them in mind.

If she wanted to know what the master bedroom looked like, she'd have to wait. After a brief stint in the bathroom to shave, he'd gone to the bedroom to dress. She started to head back to the living room when his bedroom door opened. She turned around to see him walking toward her dressed in a navy blue suit.

Something in his face or in his demeanor told her he was back to being a cop. Still, he laced his fingers with hers and led her toward the front door.

He stopped halfway down the hallway and pulled her to him. "I don't suppose I have to remind you not to go out. The whole point of you being here is for no one to know where you are."

"No. You don't have to remind me. I'll probably spend the entire day sleeping, anyway."

"You have my numbers. If you need anything, call."

"I will," she said, but she knew she wouldn't—not unless someone was breaking down the door. He had a job to do and didn't need her distracting him. "Be careful, Jon."

For a moment, he looked at her with an expression she didn't understand. Then he leaned down and claimed her mouth for a brief kiss. "I'll try to be home early."

Since she had no idea what time early might be for him, she just said, "Okay."

He opened the door and went through it. She closed it behind him and locked it.

Now all she had to do was find something to occupy her. Despite what she told Jonathan, she was too worked up to sleep. It was too early to call Joanna to tell her she wouldn't be coming to the house today to help her settle in with the new baby.

With a sigh she slumped onto the sofa that faced the TV and flicked it on using the remote. She found the local Bronx station, intent on listening to the news. After weather and traffic reports aired, the lead stories repeated. Only one of them held her attention. Apparently Reverend Robert Jones was set to hold a rally on the steps of the Bronx courthouse at ten o'clock.

Dana ground her teeth together. Who knew what that man was up to. But considering she could see the courthouse from the living room window, she'd probably hear every word.

When Jonathan arrived at the stationhouse that morning, Mari was, as usual, already at her desk. For a change she seemed anxious to see him. Despite that, the first words out of her mouth after he sat down were, "You sure look like hell."

He pulled his chair closer under his desk. "Thanks for reminding me." After he'd brought Dana to his place, he'd had to shower and shave quickly in order to get there with some sort of punctuality. Combined with the lack of sleep from the night before, he was sure he looked like the devil. "What have you been up to?"

She grinned. "Since someone ruined my evening last night, I headed over to Jackson's watering hole. Folks there confirmed that our guy hadn't started the fight."

Funny, no one had volunteered any information on who instigated what the first time they'd gone to the place. Most of the folks still around at that time claimed not to have seen a thing. But then everyone knew they were cops. Dressed as she was last night, he doubted anyone would have recognized her as the same policewoman who'd been there a few mornings before. No doubt there were plenty of things a man would tell a pretty girl he wouldn't tell a cop.

"Where did you leave it?"

"The A.D.A. is writing it up as self-defense."

While he was glad the case was cleared, he doubted that's what had Mari so eager to see him. "What else have you been up to?"

She sighed dramatically. "Nothing important. I just figured out why Moretti has such a hard-on for you."

"Why is that?" Not that he really cared, but he was curious as to both what she found out and why she'd bothered.

"Way back when Moretti had some ambition, he wanted to be seated where you are now. But he got on someone's shit list in the department, whose and how I'm not exactly sure. The powers that be made it clear that where he was was all he'd ever be."

"And he blames me for that?"

"Probably not, but you have to admit it probably sticks in his craw that you came on after he did and he's still where he is. He must have been on the job a good decade before you ever showed up on the scene and you get bumped up, not him. And coming from the same squad . . ."

He shrugged as Mari's words trailed off. Neither Moretti's stalled career or his loss of faith were Jonathan's problems. But if what Mari said was true, that probably explained Moretti's dislike of her, too. She'd moved to homicide three years ago after some city report was released claiming a lack of diversity among the NYPD's special units.

The NYPD's response had been to reassign Mari, a self-described demographer's wet dream, as she was part black, part Latina, female and short—the whole crap shoot in one little bundle. There were those who still believed she hadn't earned her shot just because of the way she got it. Mari, of course, couldn't care less.

Considering her indifference he wondered why she'd bothered to investigate. He said as much.

She crossed her arms. "Never let it be said that I don't have my partner's back. And speaking of which, what did you do with our witness?"

As segues went, that wasn't a bad one. "Somewhere safe."

"I figured as much." She let out an annoyed sigh. "I hope you know what you're doing, Stone."

He knew what concerned her. "When have I ever let anything get in the way of getting the job done?"

"Uh, never," she said in a way that suggested that's why she was concerned this time.

The sound of Shea's office door opening drew his attention. Although the blinds to the office had been closed since Jonathan walked in, he would have been surprised if anyone other than the police commissioner had been closeted in the office with him. No doubt both men wanted a briefing so that they could plan what to tell and how much to the press attending Pierce's funeral.

Shea appeared in the doorway. "Stone, Velez." He nodded toward his office.

Jonathan glanced at Mari to gauge her reaction. She winked at him. "Showtime."

Fourteen

"I understand you have something happening in the Pierce case."

That came from the commissioner, Franklin Brooks, a man it was easy to distrust on first glance. His long nose and thin face lent him the look of a ferret. As far as Jonathan knew, he was an okay guy in that he gave the appearance of putting his men's welfare ahead of his own ambitions. Whether that was true or not was anyone's guess.

Brooks was the only one sitting in the room, perched on the end of Shea's desk. Shea stood behind his desk with his knuckles resting on the blotter, looking like a bulldog awaiting word to pounce. He and Mari stood facing the other two.

"Someone made a move on the one witness we have in the case, the last person to see Pierce alive. But it's not certain the two incidents are related." He gave Brooks a brief rundown of what had happened, the same one he'd given Shea.

Brooks listened with a thoughtful expression on his face. Without missing a beat, he said, "It does appear the two cases are related, but we don't want to be premature about this. We can get Moretti up here. He can work from up here under your direction. You work your end of the case, he works his. Hopefully the twain will meet up somewhere."

If he thought it would do him any good he might argue the wisdom of cutting Moretti loose. But since he hadn't told the chief anything new, he figured the decision was made before he set foot through Shea's door.

Brooks stood and rebuttoned his jacket. "I'd better get back to my wife, then. She's giving the eulogy this afternoon."

Brooks shot him a pointed look that was unnecessary. He didn't need the reminder of the chief's personal stake in the investigation. Nor did he need any prodding to hurry the case along. Dana's life might depend on that.

"If you boys need anything, let me know."

As he walked out, Shea asked, "This witness of yours is in a safe place?"

Jonathan felt Mari's eyes on him as he answered. "Yes."

"Has anyone spoken to this Pee Wee person?"

"Not to my knowledge."

"Then let's get to it."

Shea's usually gruff dismissal. As they walked back to their desks, Mari said, "You suppose Moretti will bring his IAB tail with him or leave them back at the ranch?"

Damned if he knew or really cared. The real question was why the powers that be wanted Moretti on the case in the first place. Maybe they wanted him off his home turf for some reason. Or maybe no one wanted to admit that a bunch of gang bangers might have some connection to Amanda Pierce's death.

At least he'd have a chance to ride Moretti's ass on the case or ride over him if he chose. Somehow he expected it to be the latter.

Dana waited until the reasonable hour of ten o'clock before calling Tim on his cell phone.

"Hey, Sis. What's up?"

She heard the wariness in his voice. She should have expected that. The last time she'd called him out of the blue it was to tell him that she was in the hospital. "I'm fine," she began, to reassure him. "But something's come up. Nothing major."

"Right. That's why you're calling me the day before I'm supposed to come home."

"Really, it's nothing."

"Fine. Don't tell me. I'll be home tomorrow. I'll find out then."

"That's why I'm calling you. You remember my friend Joanna's brother Jonathan? He's one of the detectives working on my case. He thinks I'll be safer if I'm not at home while they work on the case."

"So where are you?"

That was the one bit of information she hadn't planned on sharing with her brother. "That's not important."

"Like hell it isn't."

"For the time being, I'm at his apartment."

"How convenient for him."

"Tim . . ." she started in an exasperated voice, not really knowing what to say to him. She wanted to tell him things weren't how he thought they were, but that wasn't exactly true, either. When had her baby brother become such a man anyway, with a man's sensibilities and thought processes? "He is not taking advantage of me, if that's what you're thinking."

"If you say so, Sis."

By the tone of his voice she knew he thought she was deluding herself. Maybe she was, but it annoyed her that he at seventeen thought he knew better than she. Youth was never too young to display its own arrogance. "Look, kid, the reason I called you was to find out if you can stay with the Kenners another few days."

"Why, he wants you all to himself?"

"How about I don't want you embroiled in whatever this is. You haven't been around this whole time and I want to keep it that way."

His exasperated sigh reached her through the phone. "Hold on. I'll ask."

A few moments later, Linda Kenner came on the line. " Hi, Dana. We don't mind keeping Tim another few days. Is everything all right with you? Tim told us about the shooting."

"I'm fine." And at least Tim appeared to have enough presence of mind not to let on the reason he needed to stay with them. "I have to be away for a few days. I don't want Tim getting into any trouble while I'm gone."

"I hear you," Linda said. "Even at this age they need supervision. But Tim's no problem. Let us know when you get back."

"I will."

"I'll put Tim back on, then. I hope you enjoy your trip."

"Thanks."

"Anything else?" Tim said when he came back on the line.

Hearing the hostility in his voice, Dana sighed. He had to know she kept something from him and he didn't like it. Too bad. If he knew her true situation, he'd wangle his way onto the next plane to get to her. From the time he was a small boy, he'd been protective of her. She'd always encouraged that sort of protectiveness for others, especially those weaker than himself, in him. She couldn't fault him for growing into the kind of young man she'd trained him to be.

"You don't have to worry about me, really."

"Just let me know when I can come home."

The line went dead. With a growl of frustration she disconnected the call on her end. While she was in such a jovial mood, she might as well get the other call she wasn't looking forward to out of the way. She punched the numbers for Joanna's room at the hospital and waited. Joanna picked up on the third ring.

"Hey stranger," Dana said to Joanna's hello.

"Dana? Where are you? I thought you were going to come over this morning,"

Dana gritted her teeth. She should have known that would be the first question out of Joanna's mouth. "Listen, Joanna, something's happened since I left you last night." There was no other way to say it except flat out. "On my way home someone tried to hit me."

"Oh, my God! How did that happen?"

Dana recounted the rest of the night's events to the point that Mari and Moretti walked out her door.

"So where are you now? I hope you're not still at your house. They could find you there."

"No, I left this morning." She hesitated, wondering what Joanna's reaction would be to what she said next. "I'm at your brother's place."

"Jonathan's? Why?"

"He offered and I had nowhere else to go."

"Had nowhere else to go or didn't want to go anywhere else?"

"What is that supposed to mean?"

"Tell me my brother spent the night somewhere other than in your bed and I will drop the subject."

Since she couldn't tell her that, she sighed and said nothing. But she wondered at the negativity she heard in her friend's voice, especially considering all the times Joanna had harped on her to find a decent man.

"Oh, Dana," Joanna said. "There is a reason I've never tried to set you up with any of my brothers. I love them dearly, but I know how they are. I can't explain how Barbara has stayed with Adam all these years and Zack is, well, Zack. But Jonathan? I don't know of a single woman that's lasted more than a few months with him."

Well, that explained it, but Dana wasn't about to let anyone dictate what she did, no matter what their feelings were. "And I'm not aiming to be the first. All I did was sleep with the man."

"Is that all you want there to be of it?"

Dana blew out a heavy breath. That was the question of the hour. Although he'd offered her a choice of where to sleep, she knew she'd be a fool to spend her time anywhere except in his bed. She wanted him. He wanted her. They were both adults. If all she got from being with him was a few nights of hot sex, what was so wrong with that? Nothing, as far as she could see, even if she acknowledged that, somewhere inside her, other alien feelings that had nothing to do with lust had begun to simmer. For all she knew, she'd end up with her heart broken. Oh, well, there had to be a first time for everything. All she knew for certain was she wasn't ready to turn him loose yet.

She knew she could tell Joanna to mind her own business and she would back off, but she didn't do that. Instead she offered her most honest answer. "No."

"Then I hope you know what you're doing."

Dana laughed without mirth. "That makes two of us."

Jonathan stood at the back of St. Patrick's Cathedral as the mourners started filing in for Amanda Pierce's funeral. He hadn't been raised Catholic. In fact, he hadn't been raised with much religion at all. But the beauty and grandeur of the building stood as a testament to both art and architecture if not the divine.

Outside, uniformed officers kept the curious and the vitriolic at bay, including the sort of press that packed cameras. Banks's own people would be filming the event and doling out tapes to whatever media outlets they saw fit.

Those people actually making it into the church were often people he recognized, either from the media, the entertainment industry or the field of politics. Everyone from the Bronx Borough President to the Democratic Representative from Staten Island had shown up, which surprised him. From what he knew of her, Pierce's métier was celebrities not politicos. He'd love to hear an explanation for that.

In the periphery of his vision he saw her agent, James Burke, sidling up to him. "May I have a word with you, Detective?" the man asked.

"Sure." He didn't mind talking to Burke considering he had a few questions of his own. "What can I do for you?"

"I was wondering if you have any suspects yet. Any idea who killed her?"

He told Burke the same thing he told everyone he deigned to give an answer to. "We're working on several strong leads at the moment."

Burke nodded. The grim expression on his face intensified. He nodded toward the long rows of pews that were about a quarter of the way full. "A bunch of vultures. They're all probably here just to make sure she's dead."

"You mean the Hollywood people?"

"All of them. I thought I made it clear when we talked. Amanda may have given up the political beat, but she still had her hand in things. There hasn't been a political scandal in this city in the last two years that Amanda didn't have some role in uncovering. Amanda had few friends, but she knew everybody. And she had a knack for uncovering people's dirty secrets no matter what the arena. And if you think celebriphiles get bent out of shape when their idols get toppled, imagine the average politician's response to finding out the candidate they just endorsed has a skeleton in his closet big enough to knock him out of the election. You can ask your former boss about that."

Burke moved off, going to join a tall blonde who'd obviously been waiting for him. Jonathan's gaze followed him down the aisle. He found some small satisfaction knowing how disappointed those vultures must be to find Pierce laid out in the closed coffin the beating to her face necessitated. But her political involvement added a whole new layer to the investigation he hadn't considered.

He moved farther into the church as the hour for the service neared. He wanted a vantage point from which he could see which of the mourners might show guilt, fear, strain or any combination of the three. But so far, most of those gathered here seemed more jovial than somber, glad to rub elbows with their neighbors or perhaps advance their careers in some way. The only people who seemed to actually be in mourning were Pierce's brother, her agent and a few grim faces scattered in the crowd.

Well, he hadn't come here expecting to gain much insight into Amanda Pierce's soul. As his father used to say, a person's funeral was the only time they could fully expect that ninety percent of what was said about them would be lies. But the commissioner's wife surprised him, delivering a heartfelt tribute to a woman she hadn't had much contact with since college but who she still revered as a close friend. As Mrs. Brooks returned to her seat next to her husband he noticed Mari come up beside him.

"It's no mystery who has the class in that family," she said, nodding toward the couple.

"Mmm," he agreed. All that was left of this show was the people filing out of the church. "Let's get out of here."

About noon, after her stomach had rumbled a few times, Dana went to the kitchen to see what might be available for her to make for lunch. She quickly settled on a sandwich from the cold cuts she found in the fridge and returned to the sofa. Despite what she'd told Jonathan about sleeping the day away, even a fifteen-minute catnap had eluded her. Instead she'd ended up watching two hours of ER reruns and a particularly whimsical episode of *Charmed*.

By the time she got back to her seat, it was fifteen minutes into *Law and Order*. At least on TV the cops were always righteous and they always got the right man. Outside, she could hear the stirrings of a PA system, someone testing out a microphone with what sounded like the usual one, two, three. Reverend Bobby must be tuning up his show. She turned the set up a little louder, hoping to block out his noise.

Her cell phone rang a few minutes later. Who could be calling her now? She didn't give out her cell phone number to many people. If it were Jonathan or even Joanna, they'd have called on the regular phone. She'd called Tim that morning. Reluctantly, he'd agreed to stay put with his friend's family and they'd been happy to house him for a few more days.

She dug the phone out of her purse and answered the call. "Hello."

"Dana, where are you? Are you anywhere near a TV?"

She recognized Father Mike's voice almost immediately. "Why?"

"Your friend Nadine is on the news."

Dana picked up the remote. "Which station?"

"The Bronx news. Not BronxNet, the other one."

She flicked around until she found the channel he meant. Apparently, they were broadcasting Reverend Bobby's conference live. The camera held a close-up shot of the Reverend. Despite the cooler temperature since the night before, Reverend Bobby's forehead was pebbled with perspiration that threatened to run down his face. He dabbed at his skin with a handkerchief dramatically. She wouldn't put it past the man to have sprayed himself with water before the press conference began to give himself the appearance of a man sweating it out for God.

". . . while at this very minute, another woman killed in the Bronx is being buried with much pomp and circumstance at St. Patrick's Cathedral. Where was the pomp when poor Wesley was being buried? Only a handful of mourners saw him interred in his final resting place. Where were the police in this poor grandmother's hour of need?"

Jones gestured to his left and the camera shifted to focus on Nadine sitting in a wheelchair looking more flustered than anything else. Dana's first thought was to wonder how they'd gotten Nadine up all those steps since the woman couldn't make it to the bathroom by herself. Dana shook her head. She'd seen it in Nadine's eyes at the funeral, her desire to seek some sort of vindication for Wesley. She'd also known from the moment Reverend Bobby showed up on her doorstep that his involvement could only lead to trouble. Dana couldn't imagine that toting herself out like a spectacle was what Nadine had had in mind.

"Did you find it?"

She'd forgotten about Father Mike. "Oh, yeah."

". . . and what does it say when the only witness to this tragedy will not come out and let her voice be heard?"

Dana ground her teeth together. She supposed he wasn't going to let her get away with not joining his parade without some mention of it. But if he actually used her name or trotted out that picture of his she was going to sue his sorry butt.

"What do you think?"

"I feel sorry for Nadine, but she asked for it."

"Have you heard anything new in the case?"

For an instant she debated whether to tell Father Mike what happened last night. Considering that the only thing anyone could do if they knew about it was worry, she decided against it. "Who tells me anything? I'm only the victim."

Father Mike chuckled. "Well, if you need anything, give me a call. By the way, how's Tim?"

"He's still away with friends. I sort of am, too, for the next few days. If you need me you can reach me at this number."

After they said their good-byes, she disconnected the call and put the phone back in her purse. She looked at her meal, mostly uneaten, which she no longer wanted. She clicked off the set. Let Reverend Bobby rant all he wanted. At least with the windows closed she couldn't make out the words.

About five-thirty, Jonathan decided to give it up for the day. Figueroa must have gone into hiding, since he wasn't at any of his usual haunts. Either that or no one was willing to give up his whereabouts, which was more likely. On top of that, he'd gotten exactly nowhere trying to contact the names on Father Masella's list. He'd had someone looking up current addresses for the former parishioners. He and Mari had made the rounds of those they had so far. They wanted to visit in person rather than call for the same reason they'd gone to the funeral—to gauge people's reactions. Most of the people they located weren't home. These days, even retirees had better things to do than sit around at home. In each case, they'd left a card asking the people to contact him at the station. Of the people he reached, most launched into a paean of Father Malone's virtues, but none could remember anything about the building project or about which boys in particular had been close to the priest.

Unfortunately, Father Masella's list concentrated on folks who had been adult members of the congregation. Most had moved on, many had died, none of their memories of that time were sharp any longer. That was the trouble with trying to investigate something that happened twenty-five years ago. But Amanda had to have found something worth getting killed over, but about whom?

Or maybe Pierce's research had taken her in an entirely new direction. Maybe he was just too tired to puzzle it out. He hadn't slept much since he'd gotten the case and in the past couple of nights he'd slept even less. He was anxious to get home to the reason for his lack of slumber, to find out if Dana was all right. Though she'd shown only concern for her brother and an unwillingness to involve Joanna in her situation, he knew she had to be scared for herself, too.

Even before he turned the key in his lock, he heard her. The faint sound of her singing along with the radio. She must be in the kitchen at the front of the apartment, since the aroma of something cooking reached his nose, too. His stomach rumbled its anticipation of anything home cooked by anyone's hand but his.

He pushed open the door and spotted her immediately, standing by the sink washing something under the water. He let the door close behind him then turned the locks. By the time he turned back around, she'd shut off the water and was facing him.

She finished drying her hands on a dishtowel and tossed it on the counter. For a moment neither of them said anything. He was busy letting his gaze wander over her, from her tousled hair to her sweet face to the swell of her breasts beneath the thin covering of her T-shirt to the jeans that molded to her hips and thighs, before bringing his gaze back to her face.

She smiled at him, a lopsided grin. "Would it be inappropriate of me to say I am so glad you're home?"

He chuckled. "No." Not if she didn't mind him admitting how glad he was to arrive home to find her whole, well and smiling at him with such obvious welcome. It was the sort of domestic scene he didn't usually appreciate, but today it felt like coming in from the cold. "Missed me, did you?"

"Missed all human contact."

He curled a finger urging her over. "Then come here."

Her smile took on a teasing quality. "Why?"

She knew damn well what he wanted. He didn't mind stating it plainly. "A little of that human contact you've been craving."

She bit her lip as if contemplating a juicy meal. "Bring it on."

He closed the distance between them and pulled her into his arms. His mouth found hers for a stirring kiss. After a few moments he pulled away. It would be far too easy to lose himself in that kiss. He pulled away a little bit but still held onto her waist. "I didn't expect you to cook." He wasn't complaining, but it hadn't occurred to him before he got home that she would.

She shrugged. "We both have to eat. I hope you're not trying to convince me Joanna didn't teach you how to cook. You have food in the freezer."

"I do all right, but Martha Stewart won't be calling for any recipes any time soon. How long before dinner?"

"I was waiting for you to get home before putting the meat in the oven, so you've got a few minutes."

"I'm going to go get cleaned up."

"Okay. If you like your steak rare, don't take too long."

He kissed her forehead. "I won't."

A few minutes later he stepped into the warm spray of the water. He'd started the ritual of taking a shower when he got home the day he started working homicide. A couple of hikers had found a woman's body down by the Bronx River. It was the end of summer, hot enough for the river to be almost dry. Whatever animals frequented the riverbed had discovered the body before the police had. The sight was so gruesome and the stench so rank that even hardened investigators resorted to gas masks modified for police use. All of it was made worse by the fact that the first officer responding was a rookie who lost his breakfast a couple of feet from the scene.

That day, he couldn't wait to get home to get out of his clothes. He'd tossed the suit down the incinerator. No dry cleaner could have gotten the smell out. He'd spent a good half-hour in the shower before he'd felt anywhere near clean. Days like today, the shower was more a psychic than a physical cleansing, a means of putting the day to rest.

He got out of the shower and dressed as he usually did at home, in a pair of jeans and a T-shirt. When he got out to the kitchen, Dana was taking the steaks out from under the broiler. His mouth watered, not only for the food but also from her rear view as she bent and then straightened.

"You're right on time," she said, casting him a smiling glance over her shoulder.

"What do you need me to help you with?"

"Nothing really. I figured we'd serve ourselves here then take it into the other room."

He gestured for her to precede him. She filled her plate then slipped past him out of the kitchen. It wasn't until then he noticed how much she'd cooked. Certainly more than the two of them could eat in one night. He filled his plate and stopped short once he left the kitchen. By the other room he thought she'd meant the living room where he normally ate, not the dining room he never used. He hadn't noticed before that she'd actually set the table with wine-glasses and a bottle of wine he'd forgotten he had.

"Surprised you, huh?"

"A little."

"Civilization comes to 162nd Street. Don't tell me I'm the only woman you've ever had here."

No, he couldn't say that, but for the most part he preferred to be somewhere he could get up and leave if the urge struck. He didn't know if that comment of hers was simply a throwaway or if she were fishing for information about him. But the last thing he wanted to do was discuss his other women with her. He didn't know how she'd feel knowing his track record or even how much, if anything, Joanna had told her about him. He only knew he didn't want her to judge him harshly because of it.

He cut into his steak and brought a bite of it to his mouth. The meat was juicy and flavorful. "Not bad."

She shot him a knowing look. "Fine. Don't tell me."

So, she had been looking for information. He wasn't sure if that was good or bad.

"Okay, change of subject. What did you find out today?"

"Nothing much. If I'd been much more productive I might as well have stayed home in bed."

"Well then, tell me everything. I know you suspect that Amanda Pierce was killed by whoever I saw picking her up that day, but why?"

"That's what I'd like to know, too. We believe her murder was tied up in what she was working on—researching her uncle's death twenty-five years ago."

"Who's her uncle?"

"Father Brendan Malone."

"I've heard of him. He's the one who built Trinity Houses. Aside from the religious implication, wasn't it called that because the people involved came from three fields, the church, the government, and private enterprise? Why was she researching her own uncle?"

"First, he died in a mysterious fire in his church. I pulled the file on the old case, but most of the information that should have been there was either gutted or lost over the years. At the time it was deemed an accident. Second, while he was alive, it was rumored that he and some of his cronies were skimming money from the building fund. As far as I can determine, that isn't true. I have a meeting tomorrow with one of the other partners in the building deal. We'll see what he says."

She nodded. "So you think Pierce poking around in the past is what got her killed? Most of the people involved must be senior citizens by now."

"Grandpas can't carry guns?"

"I don't say that, but they don't roll up in a gangsta car and shoot you either."

She had a point there. He didn't know how Pee Wee's crew fit into this, but he intended to be there when someone found out.

Fifteen

Dana drank the last sip of her wine and set her glass on the table. "That wasn't bad," she said, echoing his earlier words. "If I do say so myself."

He smiled. "Immodesty becomes you. And since you did the honors of cooking, I'll take care of the dishes and make some coffee. Do you want to see if there's anything on the tube?"

"Sure." She didn't suppose he had that huge TV for nothing. She tossed her napkin onto the table beside her plate. "You're sure you don't need some help?"

"Joanna taught me how to clean up after myself, too."

"Fine." She pushed back her chair and went into the living room, settling in the nearest corner of the couch. She tucked her feet under her and used the remote to turn on the set. She wasn't much of a TV watcher herself and had no idea what was on at this time on what station. She flicked around until she found a rerun of a show she thought he might appreciate. By the time he joined her in the living room, she'd gotten fairly engrossed in the show herself.

He stepped past her to set a tray laden with two cups of coffee, cream, sugar and spoons on the coffee table before sitting beside her. "NYPD Blue? I'm shocked."

She glanced up at his smiling face. "I don't mind watching cop shows on TV. It's fantasy."

She leaned down to add cream and sugar to her coffee. As she sipped from her cup he picked up his own and sampled it.

"Let me ask you something. What started this cop thing of yours? Was it the incident you told me about?" he said.

"It's not a cop thing and what incident?"

"Last night you said that when you pass some cop beating on a kid in the hallway you walk by. I assumed you were talking about something real."

She sipped from her cup. "I was."

"What happened?"

She set her cup on the table. "The usual. I was coming up the stairs in one of the buildings and on one of the landings this cop was giving it to some kid. What I found unnerving was the way the cop looked at me, like he knew what he was doing was wrong, but if I challenged him I'd probably be next." She shuddered remembering the malevolence of his glance. "Some people simply shouldn't be given that much power over others."

"There are some good guys out there, too."

She had never denied that, but it struck her that he was pleading his case to her, that it mattered to him that she didn't lump him in with those others she found wanting. She did in the beginning, but that was after knowing him for years in only a cursory manner and after he'd broken her confidence by tracking her down. She still didn't presume to know what made him tick, but she understood that what she'd originally taken as standoffishness or arrogance was a quietness of character that she found compelling. Most men she knew were so busy talking themselves up that you had to sift what they were from what they said they were. He had never tried to impress her with anything except with her own need for protection. Not until now.

For a moment, her gaze met his. Then something beyond him at the window caught her attention. A movement. Then a face appeared looking misshapen through the glass. For an instant all heat seemed to drain out of her body and her nervous system went on alert.

"Dana, what is it?"

"We're not alone."

Whoever it was rapped on the window. "Hey, Jay. You home?"

Dana let out her breath in a rapid gush. Obviously, whoever it was, Jonathan knew him. He confirmed her conclusion a second later, by cradling her nape in his palm to bring her face closer to his.

"It's all right, sweetheart." He placed a soft kiss on her forehead. "He's with me."

She nodded her understanding, not trusting her voice. Although the fright had been momentary, her nerves still jangled.

He kissed her temple. "Are you okay?"

She nodded again. "Maybe you better find out what he wants."

He muttered something she didn't catch as he got up from the sofa and went to the window. He lifted the pane. "What's up, Tyree?"

"Just wanted to hang."

She could hear the anger in Jonathan's voice and the resulting uncertainty in the other. Though Jonathan stood in a way to block her view, the youthfulness in the voice told her his visitor was a kid. She leaned her elbow against the back of the sofa. "Why don't you ask your friend to come in?"

"Sorry man, I didn't know you had company."

"Why don't you come in," Jonathan echoed, this time with more annoyance than hostility.

After a few moments in which she couldn't catch what was said, Tyree came in through the window. As Jonathan shut it behind him, Tyree came to stand beside the sofa. For a moment they sized each other up. He was tall and long limbed, handsome in a future heartbreaker sort of way. She'd put his age at fourteen or fifteen. He looked at her with interest, so she assumed he approved.

Jonathan said, "Dana this is Tyree. Tyree, why don't you have a seat?" When Tyree moved to take his place on the sofa, Jonathan added, "Over there." He pointed to the adjacent chair.

Dana hid a smile as Tyree slunk to the chair Jonathan indicated and slumped into it. Jonathan sat down, his eyes on Tyree. Whatever kind of look he gave the boy made him sit straighter in his seat.

For a moment, nobody said anything, though it was obvious to Dana the boy had sought out Jonathan because he wanted to talk to him. She searched for an excuse to get out of the room long enough for that to be accomplished. "Have you eaten, yet?" she asked Tyree.

"Nah." Another look from Jonathan and the boy amended himself. "I mean, no."

"I can fix you a plate if you like."

She saw the avidness in the boy's face at the prospect of decent food, but before he could answer Jonathan patted her thigh. "I'll take care of it."

He was on his feet before she had time to protest,

not that she was sure she would have. But she wondered why he'd left her alone with this kid who had business with him, not her.

"Hey, I know who you are," Tyree said, drawing her attention. "You're that nurse."

Is that what everyone called her? That nurse? "Guilty as charged."

"I heard what happened to you and that kid. You okay now?"

"I'm fine. Thank you for asking."

The kid flushed, probably unused to the simple courtesies of please and thank you. She hadn't sought to embarrass him though. "Do you live near here?"

"Me and my moms live upstairs."

There was something about the way he said that, that made her curious, something that seemed off. Maybe his mother disapproved of his friendship with Jon. "Does your mom know you're down here?"

"My mom's asleep." He paused, looking down at his hands. "She got out of the hospital a few days ago."

"How's she doing?"

The boy shrugged. "She's okay, I guess. She had a pretty bad accident."

He didn't look at her when he said that, leading her to believe that the only accident she'd encountered was walking into some man's fist. "Do you want me to look in on her tomorrow when she's awake?"

She could see in the boy's eyes that he wanted to say yes, but also that something held him back. The boy's gaze shifted from her to something beyond her shoulder. She turned to see Jonathan coming into the room. Maybe Tyree was afraid to say yes without Jonathan's okay.

Jonathan set the plate he carried on the coffee table

in front of Tyree. Tyree leaned forward and shoveled a few forkfuls into his mouth. Then, as if he caught himself, he started to eat at a more sedate pace.

She glanced at Jonathan, full of questions. How did he know this boy? What happened to his mother? And, most important, why had he left the two of them alone together?

He rubbed his hand along her thigh and mouthed two words: "Long story."

She'd already figured that much. She was content to wait to hear it. But her lack of sleep was finally catching up with her. She hid a yawn behind her hand.

She thought her show of sleepiness went unnoticed until Jonathan's arm slid around her, drawing her near enough to rest her cheek on his shoulder. "Hang on a little longer, okay?" he whispered against her ear.

She nodded, not knowing why her presence might matter. But since he wanted her there, she sat up and downed the remainder of her coffee. The liquid was tepid, but the caffeine would work whether it was cold or hot.

Having finished his meal, Tyree sat back. "Thanks. That was good."

"I'm glad you enjoyed it."

Another awkward silence ensued. Tyree seemed restless, as though he were ready to bolt. "How's school?" she asked him, more to prevent his leaving than any other reason.

"Makes me glad today's Saturday."

She laughed. "You sound like my brother at your age."

"Yeah?"

She told him about her brother and how he'd managed to turn himself around with a little help.

That got him talking about his school, his friends, and even a little bit about his mother. While they spoke, she felt Jonathan's hand move on her waist, a gentle strumming that had nothing to do with sex, but with a simple affection she found stirring nonetheless.

But the short-lived effects of the caffeine were beginning to wear off. She was back to yawning again. She hoped she'd accomplished Jonathan's goal in getting the kid to open up. Now it was time for her to hit the hay.

"If you gentlemen will excuse me, I'm going to go to bed." She stood, not waiting for a response from either of them. "It was nice meeting you, Tyree, and I will stop in on your mom tomorrow."

She didn't know what to say to Jonathan, so she said nothing. But in that one split second before she turned to leave she saw the question in Jonathan's eyes—exactly which bed did she plan to get into?

Had anything she'd said or done left that much doubt in his mind? Maybe he didn't want to presume to know what she wanted. That was okay. She planned to show him.

She stripped off her clothes, intending to put on the one slinky nightgown she'd packed then decided to forego even that. If she were going to send him a signal, it might as well be a clear one. You couldn't get much clearer than appearing nude in a man's bed. Leaving on only the lamp on the nightstand, she settled under the covers. Now all she had to do was wait.

She heard him enter the room a few minutes later. Though she lay on her stomach facing away from him, she didn't turn toward him. For all she knew, he'd do something like turn noble and decide he couldn't sleep with a woman he was supposed to be protecting. She wanted him and despite the fact that someone wanted to kill her she felt safe with him in or out of bed.

But he didn't disappoint her. She heard him moving behind her, laying his gun on the nightstand before taking off his clothes. She smiled as he slipped into bed with her to cover her with his big, warm body. He leaned to one side resting his weight on his forearm. His other hand roved over her back and lower over her derriere. A sigh slipped from her lips and her body heated.

"Are you sure, baby?"

"After last night, you have to ask me?"

"Last night doesn't count. That was different."

Did he think she'd only reached out to him because she was scared and she needed someone? "What do you want me to say?"

"Baby, I already know what I want. I want to hear what you want."

If she hadn't already made up her mind, did he really expect her to be capable of rational thought with his hands making such a slow, thorough investigation of her body? And if he'd expected her to get out of his bed, would he have gotten into it nude himself? He was giving her an out, slim as it might be. She appreciated that but she didn't want one.

"Tell me what you want, sweetheart," he whispered against her ear.

If he wanted to know, she'd tell him. "You inside me."

"Later."

The combination of his breath fanning her cheek and the promise of that one word sent a shiver down her spine. She closed her eyes and let sensation take over instead of reason. His hand and mouth on her breast, her belly, and lower drove her crazy. But when she reached around to touch him, he brushed her hand away, pushing her more fully onto her back. With soft caresses and gentle kisses, he set about arousing her. She'd never thought of her back as particularly sensitive, but his touch made it so.

When he entered her from behind, it didn't take long for orgasm to overtake either one of them. Afterward, they lay side by side, his arms around her and their fingers laced, recovering.

After a few moments, even though her heart still beat rapidly and her breathing was uneven, she turned to face him. He rolled onto his back and pulled her against his side.

His fingers tangled in her hair. "How are you feeling?"

She leaned up on one elbow and looked at him. "Tell me about Tyree."

"That's what you're thinking about now?"

She nodded, laughing at the indignation she heard in his voice. "Partly. What's his story?"

"You know as much as I do. You got more out of him in twenty minutes than I have in two years."

"Is that why you sicced me on him? Is that standard police interrogation technique?"

"No, but as Tyree would say, he was crushing on you. I figured I may as well use that to my advantage."

"His mother wasn't hurt in any accident, was she?"

"No."

He didn't elaborate and she figured she knew as much as she needed to.

"He's a good kid," Jonathan continued. "I'd like to do something for him, but damned if I know what. I know most social workers would disagree with me, but taking him from his mother isn't the answer. He'd carry the guilt the rest of his life that he wasn't able to help her."

She understood Jonathan's frustration but didn't have any answers either. "Don't look at me. I was trying to get Wesley to give up selling drugs. We both know where he is now."

He brushed her hair from her face. "If it's any consolation, the word is he was trying to get out."

She closed her eyes and laid her cheek against his chest. That did help. It also explained why he wasn't so quick to assume Wesley had been killed because Amanda Pierce's murderer thought she saw something. "Thank you."

The next morning, Jonathan took Dana upstairs to Tyree's apartment. Dana disappeared into the bedroom where the kid's mother rested. The apartment was still neat though the dust was starting to collect, but there was little food in the house. After her stay in the hospital, Jonathan doubted she had any money to replenish it. Under other circumstances he would have gone to the store for them himself, but he wouldn't leave Dana unprotected.

He pulled out the bills he had in his pocket, probably less than a hundred dollars, and extended them toward Tyree. "Why don't you go to the market while we're here to watch your mom?"

Tyree held up his hands as if he'd been offered something hot or dangerous. "Nah, man, I told you I don't want your money."

"I understand that. But sometimes being a man means doing things you don't want to do because they need to be done. Your mom needs to eat if she's going to get better." He thought guilting the kid a little would change his mind, but he still stood there with a belligerent expression on his face. "If you want, we can consider it a loan," he offered. A loan both he and Tyree knew he had no means of paying back.

"All right. A loan." Head hanging low, Tyree reached for the money. The kid turned and walked toward the door. Jonathan sighed, knowing it had taken a measure of the boy's pride to accept the inevitable. Somehow he'd make it up to him.

Once Tyree was gone, Jonathan prowled around the living room feeling restless. He wondered what Dana and Tyree's mom were doing. He stopped mid-stride hearing Dana's laughter coming from the other room, a full-bodied laugh unqualified by anything. To his recollection, that was the first time he'd heard that sound, which both pleased and dismayed him. There hadn't been much for her to laugh about in the last week or so. He was pleased she'd found humor in something even though he hadn't inspired it himself.

Dana was still in the room when Tyree got back. Jonathan helped him put away the food, then the two of them sat down in front of the TV to catch the tail end of some shoot-'em-up action flick Tyree had been watching.

After a few moments, Tyree asked. "What are they talking about in there so long?"

Jonathan shrugged. Damned if he knew, since that was the same question on his mind. But when Dana emerged a few minutes later, she was smiling. He was grateful at least for that.

She set her bag on the table. "Tyree, your mom wants to see you."

The kid bounded out of the room. As soon as they were alone, Jonathan asked, "How is she?"

"Whoever worked her over knew what they were doing. From what she tells me, she's lucky to be alive. But she's on the mend now, as long as nothing untoward happens."

"So what were you talking about for so long?"

She smiled in a way he couldn't begin to understand. "In some ways, she's as starved for attention as her son is. She had him when she was his age. Her mother threw her out of the house when she found out about the pregnancy. She's been making her way the best she could since then."

"But she's still making her living on her back."

"Actually, that's something relatively new. She'd been living with a man who supported her and Tyree for a long time. After he died, she didn't want to go on welfare, since that's a handout. At least the money she makes on the street she earns. In an odd way, she's as proud as her son is, too."

"That's a convolution of logic if I ever heard one."

Dana shrugged. "I never said I agreed with her. I tried explaining to her that welfare isn't what it used to be. You can't go on the dole forever, like the old days. But it would provide her with health care for herself and Tyree and they would train her to do something she could make a living at. She said she'd always wanted to be a beautician. At least then she'd make a living on her feet instead of her knees."

"Do you think you got through to her?"

"Who knows? You can't make people help themselves, but I hope so. She's a nice lady with a wicked sense of humor. She had some things to say about you, too."

"Really? Like what?"

"That," she said, with a wicked smile of her own, "you'll just have to wait to find out."

* * *

Later that night, as she and Jonathan settled into bed, she laid her cheek on his chest. For a moment she stared at his gun on the dresser, still in its holster as he always kept it, her constant reminder that her being with him wasn't some lark but as a preventive to danger.

Jonathan's kiss to her temple brought her focus to him. "So what did Tyree's mother say about me?"

That's what was on his mind at this moment? She leaned up on one elbow to look at him. "It wasn't you precisely. More about your brethren. Cops."

"What was that?"

"Only that you guys are as kinky as any pervert out there. She said most of you were control freaks and the rest of you were just plain freaky."

"Which category do I fit in?"

She noticed he didn't deny the assessment. "So far?" She lifted one shoulder in a shrug. She hadn't really considered it before. She knew that with him, she hadn't exercised her usual take-charge demeanor. In the past few days, she hadn't felt in charge of much. She'd thought it was simply a change in herself. She hadn't considered his role in the equation. "We haven't gotten into freaky yet, so you tell me."

"Are you complaining?"

"Not at all. I like what you do to me. Now I'm planning on doing a few things to you." She lowered her mouth to his chest to trail a path of soft, moist kisses to one of his nipples. She circled her tongue around the peak, while strumming her thumb against the other. She was rewarded with a low growl of pleasure that reverberated in his chest and in her, too.

She knelt between his legs and moved lower, let-

ting her mouth, her hands skim over his chest, his
ribcage, and lower, tantalizing but not satisfying.
She ran her tongue along the tip of his erection
before taking him into her mouth. He groaned and
his hands rose to hold her head in place. Even when
he was at her mercy, he strove for control. She
brushed his hands away and continued as she wanted.

She felt the tension building in his body, and the
air was heavy with the mingled scent of their arousal.
He brushed the hair back from her face. "Baby, I want
to be inside you."

That's what she wanted, too. She got a condom
from the dresser and rolled it onto him. Straddling
him, she took him inside her, both of them shivering as her body enveloped his. She didn't object
when he pulled her down to him and covered her
mouth with his. Her fingers gripped his shoulders as
they moved together, slowly, languidly, heading for
the brink. His arms closed more tightly around her.
He pumped into her more and more urgently, until
she, like him, found release, her pleasure coming in
wave after wave that made her tremble against him.

Afterward, they lay together, her cradled in his
arms. Feeling warm, safe and sated, she closed her
eyes and dozed.

Something woke her an hour later. The first thing
she saw when she opened her eyes was Jonathan
standing at the window looking out. That made it the
second time in three days she'd found him like that.
Was it some sort of ritual with him or was there
something special about those two nights. The only
common denominator she could think of was the
sound of rain against the windowpanes.

She sat up and switched on the bedside lamp.
"What are you doing up?"

"Thinking."

"About what?"

"Things. I don't know." He glanced at her over his shoulder. "You should get some sleep."

He'd said the same thing last time. But he'd come back to bed when she'd asked him to. She had a feeling he wouldn't this time. She got out of bed and went to him, slipping between him and the window to draw his attention.

His arms closed around her, but she sensed his attention still centered elsewhere.

She ran her fingers along one of his shoulders. She kissed the one tattoo she found on his body, an outline of a butterfly in black without any color to fill it in. "What bet did you lose to have gotten that?"

"It wasn't a bet."

Something about the quiet tone in which he'd said that made her look at his face. His eyes were hooded and his face grim. Obviously, there was some story behind the tattoo, something that affected him in a substantial way. Given his present mood and the closed off expression on his face, she doubted it was something he wanted to share with her, but she couldn't let it go that easily. "Tell me."

"Maybe some other time." His hands slid down to grasp her buttocks in his palms. "For now, I have something else on my mind."

His mouth found hers. She gave herself up to his kiss. If he wanted to distract her with sex, she was all for it. But whatever emotion she and the night had dredged up in him came out in his lovemaking. His hands moved over her skin roughly and there was harshness to his kiss she'd never known in him before.

He lifted her in his arms and she wrapped her legs around his waist. He carried her back to the bed, sheathed himself, and joined her. When he entered her it was with one swift thrust that brought him fully inside her. She cried out, not in pain, but with the sudden pleasure of having him fill her completely.

Then he was moving inside her with deep rapid thrusts. She wrapped her legs around his waist and took him deeper still. Her fingers gripped his back, her nails biting into his flesh.

One of his hands slipped beneath her hips to meld their bodies even closer together. It was too much. Pleasure exploded in her, making her body tremble and her eyes squeeze shut in reaction. A moment later, she felt him tremble, too, as he buried his face against her throat. She clung to him still, her body wracked with tiny aftershocks.

His lips trailed a path of kisses along her shoulder before returning the way they'd come. "I'm sorry, baby," he whispered against her ear.

"You're apologizing for giving me an orgasm?"

"The way I did. I'm usually not so . . ."

"Eager?" No, usually he reminded her of that old Pointer Sisters song about a lover with a slow hand. But she wasn't ashamed to admit that whatever way he took her he excited her. "We'll have to put that one down in the somewhat freaky category."

He laughed, but with none of the humor she'd hoped to bring out in him. "Go to sleep, Dana," he whispered against her ear.

With an exasperated sigh she lay her head on his chest and shut her eyes. Maybe she should have left him alone, since he seemed to be more withdrawn now than before. Maybe she'd manage to straighten things between them in the morning. But when she woke up he was already gone.

Sixteen

Jonathan arrived in the squad room the next morning to find Mari's chair empty. He was about to congratulate himself on getting there first until he noticed her coming back from the coffee room, mug in hand.

"Am I mistaken, or do you sleep here?" he asked as she took her seat across from him.

"Sometimes."

He shook his head. Even he wasn't that bad. "Anything shaking?"

"We got a few call backs from the folks we didn't reach on Saturday. I made a few appointments for this afternoon, after we see Rossi."

"Good." Martinez and Russell would be speaking with Stan Nichols's secretary this morning. He figured he didn't need to be here for that, since he doubted she'd provide them with anything useful. Nichols's record showed a couple of busts, but nothing major, nothing recent, and nothing anyone had made stick. If he owned a gun, it wasn't one he'd bothered to register. But Jonathan wouldn't mind finding out some dirt on her boss, however. Something that would keep him off the streets for a good long while.

"Any word on Pee Wee yet?" The uniforms had been out beating the bushes for him since Saturday morning. That's what Tyree had come to see him about. Half his friends had complained about being rousted from their usual hang out spots by cops looking for the drug dealer. Tyree had wanted to know if this had anything to do with his case. He'd told Tyree to stay home and watch his mother and Dana, fearing the teenager would do something foolish to try to impress him, or more likely, Dana.

"Not as far as I know."

Jonathan checked his watch. It was after eight. "Any word about Moretti yet?"

"He hasn't deigned to grace us with his presence yet."

Jonathan gritted his teeth. He'd known Moretti would make it as difficult as possible to work together, but not bothering to show up on time was plain juvenile. He didn't have time to waste on the man, however. He and Mari needed to leave now if they were going to make it to Rossi's place in the city by nine. He'd have to deal with Moretti later.

Sam Rossi's apartment was in a high-rise doorman building on Central Park West. The seventy-four-year-old man met them at his apartment door wearing khaki pants and a golf shirt. With his deeply lined face, Mediterranean complexion, curly salt and pepper hair, he could have passed for Tony Bennett's older, harder drinking brother. At least the image of Tony Bennett Jonathan remembered. "Come in, Detectives," Rossi said. "I hope you don't mind discussing this in my office."

"Not at all." As Rossi led them through the apartment, Jonathan looked around. There was something familiar about the décor, but he couldn't place from where.

He stopped at the open doorway to a small room that faced onto the park. "Make yourselves at home." Jonathan sat at the chair nearest to the desk, while Mari took a spot by the bookcases that lined one wall, examining their contents.

Rossi slid into a chair behind the desk, offering Jonathan an expansive smile. Rossi could afford to be magnanimous. Although a powerhouse in the underworld for most of his life, the statute of limitations on any crime the NYPD had looked at him for had long since expired.

Rossi leaned back in his chair. "Sorry to take so long to get back to you, Detectives, but my wife and I were at our country home in the Hamptons. I'm not really sure what I can do to help you. You're investigating Amanda Pierce's death, right? I never met the woman."

"You were involved with the Trinity project that Father Malone was a part of."

"We were both on the board of directors." Rossi looked from him to Mari and back. "That's what you want to know about? That happened twenty-five years ago."

"Ms. Pierce was investigating the events surrounding Father Malone's death when she was murdered."

"Why? Brendan's death was an accident. That's what the police said at the time. I'm sure that was in the report."

"There were also rumors that Malone might have been killed because he was cheating his business partners, namely you."

"Right. Let me tell you something about Brendan. We grew up in a tough neighborhood. We were tough. We had to be. East New York is no place for sissies. Brendan got straight in the can. I didn't. But so what? He was like a brother to me. I would have done anything for him."

"Including splitting whatever you were skimming off the project?"

"Hey, I wasn't skimming anything." He sighed. "But Brendan found out I was taking kickbacks from some of the unions working on the job. Force of habit." He shrugged. "But Brendan was worse than a reformed smoker. You know once they give it up they expect everybody else to do the same. He guilted me into building that playground that's in back of the place with my own money. If I'd wanted to kill him I would have done it then."

"Sounds like a real saint."

Rossi laughed. "Yeah, for the most part. Even when we were back in the neighborhood he wouldn't stand for anybody picking on somebody weaker than them. But here's something nobody really knew about him. He used to bet on the Catholic school teams, you know, basketball, football. I used to call them in to a . . . a . . . friend for him. And as for the priest's vow of sobriety, I think Brendan skipped class the day they taught that at the seminary. He could drink the best of them under the table. Always could."

These were qualities in a priest to be celebrated? Maybe not, but it did make Malone seem more human. His utter renunciation of the life he had known had always rung false to Jonathan's mind. And there was no mistaking the fondness in Rossi's voice as he talked about him. It would be hard to imagine many men who would kill a friend they regarded so highly, but Rossi wasn't like most men. "Where were you the night he died?"

"At the opera, with my wife. We'd gone out as a four-some. The soprano was bad and the couple were dead bores. I was thinking that my night couldn't get any worse until I got the call telling me that Brendan was gone."

"We'll need to check that out with your wife."

"Sure." He pressed a button on the phone on his desk and the sound of a dial tone filled the room. He punched another number, which connected to, Jonathan presumed, the house in the Hamptons. Soon a woman's voice came on. "Hi, honey. I've got those detectives here I told you about. What were we doing the night Brendan died?"

Without hesitation, Mrs. Rossi answered, "We were at the opera with some horrible couple. I don't even remember their names. Why?"

"It's nothing. I'll be home tonight." He discon-nected the call and sat back in his chair. "Will that do?"

Jonathan scanned the other man's face. Aside from his wife's convenient memory, there was some-thing disingenuous in his countenance, something he held back. Jonathan was sure of it, though he couldn't imagine what.

Mari took care of it for him. "You say you never met Amanda Pierce? She never came to you seeking in-formation about her uncle's past?"

"Yeah, but I blew her off. She didn't say what she wanted to talk to me about. I knew her reputa-tion. I was worried she wanted to write a book about me."

* * *

As they drove back to the city, Mari asked him, "Do you believe that nonsense about him thinking she wanted to write a book about him?"

"No, I don't." Not only wasn't Rossi the type of subject she preferred, but if he had so much loyalty for Malone, why wouldn't he have met with the man's niece, regardless of the situation? "Why don't you?"

"Did you notice the color scheme in Rossi's place is almost identical to the one in Pierce's place?"

That hadn't occurred to him, actually. He'd only noted that it seemed familiar somehow. "No."

"And the plants. They were all fakes, like in Pierce's place. Remember, she was an asthmatic? Many asthmatics can't tolerate plants."

"What are you suggesting? That Pierce and Rossi were sleeping together?" If that were true, there was no mention of any birth control method being prescribed by her doctor. Coupled with the m.e.'s speculation that she hadn't engaged in sex in a long while he'd assumed she wasn't seeing anybody at the time.

"Could be. I find it hard to believe that a fairly young, attractive woman like her wasn't getting any."

"Your mind is much more devious than mine."

"Don't you forget it."

Mari's cell phone rang. She answered the call, spoke for a few minutes, about what he couldn't determine, hearing only her end. When she disconnected the call, there was a big grin on her face.

"Well?"

"Some kid just phoned in a tip about where Pee Wee is. Seems he's holed up in Queens at some woman's house. They're going to check it out now."

Some kid? If it turned out to be Tyree, he was going to wring that child's neck.

* * *

By the time they got back to the stationhouse, Moretti was sitting at a desk vacated by one of the older officers when he retired. He was leaning forward, talking on the phone. His body language and hushed tone suggested the call had nothing to do with work. He looked up when they came in, but kept talking, a defiant expression on his face.

"This way, Stone," Mari said, waving him toward his own desk.

Until then he hadn't realized he'd stopped walking or that his hands had formed into fists at his sides. He knew better than to let an asshole like Moretti get to him. But knowing better and doing better weren't always the same thing.

He slung his jacket on the back of his chair and sat. He glanced over at Mari, who was skimming through one of the files. "What are you doing?"

"I'm looking through Pierce's medical file. Maybe there's something we missed."

"Like what?"

Mari looked up at him. "When are the two times a woman doesn't use birth control?"

"When she's trying to get pregnant. When she's already pregnant."

"Okay, then there are three."

"When she can't get pregnant?"

"Bingo. I wish I knew what the medical notation for that would be."

He thought of calling Dana to ask her. Actually, it wasn't the first time he'd thought of calling her, but since he had no idea what he'd say to her if he did, he didn't bother. "What's her doctor's number?" As Mari read off the numbers he punched them into the phone on his desk. The nurse who answered the call told him that the doctor was in with a patient and that she'd call back. Jonathan hung up, intending to pass on the message, but Mari was already on the phone.

"Thanks so much, Mr. Banks," she said into the phone. "Yes, we'll keep you informed of our progress. Have a safe trip." Mari hung up and grinned at him. "I'm right again. According to her brother she couldn't have kids. Her marriage broke up because of it."

"That doesn't prove she was sleeping with Rossi."

"No, but it takes us one step closer. That only means I have to dig deeper."

Despite his belief that she was barking up the wrong tree, he said, "Let me know what you find out."

"Will do." She picked up the phone and dialed another number.

The cell phone on his belt vibrated. He looked at the readout to see his brother Zack's number displayed. He couldn't remember the last time Zack had called him while he was on duty. He connected the call. "Hey, Zack."

"Hey, little brother. You got a minute for me today?"

"Sure, what's up?"

"Why don't I tell you when I see you?

"All right. Where do you want to meet?"

"I haven't eaten yet." Zack suggested a restaurant that was equidistant between their two precincts.

"See you there in about fifteen minutes."

When he got to the restaurant, Jonathan spotted his brother sitting at the bar. For the most part the restaurant was empty since it hadn't yet reached twelve o'clock. As he approached, Zack tipped his head back, exposing the beer bottle he was drinking from.

"Aren't you still on duty?" Jonathan asked as he came up beside him.

"I'm taking the afternoon off."

"Then isn't it a little early in the day?"

"Who are you? Carrie Nation? Kill the lecture and have a seat. If it makes you feel better I'm heading home after this. The only reason I stuck around is to talk to you."

Jonathan gritted his teeth. On the rare occasions when Zack got in a mood he could be a royal pain in the ass. Jonathan was tempted to walk out, except then he wouldn't know what was so important that Zack got him out here in the middle of the day. He slipped into the seat in front of him and rested his elbows on the bar. "So talk. What did I do to merit the displeasure of your company?"

"It's Joanna. I got picked as the designated talker-to. It seems she's not too pleased about you shacking up with her friend."

Jonathan let out an exasperated breath. He should have known. "We are not shacking up together. I have her with me for her own protection. You might try reminding Joanna that someone tried to kill Dana twice. I'm hoping to prevent the third time being a charm."

Zack took another swig from his bottle. "Whatever. I'm just the messenger. I think we can both agree that I'm the last person who should be giving anyone relationship advice considering I'm the owner of a freshly minted set of divorce papers."

He'd wondered what had brought on Zack's morose mood. He figured he'd just found out. "I'm sorry, Zack."

"Don't be. It was over a long time ago, except neither of us made it official."

"Why now?"

"You can't marry one guy when you're still married to another." Zack scrutinized his face. "You thought I started this?"

Jonathan shrugged.

"You know what, we made a mistake. That's all there was to it. A mistake. But I'm the bad guy because I was willing to admit that."

"Maybe if you hadn't stepped out on her no one would have blamed you."

Zack put down his beer and glared at him. "You ever try to get rid of a woman who thinks she's going to 'save you from yourself'? Reasoning with that kind of woman is futile. She needed to get knocked in the head a couple dozen times with the fact that I wasn't worth saving, not the way she meant it. Why do you think it took her so long to file the damn papers? Even after she left me she was still hoping I'd come to my senses."

And now, if she were waiting to marry another man, she must have given up. "Don't look at me to have anything to say about that. I'm not exactly the poster child for domesticity, either."

"What's your excuse, little brother? You can't make the same claim to faithlessness I can."

He shrugged again. "How about the most dreaded question in the English language? 'How was your day?' How the hell are you supposed to answer that? 'Oh, today I saw someone who'd had their face shot off or they dragged a floater out of the river after some fish got to her. You know they go for the eyes first?' So you say nothing or tell them some stupid joke you heard." Or in his case, he'd made love to her as if the world rather than just him was on fire.

He cleared his throat. "Then they claim you are

emotionally cut off when all you're really trying to do is protect them from hearing things they don't really want to know about in the first place."

Zack raised his bottle in salute. "Try working sex crimes and go home and have a decent sex life with a woman. Half the time I close my eyes and all I see is what some scumbag thought it was fun to do to another human being."

Jonathan sighed. "If I had any sense where she was concerned I would have left her alone from the beginning."

"But you are sleeping with her?"

"That's none of your damn business."

Zack grinned. "I'll put that down as a yes." Zack clapped him on the shoulder. "If you want my advice, if you make her happy or she makes you happy or you make yourself happy when you're with her—however it works out—hold on to her. The hell with what Joanna thinks." Zack picked up the five-dollar bill that rested on the bar top and put it in his pocket.

"Where do you think you're going?"

Zack stood. "Home."

"The I'll call you a cab."

"I'm not drunk."

"You think that makes the prospect of you getting on the road any less scary?"

"I'm fine." Zack winked at him. "Mood's over. Thanks for listening, little brother."

"When are you going to stop calling me that? I'm taller than you are."

Zack stood. "Yeah well, more power to ya." With a wave Zack walked out of the door.

The bartender who'd been absent while the two brothers talked came back. With a confused expression on his face, he looked from Jonathan to the empty beer bottle at the place next to him and back again. "That'll be three ninety-five."

The money on the bar hadn't been Zack's change, but his payment. Jonathan pulled his wallet out of his pocket. Yeah, Zack was back to his normal self again.

His cell phone went off again. He answered without looking at the display. "Stone."

"Guess who's in custody as we speak?"

"Who?" he said, in response to Mari's question.

"They brought Little Big Man in ten minutes ago."

So, the tip panned out. "I'll be right in. Nobody talks to him before I get there."

When he got back to the station, he was told the lieutenant wanted him in the observation room off one of the interrogation rooms. He hoped this didn't mean what he thought it meant. He entered the room to find Mari, the LT, and one of the assistant district attorneys facing the two-way glass viewing Moretti standing over Little Big Man, as Mari called him. Obviously they expected to get something out of him if they got the A.D.A. involved.

Son of a bitch. "I thought I said I didn't want anyone talking to him before I got here."

Mari said, "The Lone Ranger had other ideas."

"Has he gotten anything yet?"

"Other than a lot of lip? No. The only good thing is Pee Wee hasn't asked to see a lawyer yet."

He could tell Mari was enjoying this, seeing Moretti working himself up and getting nowhere. But since Moretti finally took it upon himself to do his job, Jonathan wouldn't interfere—unless Moretti put his hands on the other man, which he looked close to doing. Pee Wee looked the picture of calm, while

Moretti's face was puffed with anger and mottled with color.

As for Pee Wee, dressed in a polo shirt and khakis, he looked more ready to head out to a game of golf than to be in an interrogation room. His calm demeanor served as a counterpoint to Moretti's hostile attitude.

"Hey, Moretti, when'd you get the bump to homicide? Last I heard they had you chained to a desk down in the 'hood. I didn't know they let you out to mingle with the normal people."

Moretti moved in a way that blocked the view of Pee Wee. "We're not talking about me. We're talking about you. We already know you were the one who ordered the hit on Double U."

"If you think that, you don't know shit, man." Pee Wee leaned around Moretti to show his face to the mirror. "Hey, Stone, you out there?"

Jonathan pressed the intercom button to be heard in the other room. "I'm here."

"You want to get this *maricón* out of my face and I'll talk to you. Just you. Off the record."

Jonathan wondered what he'd done to earn any consideration from this man, but he'd use it to his advantage if he could. He glanced at Shea, who nodded. Jonathan hit the intercom again. "I'm coming in." He went to the door of the interrogation room and opened it without knocking.

Moretti stood where he was, glaring back at him belligerently. For a moment he thought the man would make a scene before leaving. After a moment Moretti stalked out. Jonathan guessed even he wasn't that much of a fool to pull that.

After he left Jonathan shut the door and took a seat

at the table opposite Pee Wee. "What do you want to say to me?"

"Let's just say some dude came to me with a proposition. He heard I might be ready to off Wesley and would I allow him to make it worth my while to take out someone else with him. That nurse. But he wanted it done fast. Next day."

"To which you said?"

Pee Wee spread his arms wide. "Look, I'm a businessman. If some punk don't want to work for me no more, he's free to go. And that woman ain't never did nothing to me. I told him to keep walking."

Pee Wee sat back, a smug expression on his face. "Now if some of my boys took the dude up on his offer, I don't know nothing about that. I didn't ask and they didn't tell, but it wouldn't take much to get that kid outside waiting for someone who wasn't showing up."

And when Dana came out they'd be ready. If it weren't for the shooter's poor aim, they'd both be dead right now. Anger welled in him, churning his stomach and making his temples throb. At least he knew some of the why of it, but not the who. "Who was this dude who came to see you?"

Pee Wee shrugged. "He didn't give me his name."

Which meant Pee Wee already knew who he was or what he was. "Go on."

"All I can say is, look to your own house, man." He gazed pointedly at the two-way mirror. "Look to your own house."

Seventeen

Jonathan walked to the lieutenant's office where the others waited for him. Mari stood off to one side of the door while Moretti stood behind one of the visitor's chairs. Shea stood behind his desk, knuckles resting on his blotter. The only one seated was the A.D.A., with both arms and legs crossed. Jonathan stopped a couple of feet inside Shea's door.

"Figueroa give you anything?" Shea asked.

"He claims someone approached him to include Dana in a drive-by with Evans as a target. This someone had heard Figueroa wanted to take Evans out. He says he turned this person down, but some of his crew might not have."

"Did he give any names? Who this person was? Which boys?"

"No."

Moretti said, "*I* could have gotten *that* out of him."

Obviously, Moretti was still fuming over being asked to leave. He was also implying that what Jonathan got out of him was either too little, made up, or both. Jonathan swiveled his head around to glare at Moretti. "But somehow you didn't."

The A.D.A. sat forward and put both feet on the floor. "Let's lower the testosterone level for a moment, boys. So that means we have nothing, right?"

"Pretty much. Except that if what Figueroa said is true there is someone out there who wants Dana Molloy dead and it has nothing to do with her knowledge of Wesley Evans. That was merely a coincidence that worked in the killer's favor."

"If he can be believed." Shea sat and rubbed his jowls. To the A.D.A., Shea said, "Don't worry, Figueroa's not going anywhere. When we picked him up he had a couple of ounces of cocaine on him."

"It ought to take his lawyer a whole hour and a half to kick him for that," the A.D.A. said.

Shea shrugged and picked up the phone receiver. As they filed out of the office, Jonathan could feel Mari's eyes on him. She grabbed his elbow, leading him away from their desks. "Let's get some coffee." Once inside the room she closed the door. "Okay, Stone, spill it. What didn't you say in there?"

Jonathan glanced around. Moretti had disappeared to God knew where. "Pee Wee said that if I wanted to know who approached him I should look to my own house. Then he glared at the mirror. I guess he figured you guys were still listening despite the arrangement. I wonder which of you he was looking at."

Without missing a beat, Mari said, "Moretti. Why didn't you say anything about it to Shea?"

"With him standing there? Besides, if Shea heard the accusation, he'd have to report it to IAB. As much as I can't stand the guy, I'm not willing to help fry another cop on the say-so of a drug dealer. For all I know, there's some bad blood between the two of them and the whole story was made up to make Moretti look bad."

Mari sighed. "What do you want to do about it?"

"I want to find out if there's any history between Moretti and Pee Wee and if there's any reason Pee Wee would want to jam him up."

"You mean you want me to find out."

"Uh, yeah. I don't think the animosity between us is any secret down in the 44. It would look suspicious if I tried to check him out."

"What are you going to do?"

"Work the case. Despite your Rossi angle, I'm still betting Pierce's death had something to do with what she found out about Malone."

"Then see you back here later."

Jonathan pushed off the counter. "If you find out anything significant, call me."

"You'll be the first to know."

The people on Father Masella's list had relocated to all five boroughs of the city, Westchester, and Long Island, and those were just the people they could find living in New York. Jonathan had already spoken to four of the families with whom Mari made appointments. All of them remembered Father Malone fondly. All of them had gotten similar calls from Amanda Pierce. None of them seemed to have told her anything that might incriminate anyone.

Jonathan pulled up in front of a one-family attached house on Tiemann Avenue. They called this section of the Bronx the Valley, a ten-block slope leading downhill from the peak at Gun Hill Road. He checked the address again and got out of the car. One Andrew Bickford lived at 3014 on this block.

He'd moved his family from the neighborhood a couple of years after the church burned.

Bickford met him at the door. "Come in, Detective. Like I said on the phone, I'll help any way I can."

"Thank you."

To the left of the house was a family room that faced out onto the street. Jonathan took the wing chair Bickford indicated, while the other man sat at the edge of the sofa. Jonathan had already heard all of the praise of Father Malone he needed for one day, so he figured he'd cut to the chase. "Did Amanda Pierce contact you?"

"Yes, I spoke to her about two weeks ago. Very interesting woman."

By the man's expression he deduced he hadn't been either impressed or terribly interested in her. "What did you tell her?"

"Mostly how much my family and I appreciated knowing her uncle. Now my wife, she died a few years ago, she was the real churchgoer. She'd take our girls to mass every Sunday. I'd show up for Easter and Christmas. But Father was always kind to us."

"Do you remember anything about the time right after Father Malone's death? Any of the speculation about whether his death was accidental?"

"That's what the police said. I remember there was a lot of talk about one of his partners being a shady character. Then there were a few people who blamed those boys he tried to help. They were a wild bunch."

It wasn't the first time Jonathan heard the latter opinion. When he thought about it, it made sense. If someone from Malone's past had killed Pierce, he needed to be young enough now to take on and subdue a strong young woman. "Was there anyone in particular who voiced that sentiment?"

"I'm sure there was." Bickford shrugged. "I wish I could remember more." Bickford's eyes widened as if a sudden idea occurred to him. "You know who you should talk to? There used to be this old guy who hung around the church. These days we'd call him a homeless person. Back then we called him a bum. But Father Malone used to let him sleep on a cot in the back of the church sometimes, if it was too cold or too hot."

Jonathan reached into his jacket for his notepad. "Did you tell Ms. Pierce about him?"

"As a matter of fact, I did."

"What's his name?"

"Theodore Randall. I don't know where he lives or if he's still alive."

Jonathan was glad Bickford continued to talk and wasn't really paying attention to him. Jonathan had heard that name before in connection with his case. Or rather he'd seen it, on the list of tenants at the building on Highland Avenue. As Bickford talked, he checked his notes. Randall was the old man they'd talked to in the first floor apartment at Highland Avenue, the man Dana referred to as Old Specs. Son of a bitch! Randall had to be who Pierce had visited in the building. Damn.

Jonathan stood, thanked Bickford for his time and left. Out at his car, he called Mari. "You won't believe this, but you remember the old guy we talked to when we recanvassed the building?"

"Yeah, ornery bugger."

"If I'm not mistaken, that's who Pierce went to see that day."

"Lovely. Didn't he tell us he hadn't seen her?"

"Not exactly." As Jonathan recalled, he'd asked what a woman like that would have been doing in the building, but he'd never said he hadn't seen her. "I'm going over there now."

"Listen, Stone," Mari said in a hushed tone. "I think we may have a problem. Your friend wasn't assigned the Evans case, he asked for it. He'd just caught a double homicide and asked to switch with the detective that had the Evans case. Everyone figured he was begging off the other case to get out of doing any real work. He was supposed to coordinate with anti-crime and narcotics but dropped the ball. They never heard from him."

In other words, he'd done everything he could to squelch the investigation. "How did you find all this out?"

"Seems he has plenty of other friends willing to badmouth him to whoever will listen."

Jonathan could believe that. "I'll call you after I speak with Randall."

"You think this is it, don't you?"

For Dana's sake, he hoped so. "Yeah."

"Happy hunting," Mari said before she hung up.

It would be if Randall told him what he wanted to hear.

Miraculously, Jonathan found a parking space across the street from the building on Highland Avenue. As he got out of the car he noted the telltale pair of glasses at Old Specs's window. He was home.

He went into the building and knocked on the door. He got no answer, but then he hadn't expected one. If Randall wanted to talk, he'd have done so the first time. Jonathan knocked again, louder this time. "Mr. Randall, it's Detective Stone from the NYPD. I know you're home."

Abruptly, the door was pulled open. Randall sat in his chair, a belligerent expression on his face. "Whatchu want now? Can't you people leave an old man alone?"

"May I come in? I need to speak with you."

Randall shook his head. "Anything you want to say to me you can say right there."

Jonathan gritted his teeth, but if that's how the old man wanted it. "Mr. Randall, Amanda Pierce visited someone in this building the day she was killed. That person was you."

"I told you, that gal had no business to be in here. What would she want with me? Lessons on getting old and dying? You can get those anywhere."

It was in the man's eyes that he was lying, or rather equivocating. He never said he hadn't seen Pierce; just that she had no need to be there. "She came to see you about her uncle, Father Malone. You remember him from St. Jude's, don't you?"

"I don't remember much from them days. I was a drinking man then." Randall looked down at his lap, a forlorn expression on his face. "I ain't proud of it, but that's the way it was. Whatever memories I had I drunk away."

"From what I hear," Jonathan said in a quiet voice, "Father Malone was good to you. If someone hurt him, don't you want to see this person brought to justice?"

Randall nodded, giving Jonathan the hope he intended to tell what he knew. But when the old man looked up the hostility had returned to his expression. "Don't think I don't know what you're doing, how you cops do. You're trying to trick an old man into saying something that isn't true. I don't know no Amanda Pierce. Never seen her. Now don't come

here no more." Randall wheeled himself back into
the apartment and shut the door.

Dana was sitting on the sofa attempting to read one
of the books on Jonathan's shelf when she heard his
key turn in the lock. She dropped the book to the
sofa and stood. The first thing she noticed about him
was that he looked tired, or maybe disheartened, she
wasn't sure which. Or maybe he was still preoccupied
with their lovemaking last night, but she hoped not.

She bit her lip, waiting for him to get to her. When
he got close enough, she took a step toward him and
wrapped her arms around his neck. She sighed as his
arms closed around her. She buried her nose against
his neck, inhaling the remnants of his cologne, the
aroma of a hard day's work and his own natural
scent. "Hi, stranger," she said. "How did it go today?"

He pulled away from her, enough so that she
could see his face. "You want the good news or the
bad news?"

"There's good news?"

His hand scrubbed up and down her back. "Sort of."

She could live with that. "How about you tell me
after dinner? It's almost ready."

"Sounds like a plan."

"Are you going to take a shower?"

One corner of his mouth lifted in a grin. "Are
you saying I need one?"

She tilted her head to one side considering him.
"No, but that seems to be your habit when you get
home."

"It is. I won't be long." He swatted her bottom before
moving off.

Dana looked after him as he walked away. Maybe he

was merely tired, as she'd first guessed, since he didn't seem to be in a bad mood. He'd even joked with her a little. That had to mean something. Honestly, she'd been hoping he'd be able to tell her that he figured out who murdered Amanda Pierce so she could go home, or at least get out of this apartment. She missed her brother and worried about him. He wouldn't return any of her calls, though Linda Kenner reported that he was fine. Damn that boy. He might be bigger than she was, but not so big she wasn't tempted to take a two by four to him the moment she saw him.

She needed her life back. She needed her work back. Even though she'd thought herself burnt out and frustrated only a few days ago, her job was important to her. The woman working in Joanna's place had assured her that At-Home Healthcare wanted her to take as much time off as she needed under the circumstances, but she didn't want any more time. At least not cooped up somewhere with no alternatives.

She went to the kitchen and checked the rice. It was done, as well as the chicken she'd fried and the biscuits she'd made from a mix she'd found in one of the cupboards. They hadn't finished the salad she made last night, so that would serve as their vegetable.

As she worked, she listened for the sound of the shower cutting off. Jonathan told her he had good news and bad. She didn't know what either of those might be, but with a sinking certainty, she doubted he was about to tell her what she really wanted to hear— that it was over and her life was once again her own.

Jonathan left the bathroom to head for the dining room. Dana was standing by the table with her back to him. He came up behind her and wrapped his arms around her, nuzzling his nose against her neck. "Everything looks good."

"Then sit down."

He could feel the tension in her body and in the way she spoke those three sharp words. He couldn't blame her. She must be more anxious than he for this case to be over. He did as she asked, taking his usual spot at the table. They filled their plates. He'd barely gotten a forkful into his mouth before she asked, "What's the good news?"

"I think I've found who Amanda Pierce was visiting in the building. You know him as Old Specs."

Dana's mouth dropped open. "You're kidding me. I spoke to him. He didn't tell me anything about seeing Amanda Pierce."

"Did you ask him?"

"Well, no. I only asked him about what he'd seen the morning I got shot. It didn't occur to me to ask him about Pierce. Why would she have been talking to him anyway?"

"Apparently, twenty-five years ago, he was living on the streets around the church. Father Malone took pity on him and let him sleep in the back of the church sometimes. The man I spoke to thinks he might have seen something the night the priest was killed that he told to Pierce."

"And she got killed for it? How would anyone know so quickly what she'd found out?"

Jonathan shrugged. "Maybe it wasn't the first time she'd visited him? For all we know, he could have set the fire and set her up to be killed by someone else. I don't know, but I was loath to drag an eighty-year-old cripple into the stationhouse to find out. I figured

I'd sic my partner on him tomorrow. Maybe a female will have better luck."

Dana shook her head. "He won't talk to her. He doesn't like cops, either. His son was shot and killed by the police. He told me that when you came around asking about Amanda Pierce, he lied, saying he wouldn't tell the police anything. He took a certain amount of pleasure in telling me that."

"What do you suggest I do?"

"Let me talk to him."

His jaw tightened. "Absolutely not."

"Look, Jon, he's not going to talk to you, but he's already spoken to me. You already told me that nobody in the neighborhood was out to get me. What harm could it do? If anyone suspected he knew anything he'd be dead by now."

She did have a point, but he wasn't willing to concede it yet. He didn't want her involved any more than she already was.

"What if he's the one who set the fire and is trying to cover it up? What do you expect he'll tell you then?"

"Probably nothing, but it's worth a shot."

Maybe, but he wasn't willing to chance it. Apparently she thought the old man was harmless, but he didn't. Randall's being in a wheelchair didn't make it impossible for him to wield a knife or fire a gun if the need arose. Given the level of animosity he'd seen in Randall both times, he didn't put it past the man to become violent if provoked. "No, it's not."

"Why don't you ask your partner what she thinks of my idea?"

He didn't have to. He knew Mari would want to go for it. Damn, just what he'd need—the two of them aligned against him. But it would take more than he and Mari to make this work. He'd have to bring it to

Shea, who'd probably do an Irish jig at the prospect of getting to the bottom of the case. Maybe Mari was right about him letting his emotions get in the way of his work, but he'd rather find some other way to get Randall to talk. Damn.

"If you are sure you want to do this, I would need to get it okayed. We would need you to wear a wire so that we can hear what he says."

"I know you don't want me to do this Jonathan, but I have to know. If Old Specs can tell me, then I have to try. I can't spend the rest of my life hiding."

"I'll let you know," was all he was willing to concede at the moment. But he knew he could probably get everything in place by late tomorrow morning if he wanted to. That was the question of the hour for which he didn't yet have the answer, because as much as he wanted to find Pierce's killer, he wanted Dana safe more. In the end, though, the only way to really protect her was to find out the truth.

By ten o'clock the next morning, the arrangements had been made for Dana to speak to Randall. At the stationhouse she'd been wired for sound with a small microphone taped between her breasts. Presently, they sat in an unmarked police van around the corner from the building on Highland Avenue. Two officers would accompany Dana into the building while he and Mari stayed in the van with the techs listening to the conversation. He would give the go ahead if anyone needed to rush the apartment if Dana was in trouble.

He gazed over at Dana, who had a look of determination on her face. Even though it was clear to him, he asked her, "Are you sure you want to do this?"

"You know that I am."

He held her gaze for a long moment, wishing he could think of something to change her mind, but honestly, he admired her courage.

Mari coughed, trying to draw their attention. "Let's get this show on the road before we become a neighborhood curiosity." She pushed open the van's back door and got out. Dana followed her.

Mari said, "Remember, keep your hands away from your chest, or you'll distort the transmission. Try not to cough or sneeze. And don't sweat."

"I know."

"Keep him talking as much as you can, but try to focus on Father Malone."

Dana nodded. "I understand." Then she looked at him, the expression in her eyes pleading with him to understand why she felt she had to do this. He did understand, but that didn't mean he had to like it. More than what might happen here worried him, though. She'd already proven that she was willing to risk her life to find out what happened by coming here the first time. She'd promised him she'd stay out of it, and until now, she'd kept her word. What else would she be willing to do to catch this killer?

The two officers who were to accompany her into the building joined them and she walked off without saying another word to him.

Mari climbed back into the van, sat and pulled the door closed. "You sure know how to pick 'em, Stone" Mari said, but there was admiration, not censure, in her voice.

"Thanks," he said.

* * *

Flanked by the two officers, Dana entered through the side door used by building maintenance to empty the trash. They had no idea how much Old Specs, or Theodore Randall as she had come to know him, could see from his front view and they didn't want to take any chances he'd know she was coming before she got there.

As they walked through the building, the palm of her hand clutching her nurse's bag grew clammy. She was supposed to tell Teddy that she was visiting her patients in the building and had decided to check on him. If he weren't involved in Pierce's death, it was a harmless ruse. If he were, no lie on earth would keep him from knowing her true purpose there.

She stopped in front of Teddy's door while the two officers hid from view. Having Teddy spot them when he came to the door would defeat their purpose. The moment she got inside, they would take up positions by the door where they would be able to come to her aid quickly if they needed to.

She took a deep breath and knocked on the door. A few seconds later, she heard Teddy's, "Who is it?"

She took another deep breath. "It's me, Teddy. Dana Molloy from At-Home Healthcare."

The door was pulled open. Teddy sat in his chair, a grin on his face. "What brings a pretty thing like you to my door?"

Good God, the old geezer was flirting with her. "I was in the building and thought I'd check on you. Find out how you were doing since the other day."

"Come in, child, if you've got a minute. I sure could use some company."

"Thanks, I will."

Teddy rolled back to let her enter. "Go on in the living room. You know where to sit."

She did as he asked, resisting the urge to look behind her to see if the officers were moving in. She knew they wouldn't do that until the door closed, but the temptation to check assailed her anyway.

She sat, set her bag on the floor and waited for Teddy to wheel himself into position across from her. The first thing he did was to check the view outside his window. "Can I get you something to drink?" he asked. "I've got some iced tea."

"That would be fine."

With a pleased smile, he rolled off toward the kitchen. He was saying something to her that she could barely make out about the weather, his relief that the heat spell had finally broken. She tuned him out and took that opportunity to slide her hand through the slats of the Venetian blinds. She waved to the unmarked car parked across the street, one of the signs that everything was okay that she could use if she got the opportunity.

She snatched her hand back instants before Teddy returned with two glasses of tea resting on a tray on his lap. He handed one to her. "Thanks," she said, took the smallest sip possible and set it on the table beside her. The drink held no chemical aftertaste, but she wasn't taking any chances that he might try to poison her.

Teddy took a big gulp from his glass. He eyed her with a look, part skepticism, part concern. "Aren't you back to work a little soon? They make you come in?"

"Something like that. My brother is starting college in the fall. I need the money."

"How old is he?"

"Seventeen."

Teddy nodded. "The same age my boy was when they gunned him down. I wish I could have gotten him interested in going to school instead of running the streets. Maybe he'd be alive today."

An idea seized her. Although Teddy looked to be in his seventies, drinking, the kind he must have done, aged a person. Jonathan pulled his records this morning and found out he was only sixty-seven. Twenty-five years ago, he would have been forty-two, young enough to have a son only seventeen. "Is that when you started drinking? After he died?"

His chest puffed up and he looked back at her with indignation flashing in his eyes. "Who told you that?"

"Teddy, I'm a nurse. I know these things, and I understand."

All the air seemed to deflate out of him. "Yeah, that's when it happened. I couldn't take losing my boy the way I did. Not getting any justice for his murder. They called the shooting justified, even though he had no gun, no weapon of any kind."

She could see how such a thing might push a man over the edge. Though she felt tempted to leave him alone with what was still a palpable grief, she remembered the edict to keep him talking. "What happened?"

"I lost myself in the bottle, that's what. I left my family—my wife and my daughter. I wasn't any good to them anymore the way I was. I found myself living on the street near some old church. The Father there used to let me sleep in this little room at the back of the church so I didn't freeze myself to death in the winters. He was good to me in many ways, even after he died."

"What do you mean?"

"There was a fire at that church. One of the newspapers ran a picture of the bystanders to that fire. I was one of them. That's how my daughter found me. She fixed me up, took care of me. Got me back working and got me this place."

Thinking that she might also offer some insight into what happened back then, she asked, "Where is your daughter now?"

"She died in the car accident that took my legs."

For a moment, Dana said nothing. She could understand this man's rage that his life had offered him little but sorrow. Again, she was tempted to leave him to it, but she wasn't going to walk out without getting what she came for.

"I think I've heard about that fire," Dana said. "That priest Father Malone was killed."

Teddy nodded. "He was a good man. He didn't deserve to die like that."

"How did the fire start?"

Teddy shook his head. "I don't know," Teddy said, but she didn't believe him.

"You don't know or you don't remember?"

"I remember fine. I remember those old buildings catching fire and burning and standing outside watching the whole place turn to ashes and charred wood." Tears stood in his eyes, waiting to fall. He wiped his sleeve across his nose and mouth. "I remember."

Yet she knew that he held something back from her, maybe his own involvement, maybe something else. She didn't know what. She tried the only tactic that seemed viable to her then. "Did you set the fire, Teddy? Maybe you fell asleep with a bottle? You were smoking?"

He shook his head violently. "No. I didn't have nothing to do with that." He turned to the window and looked out. When he turned back, there was accusation in his eyes. "I should have known it. They sent you in here, didn't they? Damn car parked outside my house all day. I should have known they were up to no good."

Dana sighed. She'd come so close and blown it. She tried to think of some way to salvage the situation. Maybe honesty was her only option. "Yes, they sent me in here. They think you know why someone would want to murder Amanda Pierce, something you told her."

"So what if I did. She's dead now. Ain't nothing I can say going to bring her back."

"No, but you can help the police find her killer."

"I don't give one damn about the police."

His hands worried something at his waist. Something metal flashed at her in the rays of sunlight filtering through the blinds. For a moment, she feared it was a gun until she caught sight of what it was. The cross at the end of a strand of black rosary beads. Thanks to Tim, Catholic guilt was something she understood.

"Then help me. As long as her murderer is out there, I'm in danger. I was the last person to see her alive and someone wants to kill me for that. How much longer do you have on this earth, Mr. Randall? Can you go to your maker with another death on your conscience?" She paused to let her words sink in. "Tell me what you saw that night."

His shoulders slumped and shook. "I saw them that night, those three boys. Three of the ones Father tried to help. They come strutting up to the rectory in the dead of night. I was across the street, sitting on a bus stop bench they used to have back then. I knew they were up to no good, but Father let them in anyway. A few minutes later, they came tearing out of there like the devil himself was after them. The next thing I knew I smelled smoke. Those old buildings went up like two logs on a fire."

"Why didn't you tell anyone what you saw?"

Tears streamed down Teddy's face. "I was drunk, you understand. Too drunk to get up and help him. Too drunk for anyone to believe me. I didn't tell the cops but I told one of the firemen. That's when one of those photographers got my picture. He told me to sober up and get out of his way. When the cops came by, I told them I made it up."

"Who were those boys? Where are they now?"

"I don't know. Two of them moved out of the neighborhood right away, Randy Parker and Miguel Colon. The other moved, too, but I know where you can find him. He became a cop. His name is Thomas Moretti."

Eighteen

Jonathan shared a quick look with Mari, hearing Randall's last words. "I'm getting her out of there. Get on the phone to Shea and find out where Moretti is." He launched himself out of the back of the van and jogged up to the building. The driver's side door of the unmarked car opened, but he waved its occupant back. Dana wasn't in any danger. At least not from Randall.

He walked up to the door, nodding to the two officers in a way that signaled everything was all right. He knocked on the door. "Mr. Randall, open up. It's Detective Stone."

But it was Dana that answered a few moments later. Her eyes were rimmed in red and her lower lip trembled. "Are you all right?"

She nodded, but it was clear that she wasn't. Both Randall's tale of woe and the discovery that Moretti was involved in this mess must have gotten to her. He pulled her into his arms and held her, absorbing the tiny tremors that racked her body.

She laid her cheek against his chest. "My God, Jon. What did I fall into?"

He felt the stares of the two officers on him. He nodded toward the back of the apartment. The two men brushed past him to see to Randall.

"I don't know, baby," he said. But he damn sure intended to find out. He hadn't told her this, and didn't intend to, but Mari had found out one more pertinent bit of information regarding Moretti— he was supposed to have been on duty the morning Pierce disappeared but he came in late, at least an hour after Dana saw her getting into that car. He'd disappeared later in the day, too, and no one had been able to reach him.

He squeezed her waist. "Let's get out of here." She nodded and allowed him to lead her from the building with an arm around her waist.

Once they were back in the van, she asked, "What happens now?"

"We get you to somewhere safe and we find Moretti." He glanced at Mari who shook her head. Shea didn't know where he was either. *Damn.* That didn't completely surprise Jonathan, but it complicated things. He wasn't looking forward to hunting down another cop, if that's what it came to, not even Moretti.

"What about Teddy?"

"We'll be watching him, too." Although Moretti didn't seem interested in him before, but that might have changed.

"He probably shouldn't be left alone."

"You're probably right." After his revelations today, finding himself in police custody if only for his own protection wouldn't sit well with Randall.

The car that had been sitting in front of Randall's place pulled around the corner and stopped across from them. "Come on," he said to Dana. He helped her out of the van and into the car. He exchanged a look with the driver, who nodded. Everything was in place. Jonathan nodded back. "Let's go."

Dana stared out the window as the car traveled north on the Bruckner, headed toward the New England Thruway. She had no idea where they were headed and didn't really care. With all the unspoken words and silent communication passing between the men in the car, she understood that they were taking her somewhere else to do some more hiding. For the first time she didn't mind. It was one thing when she thought whoever was after her was some unknown assailant with no luck and no means of finding her. It was another to know that this man was a cop; someone trained to kill if he needed to.

She felt Jonathan's fingers squeeze hers. She looked up at him, trying to force a benign expression on her face. He didn't need to see her fear, not just for herself, but for him. Or at least, he didn't need a visual reminder of it, there plain on her face.

He squeezed her hand again, offering her an encouraging smile. "It will be all right, sweetheart," he whispered.

She nodded, noting the irony of their situation— each of them putting on a brave face for the other. She wondered if inside, he was as terrified as she was.

After a while they pulled into the parking lot of a squat brick building and parked at the end of it, facing the last door in the complex. She recognized this place. She'd seen it countless times driving on the highway. If anyone had told her she'd spend a moment inside this place, she'd have told them they were nuts.

The driver cut the engine and he and the front passenger got out. They went up to the door, painted an electric shade of blue, and went inside, leaving the door open.

She turned to Jonathan. "This is the safe place you're going to put me? Whose idea was this?"

"Mine. The only way to get in here is through the window, through the bottleneck we just went through to get into the parking lot and through that door. There will be two plainclothes officers outside at all times."

One of the officers came back to the open door and nodded. Dana guessed that meant everything was all right. Jonathan got out of the car and came around to her side to open the door. She took the hand he extended toward her and got out. Once inside the room, she looked around. Definitely not the Ritz Carlton. Not even the Holiday Inn.

The two other officers left the room, closing the door behind them. She wondered what had prompted that. Probably some more silent cop communication she wasn't privy to.

She turned her head to look at Jonathan who stood beside her. "Is this where you usually put up folks you're trying to protect?"

He shook his head. "No."

So, it was chosen because it was a place Moretti wouldn't instantly look for her. "That's a relief. I wouldn't want to have my tax dollars going to pay for places like this."

"They're not. You pay taxes in Mount Vernon. Besides, what do you have against this place?" He looked around, appearing to take in the furnishings, which consisted only of a solitary chair, a bed, a dresser and a single night table beside the bed. "It's charming."

Hands on hips she said, "For one thing, it's a sex motel. You know, the type folks rent by the hour to cheat on their spouses. I'm surprised there's not a mirror on the ceiling."

"There was. I had them take it down."

Despite herself, she laughed. She knew what he was trying to do: leaven her anxiety with a little humor. She couldn't fault him completely, since it was working. "You're not staying with me, are you?"

"No. As I said, there will be two officers outside at all times. I'll be back as soon as I can. I'll bring your stuff from my apartment when I come back. Is there anything else you want me to bring you?"

"How about a bottle of Lysol and a can of Raid?"

"I'll see what I can do." He took her hand and pulled her closer. "Listen, seriously. Don't open that door for anyone who doesn't show you a badge through the peephole and slip his I.D. under the door."

She nodded. She'd already been introduced to the two officers outside and remembered their names.

"Put the chain on the door and the chair underneath the doorknob after I'm gone. Stay away from the window."

"I know, Jon." She sighed. He'd given her the same instructions before he'd left her at his apartment that first day. But this time she sensed in him a real reluctance to go. She didn't want him to leave either, but she knew her best chance of survival was for someone to find Moretti and lock him up before he found her. "If you have to go, go. I'll be all right."

He pressed his lips to hers briefly. "I'll be back as soon as I can."

Dana watched him walk from the room, purposefulness in his stride. With any luck, the next time she saw him, he'd still be whole and safe and this whole business would be behind them. But she wasn't holding her breath. The man out there had less to lose than he had before and he obviously had it in for Jonathan. How far would Moretti go to save himself and exact retribution? That's the question that terrified her the most.

The meeting in Shea's office was brief and to the point. "Where do we stand with this Moretti thing?" Shea asked. "Any proof, other than the word of an old rummy that he knew the priest?"

Jonathan said, "None. He didn't consider Pee Wee's conjecture proof. Did he show up this morning?"

"He came in after you left and disappeared."

Probably long enough to find out that they were talking to Randall that morning. He had to figure they'd get something out of the old man one way or another. At the very least, he'd have to answer for not mentioning he knew Malone. At worst, he was the one responsible for Pierce's death. For the fact that Moretti was still out operating without closer scrutiny, Jonathan blamed himself. If he'd told Shea about Pee Wee's intimation that a cop was involved, they would have played it differently, made sure no one outside the operation knew what was going on. Actually, Jonathan had suggested that, but Shea had arranged things the way he wanted them anyway. Now, Moretti was on the loose God only knew where. Jonathan only hoped the folks at IAB had decided to follow him that day. Damn!

Martinez poked his head in the door. "The unit

that went out to Moretti's place says it looks like he cleared out."

"Damnit to hell," Shea said.

Jonathan ground his teeth together. If Moretti wanted to implicate himself as more than an innocent party in this he'd done a damn good job.

"We'll take it from here, then, folks." Jonathan's gaze slid to the man who'd spoken, a man he recognized as being fairly high up in the rat squad food chain, but not the top. "If Moretti needs to be found, we'll find him."

If? Jonathan wanted to say. It should be obvious to everyone in this room that Moretti had every intention of disappearing into the wind. But he held his tongue and bided his time. One thing he'd learned over the years was that if you didn't ask permission to do something no one could refuse you. There might be hell to pay later, but more often than not it was worth it.

"If there's anything we need from you, we'll let you know," the suit said, before walking from the room with an air of his own importance.

After he was gone, Shea turned to Martinez, who still stood in the doorway. "You and Jerry get busy working on those other names. For all we know Moretti isn't in this alone. I'm sure the rest of you have something to do."

Shea glanced directly at him when he said that. Sure, he had plenty to do, but it surprised him that Shea seemed to be giving him the okay to do it.

As they left the office, Mari whispered. "Am I mistaken, or did the boss just grow a set of balls in there?"

She didn't need an answer to that, so he didn't give her one. "Let's get out of here."

* * *

Dana had never been one to pace the floor much, but these last couple of weeks had changed that. She'd turned on the TV set, just to have some noise in the room that didn't come from the boisterous couple copulating next door. Still she couldn't seem to sit in one place for long without getting up and worrying the carpet. Thank God she'd had sense enough that morning to wear her sneakers instead of a pair of sandals. That way her feet were protected from whatever critters might be hiding in that rug.

A sudden knock on the door made her jump and her heartbeat triple. "Ms. Molloy. It's Officer Cohen."

"Y-yes," she called back in as calm a voice as she could muster.

"Are you hungry? We've got some cheeseburgers."

Something as mundane as putting some food in her stomach hadn't occurred to her. She wondered where they'd magicked up this food from since she hadn't heard the car either leave or come back. But she understood the necessity of keeping her belly full and her wits about her.

"Okay. Show me your badge at the peephole and your ID under the door."

She thought she detected a note of humor in the officer's voice as he said, "Just a moment, ma'am."

She moved the chair out of the way so that she could look through the peephole. She decided there must be some defect in the glass, since she couldn't make out any of the details on the badge Cohen showed her, but when he removed it, she saw the car out front clearly.

She looked downward to see if he'd slipped his identification under the door. As she watched, it slid under easily. There must have been a good inch and a half of space between the floor and the bottom of the door. She picked up the ID and scanned it. He'd been the one driving.

She opened the door and exchanged the ID for a white paper bag.

"How are you holding up?" Cohen asked.

"Pretty well, I guess." She wasn't about to confide in this man that she was half worried out of her mind, a tale he might feel compelled to carry back to Jonathan if asked.

"Don't forget to lock up."

"I won't."

He smiled encouragingly. "It won't be long now."

Another brave face, but no real news. If there were anything good to report, he was keeping it to himself. She shut the door, put the food on the bed then returned to lock up. Though the cheeseburger and fries smelled heavenly, she couldn't bring herself to eat one bite.

Regardless of age, race or ethnicity, the most likely place for a man in trouble to take refuge was with his mama. Freddie Jackson had reminded Jonathan of that. But since Moretti's mother had been dead for more than ten years, they tried his girlfriend's apartment off Webster Avenue instead.

A unit in the area had been sent to watch the place until he and Mari got there. The two officers followed them inside as they went to an apartment on the third floor. They took up positions on the opposite sides of the door, weapons drawn, not taking any chances that Moretti might be inside and willing to fire on whoever was on the other side of the flimsy door.

Jonathan rapped on the door. "New York police detectives." He waited a moment. No shotgun blasts or blasts of any kind followed. Instead, the door was opened partway by a pretty, petite black woman.

She gazed back at him. "Is Tommy with you?"

Both her softly spoken question and her appearance surprised him. He wouldn't have though Moretti the type to venture over the color line, but stranger things had happened. What struck him most was the fear he saw in her eyes, not of him, but maybe of the situation. "He's not here with you?"

She shook her head. "He left this morning."

"Can we come in?"

She stepped back, opening the door wide enough for him to enter. The place was small. From the threshold he could see the living room and kitchen. No sign of Moretti. To the left was a hall that probably led to the bathroom and bedroom. "Do you mind if we look around?"

She gestured toward the back of the apartment. "Go ahead, but he's not here."

A quick sweep of the other rooms proved her right. "Do you know where he is?"

"He told me he was going to work."

"But you didn't believe him?"

She pressed her lips together and shook her head. "The last couple of weeks, he's been here a lot, but he isn't sleeping. He's not eating. This morning he gave me this." She reached into her pocket and pulled out a small key for a locker or safe deposit box. "I don't know what it fits. He told me I'd know when I needed to."

Jonathan took the key she extended toward him and put it in his pocket. How naïve could this woman be? She appeared to be in her early thirties, old enough to know that simply being Moretti's brother cop didn't mean he wished the man well. "Is there anything else you can tell us? Anywhere he might go?"

"Sometimes we'd go to the bar around the corner, but I doubt he's there." She paused, placing her hand on his sleeve. "I don't know what he's done, but I don't want him hurt. Promise me you won't hurt him."

He scanned her face, this time finding both supplication and a kind of feminine determination he hadn't expected. Something told him she knew exactly what kind of man she was involved with, and moreover exactly who he, Jonathan, was and how he fit into the scheme of things. If that were true, that made her shrewd, not gullible, as he was probably one of the few cops on the case who wouldn't want Moretti taking the easy way out of this by either eating his gun or forcing some other cop to do it for him. If Moretti were guilty of more than concealing information, Jonathan wanted Moretti caught, tried, convicted and sentenced—somewhere the population would really object to having a cop in their midst.

"I'll see what I can do," Jonathan said. But really, the outcome of this was up to Moretti.

Thomas Moretti sat behind the steering wheel of his car parked in a cul de sac on a residential street on the edge of Brooklyn. The night was dark and moonless with the only illumination coming from the street lamps and the lingering lights in a few of the houses. It was over for him. He knew that. He'd known it before Amanda Pierce came sniffing around looking for answers that were better left uncovered. He'd known it was coming from the first day he took money to look the other way when he should have been doing his job. Other people might have the kind of luck that allowed them to get away with almost anything. He never had.

Once upon a time, he'd been a good cop, ambitious, proud to be on the force. Proud to have made something of himself in the wake of his youth and in Father Malone's memory. He'd been partnered with a veteran cop who taught him everything about surviving on the streets—except what to do when your next partner puts a few hundred dollars in your hand and tells you it's your cut to keep your mouth shut about the drug dealer he tricked you into helping him roust. He'd taken the money, which he kept for years in a tin can in his closet, but he'd immediately asked to be assigned another partner. It hadn't occurred to him that a dirty cop was the worst type of enemy to have. His request coupled with a lack of explanation proved almost as damning as if he'd given one. He'd gotten his reassignment, but he'd also gained an enemy for life, an enemy that had nonetheless managed to ascend higher and faster in the police hierarchy. An enemy that made it plain that anything that he could do to thwart Moretti's career would be done.

After a while, it had occurred to him to question what he was busting his hump for when he was getting himself nowhere, when one vindictive son-of-a-bitch took it as his personal mission to make him suffer. Then one day, he'd found himself rousting some scum—taking his money and drugs off him and offering his reluctant partner a share of the take. It had come full circle.

It was time to salvage what he could, not for himself, but for the others. They were brothers, the only kinship that had ever mattered to him. His mother had washed away her disappointment in a bottle of booze. She'd barely been coherent enough to notice when her truck driver husband bothered to come home—quarrelsome and eager to take out his anger at his lot in life on the nearest person handy, usually with his fists.

Thinking back on it, he couldn't remember how the three of them had grown to be friends, except that like sought out like. None of them had a home life worth a damn. Each of them was searching, needy. He understood those kids who'd join a gang simply to have someone who offered the pretense of giving a damn about them. For a while they had been a gang, too, a gang of three, running the streets and taking what they wanted.

That was, until Father got hold of them. Something in the priest reached each of them, probably because he'd lived the life he wanted them to abandon. And for a while, each of them had—until they'd heard the rumors about Father Malone. How could a man who demanded that they walk the narrow and straight path be guilty himself of stealing from those who needed him? More than greed, they'd felt betrayal and a profound sense of disappointment in the one man they trusted.

He couldn't speak for the others, but he'd gone to the church that night hoping to be proven wrong. But Father's denials had only angered Mouse. The more he and Randy tried to calm him, the more upset he became. He'd struck Father Malone who had gone down, hitting his head on the edge of his desk. The candle burning, the symbol of Christ's presence in mass and in the Father's office, was dislodged from its holder and rolled across the floor to settle underneath the window. The sheer curtains went up in an instant. Like any frightened, stupid boys, they'd run.

But later that night, in the heat of the fire, they'd made their pact. For twenty-five years they'd kept it and their secret intact.

But he'd known. Someday, it would come back to them. He knew that Father wouldn't approve of what he was about to do, even if he was sacrificing himself to save the others. But he was determined that it would die with him. It seemed fitting that he, the least of them should take the fall. There would be no more questions, no investigation, no doubt. One way or another he'd see to that.

He took his weapon out of its holster, whispered, "God forgive me," aimed the gun and fired.

Nineteen

Jonathan pulled into the spot beside the unmarked car outside the motel and cut the engine. It was ten o'clock and he still had no idea where Moretti was or what he was up to. He only thanked God that he hadn't come here, that Dana was alive and safe. Part of him couldn't care less if they never found Moretti if it meant that would continue to be true.

He'd known almost from the beginning that he was falling for her. Why else would he have jeopardized his career and his investigation to keep her with him? Why else was it that concern for her safety fueled his determination to solve the case, much more than the vindication of the victim? Even Mari, who'd sworn after the last time she'd brought up the subject not to say anything else, noticed.

They'd stopped about an hour and a half ago to finally eat some dinner. They'd chosen to go to a restaurant rather than eat on the go as they often did, partly because they wanted to unwind and partly to go over all they hadn't accomplished in a day.

Once the waitress brought their orders Jonathan relaxed against the leather cushion of their booth.

He rubbed his eyes with the thumb and forefinger of his right hand. Weariness, both physical and emotional, pulled at him. But he sensed the opposite in Mari, an excited energy that the long day hadn't managed to sap from her.

"By the way," she said, "whatever happened with Nichols the porno king?"

In the wake of everything else, Jonathan had forgotten all about him. "Turns out his receptionist was only sixteen. He claims he didn't know she was underage, but she was the only employee he was paying off the books."

"So there would be no record he knew her age. Clever."

"Not so much. When they came to arrest him on statutory rape charges they found the two of them in the act in his office. So much for trying to salvage himself by claiming he hadn't touched her."

Mari shook her head. "Never underestimate the stupidity of the male mind once a little booty is involved." She sipped from the glass of wine she'd ordered.

So they were back to their personal battle of the sexes. "You women are no Einsteins when it comes to men either."

She made a disgusted face. "Tell me about it. Could you believe Moretti's squeeze? If I'd met her under other circumstances I would have sworn she was intelligent."

Jonathan shrugged. There really was no accounting for taste, yet he wondered what Moretti could have done to inspire such loyalty in that woman. Maybe she was like a million other women blinded by love to everything except what she wanted to see.

Or maybe there was more to Moretti than he, Jonathan, had ever gotten to see.

For a moment, he mulled that over in his mind, but quickly his thoughts returned to the one person who had constantly been on his mind.

"Why don't you go see her, Stone? We've done all we can right now. We've talked to everybody we could think of, been everywhere we could go."

"Was I that obvious?"

"Only to people who have eyes. Even the guys from this morning were taking bets on whether you were sleeping with her or not. But hey, we're cops. That's what we do. You know that."

"And you don't approve?"

"I'm not your mother. I just don't want you doing anything stupid. We already discussed how you men get." She sipped from her glass. "She's a nice lady, Jon. Sharp, compassionate. I doubt she takes any shit from you. I'm happy for you."

"Thanks."

She winked at him. "Tell me she's got a brother or two hanging around."

"Just one. He's seventeen."

"A little young for my taste, but let me know when he turns twenty-five."

After they paid the bill, he dropped Mari off at her place, went to his and collected Dana's things and started off for the motel.

Now, sitting in his car, he took the Polaroid of Amanda Pierce from his pocket and scanned the image of her broken face in the dim luminescence of the track lighting recessed in the building's overhang.

Her murder had started it all, brought Dana into his life in a way that allowed him to know her as more than his sister's friend. He had no idea what Dana's feelings were or if a relationship between them was tenable once all this was over. But those few nights spent with her had given him hope that there was something in this world for him more than the grind of the job and the solitude of his apartment.

He tucked Pierce's picture back in his pocket. It was time he gave her something back.

For the third time that day, Dana jumped hearing a knock at the door. The first time had been when they brought her lunch. The second time was when the shift changed and brought her dinner. What could they want to offer her now? A midnight snack?

"Who is it?" she called.

"It's me, Jonathan."

The three most welcome words she'd heard in a long time. She rushed to move the chair aside so she could yank the door open. She launched herself at him, clinging to his neck as his arms closed around her. She had promised herself she wouldn't act like a fool the next time he walked in the door, but she couldn't help herself, and right now she couldn't care less.

Her mouth found his for a kiss invested with her relief at seeing him, her love, and even a dose of sexual frustration. Last night, he'd held her until she slept, but he hadn't made love to her, hadn't touched her since the night before that when she'd found him standing by the window. He kissed her back with equal fervor, his arms crushing her to him.

But after a moment he set her on her feet and pulled away from her. She hadn't realized until then that he held something in his hand—his badge. He tucked it into his back pocket as he moved away from her. "Didn't I tell you not to open the door to anyone who didn't show you identification first?"

She glared at him as he went back to the doorway to retrieve her suitcase and nurse's bag and shut the door. Not exactly the response she was expecting to the hero's welcome she'd provided. Aside from that, he'd let her know they hadn't found Moretti yet. Otherwise, he wouldn't still be concerned for her safety. "Don't you think I know your voice by now?"

"That isn't the point. I don't want you to let your guard down, even if you think it's me."

She didn't want to argue with him. He looked tired and lines of irritation and frustration showed on his face. She didn't want to do anything to make his job even harder. "I'm sorry, Jon."

He closed the gap between them and pulled her into his arms. "I didn't mean to have you apologizing to me." He kissed her temple.

She wrapped her arms around his back. "Tell me what happened."

"Nothing much. I spent the day chasing a ghost. I don't know where Moretti's disappeared to. No one does."

She bit her lip. Not the news she wanted to hear. "Have you gotten any leads on the other two?"

"No. Miguel Colon seems to have vanished into thin air, and there's no record of a Randy Parker being born in any New York City hospital around that time. No school records either. Randall must have gotten his name mixed up."

"Wonderful. What does that mean?"

"The next move is on Moretti or whoever else might be involved in this thing." He rubbed his knuckles against her cheek. "Now it's my turn to be sorry."

He might fault himself for any lack of progress, but she didn't. The man obviously didn't want to be found and he'd do his damndest to make sure no one did. But that didn't make her doubt Jonathan. She leaned up and pressed her mouth to his, hoping to convey with her kiss the words of encouragement that failed her.

Something vibrated on him, tickling her, too. "Is that your phone, or are you just happy to see me?"

He shot her a droll look as he retrieved the phone and connected the call. Dana sighed. If someone were calling him at this hour, it was probably related to the case and probably important. She hadn't figured she'd have him for long, anyway. Surely the NYPD wouldn't appreciate one of its members making time on their time. But she wasn't ready for him to leave her yet. She'd spent most of the day alone, frightened, frazzled. Couldn't she have a few more minutes with him, just to have him hold her and remind her that everything would be all right?

She had to laugh at herself. If someone had told her a week ago that she would be looking to some man, a cop at that, for reassurance, she would have laughed herself silly. But a lot had changed in that short time, most of all her feelings for him, feelings she'd never thought any man would inspire in her.

A playful demon seized her, as she listened to Jonathan's end of the conversation. She leaned up and pressed one moist kiss to the side of his throat, then another. She felt him stiffen in an effort to retain some sort of decorum and ability to concentrate on what was being said to him.

After a moment, he closed the phone and clipped it to his belt. His arm closed around her and his mouth met hers. When he pulled away, much too soon for her liking, he brushed his knuckles along her cheekbone. "I have to go."

"I know."

He sighed. "They found Moretti's car, out in Brooklyn somewhere. They think he's still nearby."

She turned her head and kissed his fingers. "Be careful, Jon. I mean it."

"I will. You do the same." He took her hand, leading her toward the door. He stopped by the bags he'd brought in. "I almost forgot. I brought you a present."

He handed her a black plastic shopping bag, the kind you get at any bodega in the Bronx. He moved the other bags from in front of the door while she looked inside the one he'd given her. She burst out laughing as she removed one bottle of disinfectant and another of bug spray. She cradled the items in one arm. "Very funny."

He winked at her. "See, even when a man gives a woman exactly what she says she wants, he's still wrong." He pulled her to him and kissed her one last time. "Make sure to lock up after I'm gone."

"I will," she promised, feeling the same heaviness in her chest, the same fear, the same sense of frustration she had the last time he walked out the door. She put on the same brave face for him, but she didn't know how much more of this bravery she could stand.

Jonathan got in his car and pulled out of the lot. He took the turn that would put him on the southbound New England Thruway, but something about this situation didn't make sense to him. Worse yet, he couldn't identify exactly what. His brain was pulled in too many directions and his emotions were too chaotic for whatever disturbed him to jump out at him.

What was Moretti doing way the hell out in Brooklyn in the first place? As far as Jonathan was able to discover, Moretti didn't know anyone in that part of the other borough. Even if he did, why would he leave his car parked out on the sidewalk on a dead-end street that offered him little chance of escape? Moretti might not be the sharpest tool in the drawer, but he had to know better than that.

According to Mari, a patrol unit had spotted the car. An inspection of the interior showed a bullet hole in the driver's side headrest with the right trajectory and enough blood to suggest he'd tried to off himself. Since there was no body found, and no signs one had been carried off, according to the officers at the scene, maybe he'd changed his mind at the last minute and only managed to wound himself. If that were true, where was he? Some genius had come up with the idea that maybe Moretti realized he needed to get out of there, knew he was in no shape to drive and took off on foot. Who knew? It wasn't the first element of this case that didn't make any sense. They still didn't know why Pierce's killer had left her in a garbage can behind a pizzeria of all places.

Damn! At least at this time of night, with the roads almost empty, he'd probably make it out to Brooklyn in half an hour. With any luck, someone would have found Moretti by the time he got there. Maybe, but he doubted it.

Moretti watched as Stone drove off. By now, half the NYPD must be looking for him in some godforsaken place at the other end of the city. He'd fooled them all, but he didn't think he'd fool Stone. Not that he thought Stone was brighter than any of the rest of them, but he had more at stake, more reason to be vigilant. And he'd lose even more before the night was over.

He smiled, contemplating it. But now was not the time for musing, it was the time for action. He scanned the area one last time and saw no one. Silently, he slid his car door open and got out in a crouch. He traveled down three cars, keeping low, listening. The two brain trusts they'd left watching her had the windows rolled partway down on the car. He could hear them talking. They'd let their guard down, too, figuring he was someone else's problem now. That suited him fine.

He was close enough now to do it. He took the string of firecrackers from his pocket. He'd been watching long enough to know that no one would be interrupting their coitus to investigate the sound, thanks to the barrage of firecrackers that had gone off that day, some of which he'd set off himself. He lit the end of the string and tossed it so that it landed between her door and the car. He only needed a minute for the cops' eyes to be trained on something other than him.

While the mini explosives burst on the pavement, he walked up to the car and fired two shots inside the car. Those cops wouldn't be giving him any more grief. Now, to the girl. He didn't stop himself from smiling this time.

Dana took several calming breaths as she paced around the small room, unable to keep still. Ever since Jonathan left, a feeling of foreboding had gripped her, churning her stomach and putting her

nerves on edge. The damn firecrackers weren't helping any. Every time a new set went off, she jumped.
This last bunch sounded like they were right outside
her door. She was tempted to check what was going
on out there, but she remembered Jonathan's edict
to stay away from the windows, so she didn't bother.

Besides, the two officers were still outside. She
could still see their car through the peephole, though
the tinted exteriors made it hard to see in.

Suddenly a dark shape blocked the peephole. The
sound of someone knocking made her gasp and
step back from the door.

"Ms. Molloy? This is officer Burke. My partner
and I will be taking over. It's time for the other guys
to go home."

Officer Burke had to be a hit at the stationhouse.
He had one of those Mike Tyson voices, wispy and
lispy and too nasal for your average man to carry off
well. "Thanks for letting me know."

"Ms. Molloy, can you open the door? I'd like you
to see my face, know who I am, in case anything
happens."

At first, she didn't think anything of the request,
even though the first change of officers hadn't done
the same. Maybe something in the situation had
changed and they expected to have to move her.
"Show me your badge through the peephole and
slide your ID under the door."

"Sure thing."

She looked out the peephole but at close range
all she could make out was the glint of something
metallic. "Okay," she said. "Now slide your ID under
the door."

She stepped back and looked down. A moment
later, the edge of an ID appeared at the bottom of

the door. Considering the gap between the threshold and the bottom of the door, the placement had to be deliberate. But, why? The only reason she could think of was that whoever was outside didn't want her to know who he really was and the only person she could think of who would go to so much trouble was Moretti. But if it was him, why didn't the officers in the car stop him? Maybe Moretti had already made sure they couldn't.

That thought sent a chill of pure terror up her spine. If it were him, she had no way out of here, no weapons and no one looking to help her since they were all on a wild goose chase in another part of the city. She inhaled and let her breath out slowly, trying to calm herself. If it was Moretti, she'd need her wits. "Can you slide it a little farther under? I can't get it." Let whoever it was think she was still by the door. Instantly she started backing up, looking around for something with which to defend herself. She'd already checked her bag, which contained nothing more deadly than a pair of blunt tape scissors.

She didn't have much chance, as the door burst open a second later. If she'd been where she was supposed to be, crouched down, the door would have hit her, maybe knocking her unconscious, but definitely wounding her. Moretti stood in the doorway, his gun in his hand, surprise written on his face that she was upright and not on the floor.

Instinctively, she backed away from him, bumping into the nightstand.

Moretti stepped farther into the room and kicked the door closed, the expression on his face containing both cockiness and menace. "You know, Ms. Molloy," he said. "You're really getting to be a pain in the ass."

Twenty

As usual, traffic headed toward the Cross Bronx Expressway moved slower than a snail on a hot day. For once, Jonathan didn't mind, since it gave him time to think. The turnoff for the Whitestone Bridge loomed just ahead. He needed to make a decision before he committed himself to the trip across the water.

He pulled out his phone and dialed Mari's number. She answered on the first ring. "I was just about to call you."

"Why?"

"They've got a crew out here beating the bushes for Moretti. Haven't turned up anything yet."

"Then why were you going to call me?"

"When all the hubbub starts, the locals started to come out of their houses to see what was what. One of the men reported that his car was missing. He parked it in front of his house two hours ago. Now it's gone."

A car vanished on the same block where Moretti abandoned his? That had to be more than coincidence. But if it was Moretti, what the hell was he up to? Why bother to go out to Brooklyn and fake an almost suicide in the first place? Probably because he knew Jonathan would follow wherever he thought Moretti was. He wanted a chance to get to Dana without him around. Damn. He'd played right into the plan. He put Mari on hold and called Cohen. The fact that he got the man's voicemail decided it.

"I'm going back," he told Mari, closed the phone and tossed it onto the seat beside him. He got the dome from his glove compartment, put it on the dash and turned it on. Immediately the siren and accompanying flasher kicked in. Once the other cars moved out of his way, he took the turnoff for the Whitestone, but rather than getting on the circular path toward the bridge he made the U-turn to backtrack to the motel.

Adrenaline rushed through him, tightening his nerve endings and churning the acid in his belly. He estimated he'd left Dana about fifteen minutes ago, at the most. With any luck, he'd make it back in another five. Twenty minutes. A lot could happen in twenty minutes. His mind churned with the possibilities of it. He pushed the gas pedal a little closer to the floorboard. He only hoped that when he found her, he wasn't too late.

Dana swallowed in a throat that had gone completely dry. Her heart beat so rapidly and resonated so loudly in her ears that it threatened to block out any other sound. She started to tremble and her knees felt like water, but she was determined not to face her attacker with fear. For one thing, if he simply wanted her dead, he'd have shot her already. He wanted something else first. Maybe to torture her or rape her or just torment her a little while before he took her life. She would need her wits to survive whatever he had in mind.

He took a step toward her, causing the tremors that wracked her body to intensify. "Stay away from me," she said in the calmest, deadliest voice she could muster. "You know he'll kill you if you touch me."

Moretti stopped midstride, a smile stretching across his face as he shook his head. "No, he won't."

He spoke with such certainty that a chill traveled up from the base of her spine to her scalp, setting off the hairs at the back of her neck. How could he be so sure Jonathan wouldn't come after him, unless he'd made sure he couldn't beforehand? Had Moretti been outside all that time, waiting to ambush Jonathan? She remembered the explosion of fire-crackers a few moments before. That sound could have camouflaged a multitude of other sounds Moretti wouldn't want heard.

Tears sprang to her eyes. She braced her hands on the nightstand behind her to steady her footing. Her fingers bumped into something. Not the lamp, but something else she'd left there.

Moretti continued toward her, closing the space between them rapidly, his arm outstretched as if he intended to grab her. She slid her hand around the can, waiting, bracing herself for the optimal moment. He took one final step toward her and she acted, bringing the can level to his face and depressing the button to shoot bug spray in his face.

He screamed, his hands going to his eyes to cover them. But before she could get away, one of his hands swung out, backhanding her, knocking her to the floor and sending the can rolling across the carpet. She blinked, both from the blow and the fact that she'd managed to get some of the spray in her own eyes.

"Get up," Moretti growled.

She glanced back at him over her shoulder. One of his hands still shielded his eyes, but the other held his gun, trained on her. Damn. Her attack might have surprised him momentarily, but hadn't really done her much good. As she rose to her feet, she noticed her bag lying at the foot of the bed. Jonathan had put her heavy computer back where it belonged before he brought it to her.

She grabbed the heavy bag two-fisted and swung it in Moretti's direction. She caught him in the midsection, knocking him backward. His gun discharged and the lamp crashed to the floor, casting the room in darkness. She didn't waste a moment this time. She'd heard Moretti's groan of pain when the bag struck him, but she doubted she'd done him any real harm.

She got to the door, pulled it open and ran. She cut across the parking lot rather than circle around the edge of the building. She tried to yell, "Fire," something that would bring the occupants out of their doors, but no sound came out of her clogged throat. Tears stung her eyes as she made her way to the registration office, both from frustration and the lingering effects of the spray. Once she made it there, she tried to pull open the glass door, but it didn't budge and there didn't appear to be anyone inside. She banged on the door, hoping to bring someone, anyone who could help her.

Inside the office, a door opened and a kid came out wiping his hands on a paper towel. He sauntered toward her with the air and the deliberation of someone who has nothing better to do than take their time. She glanced over her shoulder. There was no sign of Moretti, but that didn't mean he wouldn't follow her. She banged on the glass again, trying to speed up the kid's progress.

Instead, he paused to pick a piece of toilet paper from his sneaker. "Hang on to your panties, lady. I'm coming."

"Son of a bitch," Dana muttered under her breath. The moment the kid opened the door, the strong smell of marijuana assailed her nostrils. So this kid had been taking a pot, not a potty break. That explained his lazy manner and glassy eyes. He'd be no help to her.

"What can I do for you, lady?" He looked her up and down in a way that made her want to slap his face.

"Call 911. Ask to be put through to Detective Jonathan Stone." She glanced over her shoulder again. Although she saw no one, she couldn't shake the feeling that Moretti was out there somewhere. For a brief second she considered asking the kid to hide her in the office until the police arrived, but as stoned as he was, he'd probably tell anyone who walked in that he had a lady hiding in the bathroom. Besides, she wasn't going to flee one place that offered her little means of escape to lock herself in one that had none. She had to get out of there.

She took off running, veering left to make it out onto the street. Almost immediately a pair of headlights blinded her—another car coming into the drive. The car squealed to a stop, its horn blaring. She dodged to her right, slipped on the gravel and kept running. She didn't know anything about this neighborhood, except the way they'd come in the car. When they'd made the turn down here, which was the service road for the New England Thruway, she'd seen a McDonald's and a gas station and a sign for a Dunkin Donuts a few blocks down. If she couldn't find a cop there, she really must have run out of luck.

She sprinted toward the end of the block, which would almost take her to civilization. Her lungs burned and her injured shoulder ached. But she would make it. She had to. A car passed by, heading toward the highway or whatever else lay back there, but too quickly for her to think of flagging the driver down until it passed. Considering that the driver might be just as much of a hazard as Moretti, maybe it was a good thing. She glanced over her shoulder. Still no sign of Moretti. She allowed herself a tiny smile. Maybe that heavy computer had done him more damage than she'd suspected.

She turned her head to focus on the path in front of her, and suddenly he was there. She skidded to a stop. But not before she barreled right into him.

He grabbed her left upper arm in a painful grip, right below the wound in her shoulder and pushed her back against the building. An instant later, the muzzle of his gun pressed against her throat. Moretti's face was so close to hers that his features blurred into a grotesque mask. "Do exactly as I tell you, or I will do you right here. Do you understand me?"

She nodded, having run out of any other options save agreeing with him. She had no idea if the stoned teenager in the office had bothered to call the police or was now satisfying the call of the munchies from the vending machine. Twin emotions of helplessness and dread assailed her. She knew that if Moretti took her away from here, he would kill her and whatever else he had in mind at his leisure, but she saw no way to stop him, not with the grip he had on her and his gun pressing into her flesh.

Slowly, Moretti backed away from her, removing the gun from her throat, and his grip eased slightly. She knew if she were going to act it had to be now. She eased off the wall slowly, waiting until she stood close enough to raise her knee and drive it into his groin. As his body contracted she drove her elbow into his solar plexus. It wasn't enough to put him down, but he did let go of her. The minute he released her, she ran, her feet moving, but her mind a jumble. She didn't realize she'd run into the street until the blare of a car horn forced her back onto the sidewalk. Disoriented, she ran in the opposite way she'd intended. But it was too late to change her mind. The only way to the main street now was to keep going the way she started, back to Moretti.

She glanced over her shoulder, but this time she didn't congratulate herself at not finding Moretti. She ran harder, hoping to find somewhere to hide before he found her.

Except for the sounds from the highway, the neighborhood was quiet, not even a light on to suggest someone was home and up at that hour. No one on the street to seek help from. She ran on without stopping.

But she knew she didn't have much more left in her. The shooting had taken a lot out of her. Even now, the healed wound throbbed and her lungs burned. Not too far ahead, she thought she might have found what she was looking for—a row of houses in the final stages of construction. She didn't know if Moretti would look for her in there or if he'd assume she kept going. In the distance she heard the sound of sirens. For all she knew, they'd already caught him and all she had to do was wait until someone found her.

But behind her, she heard the sound of a car approaching. She had no way of knowing if that car was headed for the highway, one of the side streets or if it was Moretti looking for her. She ducked into the house on the corner and quickly disappeared inside.

Jonathan made the last turn to head into the parking lot of the motel, but his way was blocked by a pair of police cars stationed just inside the driveway by the rental office. Dispatch had already reached him to let him know that Moretti had been here, that Cohen and the other cop had been found dead in their car. But no word on Dana's whereabouts or Moretti's. The car Moretti had stolen was still in the parking lot.

He pulled to a stop and got out. One of the officers jogged over to him. Jonathan didn't waste any time on pleasantries. "Where are they?" he asked.

"Dunno. A passerby said he noticed a woman heading in that direction," he pointed back toward the service road to the highway. "We've got guys back there looking, but no luck yet."

Jonathan got back in his car, pulled a quick U-turn and headed down the service road. If someone had seen a woman alone running down the road, that meant that Dana had to have gotten away from Moretti, for a little while at least. So where the hell would she go? To his left was another motel, but a squad car already sat outside that building. If she were there, they would have found her already.

A little farther down, cops on foot with flashlights were combing the bushes along either side of the road. The same was true on the block that followed.

They must have half the cops in the Bronx out here looking for her, and as of yet, no one had found her.

Damn. He turned left, cruising down one of the streets. By now, she had to know that they were looking for her. Half the neighborhood had come awake, probably wondering about all the unusual police activity in the neighborhood. Some of the people had even come outside and had to be sent back to their houses. If Dana were hiding here, she would have come out already if she could.

If she could. That was the part of his last thought that disturbed him. If Moretti had found her, all the knocking on doors and beating the bushes might not mean anything. But knowing Dana, her first thought wouldn't have been to go somewhere that Moretti would have put additional people in danger. At the back of the neighborhood was a maze of new houses, some of them finished, some of them in various stages of production. He doubted his fellow officers had extended their search that far yet. He gunned the engine and headed there.

He turned right at the first block of empty houses. They were complete save for doors and windows, looking like twin rows of startled, open-mouthed faces in the paleness of the moonlight. He cut the engine and listened for a moment. Any sound coming from these cavernous buildings might be amplified enough for him to hear.

At first, the only noise he heard came from the cars zipping past on the highway. Then another sound made his blood run cold—the report of a single shot being fired, coming from the direction of the buildings to his right.

* * *

Kids. Moretti gritted his teeth. He'd seen a shape in the dark and fired, expecting his bullet to find Dana Molloy and put an end to this shit already. Not only had he missed, but once he turned the corner of the house, he knew he'd made a mistake. Four kids, all in various stages of drunken stupor and undress were gathered around a couple of candles. All four of them looked up at him with startled glassy eyes.

The one closest to him, presumably the one he'd missed, said, "I was just taking a leak, man. That's not against the law."

The four of them found this hilarious, until he trained his gun on the noisemaker. "Get out, all of you."

Grousing about police brutality, the four of them took their things and cleared out. Moretti smiled to himself, the last thing he'd needed was some liquored up teenagers who might want to play the hero once he found her. And he would find her. He'd seen her come in here and he knew her type. She'd hole herself up in some closet somewhere and think she was safe from him. But he had to move quickly. He'd heard the police sirens in the distance. It wouldn't be long before they headed down this way looking for him. He edged around another corner into a large open room, searching for her in the reflected lights of a car passing on the highway. Nothing.

Damn it to hell. All she needed to do was remember. That's what Mouse feared. That's what started this whole mess to begin with. The fear that one day she'd put two and two together and realize what she'd seen. None of them could afford to take that chance, not anymore.

He was looking forward to silencing those memories, much more than he thought he would. Now all he had to do was find her.

Dana edged along the wall of what would one day be the second floor master bedroom of the house. She knew she had to get out of there. The moment she heard the shot, she knew Moretti was close by. He must have seen her go into the house on the corner, but not her escape through the downstairs window into the house next door. She'd lost one of her sneakers in the process. She'd left it where it lay and removed the other one as soon as she made it inside the house. Barefoot she made less noise. Sooner or later, he'd figure out she wasn't where he thought she should be and go looking somewhere else.

She made it to her goal, the front window, where she could look down on the street. The light from a car passing on the highway blinded her momentarily. Her eyes had already adjusted to the darkness inside the house. She blinked and refocused her gaze on the street. No sign of Moretti, nothing had changed, except that there was a car parked at the opposite end of the street that hadn't been there before. It was too far away to make out anything except that it was dark in color. She couldn't imagine who would be parked here in this deserted block, but the lights were off and the driver was nowhere to be seen, and therefore of no help to her.

She backed away from the window, intending to make her way as silently as she could to the first floor and back in the direction of the motel. She'd heard sirens before. In the still of the building it had seemed like hours ago, but in reality it must have been only minutes.

She started to turn when something passed before her face to tighten around her neck. Her hands went to her throat, clawing at the binding, at the hands that held it in place. No one had to tell her who held it. Moretti had found her and he intended to kill her the same way he'd killed Amanda Pierce. She gulped in air, surprised to find it still possible, though difficult. That didn't make sense; unless he didn't want to kill her just yet, only immobilize her.

Moretti leaned in closer, his hot breath fanning her cheek as he whispered. "Did you see the car?"

Her semi-oxygen deprived mind couldn't wrap itself around that question. "What car?" she croaked out.

The band around her neck tightened painfully. "The car Pierce got into. What do you remember?"

"Nothing." Nothing more than she'd already said.

"Too bad," Moretti said. She would have sworn she heard regret in his voice, but the band around her neck tightened, shutting off any attempt at breathing. She clawed at his hands, at the same time trying to kick back at him, but without her shoes, she had no effect on him. She got hold of a lock of his hair and pulled, tearing it out at the roots. She fumbled, trying to find his eyes, his nose, something with her fingers, some way to hurt him so he'd let her go. But all the while, the pressure in her lungs built. She felt herself growing weaker, succumbing to the lack of oxygen. He was killing her and she had no way of stopping him.

"Don't fight it. It will go a lot easier if you don't."

She had no fight left in her. Her arms slumped to her sides. If it weren't for the hold Moretti had on her she would have fallen. By degrees, the world around her went blacker and blacker until there was nothing. As she succumbed to the void, the last things she thought she heard were the howl of sirens in the distance and the sound of Jonathan's voice.

"You heard me, Moretti. Let her go." Jonathan stood almost directly behind Moretti, his gun trained on the other man's head. The beam of his flashlight caught the side of both Moretti's face and Dana's. He didn't know if Dana were dead or alive now, which was the only thing that kept him from firing. He couldn't risk hitting her instead. "Let her go," he said one last time. "Or I will shoot you where you stand."

Moretti lifted his hands and Dana slumped to the floor, landing on all fours. He heard the rasp of her gasping in air. He needed to get to her to make sure she was all right, but not yet. Not until he was sure that Moretti couldn't do either of them any more harm. For a moment, the temptation to simply shoot the man assailed him. He could always say that Moretti forced him to fire. Who would be there to dispute his version of what happened? Dana was too preoccupied with simply breathing to know what was going on behind her. Who would blame him for taking down a dirty cop? A murderer, maybe two times over?

Jonathan inhaled, willing those feelings to subside. "Put your hands on your head," Jonathan said, intending to take Moretti's gun away from him when he was in a more vulnerable position.

But Moretti had other ideas. Moretti went for his gun, but before he could fully spin around, Jonathan squeezed off two rounds, both of them hitting Moretti in the shoulder. He'd been aiming lower, but that would do. Moretti's gun clattered to the floor and a second later, Jonathan was on him. Moretti didn't struggle much as Jonathan cuffed his hands behind his back.

Jonathan picked up Moretti's gun and tucked it in the back of his waistband then went to Dana. He sat on the floor, pulled her onto his lap and held her, waiting for her breathing to normalize and for cavalry to arrive. He heard the sounds of them coming. The footsteps on the stairs, the sirens outside. Moretti, a few feet from them moaned, whether it was from his wounds or his impending fate, Jonathan neither knew nor cared. Finally, it was over. Now he could focus on his own fate and the life he wanted to make with the woman in his arms.

Dana shut her eyes to the flashing of the lights atop the row of police cars parked on the street as he carried her out of the building. She certainly wasn't going to object to his he-man routine since she doubted she'd be able to stand on her own. She felt light-headed and her throat burned inside and out from both the lack of oxygen and the pressure of being strangled. She thanked God that Jonathan had found her when he did. She'd been on the verge of passing out. She wouldn't have lasted much longer.

Once officers had arrived to take possession of Moretti, he'd brought her out of the building. She had no idea where he was taking her. She didn't balk until she realized his destination—one of the ambulances stationed at the curb. She shook her head. No hospital. Not again. She was fine, or she would be after a good night's rest. More than anything, exhaustion pulled at her. All she needed was some sleep.

"Don't argue with me, Dana," Jonathan said. "You need to be checked out."

"So—" She winced, realizing how difficult it was to speak. Her voice was little more than a hoarse rasp. "So some doctor can tell me I have a sore throat?"

"Yes, if that's what he's going to say."

She would have ground her teeth, except it hurt too much to move her mouth in any way. Besides that, she supposed she understood how he felt. He must have gotten quite a scare finding her the way he did. If nothing else, she knew he cared about her, wanted to protect her. It must have occurred to him, too, that he'd almost been too late.

She huffed out a raspy breath, her way of letting him know she'd acquiesce without having to talk.

Once they reached the ambulance he paused and kissed her forehead. "I have some things to take care of here. A policewoman will ride with you to the hospital. I'll get there as soon as I can."

She nodded. She didn't want him to leave her, but she knew he had his job to consider. But there was one question plaguing her that she asked as best as she could. "I thought you were dead."

He shook his head. "What made you think that?"

She shook her head. It would hurt too much to answer.

She let Jonathan help her into the ambulance where an attendant waited. Despite her claims of being fine, the attendant managed to get her to lie down with no coercion. Dana watched as Jonathan got out and a policewoman got in. She closed her eyes and for some unknown reason, dreamed of a fish with a broken tail swimming in a black sea.

After the ambulance drove off, Jonathan walked back to where Shea and some of the other brass were waiting for him, by one of the many squad cars still lined up outside the building. He knew what tonight's escapade would mean for him. He'd have to turn over his gun until the powers that be deemed him fit to return to regular duty, which would include the obligatory trek out to the department's shrink to make sure his head was still screwed on as tightly as it ought to be. He doubted there would be much question that his shooting of Moretti was justified. As far as his mental state went, they would have to see.

He'd never been so scared in his life, as when he'd walked into that room to find Moretti's hands holding that scarf around Dana's throat. He knew Moretti was strong enough to have snapped her neck in a second if he'd wanted to, and Jonathan couldn't have done a damn thing about it. He'd have made sure Moretti was dead a second later, but that wouldn't have helped Dana any. He supposed he should be grateful Moretti hadn't and leave it at that.

Jonathan handed Shea both his own weapon, the one he'd taken off Moretti, and the key Moretti's girlfriend had given him without being asked.

Shea eyed him suspiciously, though what exactly Shea suspected Jonathan had no idea. "How is she?" he asked.

"The EMTs say she'll be fine."

"How about you?"

"I'll be fine as soon as that son of a bitch is behind bars."

Shea grinned. "Thanks to you, he gets a trip to the hospital first."

"Poor thing," Jonathan would have said, but the sound of a single gunshot coming from the building silenced him.

And then he was running, like several of the other cops hauling ass toward the building. "Holy shit," he hard someone say, but no one was moving.

He pushed his way through the crowd to the base of the stairs. Moretti was sprawled halfway down, face down and bleeding. Fragments of the top of his head dripped down from the ceiling above. "What the hell happened here?"

One of the older officers said, a sheepish expression on his face, "He said he didn't want a stretcher, he could walk out. He talked us into cuffing him in the front because of his wound. We started down the stairs when he lunged forward and grabbed Dante's gun, put it under his chin and fired. It happened so fast."

Jonathan looked at the officer in question, Dante. A rookie who probably didn't know crap about guarding his weapon. No wonder Moretti had picked him. The poor kid looked like he was about to pass out.

Jonathan headed back out the way he'd come. For a change, this wasn't his mess to clean up. He met Shea right outside the building. "What went on in there?"

"Seems our friend will be taking a little detour to the morgue."

Out at the curb he found Mari standing by the driver's side of her car. "Hey, sailor," she called to him. "Need a lift?"

For the first time that night, a smile formed on his lips. "Could be. Where you headed?"

"Over to Monte. A good friend of mine has a lady being looked at over there."

He got in the passenger side and fastened his seat belt while Mari did the same. Without turning on the engine, she turned to look at him. "Seriously, Stone, are you okay?"

No, he wasn't okay. He wasn't ashamed to admit that. He rested his elbow against the doorframe and rested his forehead in a palm that trembled. Between nearly losing Dana and seeing Moretti's brains splattered, he'd definitely seen better days. The best he could offer was, "I'll be all right."

She patted his thigh. "I'm sure you will." She gunned the engine. "Now let's get over there and see if they've got some cute doctors in that place." Mari grinned. "A girl's got to look out for herself."

Twenty-one

Morning had already broken by the time Jonathan got Dana back to her house. The doctor had informed him that she'd been lucky that no major damage had been done to her throat or larynx and she should start sounding like herself in a few days as long as she rested her voice for the next twenty-four hours. They'd given her a foam brace to wear around her neck while the muscles healed. It hid the line of purple marks around her neck, a colorful reminder of what Moretti had done to her.

Neither of them was in shape for much of anything but sleep. Jonathan settled them under the covers in her bed, waited for Dana to drift off, then let sleep claim him. The next time he woke, darkness had already fallen again. Dana still lay cradled against his chest, her breathing even, though a bit raspy. That should ease up in a couple of days, too.

All in all, he was simply glad to have her here, alive, whole, lying beside him. He kissed her temple and she stirred, groaning in pain. "Ssh, baby," he crooned, hoping she'd settle back down to sleep. That was not to be. She opened her eyes and winced when she tried to lift her head.

"God, this hurts," she said against his chest.

"You're not supposed to talk." He scrubbed his hands up and down her back. The doctor had given her a prescription for painkillers that they'd filled on the way home. "Do you want me to get you one of your pills?"

She shook her head as much as she was able. "Ice cream."

He chuckled. They'd picked up some of that, too, plain vanilla, chocolate and strawberry, which made chewing unnecessary. "I'll be right back."

He got out of the bed and went down to the kitchen, loaded a tray with two large bowls piled high with ice cream, a glass of water, her pills, a couple of spoons, and some napkins. When he got back to the room, she was coming out of the bathroom. His eyes traveled over her nude body. How long had it been since they were together? At most it was a couple of days, but it seemed like years to him. He wanted her, and his body had no compunctions about showing her how much. But for the time being, that would have to wait.

He waited until she got back into bed, sitting up against the pillows before setting the tray over her. He went around to the other side of the bed and climbed in next to her. She dug into the ice cream, wolfing down several spoonfuls and purring in delight. She lay back against the pillows. "You're not eating."

"And you're not supposed to be talking."

She gritted her teeth and rolled her eyes at him. She leaned over and got a pad and pen out of the nightstand. She wrote something on it and turned the pad around to show him. Her note read, *You're not eating.*

He laughed. "I'm not hungry."

She scribbled something else on the pad. *Not hungry for food?* She offered him a wicked smile.

He definitely did not need her to go there. "Not hungry for anything."

She looked down his body and wrote four letters on her pad. *LIAR!*

No kidding, but what did she want from him? He needed to rephrase that in his mind. He knew what she wanted. He wanted it too, especially after the last time they'd come together. He'd shown her a side of himself he would rather have kept hidden. But she'd been through so much physically and every other way that he didn't want to risk hurting her.

As if reading his mind, she wrote on her pad and showed it to him. *Doctor didn't say anything about not having sex.* She scribbled something else. *Though a blowjob is out of the question.*

He rested his forehead in his hand. What was he going to do with this woman? His only answer was to love her the best way he knew how. He took the tray from her and lowered it to the floor. He lay back and opened his arms to her. "Come here, sweetheart."

She nestled against him, her head on his shoulder, one of her legs between his thighs, restless. Her fingers strummed across his chest. She murmured two words in that hoarse whisper of hers. "Please, Jon."

Any trace of humor was gone from her voice, replaced with a kind of desperation he understood. She thought what she wanted was release, the physical kind, but it wasn't, not entirely. It hadn't occurred to him until that moment that she hadn't said one word about what happened last night. Whatever she felt, she'd bottled up inside, and it would come out one way or the other. Either that or it would lie inside and fester, eating her up. He knew about that, too.

He tilted his head and kissed her cheek, her eyelid and finally her mouth, a soft sipping kiss that he repeated again and again. His hand roved upward to cover her breast, pressing her backward to give him better access. With his hands and his mouth, he brought her to the brink, before sheathing himself in a condom and pulling her on top to straddle him, knowing she couldn't bear his weight. Yet it felt so damn good to be inside her, it took every ounce of his control to take it slow and easy, as she needed it. With his hands on her back, he urged her down to him, so that their upper bodies lay flush. He hugged her to him, as their slick bodies moved together, drawing each of them closer to the edge.

She toppled over first, her body contracting around his, her fingertips biting into the flesh at his shoulders. He let his own release take him then, tautening his body as a wash of pure pleasure flooded through him.

He hugged her to him; aware at first only that she was trembling. Then he felt the dampness on his chest and the growing intensity of the sobs that wracked her body. "It's all right, baby. It's all right," he whispered against her ear. He stroked her back, her hair, whispering whatever nonsense he could think of that might soothe her. He held her until there were no more tears, only dry sobs and then she finally quieted.

"Better?" he asked, before remembering she wasn't supposed to talk.

"If I had a tissue."

He laughed and reached for the box on the nightstand. Now that sounded like the woman he knew. She pulled out several, mopped his shoulder then blew her nose. "Sorry," she mumbled.

"About crying all over me or about blowing your nose?"

She smacked him on the shoulder and reached for her pad. *Both.*

He squeezed her thigh. "You shouldn't be sorry about either. That's what I'm here for."

She pantomimed blowing her nose then looked at him questioningly.

"Well," he conceded. "Not that so much."

She pressed her lips together and wrote. *Don't make me laugh. Hurts.*

"What do you want me to do with you?"

She pantomimed turning on the faucet and a shower raining down.

Not a bad idea, considering the last time his body had seen water was the morning of the previous day. He got out of bed and set the shower, checked to see if there were enough towels for the two of them and went back to her. In that short span of time, she'd fallen back asleep. He couldn't say he minded. She needed her rest. He went back to the bathroom and turned the cold water up full blast.

Dana woke in the middle of the night feeling chilled. Although she was covered by a sheet and thin blanket, her bed lacked the warmth of the man she'd become accustomed to sleeping beside. She turned on her side and found him by the dim light of the bedside lamp, standing by the window where she thought he'd be. But this time, he was nude, not having bothered to don a pair of pants in order to have a place to carry his gun.

She smiled as her eyes wandered over him, her savior, in more ways than one. As a woman who prided herself on her self-reliance, she wasn't afraid to admit that she'd needed him and he'd come through for her, not only in keeping her safe from Moretti, but also a few short hours ago. She'd needed the release he'd given her, both physically and emotionally.

Ever since she woke up in the ambulance, she'd been numb, as if her emotions had shut down, like all she could remember were the events, not their impact. Last night, they'd come flooding back, mostly her fear that she would die in some unfinished building at the hands of some rogue cop and the desolation she'd felt thinking Moretti had gotten Jonathan, too.

He'd held her so sweetly, whispering bits of nonsense in her ear, soothing her. When was the last time someone held her and comforted her? Not since her mother, before the illness claimed her and took away everything that she was.

Oh, God, she was falling in love with this man. She had been long before the previous night. That scared her more than all the Morettis in the world, not in spite of what he was, but because of it: A man who was his own man, someone she couldn't dominate and didn't want to. She had no experience dealing with a man like him, and what experience she did have didn't count. The whole time they were together consisted of her doing what he said in order for her to be safe.

But now that the danger was past, how were they supposed to get along? How did she, how did anyone let someone in that close, and not find themselves subsumed by the other person? She was sure people did it, but she never had. She'd spent the majority of her life sublimating her own desires to those of others. She was done with that now. She wouldn't go back. Not for anybody.

But for now, she noted the tension in his posture and wanted to relieve it. She wanted to understand this ritual of his, whatever it was. He seemed oblivious to her, but she had no intention of pretending to be asleep. She leaned up on one elbow and said, "It's a good thing we don't live where there's a monsoon season. You'd never get any sleep."

He said nothing to that, relieving her of the notion that she could humor him out of his mood. She supposed only the direct approach would do. "What's the matter, Jon? Tell me."

He did look at her then. "It's nothing you need to worry about."

She groaned in frustration. At least he hadn't told her to go back to sleep this time. "I'll decide what I want to worry about, thank you, and it's clear something is bothering you."

He neither confirmed nor denied that. Undaunted, she asked, "Is it the rain?"

"It's nothing."

If she'd had something handy to throw at him, she would have hit him with it. Her throat hurt and his refusal to share with her hurt in a different way, as well. "I see. It's okay for you to be there for me, but not the other way around."

"I never said that."

"No, but you implied it."

He sighed and came over to the bed to sit facing her. She sat up; an unspoken sign that she was willing to listen to him. Still, for a long time he didn't say anything. He simply rubbed his left hand over his right arm, back and forth over his tattoo in a distracted way. She'd seen him do that before. She scootched closer to him, took his hand away and kissed the tattoo. "Tell me about this," she said.

Her gaze met his, and there was something about the way he looked back at her that told her she'd hit her mark. She wasn't about to let it go. "What's a big, tough police detective doing with the tattoo of a butterfly on his arm?"

She saw it in his eyes, his capitulation. He didn't want to tell her but he would. "I'd been on the job about four years, still on patrol, when we got a tip that someone we were looking for was hiding out in an abandoned apartment building. I was working nights then. The crazy shift. So we go to this building. It's pouring so hard outside and this place is in such disrepair that it's more or less raining on us inside.

"We're searching around with flashlights for this guy, when one of the officers comes across a body lying in a bathtub in one of the apartments. At first he thought it was a doll wearing a multicolored dress, except it was too big to be a doll, since the body was perfectly intact. But it was a four-year-old child, left there no more than twenty-four hours before, presumably by whoever had killed her."

Dana swallowed. She'd figured whatever story he might tell her wasn't going to be pretty, but she wasn't sure she wanted to hear about the death of a child. "Who was she?"

"To this day I don't know. There was never any missing person's report filed on her. No reports of any child unaccounted for by social services. We canvassed the neighborhood, put up flyers; there were reports on the news. I don't know how it can be that a four-year-old child is abandoned somewhere and absolutely no one is looking for her, but it was true. The officer who found her was Hispanic and gave her the name *Mariposa.*"

Dana knew that word from the Spanish she'd learned working in the neighborhood. *Butterfly.* "Hence the tattoo?"

"Well, a bunch of us, the ones still working the case, got drunk one night, the night we realized we'd have to give up on the case. We decided someone should remember her, even if no one else seemed to care." He rubbed his arm while offering her a self-mocking smile. "It seemed like a good idea at the time."

But she'd bet that little tattoo had become for him a physical representation of every mistake he'd ever made, every misstep, every unsolved case. "Why don't you have it removed?"

"I can't. We were foolish enough to make the promise that we'd wear them until we solved the case."

"Is that a possibility?"

"Who knows? Every now and then one of us will pick up the file or get a tip from someone that doesn't pan out." He exhaled. "Probably not."

He fastened a gaze on her that was as intense as it was searching. He probably wondered what she thought of him in light of the story he'd told her. She had no words to express what she felt. She recognized that he'd shared with her a part of himself that he probably didn't share with many other people. That touched her more than she could say. And she understood now what the other night had been about, all his feelings of guilt, frustration and impotence coming out in the way he'd touched her. No wonder he'd withdrawn from her after that, since he hadn't wanted to show it to her in the first place.

She took his face in her palms to place tender kisses

on his cheeks, his eyelids, the tip of his nose and finally his mouth. Slowly, she leaned back against the pillows, pulling him down with her. It was on the tip of her tongue to tell him that she loved him, but she wasn't ready to voice that sentiment yet. Instead she showed him with her body what she couldn't manage to say with words.

The next morning, after she'd showered and made him a breakfast of eggs, juice and coffee, she sat on the edge of the bed next to Jonathan and shook his shoulder. "Wake up, sleepyhead."

Mumbling something, he opened his eyes and looked at her with eyes at less than half-mast. "Hmm?"

"I said, wake up. Your breakfast is getting cold."

"Here's the only breakfast I want." He grabbed her by the waist and pulled her across him so that she lay beside him with her legs over his. He buried his nose against her neck, then stopped abruptly. He lifted his head and looked down at her. "You're not wearing your throat thingie."

"So you're awake now?" she teased. "No, I'm not. I was starting to feel like Queen Elizabeth." When he looked at her quizzically she explained. "You know with the ruff." She gestured with her hands to emphasize her point.

He brushed a strand of hair from her face. "Your voice sounds better."

"I broke down and took one of the pills." She'd given in when she discovered nearly every muscle in her body ached from overexertion of one kind or another.

"I'm glad. I thought I might have to sic Joanna on you."

"No, not that," she teased, knowing Joanna could

be just as forceful as she was when the situation called for it. She wondered what Joanna, who'd warned her away from her own brother, would say if she saw them together now. He'd never seemed to her to be the kind of man Joanna described: fickle, faithless, unable to commit to anything besides his career. If anything, after seeing him with Tyree, hearing his story last night, he struck her the opposite way—as a man who stuck once he decided to care about something. Maybe he'd showed her a side of himself he kept from his family or maybe he was different with her. "Joanna doesn't approve," she said finally.

His mouth tilted in a self-mocking smile. "I don't blame her. I've never exactly been great relationship material. After a while the most patient woman gets tired of waiting around wondering when I'm going to show up or when I'm going to do more around the house than sleep and deplete the refrigerator."

His gaze drifted downward, to her abdomen where his fingers sketched a pattern on her belly. Was he trying to warn her off, too? Or perhaps that this was the way he was and he didn't intend to change. Maybe it was time she let him know a few home truths, too. "I wouldn't sit around waiting for anybody. I'd hire a housekeeper and do what I wanted to do."

He smiled. "I'm sure you would."

From the way he said that, she wasn't sure whether he considered that a good thing or a bad one. "I haven't exactly been the poster child for great relationships either," she confessed. "I never wanted to bring guys around Tim, especially when he was younger, let him grow attached to them only to have them leave. I always kept men a separate part of my life."

He took her chin in his hand and turned her face

toward him. His gaze was intense, but at the same time reassuring. "I'm not going anywhere, Dana, not unless you want me to."

He must have misread her meaning. She didn't have abandonment issues, at least none that he figured into. If anything, at the moment, she was the one guilty of abandonment, having failed to bring Tim home.

"What's the matter, baby?"

"I want to go get my brother."

"When? Now?"

She nodded.

"That's not a problem. Why don't you give him a call and let him know we're coming? I'll go wash up."

He touched his lips to her shoulder before climbing out of the opposite side of the bed. She watched him walk to the bathroom. Damn! She had to be insane not to give herself one full day alone and conscious with him. But she missed her brother and wanted to see for herself that he was all right, that things between them were all right. She picked up the phone on the bedside table and dialed his cell phone.

"Hey, Sis," he said when the call connected. "I wondered when you'd get around to calling me yourself."

She'd asked Jonathan to call him last night from the hospital fearing he'd hear a news report about the events in the unfinished house and worry. Jonathan had told him that she'd call him as soon as she could. Now, she heard the chastisement in her brother's voice at her lack of promptness in getting back to him.

Unsure she wanted to tell him everything that happened that night, she said, "Things have been a little crazy around here since then."

Unrepentant, Tim said, "I bet."

Dana ground her teeth together. "I'm home now. Do you want me to pick you up?"

"Nah, Ms. Kenner said she'd bring me home when I was ready."

"When?"

"In about an hour, I guess. See you then."

The line went dead. She hung up the phone and threw off her covers. While she'd spoken to her brother, she'd heard the sound of the shower come on in the bathroom. She got a condom from the nightstand drawer and went to join Jonathan.

He didn't seem surprised to have her slide in the shower behind him and wrap her arms around his waist. His hands covered hers and he brought one of her palms to his lips to plant a soft kiss there. "Trying to sneak in a quick one before we have to go get your brother?"

Hearing the humor in his voice, she said, "What a delicate way you have of phrasing it, but yes. Do you have a problem with that?"

"None." He turned so that he faced her and pulled her into his arms. She tilted her face up for his kiss. For the next few moments she concentrated on nothing but the warmth of the water, the heat of his embrace and the cold certainty that, despite their own histories and personal baggages, she didn't want to let this man go without a fight.

Dana had barely finished dressing and fixing her hair when she heard Tim's key in the lock. "Hey, Sis, where are you?" he called.

She hurried down the steps to greet him. Even in

the short time they'd been separated, he seemed to have grown another inch.

He smiled when he saw her and grabbed her in a bear hug once she was close enough for him to do so. "I missed you."

She smiled against his shoulder. He was man enough to take her to task for what he saw as her deficiencies, but there was still enough of the little boy in him that he sought her comfort and reassurance.

But suddenly, he stiffened. She pulled back to look at him and noted where his attention centered— behind her, to watch Jonathan descending the stairs.

It should have occurred to her to orchestrate a better meeting between the two of them than this. She knew Tim regarded Jonathan as an opportunist taking advantage of his older sister, despite the implausibility of that assumption. Half of her wanted to shake Tim and ask him when had he ever known her to allow anyone to walk all over her. The other half of her understood his hostility. For what other reason would Jonathan have been upstairs except to share her bed? His presence on the stairs was like throwing it in Tim's face that they had just been together. Inwardly, she groaned. Dealing with men and near men could sometimes be a colossal pain in the ass.

"What is he doing here?" Tim said finally.

"He's a guest in this house and you will treat him as such."

"Yeah, right." Tim picked up the bag at his feet. "I'm going to go put my stuff away." He moved off, went to his room and shut the door.

Damn! She shut her eyes and counted to ten for patience as Jonathan's arms closed around her from behind.

"I'm sorry, sweetheart. When I spoke to him yesterday, he was so accommodating, I thought he'd gotten over whatever thing he has with me."

"That would make life too easy, wouldn't it?"

He kissed her shoulder. "Well, he'll have you all to himself this afternoon. I have to go in for a while."

She figured as much. At the very least, she knew he'd have to report the details of what happened to his superiors. "Do you need me to go in, too? Make some sort of statement?"

"How about you write down everything that happened as best as you can recollect it, for now. Moretti's dead. As far as I know, the investigation is closed."

She nodded. "That shouldn't be too hard. I got a lot of practice writing yesterday." She went to the kitchen and got a yellow legal pad and a pen from one of the drawers, then sat down at the kitchen table to write down everything she remembered. When she was finished, she slid the pad to Jonathan.

He read through the sheaf of paper she'd filled. "Why did Moretti want to know if you'd seen the car that picked up Amanda Pierce?"

"I don't know. Maybe there was something about it he thought I might have remembered that would have identified it. At the time I got the feeling that's what this was all about. He thought I saw something that would link him to the car. The irony is, like I told him, I don't remember anything. I was too busy being disgusted with seeing two yuppies flashing their wealth in the 'hood."

Jonathan stood. "Walk me out?"

She took his hand and followed him. When they got to the door she asked the question that had been plaguing her since she'd fled the motel room, but hadn't really wanted to know the answer to. "The officers who were watching me. What happened to them?"

He squeezed her hand. "They're gone."

She lowered her gaze to watch his thumb sketch a lazy pattern over her skin. Intuitively, she'd known that, but hearing it flat out disturbed her. She didn't know those men, but it seemed unfair for them to lose their lives over something they weren't a part of while she still had hers.

"That isn't your fault, Dana. That was their job."

"I know." She let out a long weary breath. "So much death, Jonathan, and over nothing."

"But it's over." He tilted her chin up and kissed her mouth. "I'll be back as soon as I can."

Jonathan pulled away from the curb in front of Dana's house, grateful that she hadn't proved to be more inquisitive than he could handle at the moment. He'd already heard from Mari that the scarf Moretti had used was probably the same one used to kill Amanda Pierce. It bore the same black-and-white pattern she described seeing.

As of yet, no one had been able to locate Moretti's two accomplices to verify his story. The key Moretti's girlfriend had given him turned out to belong to a room in a storage facility where they found Pierce's belongings, minus her clothes. Her notes verified she'd met with Randall—Old Specs—and he'd given her Moretti's name.

It was all tied up neatly with a ribbon that said, case closed. The brass seemed to want to look at it that way, but they would, considering that one of their own was responsible for at least four deaths and that wasn't even counting Malone. They wanted it wrapped up, so they could tell an edgy public that the threat to their safety had been quashed. But something niggled in the back of Jonathan's mind, just below his consciousness, that didn't allow him to let go of the case that easily.

Mari was sitting at her desk when he walked into the squad room. She leaned back in her chair with her arms crossed and surveyed him as he took off his jacket and sat across from her. "I didn't think I'd see you in here today."

"Time, tide, and paperwork wait for no man."

"I hear that. How's Dana?"

"She's fine. Still sounds like Lauren Bacall with a frog in her throat."

"She's lucky you decided not to take the trip out to Brooklyn."

Maybe so, but he didn't feel lucky. Luck would have been not leaving her at Moretti's mercy in the first place.

"Did she tell you what happened?"

Mari had to know she did and was fishing for information. He took the folded sheets of paper on which Dana had written from his pocket and tossed them to Mari. "Let me know if you notice something unusual."

Dana had written down everything, including what Moretti had said, what she thought he'd meant when he said it. He'd learned from what she'd written why some of the first words out of her mouth were that she thought he was dead—the certainty with which Moretti had promised that he, Jonathan, wouldn't kill him.

Mari finished scanning the pages and looked up at him. "Am I missing something, 'cause I don't get it?"

"I don't either. Even if Moretti found out that

Pierce was on to him, he's not that much of a hot-head to strangle a woman, or even if he was, why not use his bare hands? Why not shoot her? There are a million other ways he could have gotten rid of her body besides leaving her in a garbage can where anyone could find her." That had never made any sense to him, no matter who'd killed her. "He told Dana he knew I wouldn't kill him. He had to know that any mercy on my part was over once he'd taken her. And rather than come along like a good boy, he tried to fire on me."

"What's your point?"

"He planned on not making it out of that building. My only question is why?"

"You want me to explain to you the workings of that son-of-a-bitch's mind? I haven't the faintest clue. Why'd he kill himself? Maybe he didn't want to get locked up with the rest of the scum of the earth? To me, Moretti is just as bad as any of the other skels and gangbangers we bring in here. The only difference is he had a badge. And you know what will happen now? Every single one of his busts, every single one of his convictions will get looked at again, if not dismissed outright."

She exhaled, calming herself. "You're looking to make sense out of something that is essentially un-explainable. If criminals made sense we'd all be out of a job. Forget it, Stone. It's over. You of all people should be glad it is."

He shrugged. Maybe she was right. He was looking for explanations where there weren't any. Why would anyone go to so much trouble to hide their part in Father Malone's death in the first place? Even though the statute of limitations for murder never expired, what could anyone have proven 25 years later when almost every piece of evidence, every witness, save for an old reformed drunk, had disappeared? Only Moretti could answer those questions, and he was dead. Maybe it was time he let it go.

He filed his report and left. He managed to last a whole twenty minutes in the shrink's office before he had enough and walked out. He didn't need his psyche delved into, no matter what the department thought. He'd done what he had to do, no more, no less. What they'd trained him to do.

He knew what he needed. She was waiting for him in a little house in Mount Vernon. He got in his car and drove home.

Dana spent the afternoon out of sorts after Jonathan left. Tim obnoxiously refused to come out of his room for anything except to use the bathroom, punishing her in that passive/aggressive way men tended to adopt when they didn't get their own way.

For want of anything better to do, she'd lain down for a nap, only to dream of strange disjointed images that seemed not to belong together. After a while she got up, cajoled Tim into going to the store for her, and fixed a quick and uncomplicated dinner of spaghetti with meat sauce, Italian bread and salad.

Jonathan got back as she was getting ready to bring the food to the table. She pulled the door open to find him standing on the other side of the door, smiling. "Hey," he said.

"Hey, yourself," she said, not knowing what to make of his mood. "Did you take care of everything you needed to?"

"Almost." She stepped back as he stepped up to cross the threshold. Once inside he pushed the door closed and took her into his arms. He leaned his back against the door and ran his hands up her back to place her arms around his neck. "Did you miss me?"

With some difficulty she held back her own smile. "Maybe."

He pulled her closer to him. "Liar," he whispered against her ear before pulling her lobe into his mouth and releasing it slowly. When she pulled back to look at him, he winked at her.

She shook her head, unused to this playfulness in him. "If you're so sure of my answer, why'd you bother to ask the question?"

"Is that garlic bread I smell?"

She didn't know if it was the cop in him or the man that felt compelled to answer her questions with questions of his own. "If it hasn't burned to a cinder in the oven by now."

"Give me a minute to wash up and I'll help you." He swatted her bottom and headed up the stairs.

Dana shook her head watching his ascent. Then she went back to the kitchen and took the bread from the oven. Thankfully, it had survived with only a little charring around the edges. Before she'd finished slicing it and placing the pieces in a bowl, Jonathan was back, wearing the same clothes, though his jacket was gone and his shirtsleeves were rolled up.

She set the bread bowl on the table. "No shower?"

"Not tonight. What can I help you with?"

"You can get the salad out of the fridge."

He did as she asked. Within minutes she had the table set and the food laid out the way she wanted it. "Sit," she urged. "I'll go get Tim."

She went to her brother's room and knocked on the door. "Tim, dinner's ready."

"I'll be out in a minute to get something."

"No you won't. You'll come and sit at the table like a human being."

She waited a minute. When the door didn't open, she knocked again. "Right now."

The door opened. Tim stood on the other side, looming over her, a sour expression on his face. "Fine." He marched past her and slumped into one of the kitchen chairs.

Dana ground her teeth together. That was a teenager for you. He'd do what he was told, but he'd try his damndest to make everyone else miserable in the process. She slapped a smile on her face and went back to the kitchen.

"I hope everyone is hungry," she said in a false cheery voice. She claimed the seat that was next to Jonathan and opposite her brother. But as the meal progressed, she grew more annoyed with Tim. Time after time, Jonathan tried to engage him in conversation, asking about his time in Florida, his plans for school next year, his fascination with basketball and video games. Tim answered in monosyllabic grunts, when he bothered to give an answer at all. Finally, on the verge of braining her brother with the salad tongs, she excused herself intending to start cleaning up the kitchen.

Tim was up from the table a second later. "The game is still on." He went to his room and slammed the door shut.

Dana gritted her teeth. Tim hadn't even bothered to remove his own plate from the table. She looked at Jonathan. "What am I going to do with that boy?"

He got up from the table and closed his arms around her from behind. "Leave him alone, Dana. He's doing what he's supposed to do."

"What's that? Getting on my last nerve?"

"No, he's looking after your best interests."

She sighed. "So I should just put up with rude behavior?"

"No. I'll have a talk with him."

She'd noticed how well that had gone during dinner. "And what are you going to say to him this time?"

He nuzzled her neck. "That I'm in love with his big sister and to please cut me some slack."

She froze hearing that word coming from his lips. She supposed, given his promise to stick around this morning, that sentiment shouldn't have come as such a shock, but it did. She hadn't expected him to voice his feelings so easily, so unequivocally or so soon.

She swallowed, unsure how to respond to him. She knew he was waiting for her to say something. Any man in his position would be. But her mouth didn't seem to work, except to open and close a few times with nothing coming out. Not that she could think of a coherent thing to say. As strongly as she cared for him, she wasn't ready to vocalize that yet. Not when she'd bet she understood what kind of man he was better than Joanna did. He would never be content to exist on the periphery of her life as every other man she'd known had been. She'd known that even before the L-word came into the picture. He'd want more from her, more than she was sure she had it in her to give.

She turned around to face him, wrapping her arms around his neck and burying her nose against his throat. The desire to protect herself emotionally warred with her desire to speak the truth. In the end, neither won.

After a moment, she felt the breath whoosh out of

him, even though his hands moved on her back in a soothing motion. "It's okay, baby."

She knew she'd hurt him with her silence and she felt the need to offer him some explanation for it. But again, no words came, which was just as well, since anything she said would only be an excuse, a cop out, and therefore unworthy of her.

He stepped back from her, creating a bit of space between them and tilted her chin up with his finger. His face bore an expression she didn't understand. He lowered his mouth to kiss her cheek. "I'd better go have that man-to-man with your brother."

Twenty-two

"Come in," Tim called in response to Jonathan's knock on his door. Jonathan pushed the door open. The teenager's surprise that he, not Dana, had come to his room was evident on his face. He went back to watching his television screen and the video game being played out on it. "What do you want, man?"

Jonathan closed the door behind him. "I wanted to talk to you about your sister."

"What about her? Did she send you in here?"

"I thought for her sake we could iron out a couple of things between us."

"Really?" Tim tossed the game controller onto the bed beside him. He folded his arms in a defensive posture. "What do you think you're going to tell me about my own sister?"

Damn this kid was stubborn. For a moment he searched for something to say that would break through the kid's wall of animosity. "I'll tell you what I told her. That I'm in love with her and wish you would cut me a little slack."

Tim's eyebrows lifted. "What did she say?"

Something about Tim's reaction rang false, as if he

weren't hearing that for the first time. "You already know that, don't you?"

Tim shrugged. "Maybe." He picked up the controller again.

Jonathan sighed, wondering if this was the kid's way of saying he considered the conversation over. "Do we have a truce?"

Tim shook his head. "Tell me what happened. Dana won't talk about it. All I know is what I read in the papers and saw on TV."

Which Jonathan knew was, at best, a distortion of reality. Apparently Tim's hostility was trumped by his curiosity. "Mind if I sit?"

Tim nodded toward the chair. "Go ahead."

Jonathan recounted the story, leaving almost nothing out. Tim's one word of response was, "Man."

For a moment neither of them said anything. Jonathan remained silent, hoping it would give Tim enough room to say what was on his mind.

"Does this mean you'll still be coming around?"

At first he wondered if Tim thought that was a good idea or not, but he heard none of the belligerence in the kid's voice now. "Yes."

"Don't hurt her and don't make her cry."

How could he promise anyone something like that? In any relationship there were bound to be ups and downs, rough times. He answered Tim as honestly as he could. "That's not my intention."

Tim nodded.

Jonathan let himself out of the room and shut the door behind him. He found Dana standing in almost the same spot he'd left her. He wondered if she'd been able to hear what he and Tim talked about.

She closed the gap between them. "How'd it go?"

"We have a truce." He looped his arm around her waist. "Come walk me to the door."

"You're leaving? Is it because of what happened before?"

He kissed her temple. "No, baby. But I think your brother needs you more than I do tonight."

He led her to the door, then pulled her into his arms for a kiss goodnight. She kissed him back with the kind of fervor he hadn't seen in her since the night the car went after her in the alley. God, he wished he'd kept his mouth shut now, but the words had slipped from his lips effortlessly when he'd said them. He should have known she couldn't handle them yet.

He pulled away from her, not because he wanted to but because he knew in another moment he'd forget what he was supposed to do and drag her off to her room. He wasn't looking forward to spending the night alone, even if it were for the best.

"Good night, sweetheart," he said. "What time do you want me to pick you up tomorrow?" When she looked up at him in confusion, he added, "For Joanna's barbecue?"

"Oh. I forgot. Call me in the morning, okay?"

"Okay. Say good night to Tim for me."

He let himself out of the house and walked to his car. Considering the uncertain expression on her face when he walked out, maybe he shouldn't have left her. He glanced back at the house, but she'd already closed the door behind him, shutting him out.

For a long time after Jonathan drove off, she remained by the door, leaning her back against it. Jonathan said his leaving had nothing to do with what transpired in her kitchen, but she wasn't sure she believed him. Until then, he hadn't mentioned anything about going home. She hadn't heard what was said between him and Tim, but she doubted it was anything so earth shattering that he felt compelled to leave over it. Maybe she was being paranoid, but she feared she'd ruined things between them.

She pushed off the door and walked to Tim's door. She rapped on the surface. "Do you want to watch a movie with me?"

After a moment, he said, "Okay."

She was tempted to say, "Could you show a little less enthusiasm?" but held her tongue. Tim wasn't responsible for her bleak mood. Neither was Jonathan, really. She did that to herself by not being honest with him when she should have been.

But Tim wasn't helping any either, between his rudeness before and his surly attitude now as they settled on the sofa and decided on something to watch. Finally, at the edge of her patience, she asked, "What is with you tonight? First you're angry because Jonathan was here and now that he's gone you're still mad."

"Jon isn't the problem, Dana. You are. What you did to him tonight wasn't right."

Those were the last words she'd expected to come from his mouth. "So it's Jon, now? You had your great guy bonding moment and now he's all right?"

"Look, I know I was wrong when you first told me about him. But how was I supposed to feel? When I was growing up, you never even brought a guy around here. I wasn't even sure you liked guys or anyone, for that matter. Then all of a sudden you tell me you're in danger and you're staying with him? And you won't even let me see you. Okay, that part

I can understand. But, you've got to stop treating me like I'm still seven years old and Mom just died."

"I don't."

"Don't you? You think I didn't notice the way he looks at you? What that means? Are you so cold inside that you don't know either? My God, Dana, the man told you he loved you and you didn't say a thing."

For an instant she wondered if he'd heard that himself or if Jonathan had told him. Truthfully, it didn't matter. It never occurred to her that her brother saw her that way, distant and unfeeling. Even if he did, she didn't need this from him right now. "That's none of your business."

"You know, Sis, I don't understand you. You don't believe in anything do you? Not God, not anybody else, not me."

Her anger finally bubbled over. "I believe in me, that's what I believe in. I'm the only person I could ever turn to, count on. Who was ever there for me? You tell me that?"

"It seems to me that when that shit went down with Moretti, someone had your back and it wasn't you." He pushed to his feet. "I'm going to bed."

After Tim walked out, she pulled her legs up and rested her chin on her knees. She'd done an excellent job of alienating both men in her life, though she had to admit with Tim, each of them had given as good as they got.

She didn't have to question if Tim was right about her. She knew he was. Even her clients, like Nadine, grumbled about her lack of sympathy and sentimentality. She knew she'd been stern in raising Tim, but she'd never realized she'd shown him that side of herself, or at least not enough to make him think her callous.

She also knew that she and Tim would work out whatever disagreement they had. They always did. It was her relationship with Jonathan that concerned her, or rather her inability to be straightforward with him about how she felt. He'd deserved some kind of honest response to his declaration of love, and she hadn't given him one. What bothered her most was that she'd held back out of fear. Tim was right about that, too. She lacked the faith in herself and in him, in life, that things would turn out all right. That wasn't fair to any of them.

In the morning, she would make it right with Jonathan. She would tell him that she'd been stunned by his admission and her own insecurities held her back from returning his feelings. She hoped that would be enough.

For the first time in a long time, she climbed into bed alone and lonely. She lay there for a long time, watching the shadows from passing cars dancing on the ceiling, until her eyes closed one last time and finally sleep came.

The next morning Tim informed her that some friends had invited him to a party up in Yorktown Heights near the Croton River. Since she didn't want him making the two-hour drive twice in one day, she agreed that he could borrow her car and spend the night up there. He seemed genuinely contrite about their argument the night before, as was she. Besides, if she hadn't read the expression she saw in his eyes, a girl figured somewhere in this outing, as well.

She had no idea if Tim were sexually active yet.

That's one thing she knew he'd never tell her unless she cornered him into doing so. Given the present circumstances, she wasn't about to ask him. She'd done all she could in that regard anyway. She'd taught him how to use a condom, which was eminently more embarrassing for him than it was for her. She'd taught him what it meant to be sexually responsible, not only in protecting himself and his partner from disease, but in other ways as well. It was up to him to make the right choices.

As he headed to the door, she stopped him. "Have a good time."

He embraced her. "I will. You, too."

She stepped back from him. "You know I love you, right?"

He huffed. "Of course I do. You know, Sis, I know you sacrificed a lot to keep me with you after mom died."

True, but she never wanted him to feel guilty for that. "Whatever I did, I did because I wanted to. You're my brother."

"I know. Let me finish. I guess I was mad at first that you were with Jon. You've always been there for me. But that's kinda selfish, isn't it?"

"Just a little bit."

"I want you to know that if you have the chance to be happy with him, then you should take it."

Fine advice to give her now, after she'd probably blown it with him. "I intend to."

Tim smiled. "Good. At least I'll be sure someone is taking care of you while I'm away at college."

Dana rolled her eyes. "Look out, your macho is showing."

He laughed but he didn't deny it. "I better get going."

She couldn't help one last admonishment. "Be careful."

He didn't pretend not to know to what she referred. He winked at her. "You, too, Sis." With one last grin, he was gone.

After a night without much sleep, Jonathan pulled up in front of Dana's house. She was already sitting out on her porch waiting for him. Tyree, who'd come to see him as he was walking out the door to give him a progress report, had delayed him. Tyree's mom was back on her feet and promised her son she'd find some other way to earn a living. That was no guarantee she wouldn't slip back to her old life, but it was nice to see the hope on the boy's face.

He got out of the car and walked up the front steps. As he approached, she stood. Once he made it onto her side of the porch, she stepped into his arms and kissed him. For a long moment, he lost himself in her tender embrace. Eventually, he pulled back, looking down at her with a bemused expression on his face. "Um, where's Tim? Isn't he coming with us?"

She shook her head. "He's found better things to do than hang out with us." She lowered her gaze and when she looked at him it was with a troubled expression on her face. "We need to talk, Jon."

Inwardly, he froze. He'd dreaded this since he left her last night. He'd lain in bed last night contemplating her reaction to him telling her he loved her last night. He vacillated between the certainty that she simply hadn't been ready to verbalize her feelings and the fear that she didn't return them at all. He thought back to when he'd told her he wasn't going anywhere unless she wanted him to. She hadn't said anything to that, either, only voiced her desire for her brother to come home.

The kiss she'd just laid on him notwithstanding, if there was the slightest possibility that it was the latter sentiment she wanted to express, he didn't want to hear it. He didn't think he could handle that right now, not and go make nice with his relatives afterward. That much of a brave face he didn't possess.

"Can we talk about it when we get home? We're already late and you know how Joanna gets."

To his relief, she smiled. "Sure." She went back to the rocker she'd been sitting in and picked up her purse. "I'm ready."

During the short ride to Joanna's he noted the smile on Dana's face and decided to take his cue from her. Would she have that beatific expression on her face or would she have kissed him like that if she planned to tell him to kiss off? He doubted it. She'd been straight with him from the beginning. If he had anything to worry about, it was his own doing for trying to rush her. He couldn't explain his moment of panic, and that's what it had been, except that he'd never wanted anything so much as he wanted this woman in his life. The mere thought of losing her made him a little stupid.

When he helped her out of the car was the first time he noticed what she was wearing—a form-fitting spaghetti strap sundress that ended well above her knees.

"Why are you looking at me?" she asked, coming to stand beside him.

"I don't think I've ever seen your legs before, while you were clothed anyway."

"I'm not that big on dresses," she confessed. "In fact, I wore it for you. Do you like it?"

"Mmm," he agreed. He'd enjoy it even more once he got it off her. In the meantime, he slung his arm around her waist and walked with her up to the house. As usual, Joanna's barbecue encompassed the entire property. Some kids were already out on the front lawn tossing a Nerf football. Inside the house was packed and the back yard was nearly as bad, with folding chairs stationed around the perimeter so the grown-ups could keep an eye on the kids.

They found both Ray and Joanna in the back of the house by the grills. Ray usually made ribs, steaks, chicken, and shrimp on skewers with peppers and onions, as well as the requisite hamburgers and hot dogs—a feast that couldn't be entirely consumed no matter how many people showed up.

Joanna embraced each of them. "It's about time you two showed up," she fussed, though there was a smile on her face.

"We're only fifteen minutes late," Dana said.

Joanna made a face that said what she thought of their tardiness. "Well, help yourselves to whatever. I had most of it catered this year." She patted her belly, which was still slightly rounded from her recent delivery. "Next year we'll be back to normal."

"If we keep out of the poor house this year," Ray teased.

Joanna rolled her eyes. "I didn't spend that much, really. Now scoot. I need to have a few words with my husband."

With his hand on her waist, Jonathan led Dana toward the tables that held the remainder of the food and the drinks—everything from an assortment of sodas to beer and wine and harder stuff. "Are you hungry? Thirsty?"

"I'd love a glass of wine."

"You didn't take one of your pills this morning, did you?"

She fastened a disgusted look on him. "Tell me again who's the fussbudget in your family. I know better than you what not to mix with what."

"Whatever you say, Miz Nurse," he said. He pulled her closer, but had to release her a second later when his cell phone rang. The display revealed an unfamiliar number that he decided to ignore.

"Don't you have to take that?" she asked as he re-clipped the phone to his belt.

"I'm off duty and on vacation. If anyone from the department wants me, they can leave a message like everyone else."

But later in the evening, after they'd spent the day enjoying each other's company and the warmth of his family, his phone went off again. That made the fourth time in five hours.

"Why don't you just take it," Dana suggested.

He might as well find out who this was and what they wanted and get it over with. He connected the call. "Stone."

"Is this Detective Jonathan Stone?"

"Yes." He didn't immediately recognize the voice or the name she supplied, though both sounded familiar. "What can I do for you?"

"I need to talk to you about Tommy."

Now he knew to whom both the name and the voice belonged—the woman he'd met at Moretti's. The only time he'd seen her he'd come to peg her as a shrewd woman. He couldn't imagine what she hoped to gain by talking to him now. "Go ahead."

"Not over the phone. Can you meet me?"

He looked over at Dana, who looked back at him expectantly.

"Please, Detective Stone. I promise you it's important."

It was the urgency in her voice that won him over. "Where?"

When he got off the phone, he turned to Dana. "I've got to go."

She sighed. "I figured as much. Does it have to do with Moretti?"

"Maybe."

She walked with him out to his car. Leaning his butt against the hood, he pulled her closer to stand between his parted legs. "I don't know how long I'll be. Maybe you should get Ray or one of my brothers to drop you home when you're ready."

"Will I see you later?"

He winked at her. "That you can count on." He pulled her closer for a brief kiss.

She stepped to the side while he got in the car and started the engine. "Be careful," she said as he put the car in gear.

Considering that he really had no idea what he was walking into, he intended to be.

After Jonathan pulled off, Dana went back to the house. She was tired and her throat hurt. Without Jonathan there, she had no real reason to stay. She'd find Joanna, tell her she was leaving, and see if Ray could drop her home.

She found Joanna in Ray's study, nursing the baby. "There you are. You have everyone wondering where you disappeared to."

"I wanted a moment's peace and quiet. Between everyone stopping by to see the baby and now our usual Fourth party, I haven't had much time to myself."

Dana scanned her friend's face. She saw more there than new mother fatigue or the need for solitude. She saw unhappiness and wondered if, for the first time, Joanna might not be suffering from postpartum depression.

"Actually I'm glad to have you here alone." Joanna fixed her clothing and settled the baby on her shoulder for a burp. "I wanted to talk to you."

Dana sighed, knowing exactly the subject on Joanna's mind. The last thing she needed was for Joanna to weigh in on her relationship with Jonathan. "If you want to harangue me some more about your brother, you are wasting your breath."

"I know. At first I thought it was only some sex thing Jonathan would tire of. But I've seen the way he looks at you. And a couple of times today, I actually heard him laugh. I don't know what you did to him, but make no mistake, kiddo, he's in love with you."

Dana looked down at her hands. Even more than she didn't want Joanna warning her off Jonathan, she didn't want Joanna questioning her feelings either. "I know."

"And you don't feel the same way?"

She glanced up at Joanna, who watched her expectantly. It occurred to her to tell Joanna it was none of her business what she felt. But they'd been friends too long and Joanna was too determined to let that response slide. "I didn't say that."

Joanna laughed. "Then what are you saying?"

Dana threw up her hands. "I don't know." Even though she'd made the decision to tell Jonathan how she felt, she still dreaded the conversation they would have when he returned. She wasn't sure why. That's why she allowed him to put it off so easily. From his behavior today, she doubted he held her silence against her. It didn't make any sense to her. Maybe she should share what she was feeling with her friend. Maybe Joanna could provide the insight she lacked herself.

"He told me he loved me last night and I just stood there not saying anything. It's not that I don't love him, Joanna, because I do. I couldn't get my mouth to work. Even today, when I told myself I was going to tell him, I didn't. I don't know why not."

Joanna smiled at her as if the answer were the most obvious thing in the world. "You're scared, maybe?"

"Bock, bock," she said, flapping her arms imitating a chicken.

"I didn't say you were a chicken," Joanna chided. "But think about it. The last time you and I had a conversation about men, I accused you of acting like you didn't need anybody, of being incapable of letting any man in. That was what? Two weeks ago at the most? Then all of a sudden here comes my brother and within that short space of time you and he go from virtual strangers to falling in love? Frankly, Jonathan's behavior doesn't surprise me all that much. You know how men are. As long as you feed them and make their gonads happy that's all they require. Besides that, all my brothers tend to be a bit intense. Once they decide on someone or something, that's it. But you?"

"What can I tell you? Everything between us has happened so fast. One minute I was busy hating his guts, the next I was inviting him to share my bed . . ." She trailed off seeing the surprised look on Joanna's face.

"*You* initiated sex?"

The way Joanna spoke, Dana felt heat rise in her cheeks. "Yes. Why does that surprise you so much?"

Joanna shrugged. "Never mind. What were you going to say?"

She inhaled deeply, trying to find the words to say what she meant. "*I* wasn't going to say anything."

"Well then, let me say this. Don't let him or your own feelings rush you into doing anything you aren't ready for. If you ask me, what you need is more time, more normal time when no one is trying to shoot you or run you over. Go out, have dinner, date. Pretend you're normal people for a while."

Dana had to laugh at Joanna's assessment, but she knew she was right. Jonathan had saved her life, but they'd never so much as gone to a movie together. There was still so much about each other that they didn't know. She doubted learning more about him would change her feelings for him, though, except to deepen them.

"Understand something else," Joanna said. "Although neither of you will probably admit it, you'd each put off even trying to find someone elsc. I can't say what my brother's problem is, but I know you've always been afraid to let anyone else in. Both of you finally let your guard down and neither one of you knows how to act. He responds by trying to push forward, you respond by backing away. Why don't you both do yourselves a favor and make sure you've made the right decision before you take things any farther?"

Something about the way Joanna said that made Dana wonder if she was still talking about her and Jonathan. "Is that all you wanted to talk to me about?"

Joanna shook her head. "Actually, I wanted to talk to you about Ray."

Dana went rigid. Don't tell her that she'd finally accepted that Ray was one of the good guys only to find out that he was mistreating her friend. "What about him?"

Joanna sighed. "Ever since the baby was born, he's been . . . different. More moody, more withdrawn. He took time off from work to spend with me, but he spends half his time holed up in here doing God only knows what." Joanna shook her head.

Dana looked around. The room was tastefully furnished with a desk in the corner, on which a laptop sat, the chair and sofa she and Joanna sat on, a TV, a stereo system, and that was about it. Dana couldn't imagine what kind of trouble Ray could be getting himself into in this room, other than tossing back a couple of beers from the mini-fridge in the corner and trolling for nudie pictures on the Internet. For once, Dana figured her friend's fears were for nothing. "He's probably got a bad case of it's-too-soon-for-my-wife-to-have-sex-with-me-itis. I hear it's the masculine equivalent of postpartum depression."

Joanna laughed, disturbing the baby sleeping on her shoulder. She settled the baby in her arms and quieted her. "Do you think that's all there is to it?"

Dana shrugged. "Either that or he's catnapping and doesn't want you to know it."

Sighing, Joanna rocked the baby. "I hope you're right. I know I've made some foolish choices where men were concerned, but I'm not about to put up with any man's nonsense anymore." Joanna glanced up at her. "I really don't want to end up raising my baby alone, again."

Dana swallowed, saying nothing. Things must really have deteriorated between Joanna and Ray for Joanna to be talking this way. Whatever the real story was, Dana knew she hadn't heard the whole of it, only what Joanna felt comfortable telling her.

"I tell you what," Dana said finally. "I'll come over tomorrow afternoon, when there aren't so many people in the house and see if I notice anything."

"Okay." Joanna nodded. "For now, I'd better put the baby in bed and see if the guests need anything."

"This guest needs to go home. Jonathan had to leave and I'm beat."

"No problem. I'll have Ray drive you home. Wait here and I'll go get him. I don't want to have to search through this crush to find you."

Dana watched Joanna leave. She wasn't fooled by her friend's easy agreement to fetch her husband. She figured Joanna hoped she'd ferret some information out of Ray that would explain his change in behavior. Fat chance of that considering that until recently, she and Ray weren't exactly speaking to each other.

Feeling restless, she got up from the sofa and walked to the bookcase along one wall. Most of the shelves were taken up with copies of medical journals, texts or books written about the medical field. Only one shelf housed a variety of hard cover and paper-back novels. She scanned the titles—all mystery or gory horror, the type of stuff that usually bored her. She saw enough real horror every day to not be fazed by made up stuff.

The edge of what she thought was a square piece of paper jutted out from among the books. Without thinking, she pulled it out and immediately real-ized what it was—a photograph. Given Joanna's con-cerns, she wouldn't have been surprised to find a woman's picture there. But the photograph was an old one that depicted three boys, teenagers with wild hair and leather jackets and a look of mischief in their eyes. Someone had scrawled "Us 1979" as a caption on the back.

She recognized the boy on the left as Ray. Next to him stood a shorter boy who looked Hispanic, complete with a mustache that hadn't quite grown in. There was something familiar about that boy's face. Maybe the grown up version of this kid was one of the guests outside. She focused on the third boy, taller than the other two. His face bore a cocky expression she'd seen before, more times than she'd wanted to. She knew those eyes and that mouth twisted into a cruel smile. Her head swam, her brain trying not to comprehend what this picture might mean for all of them, since she knew without a doubt she was looking down at the teenage face of Thomas Moretti.

Twenty-three

"Joanna says you're ready to go home."

Hearing Ray's voice behind her, Dana jumped. She still held the damning photograph in her trembling fingers. She didn't know what Ray would do if he knew she'd seen it, but she didn't want to find out. Casually, she tucked the photograph into her pocket as if she were straightening her skirt. She turned to face him. "I don't want to drag you away from your guests. Maybe Zack can take me."

"Nonsense. It's no bother. If you want to know the truth, this party is more Joanna's gig than mine."

He smiled at her benignly, his face showing no trace of malice or the knowledge that she'd discovered his secret. Besides, he was a doctor. If he wanted to get rid of her, he could have slipped something into her food or drink, either here or when she'd visited Joanna in the hospital. He'd have to be a fool to try to harm her now when Joanna would know the two of them were together. But she couldn't take that chance.

"Really, Ray, I was just in a mood because Jonathan had to leave. I think I'll stick around until he gets back."

Ray shrugged. "Have it your way. If you change your mind again, let me know."

She walked toward him, her nerves screaming, wondering if he'd try to hold her back or let her pass. When she got to the doorway where he stood, he stepped aside, saying nothing. But she didn't let her breath out until she'd made it inside the small bathroom by the stairs and shut the door behind her. With trembling hands she splashed some water on her face and patted it dry with a towel. She had to get out of there. If Ray hadn't noticed she'd taken the picture before, he must surely know by now. She didn't intend to wait on anyone else to take her. She made her way to the front of the house, slipped out the front door and walked the block and a half to an all-night diner. She called a cab from there.

Sitting in the back seat, she finally relaxed. As soon as she got home, she'd call Jonathan, as she hadn't bothered to bring her cell phone with her. He'd know how to handle this. She paid the driver, got out and hurried toward her house.

Once inside with the door closed, she leaned against the wooden surface, and exhaled her pent-up breath. She was safe. All she needed to do now was to call Jonathan and make sure he got back here as quickly as possible.

She started to push off the door, when the bell rang, startling her. She turned and opened the door, only to gasp, finding Ray standing on the other side. In the short time since she'd seen him last, he looked changed—weary, with lines of stress evident around his eyes and mouth. Or maybe that was a trick of the stark porch light. Something about him frightened her, beyond what she thought she knew about him. But she refused to let him see that she was afraid. In a stern voice, she demanded, "What are you doing here, Ray?"

He extended his hand toward her. "For starters, I'd like to have my picture back."

Jonathan met Andrea Weathers at the bar around the corner from her house, ironically the same bar in which Freddie Jackson had almost met his eternal reward. The name of the place was the Hazard Inn. Jonathan figured that was as good a name as any for this place.

Ms. Weathers was already seated in one of the booths when he walked in. He slid in across from her, noticing from the redness in her eyes and the puffiness of her face that she'd been crying. Why she, why any woman would waste her tears on a piece of trash like Moretti, he couldn't fathom. He didn't have any sympathy for her and didn't try to pretend he had any either. He only hoped she hadn't gotten him down here on some wild goose chase or to try to convince him that Moretti wasn't so bad. "What do you have for me, Ms. Weathers?"

She dabbed at her eyes with a tissue. "First I wanted to say how sorry I am that Tommy hurt so many people. I knew he wasn't a saint, but I didn't know he had that in him."

He didn't know what to say to that, so he said nothing. He wasn't about to debate the merits of Moretti's character with her.

She licked her lips. "But the one person I know he didn't hurt was Amanda Pierce."

For a moment he stared at her nonplussed. He hadn't expected that, nor did he believe it. Still he asked, "How can you know that?"

"My mother had a stroke the night before that Pierce woman got killed. Tommy was with me at Mercy Hospital. You can check with the doctors there. He didn't want to leave, but my mother was better and I didn't want to get him in trouble at work. But he didn't leave until nine-thirty, at least a half hour after that woman was picked up."

Adrenaline whooshed up through Jonathan's system, putting his nerve endings on alert. If Moretti hadn't picked up Amanda Pierce, then someone else had, someone Moretti had covered for to the point of taking his own life. One of his old running buddies, no doubt, or maybe both of them. If they'd really killed Father Malone, none of them would want that getting out. But as far as he knew, no one had found out who those other two men were or if they were still alive or in the area. He wasn't even sure anyone was still looking.

"Who was he covering for?"

"I don't know. He got a few calls that he left the room to take. I didn't hear him use any names. I thought it was another woman."

Damn. He was no better off now than he had been when he walked in the door, except that if another person was involved, Dana was still in danger. He pulled out his phone and called his sister's house. Joanna came on the phone to tell him that Dana had just left with Ray.

"Do me a favor, Sis? Call Ray and ask him to wait with Dana until I get there." He didn't want to call Dana and risk upsetting her when he wasn't there. He would have preferred it if one of his brothers had seen her home, but Ray would have to do in a pinch.

"Is everything okay?"

He didn't want to upset his sister, either. "Yeah. Just do what I ask, okay?"

"Sure. Call me later?"

"Will do." He clicked off the phone and clipped it to his belt. He looked at the woman sitting across from him. "I have to go."

She nodded.

He slid from the booth and walked out. He could probably make it back to Dana's in less than ten minutes. Even though Ray was with her, he wouldn't breathe easily until he saw Dana again for himself.

Dana reached into her pocket and pulled out the picture. She handed it to Ray. "If that's all you want, please go. I'm tired and I want to go to bed."

Ray looked down at the picture before slipping it into his shirt pocket. He looked up at her, his face bearing the bleakest expression she'd ever seen. "Don't worry, Dana. I'm not here to hurt you."

She'd believe that when he got his behind off her porch and left. "Go home, Ray. Joanna needs you."

He shook his head. "I won't be going home. Maybe not for a long time. When will Jonathan be back?"

She lacked the presence of mind to lie. "I don't know."

"Do you mind if I wait for him?"

"Here?" she asked, meaning the porch.

He nodded. "Can I have something to drink first?"

She scanned his face again. His expression seemed more desolate than dangerous. She didn't know what to make of that. She still didn't trust him, but to some extent she felt sorry for him. Whatever his role in all this, his life as he knew it was over. She'd see to that, even if no one else did. "I have some iced tea," she ventured.

The look on his face told her that wasn't the kind of drink he had in mind. "I'll be right back." She went inside, closing the door behind him, shutting him out. She was tempted to call the local police and have him escorted from her property. She called Jonathan instead, who picked up on the third ring.

"Hey, sweetheart," he said. "Is Ray with you?"

Jonathan already knew he was there? That changed things. "Yes. He's out on the porch."

"Make sure he stays there until I get there, okay? I'll be home in five minutes."

"All right."

The line went dead before she finished speaking. It was probably best he got off the phone since he was driving, but the abruptness with which he ended the call left her with a bad feeling. Something wasn't right. That much she knew, though she couldn't tell if it was Ray's being here or Jonathan's distractedness. But she would do as Jonathan asked and keep Ray here.

She got a tumbler from the cabinet and filled it with a mixture of ice and scotch, the drink Ray preferred. She tucked her spare house key into one of her pockets. Looking down at the drain board beside the sink, she got another idea. She tucked the small paring knife into her other pocket. The blade wasn't long, but it was sharp enough to do some damage.

She went back to the porch and shut the door behind her. Ray was sitting in a rocker looking down at the picture she'd taken from his house. Whatever thoughts ran through his mind, they engrossed him enough that he didn't react to her return. "Ray?" she said finally.

He wiped his hand across his face. When he reached for the glass she offered him, she noticed twin trails of moisture on his skin. He gulped down half the drink, before setting the glass on the floor beside him. "Thank you."

She didn't know what to say to that, so she didn't bother. She slipped into the rocker across from him, turning it slightly so that she could watch him. At first he remained silent, but she sensed in him a desire to speak, to unload whatever burden he carried. "Why are you here, Ray?"

"Because I'm tired, Dana. I've been running from this thing for twenty-five years. It's past time to put it to rest." He turned his head toward her, showing her the picture in his hand. "Growing up, these were the best friends I had. Me and Tommy and Miguel. They knew me by my given name, Randy, and we used to call him Mouse, a take on Speedy Gonzales, you know, the cartoon. He was a pipsqueak, and man, could that boy run. We used to get him to take things from the local stores, because even if they knew who did it, no one could ever catch him."

He spoke with such nostalgia that she wanted to shake him and ask him what made him think she wanted to join him on this trip down memory lane. At least one of these men, his friends, was responsible for a number of deaths. For all she knew, he was, too. If that's where this was leading, she'd prefer to hear the truth of it now. "What did you do, Ray?"

"Me? I didn't do anything."

Rather than sounding like a denial of culpability, his words sounded more like self-condemnation. "What do you mean?"

"I didn't do anything to stop them, not now, not twenty-five years ago. When that fire started, I didn't want to leave Father there. Mouse hit him and he fell, but he was alive, Dana. We left him there to burn to death because Tommy said we'd go to jail for assault and for setting the fire if Father told on us, even though it was an accident. Despite all the nonsense we pulled, none of us had spent so much as a day in juvenile hall. I was scared and I let them talk me into leaving him there.

"I never forgave myself for that. Never. But I was determined to straighten myself out. I thought we all were. At least something good could come of Father's death. A year later, my mom remarried. She met some rich guy on her job. He was good to us. He even adopted me, like I wanted to do with Joanna's kids, though I was almost eighteen at the time. I thought I had put it all behind me until Tommy called me to tell me what Mouse had done to Amanda Pierce. They left her behind old man Mario's pizzeria, a payback for all the times he told us all we'd ever amount to was trash."

So, neither Ray nor Moretti had anything to do with Pierce's death, though Moretti had been guilty of helping to cover it up. If that were true, why hadn't Moretti turned Mouse in? She voiced that question to Ray. "Was he afraid Mouse would tell what he knew about Father Malone's death?"

"No, all three of us vowed to take what happened to Father Malone to our graves. Turning Mouse in would have been like betraying a member of our families. For a long time, we were all each other had. They considered me a turncoat since I wouldn't go along with their plans to get rid of you. You didn't know it, but you'd seen Mouse, seen the car. You didn't seem to remember much, but you might have. We'd all made decent lives for ourselves. Neither of them wanted to risk losing what they had, Mouse especially."

"So you were willing to let them kill me to keep your precious secrets?"

He averted his gaze. "I tried to keep you out of it, Dana. But you kept putting your nose back in it. Tommy told me where those gangbangers had dumped the car they used in the drive-by. After you left the hospital, I got in the car and went after you. I wanted to warn you off getting involved any further, but I would never have hurt you. Once I found out you were staying with Jonathan, I figured he'd keep you safe. I didn't know how far Tommy would go to keep you silent."

Dana didn't know what to say to that. Her head swam, trying to assimilate what Ray had told her. She could understand a childish reaction to a dangerous situation. Those boys had probably been as frightened by the fire itself as they had been about being discovered. In her mind, she didn't excuse their behavior, but the logic of it reached her.

But three grown men destroying the lives of so many others for no other reason than to keep a past crime from being discovered she could not. Ray might not have actively participated in trying to cover things up, but there was such a thing as a sin of omission. He could have gone to any of his brothers-in-law seeking help, he could have warned her more directly, even if he did so anonymously. Anything. Now she understood the self-condemnation in his voice when he said he hadn't done anything. At least he had enough character to feel remorse.

She knew everything she needed to from him, except one thing. "Who is the third man, Ray? Who's Mouse?"

"I figured you'd get around to that question sooner or later."

The voice, coming from the other side of the glass door, held an eerie quality that made the hairs on the back of Dana's neck stand up. The door opened and Father Mike stepped onto the porch. He let the door swing closed behind him. It clattered back and forth a few times before settling into its proper place. Each clang reverberated through her like the knell of a large bell.

For a split second, her mind whirred, as images from her dreams flooded her consciousness—the fish swimming in a sea of black, a frozen flame. She knew where she'd seen them now. On the back of Father Mike's car, the one Moretti had questioned her about seeing. The flame, which represented a burning candle, was the emblem of St. Matthew's. Bring a light unto the world, was the school's motto. It was emblazoned on a bumper sticker on the back of the black sedan right above one of those metal fish that Christians affixed to their cars as a symbol of Christ. In Father Mike's case, one of the twin tails had broken off as the result of someone rear-ending him.

Her subconscious mind had been screaming at her in her dreams. If it weren't for Father Mike standing there now wearing one of the school's sweaters she probably wouldn't have figured out how to fit those images together. But now that she had, she rose to her feet, truly frightened. Despite his dress, there was nothing holy about Father Mike's appearance. His hair was as wild as his eyes, and she feared something in him had snapped.

He turned his attention on Ray. "I see you told her everything, Randy. Tommy was right about you. Traitor!"

Father Mike's voice reminded her of an adolescent's whine at injustice, which only frightened her more. Adolescents were unpredictable, and sometimes inexplicably cruel when betrayed. If in his mind he'd gone back to the time they were boys together, there was no telling what he might do.

Ray rose to his feet. "You didn't have to come here, Mouse. I only told you I was coming here so you'd be prepared. I didn't plan on giving them your name. You could have—"

"I could have what? Run? Disappeared? Given up the life I'd created? Just because you couldn't keep your mouth shut? Tommy died to protect us and you want to make his sacrifice for nothing?"

Ray shook his head. "Tommy took his life because he knew they had him. He was going down long before he took it into his head to make this noble sacrifice. You know that as well as I do."

As the men spoke, Dana inched herself backward, toward her front door. She regretted now not leaving it unlocked. If it were, she would have bolted for the door and left the two "friends" outside to quibble about their past. Now she'd have to worry about unlocking the door, which both men would notice. She felt confident Ray would let her go. She had no idea what Father Mike would do. But as far as she knew he wasn't armed, so she was going to chance it. When she got close enough to the door she turned, key in hand. She'd just slid the key into the lock when a bullet whizzed past her and embedded in the surface of the door, next to her head.

She glanced over her shoulder to see Father Mike standing beside her, a revolver in his hand. "Get away from—"

That's as far as Father Mike got before Ray was on

him. As the two men grappled for possession of the gun, Ray said, "Go, Dana."

She hadn't realized she'd stood there frozen watching them until Ray spoke. She turned back to the door, trying to get the uncooperative key to turn. She'd had this spare made, but never used it. She fiddled with it trying to get the tumblers to turn, her panic rising to a crescendo when a single shot sounded behind her and an instant later the slump of a body hitting the floor. Of the two men, Father Mike was the stronger and the more desperate. She hadn't counted on Ray overpowering him. When she heard Father Mike's voice she knew her assessment had been correct.

"Now, it's just us," Father Mike said. "Now come away from that door."

Dana turned around, but didn't move otherwise. Ray lay on the floor sprawled on his back, blood seeping from a wound in his belly. She couldn't let him die there like that. "Let me help him," she said.

"He's beyond your help or mine. Let God take him."

Tears welled in her eyes. Who was this man who'd helped her get Tim through school, the man who she had started to call her friend? A supposed man of God who was also a madman. "How can you do this?"

"I didn't want to hurt him. He gave me no choice. I can't go back to being what I was. I worked too hard to leave it behind. I changed my name, changed everything. Miguel Colon is dead."

He'd escaped into being Michael Coyne, your friendly neighborhood priest. "And that gives you the right to take someone else's life?"

"I didn't want to kill Amanda Pierce. I'd heard she was looking into Father Malone's death. I wanted to find out how much she knew, maybe put us off investigating further. But she already knew our names. It was only a matter of time before she exposed all of us. I couldn't have that. I've spent most of my life devoted to God, dedicated to helping those boys. Didn't that count for anything? Didn't that make up for the death of one old man?"

She didn't have an answer for that. Even if he'd lived his life as a penance for what he'd done to Father Malone, his killing of Amanda Pierce had been nothing but a selfish desire to preserve what he had. There was no excuse for that.

"I tried to talk her out of investigating further, but she kept telling me she'd do what she wanted. She turned to walk away and I grabbed her scarf."

Father Mike lowered his head. "I thought I'd left it all behind. Left behind the boy I was, all the anger, the shame. But it was still there. I'd never been tested before. I'd never had to look inside my heart and decide. And I failed."

He was talking now as if to himself or to open space or maybe to Ray, prone on the floor. She wondered if he was still aware of Ray's presence. While he had the gun at his side, she was going to chance that he wasn't. She turned and grabbed the key. Finally the lock turned, but she didn't get a chance to turn the knob before he grabbed her around the waist.

"I can't let you go, Dana. You know that."

His hold on her made the knife in her pocket chafe against her leg. As he tried to pull her from the door, she fumbled to get her hand in her pocket. She raised the knife and stabbed him, missing his throat and hitting his shoulder. He screamed and drew back from her, enough so that she could get the door open. She fell inside the open door. He lunged after her, catching her legs and tripping her as she tried to gain her feet. She kicked back, aiming for his shoulder where the knife still protruded. Hearing him scream again, she knew she'd hit her mark.

She scrambled away, both her arms and legs fighting to right herself. She raced down the hall, knowing she'd only have a few seconds at most before he followed her. She ran to the back door and unlocked it, leaving the door wide open. But rather than go out, she withdrew into the small bathroom to the left and shut the door. With any luck, Father Mike would think she'd run out of the house to escape him. He wouldn't look for her back here.

A second later she heard footsteps in the kitchen and the sound of something clattering to the kitchen floor. She held her breath for a moment, hearing nothing but silence. She shut her eyes hearing the footsteps again, closer this time. If he found her, she had nothing save a toilet brush with which to defend herself. But the footsteps veered off, and she heard the sound of the back porch door slamming.

She let out her breath, willing her heartbeat to normalize. He'd taken the bait and left. It occurred to her that she should go out and lock both her doors. She'd wait a minute to make sure he'd really left and hadn't slammed the door on purpose to trick her.

Leaning her back against the door, she slumped down to the floor. Where the hell was Jonathan?

Jonathan's first clue that something wasn't right at Dana's house was that the front gate was open. She always closed it. The porch light was on, but from the street he couldn't see anyone occupying it. Beyond that, the front door was ajar.

He pulled his weapon as he walked up the front steps. He didn't hear a sound from the house, nothing to give him a clue as to what had gone on. He pulled open the glass porch door and immediately saw Ray lying on the floor. There was so much blood, Jonathan's belly roiled. Keeping his eye on the open front door, he knelt next to Ray and felt for a pulse.

Ray's eyes opened and his mouth worked. Jonathan leaned in to listen.

"Mouse . . . help her."

Jonathan assumed the her was Dana, but mouse? Ray's eyes closed. Jonathan shook his shoulder. "Ray, what's happened? Where's Dana?"

Ray winced, but when his eyes opened again he fastened a clear-eyed lucid gaze on Jonathan. "T-tell Joanna I'm sorry."

The look in his eyes went vacant. Jonathan used his middle and index fingers to close Ray's eyes. For a moment, Jonathan shut his eyes, while Pee Wee's words rang in his ears. *Look to your own house.* He'd never imagined the man meant it in a literal sense. Had Pee Wee known about Ray's involvement or had he just been talking about Moretti?

Either way, there was nothing more he could do for Ray. Now he needed to find Dana. He got to his feet. The knee of his pant leg was soaked in Ray's blood, leaving Jonathan with a cold, clammy feeling throughout his body. A feeling of death. He knew the man he hunted now had to be Miguel Colon, the third of the friends that had killed Father Malone. If he were willing to do this to Ray, what would he do to Dana?

Slowly, Jonathan started toward the house. He noticed another blood trail that started right outside the door and continued down the hall. Had Dana been wounded or had she managed to wound her attacker?

He continued down the hall to the kitchen. The light was on and the back door was open. The blood trail, that had been fizzling out, was stronger toward the opening. Jonathan advanced toward it, until he stepped on something at the edge of the table—a short, bloody knife. This scene made no sense to him. Had one of them been wounded by the door and the other here by the knife? If so, why did there appear to be only one blood trail? He'd puzzle it out later. He continued toward the back door, until he heard a clicking sound to his left. He spun around, his gun poised to fire at whoever made the sound.

He'd forgotten about that little bathroom off to the side that Dana rarely used. She poked her head out. When she saw him, she drew back, with a cry of surprise. Then she launched herself at him, wrapping her arms around his neck. For a moment, he hugged her trembling body against his, as words poured from her, tripping over one another, so that he couldn't make out much of what she said. The only thing he did grasp fully was that her assailant had gone out the back door.

He set her on her feet and closed and locked the back door. He turned around to find Dana staring transfixed at a man, a priest, standing at the opposite end of the kitchen.

"Put your gun on the floor, Detective Stone," he said. "Slide it to me."

Jonathan shook his head. He recognized in the man's face a mind that wasn't quite right. There was no way that he was going to leave himself and Dana at his mercy. He stepped forward, his arms raised but his weapon still in his hand. He wanted to appear non-threatening, at least until he managed to put himself between this madman's aim and Dana. "I can't do that, Father."

"Then you're not leaving me any choice."

Jonathan stepped in front of Dana, aimed and fired. His shot hit its mark, the center of the priest's forehead, but not before the priest squeezed off a round.

As the priest slumped to the floor, Jonathan looked down at his side. His flesh burned and blood oozed from a wound in his side. "Damn."

As if from somewhere far away, he heard Dana calling his name. He blinked and the next thing he knew she was leaning over him, her face a mask of concern. He lifted one hand and brushed her tears away. "Don't cry, baby."

She knocked his hand away. "Don't you dare die on me, Jonathan Stone, or I'll kill you myself."

He tried to laugh at the incongruity of her words, but it hurt too much. A kind of internal frost claimed him, making him shiver. He tried to open his eyes, but it was damn difficult. He squinted up at her, wanting to tell her not to worry, but no words came.

"Don't leave me, Jonathan. I love you."

"I love you too," he whispered then succumbed to the blackness that claimed him.

Twenty-four

Dana paced the small hospital waiting area, waiting for news of Jonathan. He'd been taken into surgery the minute the ambulance had pulled up to the hospital. That had been two hours ago and no word since. She knew these things took time even when they went well, but with each passing minute, her sense of dread increased.

Even though the waiting room was crowded with Jonathan's partner, his boss, and assorted family members, she felt alone in her misery. She knew what he'd done. He'd stepped in front of that madman's bullet and taken it himself. If it weren't for him, she'd be the one lingering near death instead of him. She loved him for that, but didn't want to lose him because of it.

Her mind drifted to Joanna, who'd arrived at the hospital with the others to find out that Ray was dead. She'd been so inconsolable that Adam had taken her home. Tears formed in her eyes. How would she react if she were given similar news?

She brushed the tears away. She couldn't think like that. Jonathan would be all right. He had to be.

A doctor in green scrubs with a surgical mask pulled to the top of his head entered the room. From the expression on his face it was difficult to tell if he bore good news or bad. She walked toward him. "Do you have news for us?" she asked, her voice shaky.

He fastened a weary gaze on her. "Mr. Stone is out of surgery. He's lost a lot of blood and he's weak, but other than that, he's all right."

Relief flooded through her, renewing the sting of tears to her eyes. "Thank you, Doctor."

"Are you Dana Molloy?" he asked.

"Yes."

"He's been asking for you. He'll be in postop for a while, then you can see him."

"Thank you."

After he left, she scanned the faces around her. She knew the happiness most of them felt learning that Jonathan was okay was tempered by Ray's loss. She felt it, too. He'd tried to protect her and lost his life because of it. He wasn't blameless in Father Malone's death, but of the three men, he'd been the only one moved by his conscience rather than his own desire not to get caught.

It was as she'd always believed, that the truth, no matter how carefully hidden, always sought the daylight of discovery. Nothing stayed a secret forever. But was any secret worth so much destruction—even the havoc they'd created in their own lives? They'd made a pact to change, and outwardly, they had. A priest, a doctor and a cop—three men you were supposed to look up to. But inside, Moretti had reverted to his old ways; Father Mike let the guilt drive him over the edge. And now they were all dead and their past laid bare. There had to be some irony in that, though she'd be damned if she could find it. All she knew was that she wouldn't be content until she saw Jonathan again for herself.

When a nurse came to take her to Jonathan's room, she followed the woman on legs that trembled. The doctor hadn't elaborated on his condition and she hadn't asked, not wanting to alarm the rest of the family. She knew that bullet must have done some internal damage. The extent of that remained to be seen.

The nurse left her at the door to his room. She took a deep breath and plastered a smile on her face before opening the door. He didn't necessarily need to see how concerned she was.

He lay on a bed directly in front of her, his face turned away from her, his eyes closed. She walked over to him. "Jon?"

Slowly his head turned and his eyes opened. "Hey, you."

"Hey, yourself," she said. "How are you feeling?"

"Pretty good now. The stuff they give you for the pain is excellent."

If he weren't lying in a hospital bed she would have hit him. "You know what I mean."

He lifted his hand and with a surprisingly strong grip pulled her to him. She sat on the edge of the bed, as he seemed to want her to. "I'm pretty doped up right now, but I could swear I heard you tell me you loved me."

That's what he was concerned about? She'd nearly lost him and he was worried about what she'd said while she was trying to keep every ounce of his blood from ending up on her kitchen floor. "I did."

"Did you mean it, or was it just something to say?"

She answered him honestly. "I thought I wasn't going to have a chance to say it later, but I meant it."

His thumb brushed against her palm and a faint smile formed on her lips. "I told you I wasn't going anywhere. You should have believed me."

She lifted his hand and kissed the back of it. "I love you, Jon. I would have told you earlier, except I was afraid."

"Of what?"

"Losing myself again in what somebody else wanted."

He made a noise that sounded almost like a laugh. "Baby, you're the strongest woman I know. And I would never ask for more from you than you were willing to give."

"I know, but everything between us happened so quickly. I need time to adjust."

"Do you think I was ready for you to come into my life and turn my world upside down?"

She lifted one shoulder in a shrug.

"Let's take it one day at a time, okay? We've got our whole lives."

Smiling, she nodded.

"Good. Now kiss me and send Mari to me. She's probably chewing the furniture waiting for her turn to get in here."

The door pushed open. "I heard that, Stone. You'd think I'd get a little credit for leaving a tender moment alone rather than bursting in here like I wanted to."

"You'd think," he said, sleepily.

"Just remember what I said about having to work with those other yahoos. You'd better hurry up and get back on the job."

"That's up to my nurse, here." He squeezed her hand. "Are you going to nurse me back to health?"

She leaned down and kissed his cheek. "Hush, dear. The drugs are making you stupid."

He mumbled something she didn't catch. She drew back to find he'd closed his eyes. "We're going to leave you now to get some rest."

He didn't respond to that, but since none of the monitors signaled anything was wrong, she figured he'd already fallen asleep. She kissed him again and stood. He'd be fine for tonight, but she wanted to see to Joanna now, who needed her at the moment more than he did.

"I'll be back tomorrow," she told him, just in case he could hear. Then they could start, one at a time, on those days—all the ones that would make up their lifetime together.

Dear Reader,

I really hoped you enjoyed *Body of Truth*. This book was a real labor of love for me, as it is set in my beloved hometown, Bronx, New York. I have to admit I took some liberties with street names, precinct numbers and the like, as a means of changing the names to protect the innocent. But my real goal was to provide the essence of the Bronx, which I hope I've done. You'll see more of the Bronx, and more of the Stone Brothers in the rest of the series. Next up is Zachary Stone, who meets his match with a lady from his past.

I'd love to hear from you. Please contact me at aboutdeesbooks@aol.com or write to me at: P.O. Box 233, Baychester Station, Bronx, NY 10469.

Also, please join my list for readers: http://groups.yahoo.com/group/ladiesinred/ This is the place for discussions of my books, giveaways and much more. Hope to see you there.

Wishing you all the best,
Deirdre Savoy

ABOUT THE AUTHOR

Native New Yorker Deirdre Savoy spent her summers on the shores of Martha's Vineyard, soaking up the sun and scribbling in one of her many notebooks. It was there that she first started writing romance as a teenager. The island proved to be the perfect setting for her first novel, *Spellbound*, published by BET/Arabesque books in 1999. *Spellbound* received rave reviews and earned her the distinction of the first Rising Star author of Romance in Color and was voted their Best New Author of 1999. Deirdre also won the first annual Emma award for Favorite New Author, presented at the 2001 Romance Slam Jam in Orlando, Florida.

Since then, Deirdre has published nine books, all of which have garnered critical acclaim and honors. Deirdre has been featured in a variety of publications including *Black Issues Book Review, Romantic Times, Affaire de Coeur, Blackboard Bestsellers List* and others. Many of her titles have been issued in hardcover by Black Expressions.

Deirdre is the president of Authors Supporting Authors Positively (ASAP) and the founder of the Writer's Co-op writer's group. She lectures on such topics as Getting Your Writing Career Started, Taking Your Writing to the Next Level, and other subjects related to the craft of writing. She is listed in the *American* and *International Authors and Writers Who's Who*, as well as the *Dictionary of International Biography*.

Deirdre lives in Bronx, New York, with her husband of ten-plus years and their two children. In her spare time she enjoys reading, dancing, calligraphy, and "wicked" crossword puzzles.

Check Out These Other
Dafina Novels

Sister Got Game
0-7582-0856-1

by Leslie Esdaile
$6.99US/**$9.99**CAN

Say Yes
0-7582-0853-7

by Donna Hill
$6.99US/**$9.99**CAN

In My Dreams
0-7582-0868-5

by Monica Jackson
$6.99US/**$9.99**CAN

True Lies
0-7582-0027-7

by Margaret Johnson-Hodge
$6.99US/**$9.99**CAN

Testimony
0-7582-0637-2

by Felicia Mason
$6.99US/**$9.99**CAN

Emotions
0-7582-0636-4

by Timmothy McCann
$6.99US/**$9.99**CAN

The Upper Room
0-7582-0889-8

by Mary Monroe
$6.99US/**$9.99**CAN

Got A Man
0-7582-0242-3

by Daaimah S. Poole
$6.99US/**$8.99**CAN

Available Wherever Books Are Sold!

Check out our website at www.kensingtonbooks.com.

Look For These Other
Dafina Novels

Grab These Other
Dafina Novels
(mass market editions)

Available Wherever Books Are Sold!

Visit our website at **www.kensingtonbooks.com**

Grab These Other
Thought Provoking Books

Adam by Adam
0-7582-0195-8

by Adam Clayton Powell, Jr.
$15.00US/$21.00CAN

African American Firsts
0-7582-0243-1

by Joan Potter
$15.00US/$21.00CAN

African-American Pride
0-8065-2498-7

by Lakisha Martin
$15.95US/$21.95CAN

The African-American Soldier
0-8065-2049-3

by Michael Lee Lanning
$16.95US/$24.95CAN

African Proverbs and Wisdom
0-7582-0298-9

by Julia Stewart
$12.00US/$17.00CAN

Al on America
0-7582-0351-9

by Rev. Al Sharpton
with Karen Hunter
$16.00US/$23.00CAN

Available Wherever Books Are Sold!

Visit our website at **www.kensingtonbooks.com**